Acclaim for *Tho*

"I'm delighted to see this publication of Marilyn Brown's novel *Thorns of the Sun*. Both books, *Thorns of the Sun* and *Shadows of Angels,* make a major contribution to Mormon historical fiction and should achieve the wide audience which they so justly merit."

Richard Cracroft, Compiler of Mormon Literature

"A powerful book: very interesting characters, the background carefully researched. Good reading material for anyone interested in the history of the West."

Kathryn Gardner, Library Scientist / UELMA

"Like nested baskets, this densely woven family saga poises the mysteries of human love and human faith. Beginning with the origins of Provo, a precarious village by a Utah lake, Marilyn Brown constructs a language of containment for the tender miracles of faith and love, even when the tenderest miracles are bracketed by deceit and ruptured by violence. And nesting most securely at the heart, in a voice that speaks authentically from Mormon experience to Mormon experiencers, is the greatest miracle of all: the ability of the present to forgive the past."

Lavina Fielding Anderson, Author / Editor

"I will be very happy to see Brown's work published. *Thorns of the Sun* and *Shadows of Angels* bring together the early Mormon pioneering experience, the family experiences with polygamy, and the struggles with the Indians without mitigating the prejudices or condescensions. . . . Both books should get the wide circulation they deserve."

Marden Clark, Author / Poet

"Marilyn Brown's *Thorns of the Sun*, like Faulkner's writing, weaves stories around a specific locale—central Utah—during its settlement years. Its characters, though fictional, come alive through the rich detail and moving stories, and interact with historical figures. For the readers familiar with the locale, the book provides a rich look at early Utah history; for the student of early Church doctrine and practices, the novel shows how this small group of Saints lived from day to day; for readers who just want a good story, the novel thoroughly satisfies that desire. The characters are unforgettable, the setting well drawn, the action realistic—sometimes startling, the dialogue believable, and the theme significant. A classic in Mormon fiction, *Thorns of the Sun* is a must for everyone interested in the development of Mormon literature."

Sally Taylor, Writer / Professor

"Marilyn Brown takes us from history to the human side of the interaction of the Anglo and Indian cultures on the American frontier with sympathy and understanding. Introducing characters with great skill and clarity, the story unfolds the power of love and the full range of other human emotions, always maintaining the heartbeat of the Mormon faith as it manifests itself in the lives of individuals."

Edward L. Hart, Author / Poet

"*Thorns of the Sun* extends Marilyn Brown's poetic figures for the phenomenon of *connection* in the early period of Indian-Mormon relations. The organic form echoes the unifying forces she suggests will bond all the people of the earth: a leveling of hierarchies, both lingual and biological insemination, compassion and submission."

Clinton Larson, Poet / Playwright

"This novel helped me consider the Indian-white relationships in early Utah: the challenge of adopted Indians, the fears of Indians escaping capture from other Indians, their distaste for white domestication, their vulnerability to renegade whites. The 'feed them instead of fight them' advice from Brigham Young does not consider the many nuances between the Mormons and the Indians. Brown explores these human dimensions."

Douglas Alder, Writer / Teacher

THORNS
OF THE
SUN

Part I of a Pioneer Saga

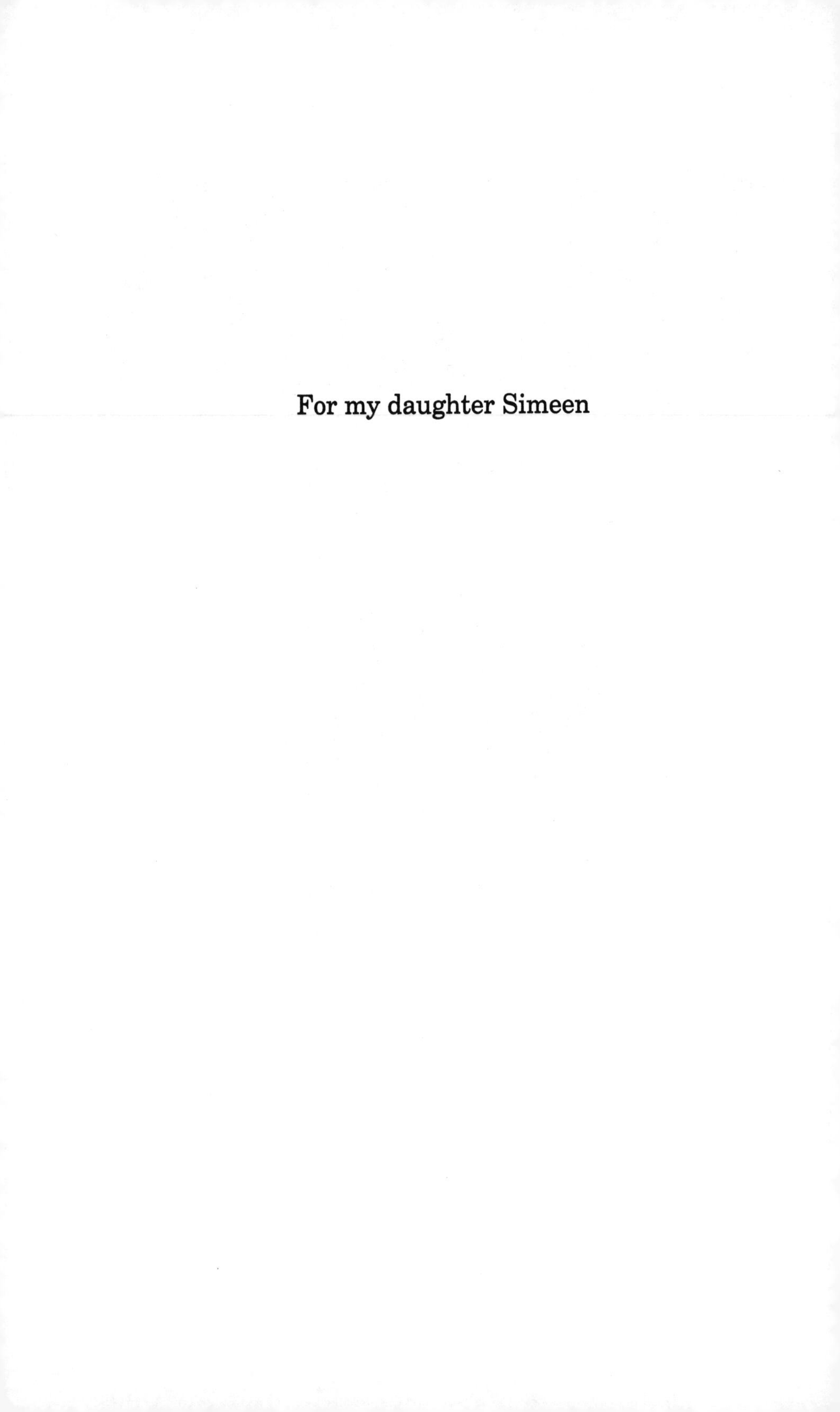

For my daughter Simeen

THORNS OF THE SUN

Part I of a Pioneer Saga

A NOVEL BY

MARILYN BROWN

Printed in the United States of America
Covenant Communications, Inc.
Library of Congress Catalog Number 92–071088
Thorns of the Sun
First Printing August 1992
ISBN 1–55503–394-6

Chapter One

While the militia was returning in the night, it rained. The swollen waters broke along Emigration Canyon and slipped down the slick face of the mountain like tears. The rains brought with them a new season. The earth seemed to heave and turn, shifting under its coverlets of snow. The shallow ice shrank back from the great black flanks of ground where the dirt of the hills slipped down with the water and mixed into a thick mud. The horses and the militia stirred doggedly through the roads from Provost's Hole, bringing with them the fruits of their spoil clinging to them like the thorns of burrs—the ragged women and children—Indians—their faces blank with the bewilderment of upheaval.

The girl Mara, who knew the home boys would be returning by the south road—and one particular boy with them—ran out of the house in her nightgown to fetch the water from the well, hoping she would be in the yard to hear them coming. She had forgotten her father's warning never to leave the house without being dressed. She paid no attention to the cold. All she thought was that finally the sun was shining. The hills seemed so warm and so bright that she ran to embrace the spring. She had forgotten the reason for her father's concern until she stood at the well and could see in the distance, above last summer's withered roses, the eyes in the bedroom window.

She knew their neighbor was watching her again.

It was too late to go back without his noticing that she knew she had made a mistake. She leaned over the well, unhooked the bucket, dropped it and listened to the shattering ice. She could still feel the staring eyes from the back bedroom window where the man's wife lay too sick to move, where the unhappy Ivie Richards moved back and forth, back and forth in front of the thin glass, his gaze summoning her through the distance of the pasture, through the misty sunshine at the well.

As she hurried to raise the pail, she thought, "Let him look." He could see as well as she could that there was sunshine in the hills. He was just a cranky man. He had begged Bishop Hunt—now Captain Hunt—for permission to marry a second wife, but he would never receive it. The new bishop, Brother King, remembered too well that Ivie Richards had quarreled with Hunt over the Wright girl.

Mara ducked slightly behind the rope and behind the well and remembered that when he had looked at her at church, she and Nancy had been laughing at him when he stumbled—he had been watching them instead of where he was going. And he had glared from beneath his bushy dark brows and said, "You are taking chances, girls."

She stood behind the bucket and listened to the other sounds of the morning: the wind, the whisper of the rope. Suddenly she thought she could hear feet pounding. She lifted the bucket, then let it go. As it dropped back into the well, she heard someone running up the road.

Shivering, she backed up to the house in her thin nightgown and opened the door. Still feeling the cold eyes from the window, she ducked behind the door and leaned out to see as far as she dared. A group had gathered at the crossing. The militia was here! And someone was running toward the house. As the figure drew nearer, Mara could see it was not Bret Hunt. She tightened her fingers on the door. It was not Bret, but Bret's foster brother, Sully.

She ignored the eyes in the window and the bucket at the well. Slipping and sliding, she vaulted across the floor of the back porch and into the back room. Knowing her father would scold her for going into the yard undressed, she took his coat off the hook on the inside of the door and pulled it around her shoulders. Before she shut the door, she turned to the backyard and stuck out her tongue. Then she hurried inside. "Mama! Papa!" she called. "They're here! Sully Tuttle's coming up the road!"

"Bless me!" Mama stood up quickly from the flour board. With her fingers still buttery, she hurried to the front window. Nine-year-old Ashel followed her. Sophia and her husband John peered down from the loft. "How do you know?" Sophia leaned over the steep stairs.

"How do I know? Sully Tuttle's in the road." Sully—the boy who had been raised in the alley behind London's Blackthorn Saloon, his father drunk and his mother dead, whose luck changed when Bishop Scott Hunt had taken him in and brought him to America and across the plains with his own boys. Sully, who had the cheek to wish Mara would be his girl. But she just felt like laughing at him.

Papa was so large that when he moved fast there wasn't enough space to hold him. He rose from his chair so quickly that the newspaper flew to the floor. He seemed to fill the entire room. When he breathed in, the buttons looked like they would pop off of his vest.

"They're here all right," Mama said, watching Sully turn toward the house. Ashel, still wrapped in his blanket, pressed his face against the glass.

Papa moved ponderously to the door and opened it before Sully had a chance to knock. "Well, birds and bee feathers!" he said.

"Mr. Eastman, sir." Sully stood, his hand raised, ready to knock on Papa's nose. Ashel was laughing.

"Well, boy!" Papa thundered. He turned and walked back into the room. Sully burst over the threshold as though he were announcing the birth of a new world. He was so thin it seemed there could be no strength in him. But when he banged the door behind him, he hit it so hard it bounced open, so he hit it again. Then he crushed it against the jamb with a furious violence and to keep it shut, backed up against it. Papa's drawing of the house in Hoboken snapped off the wall, and Mama picked it up, brushed it off, and hung it gently back in place. Mara, feeling like she would burst from the desire to laugh, forced her face to stay straight.

"We're back, sir," Sully said, breathing hard from running so fast. Beads of sweat had broken out across his forehead. He was pale with thick, curly sandy hair that stood straight up along the top of his head like a piece of carpet. Mara watched him as he came into the room. She suspected it would not be long before his clear watery eyes found her. And she was right. She moved behind Papa, back against the wall. Feeling naked, she pulled her father's sheepskin coat more tightly around her shoulders.

"All of you back from your Indian war? Did you save the cattle?" Papa said.

"The cattle was dead, sir."

"Dead! What has happened, then?" Mama asked.

Sully looked away from Mara for a moment. "We ambushed 'em, ma'am, and demanded surrender. But they fought till they was all killed. Except the women and the children. Can you take some?" He threw the question at

Mama hastily, as though if she did not hear clearly she would say yes.

Mama moved forward. "What, Sully?"

"They was all dead but the women and children. Can you take some?"

"My boy," Papa pulled up to his full height, his shirt protruding through where a button was missing on his vest. He wore leather pants with a gold kerchief straying from his worn pocket. He pulled the kerchief out, flourished it, and rubbed so hard he squashed his nose into his face. "You mean to say you brought those Indians here?"

Mara listened, alert to the tension in her father's voice. Indians! Why had they brought the Indians here? These Indians. Utes. Dangerous. Wild. Savage, like animals.

"Some of 'em. Some Indian customs is they don't take care of widows and children. Can you put some up?"

"Why, of course, Sully," Mama said quickly, not even looking at Papa's face.

"I've got to leave and tell everyone," Sully said in a rough voice. "They'll be down at the State Street crossing in half an hour.

He turned so swiftly, Mara thought he might break. He was so thin and bony it was a wonder his body could support his large head. She watched him as he stumbled over his long shoes. He would never have been one of the survivors in the back streets of London. He turned to look at her once more, then Papa closed the door. She breathed a sigh of relief. She hadn't laughed out loud.

"So they brought those Indians here, eh?" Papa turned around and leaned against the door latch. "I'm feelin' a new ache in my bones."

Mama sat still in the rocker, her head leaning back against Aunt Caroline's afghan. Her eyes were halfway closed in pain, in an intense expression that Mara remembered seeing only when Mama had gone into labor with her brother Ashel. "Oh my. I thought we wasn't to kill anybody. I thought they promised Brother Brigham they wasn't going to kill anybody."

For a few silent seconds Mara stood watching Mama's eyes and listening to her faraway voice. No white men were killed. They were only Indians, Mama, she wanted to say. The Indians need not mean anything to them. Mama's concern sounded like the same worry she managed to stir up over curdled milk or fuzzy cheese. Yet Mara could feel something different in the air—something heavy. When Papa came toward her to get his coat, she flinched and drew back, seeing something sharp in his eyes. Mama brought her a robe and stood between her and Papa as Mara slipped out of the coat and gave it to her father. No one said anything. John, her sister's husband, wound his big scarf around his neck while Papa grunted and pushed his arms through the heavy sleeves of his coat. Tow-headed Ashel climbed out of his blanket. Even Sophia, fully dressed, backed down the stairs. Deciding not to be left out, Mara flung herself up the steep stairwell and into her gingham frock as quickly as she could, whipping her long dark hair into a ribbon behind her. She snapped her shawl off its nail and flung it around her neck. But at the bottom of the stairs she met Mama.

"Did you fetch fresh water, girl?" Mama said. "You need to bring in that water before you do anything else, Mara. It won't take you long."

"We'll go ahead," Papa was saying. "I'll take Ashel with me. You and Sophia get them loaves in the oven and come out when you can." But Sophia was already following John.

Mama was standing in Mara's way. "I'll come now," she

said to Papa. To Mara she said "After you bring in the water and set it to boil, you can come, honey. We'll wait to put the loaves in. But the boiling water. . . ."

Mara stood very still. She remembered she had dropped the bucket into the well. She would be late. She felt her mother was not being fair.

"Hurry." Mama pulled Aunt Caroline's afghan out of the big chair and wrapped it around her shoulders, then left.

Mara looked after her from the window, then narrowed her eyes and looked down the road. The townspeople were moving toward State Street. In a moment the house was quiet. Still stunned and feeling angry, she decided to hurry. Fully dressed now, she ran to the well and drew the bucket up as quickly as she could without spilling it, poured the water into the pan, and made her way awkwardly back to the house, with the pans swinging side to side. At the back door she thought she heard steps on the wooden floor inside the front room. Her neck felt cold. "Who is it?" she called.

Nobody answered, but the steps on the floor stopped. She set the water on the stove and pulled her shawl higher around her neck. "Who's there?" she repeated. She thought she saw a big shadow near the door.

"Oh, it's just me," a voice said. "Hello. I saw your Pa on the road. Told me I could get my ax he borrowed. I need it now. I didn't know you was here."

She turned the corner into the room. She saw the same eyes she had seen through the winter roses—Ivie Richards! Cold gripped her hair. He leaned down to the tool chest behind the door and pretended to rummage through the tools.

She tightened the shawl over her dress. "Well, I'm here," she said, narrowing her eyes and trying to stop her heart from bumping against her breast. "I wish you would have knocked."

Papa had said something strange seemed to be happening to Ivie Richards since he lost three little children on the trek west. The two older boys were from his only wife's first marriage. What he wanted was a son of his own.

From beneath the dark bush of hair, the black eyes clouded as he gazed at Mara. He had wanted that second wife like he never wanted anything else he ever asked God for. Everyone had been stunned when Bishop Hunt, who already had three wives, married Kate Wright for himself. Richards was a walking volcano.

Her father had said, "Never bait Richards. Some people will never be saints no matter how many times they get baptized. No matter how many times they try to wash their sins away. Their sins stick to them like a stain." Richards told anyone who would listen that things were going to change.

"So they're back, are they?" He raised his head and looked askance at her. "Ain't you going?"

Mara backed up against the door. "Yes, if you'll get out of my way," she said.

"You got my ax?" he said.

"I'll find your ax," Mara said. She knelt at her father's tool box and dug around in the tools. The ax was not there.

"It's there somewhere, girl," Richards said, coming up behind her, his body so close that she could feel his coat against her shawl. His hot breath touched her hair. "Ain't it there?" He put his hand on her shoulder.

She felt his rough hand through her dress like a claw, and for a terrible moment she didn't move. Then she turned, her eyes flickering, dark. "Don't you dare touch me," she said between her teeth. She wrenched herself free.

He laughed and drew back to stare at her. "You're not scared of me, are you?" He laughed again.

Mara turned around to stare back at him. She froze.

"Now, if I married you, you wouldn't be scared of me, would you?"

Mara was stunned. She shrank back, not believing what she was hearing. Her lips stiffened. Slowly she spoke. "You already have your ax, don't you?"

"Things change, girl," Richards said. "I already been to Brigham Young." He smiled a strange smile.

Mara wanted to say something, but her voice was locked. No sound came out to make words.

Richards reached toward her face and touched her hair. His hand was hot. He touched her cheek, drew his fingers down her neck and shoulder. Afraid to move, she felt him grip her arm.

"You're a woman now, girl," he said. He was big, like Papa. "You been kissed yet?"

Mara found her voice. "You wouldn't dare." She twisted her arm away from him.

"Maybe not now. Not today." He laughed again. The sweat began to run from under his hair down his slick brow. A sweet-sick odor steamed from him. "Sure you wouldn't like a ride to the crossing on the back of my horse?"

"No, sir. Good-bye, sir!" Mara was so hot inside she thought she would burn up. With the strength of his grip on her arm, he could have easily thrown her to the floor. She would place her faith in silence. She did not breathe.

Whether it was the prayers she said in silence between her teeth and in her eyes, she did not know. She felt suddenly unworthy of uttering them. But he relaxed his grip. He laughed. "You look scared, girl. Well, I'm not that kind of man. This is neither the time or place. I'm a church-going man, remember?" Then he smiled. "But this is not good-bye, Mara Eastman." His horse was just outside by the stoop. He flung himself over it and kicked it into the walkway to the road. He looked back at Mara who stood still in the house. Slowly she shut the door. For a moment she stood without moving, without tightening her shawl, without breathing. She waited to go to the window. She saw Richards disappearing round the bend toward the State Street crossing. Now she could go. But she went slowly, feeling empty and drained.

By the time Mara had caught up to them, Papa and the others were moving down the muddy slough of State Street, their eyes fastened on the gray distance where the tiny string of men were tramping home from the massacre of Indians near Provost's Hole. "Would they have killed them if they had not stolen our cattle?" Mama wanted to know. "Why didn't they surrender?" Her voice hovered on a whine.

"Why did they kill *all* the men?" Ashel ran alongside Papa to keep up.

Papa said, "Bee feathers," he didn't know. He couldn't answer all of the questions. He was just a visitor in this god-forsaken place.

Riding and on foot, the thirty or more local men of the militia led the small group of Indian women and their children northward toward the center of Salt Lake City. As they came closer, some of the townspeople slowed their pace. Some on horseback, like Richards, rode out to meet them. Richards dismounted from his horse alongside a tired old Indian woman whose feet were buckling under her. He scooped her into his arms and set her up in his saddle. Some horses in the returning group carried two old Indian women apiece. Most of the horses belonged to Captain Hunt. Hunt led one horse at the head of the party. Behind him, Mara saw his son, Bret. She felt her tongue go dry in her mouth. Bret carried an old woman and her young daughter on the back of his horse. Three other of Hunt's younger sons had gone out to meet the party and now rode smartly with Indian women behind their saddles, following their father, strutting as though they had also been on the expedition and were going to share the spoil. In an intense moment one of Chloe's youngest boys fell off his horse in the mud. Laughing, Scott Hunt scooped him into his own saddle. Everyone cheered.

Scott Hunt was the man everyone had expected that Brigham Young would call to stop the cattle robberies at Provost's Hole. After all, Bishop Hunt had, in the scant seven months since they had crossed the plains, carved out a cattle ranch unlike any other in the valley. With his six large sons and his adopted boy, Sully, he had fenced his place in one week and raised his barn in two. Timber had been cut for his house in October, and by November it stood its three imposing stories high on the east side of Main Street. In December, wagons from the East brought glass, and before the snow came in January the house was painted white—a glaring white that turned away the sharp rays of the sun. Only Brigham Young and a handful of the Church leaders on South Temple Street had as much to show for their efforts by the spring of 1848.

During January, Ella Hunt and the three younger wives—the youngest of them Kate Wright—had gathered their goods and children into the new home. Mara went there once with Papa and Ashel to visit. The fine spreads, carpets, drapes, needlepoint cushions, linens, old cut glass, prized clocks that had come in the big wagons from Nauvoo, reminded Mara of their old life. There was a softness inside the Hunts' white clapboard.

By the time Hunt's party reached the center of the City, the sun stood high, burning holes in the mist of the spring sky.

"Halloo!" Scott Hunt called to Papa and to their new

bishop, who stood chattering with cold at the edge of the group. Someone had gone to fetch Brigham Young, who would probably come to see things handled correctly, but for the time being Bishop King was in charge, his white beard jittering with the clatter of his jaw.

"Well now, Hunt. We heard from your foster boy that we're to put up these here Indian women."

"That's correct," Hunt said, after he shook the bishop's big fox-skin glove. "The Indians don't want their widows. They leave them to die." He greeted people he knew one by one, smiling and giving Papa a smart salute.

Mara stood with Ashel at Papa's elbow, trying to keep Papa's big body between her and Ivie Richards. She kept her eyes on Bret, Hunt's oldest son, until he finally nodded and smiled at her. With his father and his brothers, he lifted the Indian women down from the horses and stood them all together in a ragged row.

Some of the women huddled together to keep warm in the cold, their eyes staring from stunned faces. They were a mixed group, some dressed in shaggy buckskin ponchos, old patches of leather tied like bundles to their feet. Some wore moccasins of surprisingly fine quality. Three young women and a hunchbacked grandmother seemed to stand out from the rest. Their moccasins were beaded and fringed with soft doeskin. Two of the young women carried children. The third young woman, taller than the others, stood alone. Though the other Indian women seemed bent and broken, this one was obviously angry, her head high. A braid of thick hair fell to her waist. Tied over one of her shoulders was a large warm wrap that looked as if it had been made from the skin of a beaver or bear. She wore a necklace of teeth and sharp beads around her neck.

From his saddlebags, Scott Hunt took some small bundles wrapped in scraps of burlap or cattle hide. The old woman and the two others who stood beside her reached for their bundles greedily. The tall girl did not move. She did not even turn her head to look at the others nor did she heed the prodding of the old grandmother. Her wide black eyes stared straight ahead.

As Hunt led a thick-waisted older woman and a girl of about twelve to Papa, Ivie Richards leaped down from his horse in front of the tall Indian girl. He stood looking at her for a moment. She glowed, her skin a deep olive color. Her features were more delicate than the features of the others. Richards did not touch her but slowly walked around her. The grandmother and the two others backed away. Mara's heart pounded. She thought she could feel how hot his breath was against the tall Indian girl's cheek. The girl did not flinch, or blink.

Hunt stood off to the side distributing the other Indians among the townspeople. Bishop King was writing it all down with a stub of chalk on an old stone slate. As his nose ran, he wiped it with the back of his glove.

Richards spoke to Hunt, his old enemy, as though he were still in good favor. He spoke with a cool voice. He had managed to stay in the church; he had managed to face the other members as though nothing had ever happened among any of them. "Hunt," Richards said stiffly. "You did good, Hunt."

Hunt turned toward him and saw Richards standing by the handsome girl. "She's going with me," Hunt said in a loud voice. "She and the other two sisters and the old woman Hawk Feather." Hunt's voice carried authority. He was Richards' size, his hair blond, his eyes clear blue. His face was clean shaven, except for a light red moustache, and he wore a sharp white felt broad-brimmed hat that stood out against the black hills like a white bird with curled wings. Mara loved Mr. Hunt and all his family—all his wives, the little blond-headed children of his younger wives, the six tall children of his first wife, Ella. The Eastmans were all grateful for the Hunts, who from the beginning had seen to it that the Eastmans' stock was well cared for, until John Smith had come along to marry Sophia and help out. But it was more than family gratitude that Mara felt for Bret. When his eyes met hers she felt weak. She shrank behind Papa.

"My wife's ill and I need help," she heard Richards say. "I've already talked to Brigham Young."

"She's going with her grandmother and the sisters," Hunt said, an edge to his voice. He turned around and gave another older Indian woman to Eastman's neighbor Sadie Harper.

"I could take one of the women with children," Sadie chattered the way she always did. "My daughter will be over and she has children. Why don't you let me take the young one with the baby and the little boy? I'm not so busy I couldn't take care of them myself." She pointed to one of the two sisters with Hawk Feather. The young woman had a small baby in a cradle fastened to her back, and she was leading a little boy by the hand.

Hunt looked over at the group of women standing with Hawk Feather. Richards was still waiting, his thick arms folded across his chest. "Well, I'm not sure," Hunt said to Sadie. "I was planning on taking them together. . . ." His voice seemed forced, hesitant.

"Give them their opportunity to reap blessings," Bishop King said suddenly, his chalk raised over the slate. "Give them their blessings." He snorted when he sucked the air through his nose.

Richards began to smile at Bishop King. He stood over the Indian maiden, his large arms only inches from her black hair. Mara watched him. It seemed as if she herself was standing there in the moccasins of the beautiful girl, feeling his breath in her own hair. Only once did his gaze meet hers. She was sure he was laughing at her behind his eyes.

Now Scott Hunt turned toward Richards angrily. "You. . . . you wouldn't dare, Richards." His anger and his words stunned Mara.

"But you would," Richards sneered at Hunt, his arms still folded. "You would dare, wouldn't you?" Every indignity he had suffered at Hunt's hands—particularly Hunt's marriage to Kate—burned in his eyes.

Hunt flushed, the color rising along his temples.

"I went to Brigham Young."

Now the people in the circle drew back. Once there was a rumor that Richards had threatened Hunt with a knife. The crowd was quiet, including Bishop King. Everyone watched in silence while the bishop gave up the beautiful Indian girl to Richards.

Mara watched Scott Hunt. For a moment she thought he was going to say something. His face grew red. But he kept his lips closed. Bishop King wrote down with his piece of chalk that the Hunts would take Hawk Feather and the sister Angel Lip, the one with the big baby, and Richards would take the tall Indian girl. Her name was Blueflower.

Richards put his large hand on the girl's neck and said, "You come with me." She jerked her head away from his touch, her eyes flashing. The necklace snapped. Some of the beads flew to where Papa was standing with the little old Indian woman and her daughter. The rest of the beads slipped down the Indian girl's leather dress into the mud. Richards did not bend. When she scrambled for the beads, he jerked her arm. The little old wizened woman in Papa's care knelt in the mud and recovered some of them, but the dark ground sucked them under as if reclaiming its property.

Hunt turned to Hawk Feather and Angel Lip and

spoke in broken Ute. From his frustrated gestures Mara could see he was trying to explain to them that Blueflower would live close by—that they would see each other.

The old Indian woman Hawk Feather turned from Hunt and ran to Blueflower to clutch her robe. Her twisted hands sank into the thick fur while Richards tore the girl away. Reaching for the old woman, Blueflower pounded Richards, her hands beating at his arms. "Kah cheeg, kah cheeg," she cried. Then she shuddered and moaned, clutching at her broken beads. Richards pulled her up into his arms and lifted her to his horse. She sat stiffly on the saddle and stared straight ahead. Richards mounted behind her and shouted something to Scott Hunt that sounded like "Crawl into the ground."

Mara watched Richards lean his head back against his stiff collar as though he were laughing at all of them. She could not take her eyes away from the Indian girl, whose hair streamed behind her. She felt a terrible fear. Finally Richards turned, cut his heels into the horse's flanks, and was gone.

"So this is what God made out of the earth around here. This is it," Papa mumbled on the way back to the house, his kerchief flying like a flag out of his back pocket. He was keeping his distance, but he could not stop looking at the old toothless woman and her twelve-year-old daughter who walked behind them.

What Mara noticed most was the smell. Not an unpleasant smell at a distance, but close, it was strong: woodsmoke and juniper berries, a gamy sweet and overpowering odor that reminded her of wet cattle in a hot barn, their steaming hides sweating and stinking.

The old woman wore a leather thong on her pepper-gray

head and a covering of paper-thin deerskin. She walked with a thudding step, her knees straight and her feet flat. The young girl clung to the fringe of her cape and half ran, half stumbled trying to keep up. She was thin, with black puffed circles under her big eyes. At the ends of her gaunt limbs hung large dangling hands and wide feet. But she had the same sleek black hair of the Indian maiden, a fine thick cape of it tied in a piece of leather below the back of her neck. Ashel stared at them often and stumbled because he was not watching the road.

"So this is what the sun stirs up out of this ground out here—this sharp hot sun clingin' to the earth stirs this up out of the soil and the rain makes it grow." Papa squinted at the sun and he spread his hands. In the distance were the lakes and rivers, the barren sage-covered foothills fed by the rain. He often thought he saw the colors of the ground in the life on it. It was the land that gave you life. It was this land that stood inside the Indians. All of this had given them their lives, and Papa couldn't get over how they had sucked up the land in the very roughness of their bodies—the skin of their hands and faces burned and scarred by years of this sun and wind.

Mara thought it would have been all right if they had been assigned the tall Indian girl Blueflower. But she thought these small dirty ones should have been left where they came from, and she said so, adding, "They need a bath."

"Yes, they do smell like they been crawling in and out of a rabbit hole—or a bear pit," Papa said.

At the door stoop, Mara ran ahead of everyone and opened the door. Sophia and John entered first and Sophia headed for the water on the stove. The Indian woman stopped at the steps, her hands clutching the deerskin cape.

"Come in?" Mara asked, holding both the door and her breath. The Indian girl moved closer to her mother. But the old woman did not climb the stairs. Mama, still behind, put her arm around the woman who had not yet said a word. Her eyes seemed half closed, hidden behind high cheekbones and the thickness of her eyelids. She gazed with a pinched look.

"It's all right," Mama said. But the woman did not budge. She stood at the foot of the steps and just stared.

"Well, pickles and bird feathers!" Papa hooted. "She don't want nothin' to do with any pale-faced white folks, I'll wager. I swear . . . around this brown country it's true we don't fit. Look at this." He walked toward the window and thrust his gingery whiskers into the reflective glass. "I got a face white as a ghost. You start getting an eyeful of brown faces and your own looks transparent. I ain't sure I'm even present."

Papa thought it was terribly funny to reflect on his status as an "outside visitor" as he put it. "In this country we're like babies. Don't know how to trap bears. Don't know how to eat roots or rats. How do you suppose these Book of Mormon folks have been living all this time if they didn't know how to wrestle the life out of this very ground?"

Mama quickly got the hot pail off the fire and stirred suds into it. She was fixing to scrub the old woman—Mara knew it. Sophia had got down brushes and a few old rags out of the cupboard.

"You going to wash the very life offa' that old lady?" Papa grinned. "She won't recognize herself. She don't care about living like any of you supernatural apparitions that don't know nothing about this noplace." Papa swept his hand across the view out the window again, the naked brown and black hills. And he laughed a full-throated laugh.

Mama took in the kettle. "You go fetch her in, Hart."

"Oh, I'm not fetchin' her in. You invited her. You fetch her in. She just don't want to come. Let Mara fetch her in. She can give them her clothes. Mara's a little bit wild just like 'em. Seems like she don't need her clothes, do you, girl?"

Mara looked at his eyes. They were bright with a sharp fire. She knew he had seen her from the back window this morning before she had grabbed his coat. She sucked in air and held it, expecting a scolding. But it was all he said.

"John, then you fetch her," Sophia spoke up.

"Not me. You women are the ones on this project. Pa and me and Ashel are due at the south field."

"We do need to get going, Martha," Papa said, looking one last time into Mara's eyes. She did not move. The men buttoned up their coats, took some old bread in big chunks and some cheese. Papa warned Ashel to wrap up better, and they were gone. They left in a gust of cold that came like a cloud through the doorway. Mara watched them pass the old woman and her daughter still standing near the stoop.

"Don't you let those women get you," Papa said, although his teasing fell on deaf ears. The old woman and her child still stood unmoving, their eyes almost unblinking. The old woman's fists began shaking in the cold.

Sophia and Mara stood at the window watching while Mama gave orders. "Help me with this bucket, get out the mop stick, take the mop part off of it."

The old Indian woman huddled more deeply into her deerskin as Papa, John, and Ashel left. She turned as though she were uncertain as to what she should do, and then she began following them.

"She's leaving, Mama," Mara called.

Ashel turned to watch them, and he tugged at Papa's sleeve. Papa sidestepped quickly through the gate and shut it to stop her.

Mama ran to the window. "Oh, that will never do. Poor soul."

"I have a better idea," said Sophia. "Get the bread and cheese, quick."

Mara ran for the bag of dry bread and lopped a big chunk off the white cheese. Sophia opened the door and called "Wait!" But it didn't do any good. The old woman and her daughter had reached the shut gate before Mara could catch up to offer the food in her hands.

"Here you are. Here you are," Mara said, still holding her breath and coaxing as though to a wild animal. The old Indian woman turned clumsily, her pinched eyes filled with fear, wonder, uncertainty.

"Here now. Something to eat." She called back to Sophia who was trying to get through the doorway with a tray. "Heat the milk, Sophia. It's so cold."

"Mama heated the milk," Sophia said. She brought the pitcher and two cups and set the tray on the ground. "Here you are. Eat and drink," she said softly, pouring the warm milk into the cups.

The young girl's eyes brightened. Her big hands moved nervously on her mother's wrap. But no smile crossed her thin lips. Both mother and daughter barely moved, only enough to turn toward the house. They still stood, staring.

"Bread," Mara said, handing a hunk of bread to the daughter. The girl did not move. "Eat like this." Mara took a small bite out of the bread.

"Oh, she is so cold," Sophia said, putting the pitcher on the cold ground. Though the bright sun stood at noon, the creatures shivered like newborn children naked in a strange world. Holding a cup of warm milk in one hand, Sophia reached out with the other one and took hold of the old woman's tightened fist. "Here is some warm milk," she said softly. "Take it. Drink it." The woman's eyes searched Sophia's. Sophia tried to open the old fingers, but the woman drew her fists under her robe. Sophia placed the cup to the woman's lips. Slowly, eyeing Sophia with guarded eyes, the woman finally parted her lips on the warm glass. The milk, steaming in the cold, clouded her face, her cold cheeks, her nose. With the sound that cattle make when drinking, she gulped the milk. She drank all of it. Then Sophia tried to guide her toward the house. She began to step cautiously under Sophia's urging. But when she reached the stoop, she shook her head. Sophia gave her a gentle push, but she shook her head and sat suddenly on the first step, still hiding her fists under her robe. Surprised, Sophia held some bread out to her. The woman looked at it hungrily, but she would not eat. Instead, she held out her fist and opened her hand.

As the old woman opened her hand, she looked out from under her brows with a defeated gaze. Inside, on her muddy palm, lay a bear's tooth and a thorn from the broken necklace. She leaned over the beads in her palm and began to moan.

For a long moment Sophia and Mara waited, feeling helpless, while the woman cried, no doubt for the past. She cried for her husband, for her own death from a life that would never be the same again. Primeval, her cry seemed to sound from the deepest center of the earth. Mara had never heard anything like it before. The old woman rocked forward on her haunches and leaned her head over the beads in her hand. Hesitating, Mara rested her hand with the bread in it on the woman's thigh. A gasp cut off the sound in the old woman's throat, and a tormented moment of silence burned under the sun.

Suddenly, while they were not watching, the child, who had followed them to the steps, took the bread from Mara's hand. Surprised, Mara drew back and smiled. When the old woman, silent now, saw the child eat, she tucked the beads into a seam of her moccasin and took the bread and cheese from Sophia. Mara and Sophia looked at each other but did not speak. Mother and daughter sat on the step as comfortably as they could in the cold of the March afternoon. They began timidly, as tiny animals begin on nuts, with both hands. But it was not long before they tore into the bread like wolves.

When the men returned at five o'clock that evening, Papa thought it was awfully funny that Mama and the girls hadn't yet been able to get the two Indians to come inside the house. Mama and Sophia had given them extra blankets which they had carefully spread over their backs, both to keep them warm and to protect them from the sun. When Papa opened the gate, they were sitting like carvings on the stoop. They would not budge when the men came in, either, and Papa laughed when he stoked the fire.

Mara took them big chunks of bacon from the dinner table, which both Indians grabbed with delight. After their supper, the Eastmans sat in the front room talking. Most of the conversation was about Provost's Hole.

"Next I suppose Brigham Young will send colonizers to brave the Utes," Papa said.

"I don't want to go," Sophia said, putting final tucks into a baby's shift. She was almost four months pregnant.

"Sophia," John spoke softly. "We'll go if we're called."

Still stunned by what had happened during the day, Mara didn't say a word, but sat watching the flames in the cooking fire, stroking the house cat. She thought about Richards and the Indian girl. Thinking of her there, in the house through the back roses, she shuddered.

It was a few moments after dusk. Papa got up to yawn and stretch and check on the Indians. But when he looked out the window he saw no Indians.

Mama gave a short cry. "Oh dear, oh dear! What will happen to them now?" she whined. The men left the house to look around the yard, but they saw no one.

"We go to all that trouble to take them in and now look what's happened. *Nothing* ever works out right. Nothing."

Mara turned from her mother's complaining and slipped upstairs away from her voice. If there had not been so many disappointments, Mama might have been a cheerful person. As it was, there was always something that hurt her or was too hard for her to bear. Mara was tired of it. The whining voice was a refrain in her memory even as far back as Kirtland, when through the fog of past years she remembered her mother pulling Sophia and herself under the table because mobsters were knocking at their door and peering through their window.

"Why did you marry me, then?" Mara sometimes heard Papa ask, gruffly.

"I don't know. I don't know," Mama would cry.

Mama was an only child from a wealthy family in upstate New York. She had fallen in love with Papa at first sight. When she had decided she wanted to join the Mormon Church and come west, her family had disowned her.

"You chose to come with me when you knew I was interested in the Mormons. And you joined the Church, too. You made your own decisions," Papa always said.

"Not this! Not this!" Mama would say, especially on the trek west in the old broken wagon.

Mama's whimper hurt Mara. She began to believe her mother was often unfair.

"If it's so, Mama . . . if you're here with Papa, and we're all here together, then it is what it is. Why don't you just forget the past? Let it go." But Mama didn't let it go. She clung to it. She told too many stories about the past, about Aunt Caroline, her father's sister who would now inherit the foundry and pass it on to her reckless son. She talked about how Aunt Caroline's son had made loose with family property and had married a Boston socialite and would have a houseful of heirs.

Mama told about the great pain her father, Papa Hanson Harding, had felt to see his fortune pass to his sister's family, about the great pain he felt at losing his only child to the Mormons. He begged with Martha to be wise and stay where she belonged, but when he saw that she was determined to make her own life, he let her go. Hanson Harding had died before Martha and Hart Eastman left New York. Mama told how on his deathbed he had said, "Go with God's people, like an Israeli princess. If that's what you want, Angel, that's what I want." Mama told that story over and over. But always she hesitated to tell that he had disowned her after all.

And now, beaten and dragged from place to place—Kirtland, Far West, Nauvoo—Mama had gone with God's people. Mara had to admit her mother was strong. The less sturdy ones gave up altogether. Mama never actually turned back, but her voice full of complaint betrayed her weakness. When Papa tried to cheer her up, he talked about the future. But things never happened fast enough for Mama. Mara thought she was happier here in Great Salt Lake City. But complaining had become a bad habit. Mama's fretting spilled over into a sort of anxious charity for all who suffered. And because she *was* strong and capable, she was constantly doing—perhaps too much—for her family and for anyone she could see who needed help. Mama believed that if a little was good, a lot was better. Whatever could be done, she did, but sometimes over and over again, several times too many.

"Mara!" Mama called up the stairs. "Come on, girl! We've got to find those Indians!" And dragging Mara and Ashel with her, Mama knocked on doors, called out, and asked questions until she was convinced no one in the area had seen them.

It was a long futile search. Mara resented having to ask so many people the same question only to hear "No."

"They are somewhere," Mama said. "They are somewhere. If we've done all we can do, the only thing left for us to do is to wait."

Waiting would be hard. Mara watched her mother gear herself for it, tighten the muscles in her fingers and in her back as she leaned against the hard wood of the rocker, pushing the floor with her foot. It was almost midnight when Mama's eyes grew heavy and she finally began to nod. Ashel was curled up by the fire sound asleep.

"It's time to go to bed, Martha," Papa finally said. "It won't do you no good to lose a night of sleep."

She jerked at his words, as though wakened from a vivid dream. "Oh dear," she shook her head and blinked her eyes. "Help me up, then, Hart. I thought I saw the Indians in a pit like the quarry pit we explored near Papa's foundry, and I tried to get down to them, and I was slipping . . . ready to fall."

"You're slipping into sleep," Papa said good-naturedly. "Everyone else wants to go to bed. Ashel's asleep. I'm tired, myself."

"I don't know what we're going to do if we can't find them."

"Don't get started your worrying out loud." Papa sometimes tried to stop her before she escalated into a full-fledged whine. He called it "worry out loud." Sometimes he said, "Into every life some rain will fall," but he didn't say that tonight. Instead, he got her by the hand and pulled her to her feet. With his old charm he pulled her gently into his arms. "We'll find them sure enough, Martha. In the meantime, have faith and sleep a little."

Puzzled, Mara watched her mother jerk suddenly and pull back from Papa's embrace, her eyes bright with the reflection of the dying fire. "That's it! That's where they are, Hart Eastman. Wouldn't you know it! In the pit!" she exclaimed.

"In the pit?" Papa looked amazed and confused at the same time.

"In the root cellar! Don't you see? They still need to be near the earth. I left it open this afternoon. They probably saw me going in and out." While she was talking, she was busy pulling the shawl around her arms, grabbing and lighting a wax candle, and getting to the back door. Papa grabbed her coat and his coat and another candle and padded after her just as she flung into the back porch. Mara and Sophia and John followed them.

In the cool, open darkness, lighted by a thin yellow moon, the family made its way across the cold ground. Beyond the well, the potato cellar loomed like a mouth the earth had just recently opened. The giant mound fit into the earth behind a wooden door still green from its cut of young timber.

"I'm sure of it, now. I hadn't shut it, and here it is shut," Mama said.

At the cellar door Papa handed his candle to Mama, who stood lifting one shoulder higher than the other trying to keep her coat from slipping off. The others strained to see. Papa tugged at the door in its fresh wood frame and, without much trouble, wrenched it free. Mama thrust the candles forward and lost her coat, but she let it fall while she stooped to peer into the hole.

"Hello," she called softly. "Are you there? We won't hurt you. Are you there?"

Mara saw a slight movement behind the pork barrel and said, "There, Mama!" Mama brought her candle farther into the pit and lifted it so that the light chased the shadows to the floor. There they were, against the dusty cellar wall. The child was asleep on her mother's arm. The mother stared, as though just awakened, through large, frightened eyes. It was when Mara saw those eyes that she realized the Indians were frightened people who might always have hidden in the earth, afraid to come out into the light. Mara felt a strange feeling of loss for them. The earth was where they would rather have stayed. But her mother would not let them stay here. She meant well.

"Oh, you poor things," Mama clucked, stepping over some apples and a burlap bag filled with red beans. "Oh, you poor dear things." The old woman seemed to draw herself into the wall as Mama tried to make her way back to them.

"Martha, be careful," Papa said.

"Come with us," Mama said to the Indian mother, setting both candles on the pork barrel and stretching out her arms. "Come inside where it's warm!" The old woman clutched the child closer and stared at Mama from the pit of darkness near the wall.

"Come inside and take our blankets. Sleep near the fire. Won't you come?"

Knowing they didn't understand her words, Mama kept her voice soothing, trying to win by kindness. The Indian mother only drew back farther against the dirt.

"Martha don't beggar them. They don't want to come, and it is warm in here. Let's leave them until morning."

"Oh, they can't sleep here," Mama whined softly.

"It's probably warmer here than it ever was in their own home."

"I don't know what to do." Mama said. Picking up one

of the candles, she leaned down closer to the dark faces, holding the light toward the gnarled hand of the old woman, then raising it to light her eyes.

"Oh, please come," Mama said again. Without warning, the old woman's hand shot forward against the candle knocking it from Mama's grasp. Sputtering, it flickered to a feeble ash in the apple barrel and went out.

"For the name of little green pickles, that's it," Papa said, and he took up the other candle from the pork barrel. Holding his hand around the flame, he moved back toward the door. "That's it, Martha. Let's go. They don't want to come with us. They're afraid. Don't force it. Give them time."

Mama backed up awkwardly, jerking her coat and shawl around her shoulders. She coughed a small cough and turned toward Papa. "They don't even want the comfort we can give them." She didn't whine. Her voice was quiet and raspy.

"They don't want us, anything of us," Papa said. "But now that we are here, we are theirs. They will have to learn." Sophia, John, and Mara climbed out of the cellar first, then Papa. Mama stepped behind them. Papa clutched his coattail and carried the other candle without relighting it.

"Maybe if you'll let 'em set awhile and then take 'em out in the hot sun and plant 'em, they'll bloom," Papa said as they went into the warm house.

"Yes, I know," Mama said, "and into every life a little rain must fall."

The Indians had arrived in the Salt Lake Valley on Thursday morning after the rain. The weather in the next few days grew fairer. A warm March wind blew up from the south; the morning sun flattened the frost into dew. For hours during the warm day, the Indians continued to sit on the stoop as though waiting for their husband and father to come for them from his Battle Creek grave. Ashel and Mara took them biscuits, tankards of porridge, some bacon. They ate like wild dogs, tearing, almost grunting in their hunger and satisfaction.

From the window seat inside the house, Mara and Sophia knit while they watched. Friday about noon the two visitors toured the yard looking for fresh leaves close to the roots in the spring ground. Later they stood behind the house beside the chicken shed picking bits of dry corn from the hay. Ashel scouted around the coop and tried to get the girl's attention by cracking Papa's red horse whip. The girl took her eyes off the corn in the hay and watched. But the Indian mother grabbed her daughter by her large hand and pulled her down to squat in the dirt.

On Saturday morning, Mara saw the bishop's counselor Dimick Huntington riding by on the road. He stopped at the Eastman gate and hitched his horse to it. Mara stepped quickly from the window seat to open the door to him but he stopped at the stoop in front of the old woman, who did not look at him, but kept her dark eyes lowered to his boots. Mara opened the door a crack and heard Huntington say something in the smooth yawning language of the Utes. He was asking a question. He repeated it several times, but the woman would not answer. When he saw Mara, he lifted his eyes to her.

"Did they tell you their names?" he asked her.

"No, they didn't," Mara said, widening the door. She had not really thought of them as having names. She had felt them to be pitiful, stray, nameless things. Once something was named, the clarity seemed to diffuse the haze that made it still unreal somehow.

Huntington questioned the old woman again, finally lifting her face with his hand. She jerked from him, so he knelt beside her, asking the question in Ute over and over again.

The woman stared at him with dazed eyes. Then she spoke, the first word Mara had ever heard her utter. "Si-pa-pu." Her voice was low, rasping. She tried to clear her throat. "Sipapu, Sipapu." Then she pointed to her daughter. "Wai. Mi-pu-wai. Mipuwai."

"Rain, Little Rain," Huntington said slowly, staring at the young girl. "But Si-pa-pu. Sipapu is not Ute. It reminds me of Piute. Spirit of Earth. Bia du-weep?" He turned to the woman again and asked more questions in Ute.

"Pi-ute," the woman finally answered him.

"She was born Piute, taken by Utes when a girl. Sipapu. Mipuwai. Spirit of Earth and Rain."

The woman nodded and then looked at Mara with flat gray eyes. Mara wished suddenly both of them were gone. With names, with histories, the Indians suddenly, more than ever before, became real people. She felt she ought to care about them. Yet she could still taste the raw smell that stirred in the air somehow. By this time, Mama who had heard Huntington on the porch, had come to stand by the door, Sophia behind her.

"She doesn't understand who we are or what we are trying to do. She knows Piute—can't understand Ute very well. But I think she'll come in, now," Huntington said. Mara's heart sank. She had never understood why her mother had been so anxious to have them come into the house.

The old woman turned toward Mama who stretched out her hand. Huntington said a few more words to her, and she walked awkwardly, pushing her large flat feet across the door stoop. When she entered the front room, Mama smiled and put her arm around her, ushering her to a chair as Sophia hurried to get her knitting out of the way. After Huntington's visit, the two guests spent the nights by the warm front room fire on a divan cot and cushions on the floor—adopting their new names—Spirit of Earth and Rain.

Chapter Two

Sunday morning Papa predicted that Brigham Young would call families to settle Provost's Hole that afternoon, and he was right. In sacrament meeting after a long speech by Bishop King, Brigham Young appeared after having settled some business in another ward in the city and moved to the front of the chapel drawing everyone's gaze and a noisy ripple of whispering after him.

"Now I know of the sacrifices that have already been made. You have been called from the far East to Kirtland, Far West, Nauvoo, finally to a place of refuge in the West. But your blessings, my brothers and sisters, have only begun."

Mara noticed that Mama shifted uneasily in her seat, her fingers pulling at the edges of her shawl.

"I know many of you have already built homes here. I know this." He paused and lowered his eyes, but lifted them again immediately. "The kingdom is ready to expand from here to the north, to the south, to every land on earth, and mark my words, the work of Jesus Christ will go forward to plant the truth in every dark corner of this earth."

His voice shook the congregation. "And it is time, my brothers and sisters, to send our people out from this valley into the surrounding territory to disseminate the gospel, to teach it even to the natives of this land." He stopped then, and continued in a more practical voice. "Now, I'm not one to say we will yet be able to bring these Indian peoples into our churches, though they are welcome to come, of course." Mama had tried to bring Spirit of Earth and Rain with them to church today, but they would not leave the yard. "I'm not expecting conversion or baptisms. But by example, brothers and sisters, we may begin somewhere, begin by teaching them to till the soil, to build, even to treat each other with civility and courtesy." Mara held her breath, expecting to hear Mama's whine begin. But Mama was staring, as though she were numb.

The speech ended with a calling for thirty-three families—about one hundred fifty people—to prepare their material goods and settle in the Utah Valley near the "hole" of the French trapper Provost. The Eastmans were among those called.

On the walk home, Mama didn't say a word. She pulled at the corner of her shawl, kept her eyes fastened on the road. Nobody talked much. Sophia and John, who had also been called, whispered to each other. Sophia told John she wanted to do what the prophet told her, but she wondered if he knew she was going to have a baby.

Bret Hunt stopped Mara only a few yards from the church before he turned home. None of the Hunt family had been called to go. "I noticed your father and brother-in-law were on Brigham Young's list, Mara," Bret said.

Mara slowed to fall behind her family. She thought she was going to be sick. Her heart was pounding. She wondered if she could make her voice sound normal. "I'm afraid Mama and Sophia don't want to go," Mara said.

"And I don't blame them," Bret slowed to match his stride with Mara's. He dug his hands into his pockets and stared at the road as he walked. "If my Pa hadn't had a special assignment with the militia, Brigham Young would have called him, too."

"I don't want to go either," Mara said.

At Bret's silence she felt a stab of fear. She wasn't sure what he would think.

The silence seemed to last forever. Finally he spoke. "My Uncle Jeb and I have been called to go on missions. In July. To England."

The pain she felt at his words astonished Mara as much as his announcement itself. She was suddenly very conscious of his stride alongside hers, the shadow from his head that stood between her and the sun.

"England?" she said, her voice thick. "That's a long way." Her palms grew clammy. She wondered if he knew how she felt. What was he feeling? Was he merely telling his news to a childhood playmate of his younger brothers or was he trying to say something more?

"There are twenty men called to go to England in July. I think we're lucky," Bret continued. "My pa has enough sons to send somebody to every mission of the Church."

"While you are in England, I'll be feeding Indians at Provost's Hole," Mara said, trying to sound matter-of-fact.

"Papa wondered if your family might take some of the Indians back with you?"

"Don't you want to keep your Indians? Or don't they want to stay?"

"Even though it may be hard for them, I think they want to be with their own people," Bret said.

"I'm sure we can take them with us," Mara said quietly, not really thinking about the Indians, but about Bret—about the tremor in her heart.

"I hope you don't have a lot of trouble, robberies or killings," Bret said. "They don't like us."

"I know." She knew that Old Hawk Feather and Angel Lip with her baby had tried to run away from the Hunts twice. She smiled. "Ours wouldn't come in until yesterday."

"Then what's the point?" Bret said, the words barely audible. "If they don't want our help. . . ."

As though she were afraid God would hear her, Mara said too quickly "I agree, why should we try?" As soon as she said it she hated her weakness.

"We can't let them alone to kill our animals," Bret assured both of them.

"No," Mara was afraid of saying too much.

"But maybe we could leave them to live their way, instead of carrying them on our shoulders."

Mara looked at him. Was he, too, admitting God had asked too much of them? She had read the passage from the Book of Mormon a dozen times. The Saints were supposed to carry the native people into the future. But it wasn't going to be easy.

"I have to admit I don't like them very much," Bret said.

"I don't either." Mara agreed so quickly and with such force that she felt herself blush from her rashness.

"But I think we ought to be kind." We ought to be kind. Bret's words stung her. It was as though he had planned to discover her uncharitable feelings and then shame her. She shrank back from his gaze. She was almost glad when he turned up the walk to the big white house and left her standing at the gate. He lifted his hand to wave to her without looking back. She sucked in her breath, squinted in the too-white reflection of the sun on the shingles. The brightness hurt her eyes.

Late that evening Scott Hunt rode by Eastman's with Bret and his third son Caleb, the one who was Mara's age—fifteen. The big man with his two big sons seemed to fill up the house, bringing in a draft of cold evening air. Scott was still wearing his black Sunday suit, pressed and brushed clean except for the horse hair on his pant legs. Bret and Caleb had changed into overalls.

"What I want to do is make sure they have something to go to if there's no way to make it with the old chest-beater . . . what's his name . . . Little Chief." Little Chief, Hunt told the Eastmans, had been the one who knew where the thieves were. They were renegades from his own tribe. He had sent his son with the militia to show them the way. When Hunt had returned and reported to Little Chief that all of his robber tribesmen were killed, the old man had beat his chest and wailed: "To think I sent you there to kill them. They have come to such a bad end!"

Some of the Indian wives had wanted to stay with Little Chief, but he was still suspicious enough of them and their thievery not to want them. Women and children without husbands and fathers to care for them were a burden on a chief and his tribe. Crying and pounding his chest, he had waved them away. So Hunt's militia had returned with almost all of them, except a very few who had run away.

"Then we'll take them," Hart Eastman told Hunt. "We're leaving Monday, week from tomorrow."

"I'd be grateful." Hunt rubbed his hands together. His hands were large, his nails well groomed and clean. He glanced toward the corner where Spirit of Earth sat with Rain close by her side. "Of course you'll also take these two with you."

"Of course," Mama said. "Will you stay for some hot milk and biscuits?"

Hunt looked at his sons and said, "Yes." The room was crowded, so Mara went into the kitchen with Mama and

Sophia to pour the milk into cups. Ashel carried the dinner scraps out to the pigs. Bret came into the kitchen, too, offering to help. Mara began to feel that same tremor under her heart.

"Will you be taking all your goods, Sister Eastman?" Bret asked Mama, politely, as if trying to make conversation.

"Everything I own," Mama said.

"Some families were going to keep them in storage until places were built."

"Our place will be built," Mama said, not looking up from washing out the cups at the dishpan.

"Their eighth home in fifteen years," Sophia sighed. Mara stiffened, hoping Bret wouldn't see how unwilling Sophia was to go where she had been called.

"Brigham Young told you it would be your last calling?" he ventured with sympathy in his voice.

"Our very last calling," Mama said, and Mara remembered how often he had heard that. Usually, Mama complained bitterly and listed all their previous "last callings." Now she seemed too bitter even for complaint. During the afternoon Mara had caught her touching things in the new house, running her hands over the new wooden doors. They would be leaving next week.

"If there's anything we can do to help," Bret began. "Let us know. . . ."

"Carry this," Mama said abruptly, without smiling. She thrust the tray with the cups of milk toward Bret. Mara felt embarrassed, but Bret took it willingly and walked into the front room. Mara gave each of the Indians a cup and they drew the hot milk into their throats greedily without speaking. Very soon, the Indian mother lifted herself awkwardly from her spot by the fire, took the hand of her daughter and stood silently at the front door until someone opened it for her. They left.

"Hardly what I would want in my front parlor," Scott Hunt said as though he had not meant to be heard. "But we must be kind."

"If only they would consent to bathe," Papa said.

"Oh, they're helpless and uneducated, like children," Mama answered, excusing them. "They're poor people." Mama's face filled with a compassion that for a moment erased the bitterness that had been there since Brigham Young's call.

The back door sprang open for Ashel as he came in with the scrap bucket. From the yard through the open door they could hear the dog yelping.

"Ashel?"

"Mama, something's out there back of our fence in the bushes," Ashel said, breathing hard as though he had been running. "Behind us in Ivie Richards' yard. Something's there, and the dog won't stop barking."

"Land sakes!" Mama said, wiping her hands on her apron. "What is it?"

Curious, Hunt and his boys each took some biscuits with their milk and walked through the kitchen to the windows and the door. Mara followed them. In the back yard they could see Spirit of Earth with her daughter walking toward the back fence. The dog, barking at a broken spot in the fence, went crazy trying to claw himself through the thorns.

The men left the house, Mara and Ashel following them. At a place in Richards' fence where the growth lay thickest, one of the slats was broken. Spirit of Earth knelt on the ground and tried to pull it away. The men came up behind her. Something moved on the other side. Through the triangle, they could see the brown face of an Indian lying on the ground under the bushes, reaching toward Spirit of Earth. At once Mara saw who it was. It was Blueflower. She had tried to crawl through the broken slat. She was trembling. Her eyes were large and dark. The thorns of the roses had pricked her face. Mara stood back. It was the first time Mara had seen the blood of an Indian. It was a strange moment, for she had not supposed—no one had ever told her—it was the same color as her own.

Scott Hunt said something Mara couldn't hear. Then he began to tear at the broken slats of the fence himself.

"Stop!" The shout startled Mara. She looked up to see Ivie Richards coming out on the gravel at the back of his house. He carried a gun. As he stomped toward them, he held it as though it were alive in his hands. "You didn't know she's married to me," he said.

Quickly he crossed over to the Indian girl and stood above her. "You're hurt," he said, bending over her. "You've cut yourself." Blueflower raised her face and brushed it with her hand; the blood mingled on her cheeks with the tears. While the others watched, feeling helpless, Richards brushed the tears and the blood away from her eyes with his hand. Mara felt stung by his touch; she felt the rough hand on her own cheeks. She saw Blueflower's glance of terror and fear. Blueflower! She watched the man's hand brush the dark cheek with a terrible tenderness. Mara knew. Then he took her arm. Stumbling, the Indian woman turned to follow her husband as he walked back across his yard and into his house. The door slammed shut behind them.

Spirit of Earth lay on the ground, her arm still stretched between the slats of Richards' fence, her hands cut by the thorns. Out of her mouth came the same wail that Mara had heard once before, the same deep guttural moan. It frightened her. The girl, Rain, knelt at her mother's side and clutched at her back.

Mara turned away, her stomach twisting inside of her. Hunt was the only one who spoke, his face drawn in pain. "If God wills, he'll let her go," he said, stepping back toward the house, opening and closing his fists as he walked. "He must eventually let her go."

Mama came out now, wondering why everyone was taking so long. She saw Spirit of Earth and Rain lying on the ground. "Are they hurt?" she cried, running toward them. Mara, Bret, and Papa helped her lift them to their feet and led them back into the house.

For seven days before departure, the thirty-three families prepared to make the trip to Provost's Hole. For the Eastmans, there was the matter of clearing out the cellar, packing all of the foodstuffs and utensils in the wagon, wrapping the seeds and tools in storage boxes, packing dishes and silver, linens and clothing.

Only Sophia, who was feeling ill most of the time, was unable to do her share. She complained often to Mama and Mara. During a few long anxious nights, Mara could hear her in the upstairs bedroom turning and twisting, trying to find comfort while she slept. John had always been good to her, but at the most difficult moments in these recent days it seemed that he had begun to leave her to battle her discomfort on her own. A few times, however, after dinner, while the family was sitting around the fire, Mara could hear him whispering encouraging words to her. Once he asked her if the baby was all right.

"I think I am the baby," Sophia said. "And I'm not all right."

John tried to brighten her by talking about other things. "Tomorrow night they're giving us a party at the bowery." The farewell party seemed to be the only bright spot in the future, and anticipation of it was exciting to everyone in spite of the event it celebrated. "If I saw Brigham Young maybe I could ask him . . . if we could stay." John paused for a moment. "Or at least maybe ask him if we could wait. Maybe just until the baby comes."

Mara heard Sophia's breath catch. "Oh . . ." she said, "do you think. . . ?"

"I'm not sure," John whispered. "But if you're not feeling better, we really ought to ask someone if we could stay."

But Sophia sighed. "Oh, it's all right, John. I'll surely be better soon. Never you mind."

March fifteenth was a bit early for the first party of the year at the bowery. But it was not as cold as everyone might have expected. The dark streets seemed bright with moonlight, and a warm salt breeze swept in from the lake. While Papa hooked up the Eastmans' only horse, Sequel, to the wagon, Mara went to ask Nancy Allen if she would like to ride. Sophia wore a new smock Mama had made for her and let Mara wear the lawn dress she had brought from Boston, which was now too small for Sophia. Mara floated down the block toward Nancy's, excitement exploding in her head.

The Allens had also been called to go to Provost's Hole, as had the Wilsons, the Olsens, the Wrights, and twelve other families Mara knew. Caroline Olsen and Hannah Wright were with Nancy when Mara reached the Allen door. The three girls giggled with Mara, glad when she offered them a lift in the Eastman wagon. Papa came by only a few moments later, stopped, and called to Mara.

"Can you take all of us, Papa?" Mara called back.

Mama, looking regal in her old red silk cape, smiled. Sophia and John in the back seat drew up close to each other.

"We've got enough room! Climb in all of you. Hang on!" Papa yelled, with a laugh.

The girls had barely thrown themselves and their dresses into the wagon like clumps of flowers into a big box when Papa jerked Sequel forward and everybody tipped back, clinging to their hats and screaming. They laughed until they cried before they settled down in their perfume and twitters as Sequel clattered down the street. From two blocks off they could see the halo from the bright lights near the center of Temple Square. Just one block away, they could hear the fiddle and clapping, and at last they could smell hot cider and buns.

Papa pulled Sequel up with a jolt at the bowery. Everyone fell over again, and it was hard to know whose skirt was whose as they untangled themselves. Mara leaped from the wagon feeling lightheaded. She wanted to run to the bowery floor so she would be there when Bret made his list. The programs were passed out early. She waited impatiently by the wagon for her three friends to get themselves down and smooth out their dresses.

"What's going on over there?" Hannah was pointing to a circle of boys off to the north side of the bowery.

"It's a fight, I think," Nancy said, straining to see into the circle.

"Ignore it," Mara said, turning to go into the bowery. But just then she caught sight of Bret standing off to one side of the fight. "Well, maybe we could go see who it is," she said.

It was Ivie Richards' red-haired son Tony and Bret's younger brother Joshua. Though a year younger than Bret, Joshua was bigger—bigger at eighteen than Scott Hunt himself. And he was giving Tony Richards a pounding. Mara's friends stood straining to see the fight, and Mara pretended to do the same, though it wasn't the fight she was straining to see. Bret had vanished. There was a jostling at the other side of the circle, and Bishop King appeared in the center.

"Now, brethren, we don't settle our differences with

fisticuffs." He seemed unafraid, even though both boys towered over him. Papa Eastman broke through the circle behind Bishop King and put his hand on Joshua's shoulder while the bishop took hold of Tony's right hand. "Come on, boys. Let's go have a good time," Bishop King said.

The circle broke up, and Mara turned around to find herself looking into the clear, blue eyes of Bret Hunt, who had been standing behind her! "May I have my share of dances?" he asked, smiling.

Mara's heart leapt, and she felt as though the wind had been knocked out of her. She opened her mouth, but no words came.

"A few dances—on your program," Bret repeated, still smiling.

"What's . . . what's been going on?"

"A party," he teased her.

"You know what I mean . . . with Joshua . . . and Tony Richards."

"Oh, it's the same old family feud," he said as he led her onto the dance floor. "Only this time Tony went too far." She heard what he said but his words meant nothing. His arm under her hand was like fire. "Tony Richards called Pa a bastard Indian lover to Joshua's face," Bret whispered in her ear as the fiddler struck up a Virginia Reel. "I think Pa is right to be kind to the Indians. They are people. If we are kind to them, they'll be kind, too."

Mara wasn't sure that one always followed the other. For a moment she wanted to ask questions. But when she looked at Bret's smile, every question left her. Her blood was dancing and this was her only chance, maybe forever, to be in Bret Hunt's arms. She wanted him to drop the subject of the Indians. He should have been saying "You are the best looking girl here, Mara, and if I had my way, I'd dance every dance with you for the rest of the evening."

She was not sure how it happened, but she found herself close to him dancing the reel. It was exhilarating: Bret Hunt's arms touched her wrists; his legs brushed her dress. He was taking her hand in the Virginia Reel, and leading her around under the bridge of arms! She smiled at him. She felt giddy. Her hair bounced. She let it bounce and fly.

The rest of the evening she lived only for the three dances she had scheduled with Bret. Annoyingly, Sully Tuttle took two dances near the end. During the Irish jig he tripped on her skirt and fell face-flat on Papa's boots. "Bee feathers," Papa said, and began to watch them both warily. He had watched her at dances before, scolding her if she danced too close or pulled her skirts too high. She stood fuming and red-faced while Sully picked himself up and apologized. She sidled away from him and danced with Joshua and Caleb Hunt, Nancy Allen's brother Randall, and even Tony Richards. Randall Allen begged her to have refreshments with Nancy and Caleb and himself, and she couldn't find a respectable reason to say no. Mama and Papa came to sit with them at the side table. Papa seemed to rejoice in her fun, but he kept his eyes fastened on her face. In a moment alone with her, Papa said "Don't let those young snips hold you too close, Mara. Don't let any of them get no ideas." Papa seemed unusually concerned about her tonight, as though she was going to be kissing somebody in full view. "I want you gone with us before the party ends. Hear that, now, Mara?"

Later, from the corner of her eye, while she whirled across the floor in the arms of the orphan boy Sully, Mara watched Bret dancing with Hannah and felt a deep ache. Papa came by after Sully stopped her on the floor and said, "We're leaving now, Mara. Get ready to go." Her heart sank. Sully took her hand and pressed it cautiously. His eyes were very large, and his mouth hung open.

"Mara. Do you have to go? I could see you home safe if your folks has to go."

"Sully, I'm sorry." The music began again; Bret was still standing with Hannah. Now all Mara wanted to do was retreat. Trying not to be too rude, she pulled her hands softly out of Sully's thin, trembling grip. "Please, Sully. I need to go." Her eyes were still fastened on Bret. Just as Papa took her arm to usher her outside, Bret finally turned and saw them. She waved at him, a brief, sporting wave.

"Just a moment, please," Bret said to Hannah, and he left her quickly. "Mara," he called. "Are you going so soon?"

Papa said firmly, "We're going, son." Bret did not attempt any argument.

"Good-bye then, Mara," he said, smiling.

She reached for his hand, but Papa turned her away.

"You've had quite enough, my lady. Get going. Your friends really shouldn't stay, either. We'll be no good to make a trek Monday. We've got to be hale and hearty."

Out on the street Papa was gruff. "Mara, you dance too close to the boys," he said as he lifted her into the dray. She had wondered why his happy-go-lucky mood had changed. She had danced only three round dances, two with Bret, and the last with Sully. "When we were boys, we were never allowed to touch young ladies, or ladies young men, until we were old enough to be married. I couldn't believe the way you were dancing with that Bret Hunt . . . and then you and that boy Sully."

Mama and Sophia and John were already waiting in the wagon. Sophia looked very tired. Mara could tell that John had not been able to corner Brigham Young.

Papa clucked loudly to Sequel and slapped the reins. Except for a few brief words of thanks to Widow Harper when he stopped to pick up the sleeping Ashel, all the way home Papa said nothing more. He kept blowing into his handkerchief and pushing his nose flat into his face. When he spit, Mara turned away.

By Sunday, everything was stacked and ready to go. All that remained would be loading the wagon, getting the stock ready, and hooking up the oxen. Mama could not find her potato peeler but finally remembered she had packed it with a box of utensils. Sophia complained of pain in her lower back and could not help with the chicken dumplings.

Mara's thoughts were totally occupied by Bret. She tried to see him in the morning at church, but protective Papa, with a stubbornness unusual even for him, wouldn't leave her side. Outside of the meeting house he talked with Bret and Scott Hunt together, arranging for the Indian women who were staying with Hunt to meet the Eastmans in the morning on Main Street.

"We'll be glad to take anyone else who wants to go," Papa said.

"I'm not sure any of the others want to send their visitors back," Scott Hunt said. "Of course, some have already run away."

After church in the evening, Sully and Bret both wanted to walk Mara home. They stood in the churchyard looking at Mara while Papa and Mama talked endlessly with their friends.

"I think I'll just go home myself," Mara said lightly.

"Hang on," Papa kept saying. "I'll only be a minute."

Mara waited, nervous, looking from one boy to the other, nodding to neighbors who gathered to wish them well.

Finally Scott Hunt walked up to Papa. "Well Hart, this is good-bye, then. We'd see you off in the morning, but Brother Brigham wants the militia to participate in a house-raising on the other side of town. I guess the boys and I will need to go over." Mara's heart sank. This might be the last time she would see Bret!

"Come on, boys. Bret, Sully, Joshua, Caleb." The boys came quickly to attention at Scott Hunt's order. Hunt reached out to shake Papa's hand. "God bless you all," he said. He shook Mama's hand, then John's, then Sophia's. Mara's head felt heavy and hot, her throat tight. This just couldn't be it! He wouldn't just take Bret away now. There had to be more! She felt two big warm hands cover her hands. "God bless you," Scott Hunt said again. Mara knew her face was red. "Thank you," she murmured. Did he know? Was he angry, as Papa was? He didn't seem angry, only kind and a little sad. He let her hands go and turned to his boys.

"Well, come on then, boys. These folks need to get home and prepare themselves for tomorrow." Sully stood shifting from one foot to another. Caleb and Joshua shook her hand shyly and turned to follow their father. Bret was talking to John. Now he was turning to her. Her heart beat so hard she could hardly hear what he was saying. He was shaking her hand in a firm, hard grip.

"Good-bye, Mara. Good luck with the Indians!" He laughed a little. Mara was annoyed that he was talking about Indians at a time like this. Why didn't he kiss her hand and whisper to her how he really felt, softly, so Papa couldn't hear? But his eyes were shining and her hand was in his. What could she expect in the glaring Sunday sun with the whole world standing around?

"Mara! We'll be going now!" Papa was waiting for her on the street.

"Coming, Papa." She still looked at Bret. This is it! What shall I say, she wondered in her reeling brain. "Good luck on your mission" was what came out. Then she turned and ran to her frowning father. Mama and John and Sophia were already a block away. When she looked back, she saw Scott Hunt talking to Bishop King, Caleb and Joshua at his elbows. Sully still stood watching her, scratching one ankle with the toe of the other boot. Bret was talking to Randall Allen. What was happening! He could be gone for years.

All afternoon Mara was restless with longing. To keep busy, she offered to peel Mama's potatoes with a paring knife. She took the potato bucket out to the back stoop. Close by, Spirit of Earth and Rain were hunched together over the edge of the first step, picking some seeds out of an old dried-up sunflower. They looked so dirty and smelled so awful. Mara wanted to go back into the house, but she thought they would know why she did it. "We ought to be kind." She could hear Bret's words in her mind.

Spirit of Earth looked up to Mara, holding out a small handful of shelled seeds. Mara's stomach turned at the seeds in the woman's dark palm and the gamy-sweet odor that rose from her. But she swallowed hard and smiled. I will be kind, she thought to herself. She took the seeds. "Thank you," she said.

Spirit of Earth pointed to her own tongue, then touched the seeds in Mara's hand. She had given Mara food, and she wanted her to eat it—now. The old woman was nodding her head and clucking her tongue as though to say "very good." Not knowing how to refuse, Mara put one of the seeds in her mouth and chewed it. Spirit of Earth nodded and smiled. Mara smiled weakly, tasting the sweat from the woman's hand. Spirit of Earth gave some seeds to Rain, and they all three sat on the steps eating the seeds without saying a word. Mara thought she felt the seeds stirring inside of her. She shaded her eyes from the sun.

When the seeds were gone, Mara picked up her bucket and began to peel the potatoes. Spirit of Earth and Rain went back to shelling the sunflower seeds, the mother rocking back and forth on the stoop, crooning as she worked. Mara looked at her. She was dirty and foul-smelling, but she was a woman, a generous woman who could share what she had with another. She was a human being, and Bret was right. We would all have to be kind.

When she thought about Bret in that moment, she knew—though she did not know how—that she would see him once more.

After supper, Mara avoided her father, who had seemed worried about her all day. He had followed her into the yard once and ordered her to come into the house to finish putting away a few dishes properly.

"They don't go in the cupboard, girl. We're leaving in the morning," he said impatiently. "You're in a daze, Mara. Wake up!" He snapped his fingers in her face. It was true she had not been thinking when she put some of their dishes back into the cupboard. Mama had made a special point of telling her to pack them in the boxes.

Now, as she took the dishes from the cupboard, one of them slipped from her hand. It fell across the washtub and then to the floor, shattering in a hundred pieces.

"Birds and bee feathers! What's got into you, girl! I swear, never do I see it fail. A young girl cozy with the boys one day is cloudy the next!" Papa stormed into the front room. "Martha, I can't handle it," he said. "Take that daughter of yours to task. I am not worth a tinker's pickle at it."

Tears came to Mara's eyes. She hadn't seen him like this since John was courting Sophia. Why was he so overprotective? Without waiting for Mama to come into the kitchen, Mara scrambled out the back door. Her eyes stinging, she ran to the barn. Ashel had just come back from an errand for Mama, and Sequel was still in his bridle. She felt across his neck for the reins. Quickly, without trouble in the dark, she hurried Sequel out of the barn. There was no time for the saddle. It would not be long before Papa would come looking for her.

"Mara!" His voice died on the damp night air. "Mara, come back here, girl."

Across the thick shadows that lay between her and the dim light of the house, Mara could see her father leaning against the door on the stoop; the light from the kitchen lit his face.

She dug her feet into Sequel's flanks and edged him quickly out of the barnyard into the front road. With another kick to his flanks the horse heaved toward the gate and flew over it. She felt herself slipping and so leaned her cheek close to his withers and held tight to his mane. He dashed under a tree and winter leaves broken by the wind, fell into her hair.

"Fly, boy," she whispered. The animal lurched into the wide streets, pummeled across the gray dust toward the shadowy ridge of the mountains in the east.

"Mara. Mara." In the distance Papa's voice still filtered through the night. He had been angry, and she would be punished when she got home. But tonight, she did not care. They were going to Provost's Hole in the morning; nothing Papa could do to her could make her feel worse. The damp air caught in her throat and choked her. She brushed the leaves out of her hair.

Provost's Hole. Indian country. There would be little for her at Provost's Hole. "Good luck with the Indians," Bret had laughed.

The road rolled under her. Almost without touching the earth, Sequel sped into the blackness of the foothills. In the wind that bit her ears, it seemed she could still hear her father's angry voice—"A girl cozy with the boys one day is cloudy the next! Martha, take that daughter of yours to task." Had it really been so obvious? She had never breathed a word about Bret to anyone. Why was Papa so upset? Bret was so wonderful, so fine. And he was to be gone on a mission—for who knows how long—to England. And she—tomorrow she would be leaving for Provost's Hole. Forever!

Sequel's hooves pounded the road. There, to the south, was the unknown, the Indian Country that was Provost's Hole. Indians. They could steal everything you had. Cut your throat in the dark. They could do terrible things to a woman when her menfolk were away. A woman. In a terrible flash she remembered Blueflower's blood and tears.

"I am a woman now." Mara said it out loud. And she thought about Blueflower. And I will not—I cannot—be a slave to anyone. She fought back tears. Even to Papa. Papa will have to understand that and accept it, she thought. I am a woman, and I know my own heart. She rode on in the dark, fast, like a hurricane wind. But she was crying. Tomorrow she would be gone from here, from these streets, from these familiar houses, from Bret Hunt, perhaps forever. "I *must* see him," she said to the night.

Sequel's neck was not even damp when she reached the Hunt home on South Main Street. But he was panting. Her own lungs were heaving, her throat sore from the wind. She pulled the horse to a stop in the carriage way. The house was still bright from the blazing fire in the hearth.

There was not a sound in the barnyard. The barn loomed black against the night sky. She jumped off Sequel's back and led him up close to the fence. She stood still, watching, breathless. What was she doing here? She must be insane. After several moments she saw the back door open. It was Scott Hunt. She was glad he could not see her as she watched him. He filled the door. He did not come out into the yard. He just stood there. Perhaps he had heard her in the drive. Finally he stepped back into the house saying something to someone. She breathed a sigh of relief.

After a few moments she heard the door open again. Now a younger figure stepped out into the night. Her heart began to pound. But it was not Bret. It was Sully. Mara bit her lip. Why him? He was stooped, leaning over the slop buckets. "Where he belonged," Mara thought as she watched him. Sequel skittered, and his hooves sounded against the gravel. Sully heard it and stopped before he entered the barn.

"Who's that?" Sully whispered coarsely. Mara did not breathe. Her body, from her shoulder muscles to her feet, froze. Sully was coming toward her.

"Who's that? Don't move or I'll send the dogs after you. Speak out."

Mara's tongue dried up in her throat. "It's me, Mara Eastman. I was just out riding. I . . . saw the lights from the house. . . . I . . ." She felt foolish and angry. Why had *he* been the one to come?

By now Sully had reached the fence. In the dim moonlight she could see his face. "Mara!" For a moment he did not say anything else. "I'm glad you came here. Don't you want to come in?"

"Shhh. . . ." Mara's heart pounded. She wanted to turn, to run, but she could not even move.

"I'm sure the family would like to see you. Come on in."

"I can't, Sully."

For a moment Sully was quiet. Then he said in a voice so quiet Mara could barely hear, "You got leaves all over your hair." Before she could answer he said in a louder voice, stammering, "If you won't come in and say good-bye, what did you come here for, anyway?"

"Oh, Sully. . . ." Mara pulled at the leaves in her hair. She saw Scott Hunt at the window, peering out into the blackness. He could not have avoided hearing Sully talking in the yard.

"Mara, does your papa know you're here?" Sully looked up at her again.

"Shhh. No." Mara's heart began to pound again. "I've got to hurry."

"With you all going away in the morning," he paused, "you ought to get some sleep. Shall I show you home?"

"Oh, Sully," Mara breathed hopelessly. "No, Sully. I've got to go. I *must* go."

"You just come to say good-bye?"

"I guess so." Mara's heart pounded. She could see Scott Hunt leaving the window, then Ella Hunt, some of the brothers, and finally the dark-haired Indian woman Angel Lip and her baby moving close to the glass in the fading lamplight. Then behind them she could see a light head of hair. It was Bret. And this would be her last look at him—probably forever.

"Well, good-bye then. Please stay safe at Provost's Hole." Sully was standing closer to the fence now, staring at her with wide eyes. "There's going to be fights. You know that."

"I know," Mara said, hoping that if she stayed long enough in the road, Bret would come out. But she did not know what she would do if he did.

"I'd go if Brother Hunt didn't need me with his boys for the militia here," Sully paused. "I might be going one day, Mara." He seemed to want her to say something.

What was she supposed to say? "Someday I'll be leaving the Hunts. Brother Hunt promised me money or a parcel of land or something."

What was Sully saying? Why was he looking at her that way? She could feel the leaves still bristling all over her head.

"Is your Pa prepared for shooting?"

"Oh, I don't know, Sully." She was restless with all his talk. The horse under her seemed restless. She wanted to go. But the back door was opening again, sending a long sliver of light out into the yard. Sully turned. A tall figure leaped down the back steps in one easy stride.

"Sully?"

"Yeah."

"Who is it, Sully?" It was him! It was Bret.

Without another word to Sully, Mara gathered Sequel's reins.

"It's . . . you know, that Eastman girl." Mara dug Sequel's sides with a vicious kick.

"Mara?" She heard Bret say her name as she turned into the road. "Sully, was it Mara Eastman?" She dared not even give her horse a command, but beat him into a furious gallop.

She rode as fast as she could, north, up Main Street. She wished the earth would open and swallow her. She heard a shout, "Sully, tell Pa I'll be back in a little while!" and then she was not sure . . . but then she *was* sure—there was the sound of another horse behind her.

"Mara!" It was Bret. She kicked Sequel again. "Mara! Slow down!" The wide streets were empty. She heard his horse gaining on her. They were near South Temple and Main. Mara's head was spinning. She thought she might fall off her horse if she kept going this fast. "Mara, stop!"

She stopped Sequel at the side of the road, just at the surveyor's rope that marked the temple site. Bret pulled up beside her, riding Hobo, his favorite stallion. "Mara. Why did you run away? I wanted to see you. You should have come in. Didn't Sully invite you?"

Mara felt the blood leave her face. She must have looked like a ghost in the moonlight.

"You look so pale, Mara. Are you all right? Did you come to say good-bye?"

Mara nodded. She had no voice.

Bret slid off Hobo and reached up to her. "Come on. You'd better get off. You look like you're going to fall." She sat still, afraid to move. "All right. I'll come up." He threw one of Hobo's reins around Sequel's neck, tied it, and swung up onto Sequel's back behind Mara. "Shall I take you home?" Still she couldn't speak. "All right, then, let's go for a ride."

She felt him at her back, pressed close to her. He drew his fingers through the leaves in her hair without saying a word. He reached around her to take Sequel's reins. She shivered. His warm breath was in her hair. "It's dangerous out at night for a woman," he said. She was suddenly afraid when he said "woman." "Even if you're not in Indian country yet." Mara froze with joy. She wanted to lean back against Bret's chest and melt into him. "And besides," he was saying, "I know your father, and he'll kill. . . ."

"I don't care!" Mara spoke for the first time.

"No, I guess you don't," Bret laughed.

"What does it matter what he does when Provost's Hole is going to kill me anyway?"

Something sharp in the night air seemed to settle on them all at once. Bret was quiet and then in the silence he said: "No, no!"

Mara was not sure what cold ice was freezing her up. She hunted for words. "We'll go down there and we'll all die."

"You don't know."

"I know it. Some of us are going to die."

"We all have to die."

"I don't want to go."

"We don't always get what we want."

"No."

They were almost home now. Hobo began to yank at the rein. He broke free and turned off in the direction of the Hunts'.

"Here boy, come on back," Bret called. He leaped from Sequel's back and his hat rolled in the road. He ran to catch up with Hobo and scooped his hat off the ground. He hollered like a pig farmer, led him back, and tied him to the fence a few yards from the Eastmans' front gate. He turned to Mara. His face was glistening; he was grinning. He waited for a long time, just watching her, breathing hard. "Now, come on down here and tell me good-bye."

"I told you good-bye this afternoon," she said, trying to sound cold. But her voice caught, and she was afraid she would cry.

"Don't be like that. Come on down." He reached up for her. She let go of the reins and leaned down to him. His hands on her waist, he lifted her down and drew her close to him. Her breath caught. Her head spun. She felt the blood warm in the tips of her fingers. He was holding her close. He lifted one hand to brush her hair from her face. She smoothed it, too, with a shy gesture, aware that it was whipped into a tangled mass thick with leaves and the wind.

"You're beautiful," he said, his hand on her cheek. He looked at her so long she knew she must turn and run or melt into the earth. "Mara, promise me something," he said slowly. Her heart rattled inside. She caught her breath, unable to control the shaking in her blood.

"Think about being alive, not about dying," he said, and he paused as though to frame the words in the moonlight.

She was not sure what she had expected him to say. She could not say anything in return.

"If I hadn't promised Uncle Jeb I'd go with him to England . . . I . . . want . . . to preach the gospel . . . but I. . . ." Both his arms were around her again. "Mara, if I kissed you. . . ."

"Oh, I don't think . . . I . . . Papa. . . ." And then she felt him pull her closer. She closed her eyes. He held her against his chest and she thought she could feel the pounding inside of him as she felt it inside of herself.

"Mara," he said, holding her by her shoulders. Then he held her chin. "Good-bye, Mara," he said, and he kissed her. For some reason she felt like a child. Her head spun.

"Good-bye," he said again. She turned from him and ran toward the house, stifling the sobs that rose in her throat. He did not follow her. She opened the gate and ran to the porch. She stumbled up the front steps and stood leaning against the doorpost, breathing deeply so that she would not cry. The door opened and Mama looked out. "Is that you, Mara? Mara, is that you, girl?" Bret was riding away on Hobo. Sequel stood grazing at the front gate.

Mama saw her. "Mara! Mara girl! Where have you been? We've been so worried about you! Come in here this minute!" Mama held out her hand, took Mara by the shoulder, and led her in.

In the middle of the room stood Sophia, John, and Ashel in his nightdress. In the corner sat Spirit of Earth and Rain on burlap. Near them stood Papa, his eyes red, his mouth tight.

"I'm sorry we can't trust you, Mara," he said in a cold

voice. She fled to her upstairs bedroom, tired, sick in her heart, yet still feeling the softness of Bret's lips on her own.

Chapter Three

March 17, 1849 began with a sharp and bitter chill under a distant sun. Papa began the final packing at dawn, giving his orders to John and Ashel with a cracked voice. Some crates had already been packed into the wagon. Now the last items of furniture were stacked on the crates, and dishes wrapped in towels were stuffed round them. Mama moved quickly, banging things, saying nothing. She fed the Indians hunks of bread and gave them tankards of milk.

Even with an early start, they were not able to get away from the house until nine o'clock. At Main Street and Fifth South, they waited another half hour until Chloe Hunt, walking slowly with two of her little children, brought Hawk Feather and Angel Lip with her big baby to travel with the group. A half hour after that, the Allen family arrived with their eleven children. Finally the Huntingtons, Hansens, and Olsens arrived. It was after eleven when the newly called Bishop Higbee made a final check, and, finding no one missing, ordered the first wagons to roll.

All morning, Mara, feeling broken and drained, stood at the edge of things, watching her father from a distance, staying with Nancy or Hannah and their families as orders or roll calls were read, as last-minute repairs to wagons or yokes were made, as some went back into town to get more seed or borrow this or that tool from a neighbor.

Though the sun was warm by noon, a cold wind came up and sent a chill through those who had not worn warm clothing.

Mara and Nancy, with Hannah and Mary Jane Wright, walked behind the others, talking about the party, about the people in the group, about the single young men called to go. When Nancy's little sisters weren't perched on the Allen wagon, they tagged along with the older girls, begging to hold their hands.

Mara watched the sun spin over the far hills, finally throwing shadows that grew blue and velvet in the dusk as they fell across the plain. The mountains to the left rose tall. Mara had never until now thought she could overcome the feeling that the mountains would fall on them all some night when they were asleep. Bret's words still pounded in her head. He would have told her it was a death-wish. And now there was nothing on earth she wanted more than to be alive with him.

At six o'clock, Bishop Higbee ordered the train to stop. They were at the edge of a yawning canyon that had suddenly opened up before them. Brown cliffs sprinkled with scrub oak and purple sage fell steeply to an almost invisible end. Below, in the dark chasm, lay a tiny lake.

"An old lake was here," Papa said, breathing hard from his long walk. "Ashel, look around you." He spread his arms wide to take in the valley and the mountains vaulting toward the graying sky. "All of this was once water when the earth was born. Do you see? Snail shells, fossils, the remnants of a vast body of water so large you could not see its end. And now the sun has dried it up until it is a pinch of salt in a mud hole." Papa squatted down and picked up shells and pieces of old fossils in gray stone that lay everywhere.

"Close mountains, a narrow neck of land," Bishop Higbee said, indicating the nearness of the hills now on both the left and right. The settlers drifted to the business of their camp, pulling dishes and pans from their storage, pouring water, and building fires. The dusk closed over them. In the west a sharp flame of red fire followed the sun over the ridge, caught the clouds swimming in magenta and orange.

"One thing I will say," Mama said, almost without any breath. "I do like the sunsets here."

All of them watched. Robert Egbert strummed his guitar; a few people sang. Soon all of them joined in singing the rousing words "Come come, ye Saints." They sang Irish jig songs and "Greensleeves." They were laughing and some of them danced around the fire. As the sun left the sky, Mara felt the same kind of chill she had felt in Nauvoo before they had crossed the Missouri River that cold season; a flat cold sheet of wind slapped against her cheek like a wing of ice. Gusts of dry, sharp cold blew up onto her legs, across her back. Her thin coat was not enough, and while the others were soaking their bits of bread in the warm stew, she went to the wagon to see if she could find an old quilt.

In the gathering darkness, outside the central light of the fire, she could see dark figures standing against the wagon wheels. She approached them cautiously. By the pale light still left in the sky she could make out the leathery brown of Spirit of Earth's wizened face. Beside her stood Rain, and nearby were Hawk Feather and Angel Lip. They turned away from her as she approached them as though they were hiding something. Mara watched them for a moment. It looked like they were wrapping blankets from the wagon box around their shoulders and around the shoulders of someone else. Trying to hide behind the others was another Indian, tall, her black hair shining in the flickering firelight above the other heads. In the darkness, straining her eyes, Mara recognized Blueflower. She stood as straight and slender as a reed against the wagon, her hands clutching a bundle wrapped in what looked like one of Ivie Richards' old plaid shirts.

Mara smiled to the women, nodding that it was all right for them to take the bedding. Not wanting to interrupt or stir them up, she said nothing. Cautious, she turned swiftly back to camp.

"It's Blueflower," she said to Nancy on her return to the camp circle. "She's followed us!"

Nancy looked alarmed. "Richards' girl!"

"I'm sure of it," Mara said. "We ought to tell Papa, I guess."

"Or Bishop Higbee, or someone," Nancy breathed. "She came here all this way on her own! I wonder how she got away! Well, it's probably best for her."

Mara was surprised at the joy and relief she had felt when she saw Blueflower. She was free!

Mama was the first one they told. "The pretty Indian girl Richards took?" Mama said, wrapping herself more tightly in her wool shawl. She got up from her spot by the fire and went with the girls to the wagon. "Poor thing!" she said softly. "Poor thing. All this way!" Papa followed her when she beckoned to him to come.

When they returned to the wagon, the Indians were gone. Papa was worried more about the fact that they took the bedding than he was worried about the Indians themselves. The wagon box was stripped of every piece.

"We'll look for them," Papa said, angry. Mara worried, thinking to herself that if she had only acted more quickly, neither the Indians nor the bedding would be gone.

"They couldn't be far, yet," Mama said, still clutching her shawl.

Papa stood up straight and looked out across the barren land. "No telling, no telling," he murmured. "There are, no doubt, bands of their own people close by. They could be gone—poof!"—he snapped his fingers—"as though they disappeared into the very earth they came from."

There was still some twilight, and the rising moon was bright, so Papa rounded up John and Mr. Allen, and then Hansen and Wright. Finally most of the others wanted to help. The women lit the few oil lamps available, and candles, and the small bands of searchers spread across the barren sun-scarred range.

Mara and Nancy followed Papa and Mr. Allen with Ashel and John and Nancy's married brothers Stewart and Abe into the dark recess of the mud hole. They could not go far without losing the light.

"They could be hidden among these oaks," Papa said, sounding discouraged. Arroyos and washes curved between small hills; there were innumerable places where many people or cattle could hide.

"While we're investigating every corner, they will no doubt be speeding somewhere," Brother Allen said.

"And we'll never know," his son Stewart added.

Sleeping without enough bedding (the Eastmans had had to borrow what they could) was not as troublesome to Mara as her dreams. They were the same dreams of fear she'd had as a child in Nauvoo, after Papa and the others had been taken out at night and beaten by a mob. She slept fitfully, seeing the angry faces, feeling hands on her back, starting awake to nothing but darkness, her heart beating hard. Awake, she listened for Indians, afraid at any moment she would see eyes shining in the darkness, would feel a knife at her throat. To make the fear go away she prayed, her eyes shut tightly. "Dear Father, watch over us and keep us safe from all harm."

And then she would call up the image of Bret's smiling face, try to feel his arms around her, his mouth on hers. Then she dreamed of his coming home to her, grown into a man as big and confident as his father, taking her in his arms and whispering, "Oh Mara, I've waited so long for this!" Dreaming of Bret, she would fall asleep, only to lose him to the fear her sleeping mind would imagine once again.

She woke tired, feeling dirty and smelling like the charcoal in the spent campfires. She raised her head from her pillow. A flock of sparrows shot past overhead; a few cocks carried by poultry farmers in the company cackled loudly.

Many others in the camp were already up. Mara dragged herself from her blanket and smoothed down her hair and her wrinkled dress. She was brushing her hair vigorously while Ashel and Papa stoked the fire. Breakfast was Johnnycakes and hot Brigham tea. Papa was warming the water for washing the dishes, and Mama was just about to throw the last of her lumpy dick into the flames when out of nowhere black bobbing heads appeared over the horizon.

"Land, there they are!" Mama breathed hard, her eyes widening.

Mara turned around quickly and saw Old Hawk Feather and Spirit of Earth, Angel Lip with her big baby on her hip, and Blueflower trailing behind them. Rain was dawdling in the distance. They were dragging the Eastman blankets over the sage and chit-grass, heedless of the damage they were doing them.

"Trust them to come for breakfast," Papa said quite good-naturedly, his hands on his hips as he waited for them to stumble into the camp.

Mama hurried to the flour keg and made more lumpy dick, stirring vigorously. The others in the camp saw the

Indians now and nodded, smiling at Mama. As though they were her own children, lost and now found again, Mama clucked with affectionate disapproval over her crock.

"Spirit of Earth," Mama finally said, setting the crock on the ground near the fire and gliding to the old woman. "Where were you? You must have been cold. Land, these folks didn't eat last night, I don't believe," she said to anyone who was close. "Are you hungry?" she pointed to her mouth to indicate "eat." Sipapu nodded dumbly. Angel Lip jogged the baby on her hip and smiled. "Well, we have plenty, and it's time to eat. Ashel, bring me the plates when you've washed them clean, and the cups and spoons." She put her arm around Spirit of Earth's shoulders to lead her to the camp circle. "And Blueflower, I'm so glad to see you, dear. Are you all right?" Not understanding a word, Blueflower stared without expression. But she understood Mama's hand. Mama's arm came round her shoulder and brought her in close. The girl moved without objection into the circle of Mama's welcome. With Indians on both sides of her, Mama walked to the fire, sat them on the ground and began dishing the flour and water mixture to the hot griddle over the fire. Her voice was like music, a crooning Mara had often heard in the night when she or Ashel awakened with bad dreams and Mama came to comfort them.

"We'll take care of you," Mama said to the Indians. "You'll need to eat. We thought you had left us. But we have no intention of letting you go back to your hostile people if they don't want you. Where were you? You must have been in a wash in the canyon. We called you last night. Didn't you hear us? And here you are, Blueflower. You have come a long way alone. You must be hungry. Here, can you drink this?" She placed a warm cup of Brigham tea into Blueflower's slender hands. The girl looked at Mama as she sipped. When she lowered her eyes and drained the cup, Mara saw the small red scabs on her brow. She felt the presence of the Indians like hot sunshine. They were going into country where there would be more of the same. But she didn't believe that now she would be afraid.

As usual, the Indians ate voraciously. After the first batch of Johnnycakes had gone, Mama made the mistake of asking in unmistakable sign language if anyone wanted more. Sipapu nodded yes and held out her tin plate. The others followed. Mama was cooking long after everyone else had put things away. Papa and Mara folded the bedding and organized the crates in the wagon, making room to pack the dishes and the griddle and pans at the last minute. When the Eastmans were finally ready to go, many of the other families were already on the trail.

With gear and stock, the travelers made slow progress. Mara watched for Indians behind every rock, every tree, every hill. Finally, on the morning of their third day on the trail, she saw one. They had been on the road for less than an hour when she saw him in the distance on an Appaloosa pony, a young Indian riding furiously toward them from the south, his feet pounding the horse's foaming sides, the wind sending his long hair flying.

Bishop Higbee ordered the settlers to stop. Dimick Huntington rode to the front on his pony and waited beside the bishop. The people stood stone still as the Indian boy on the flying horse drew near to them. Mara felt a fear she did not want to feel, not because one Indian boy sped toward them like an angry warrior, but because she knew from her long trek from the East that many hundreds of them might be lying in wait around some ridge or in a thatch of trees.

The Indian, a handsome boy of about eighteen, carried a spear high over his pony's back. Tied to one end of the spear was a scrap of deerskin. Though they could not be sure, Bishop Higbee and Brother Huntington announced they felt the makeshift flag meant peace. Huntington had raised his own flag—one of his white shirts buttoned to a poker. Though the Indian bore down on them with tremendous speed, he drew his horse up sharply just before he reached Higbee and Huntington; the horse's hooves raised the dust into the faces of those who stood nearby.

Mara could hear Dimick Huntington's smooth Ute, and it sounded like music to her. What would they do if no one could speak to the Indians! He also used his hands.

"Angatewats," the Indian youth said loudly between his teeth, beating himself on the chest.

"Does he want to fight?" Nancy wanted Mara to tell her.

"Sh-h-h. I don't think so," Mara said.

Then Mara saw the youth catch sight of Hawk Feather and Spirit of Earth—then Blueflower, Angel Lip, and Rain. He stared for a moment, before he continued to speak to Dimick Huntington. He pointed to the Indians and then spoke angrily to Huntington. He pointed to the group of settlers, and then toward the south and east. He made signals with his hands.

"He wants us to go before his people's council," Huntington said to Bishop Higbee and to Papa and Brother Allen, and the Wheelers and the Wrights, and the Beans who all stood close by. "He cannot trust us. His people's council wants to be sure we come in peace, and they want to extract some promises. They want us to return our *prisoners*." Huntington pointed to Eastman's Indians, standing like stones without emotion on their faces.

Mara looked at Blueflower. There was anger in those dark eyes. Above her eyes, on her smooth brow, the row of tiny scabs stood out like the buds of flowers. From time to time she touched them and looked obliquely at the members of the camp. Her mouth turned down as she stared at Angatewats. Did she know him? Did she hate him? Who was he? Mara wondered.

"He wants us to promise we won't come any further until we talk with the council," Huntington was saying.

Bishop Higbee looked at Huntington for a long moment. "Then tell him we will wait," he said.

In only a few moments, Angatewats brought six Indians back with him, all on smart ponies. They were armed with wooden spears. One tall dark Indian with a string of colored eagle feathers around his neck was obviously in charge. Angatewats spoke to him excitedly, pointing to the settlers, and then to the Indian women huddling near the Eastman wagon.

"Arrapene. Walkara's Arrapene," Angatewats pointed to the Chief and he continued his volley of words. Huntington nodded. "Arrapene, your chief, Walkara's brother, wants us to stay away, to give you prisoners. . . ."

"We can't stay away," Bishop Higbee shook his head. "Tell them we come to them in peace. We don't want to stir up trouble. We will not harm them. All we wish to do is plant seeds in the earth that will grow with the sun and the rain. To grow food, to live . . . perhaps to teach them . . . to help them raise food. . . ."

As Huntington spoke, Arrapene's dark eyebrows knit; his face tightened. Huntington reached into his pockets and held out a handful of corn. Angatewats held out his hand and Huntington poured the corn into it.

"Corn," Huntington said in English.

Arrapene did not change the expression on his face. But he took the corn from the young brave.

Huntington said something to Arrapene, softly, bringing his palms together and holding them close while he spoke, then extending his right hand. "We can live peacefully together," he said in English.

On the left of Arrapene, a wizened little Indian with graying braids and wiry white eyebrows nodded his head. Arrapene stiffened and turned. Behind him sat a large Indian whose eyes glared with hostility.

"Squash says no," Huntington translated softly. Squash must have been the fat Indian buried in rolls of flab. His eyes peered through slits in the folded flesh of his face. He slowly moved his great head from side to side. "No." The gray-headed one did not pay any attention to him. Arrapene turned from one to the other, then stared at Huntington, his eyes fixed.

Angatewats continued the angry clipped words he had been speaking.

"But Old Bishop says it's all right," Huntington nodded at the wizened smiling old man. "Old Bishop says he wants . . . the girl," He translated slowly, then he stopped, disconcerted, and stared at Old Bishop. The Old Indian's gaze was fastened on Blueflower. He was nodding at her.

Every nerve in Mara's body jackknifed. Blueflower still stood straight, her shoulders flung back under the thick silk of her hair. She knew what had been said, but no emotion other than quiet anger crossed her face. Her eyes stared straight ahead as though transfixed on Arrapene.

"They'll take the prisoners. We may go on," Huntington said without enthusiasm. Angatewats leaped from his pony and walked toward the Indians, but Mama was already standing her ground in front of them.

"Oh no you don't!" she said, flinging her arms out. "No, you don't. Get back, I tell you." Huntington was leaning toward the women from his horse, asking them questions in Ute. Hawk Feather and Spirit of Earth nodded slowly, agreeable to the arrangements. Angel Lip bounced her baby, who had suddenly cried out and clutched his mother's hair when Angatewats dismounted. Rain stood close to Spirit of Earth, her eyes afraid. Blueflower still stared straight ahead.

"It's all right," Huntington said to Mama. "Let them go. They agree to take them to their tribe or to keep them with Indian people." He glanced at Old Bishop, whose eyes were narrow black coals barely alive in his weathered face.

"They can't take these women. No one will treat them better than we do! No! Spirit of Earth. . . ." She turned to the tiny Indian who looked to Mara like an old brown sweet potato. "Don't go!" But Spirit of Earth could not understand what she said. She wasn't paying any attention to Mama anyway. Mara didn't blame her. Mama was beginning to "worry out loud."

"Leave 'em alone," Papa said firmly to Mama. Mama was crying. He took her elbow and led her away from them. They lumbered slowly like old sticks toward the brown wiry men on the tall ponies.

"What will they do with them?" Mama cried. Papa put his arm around her.

Without words, the Indians tied ropes to the women's wrists and looped the other end around their own or tied them to the horses. Old Bishop did not get off his horse. He took Blueflower's rope from Angatewats and yanked it almost viciously. She still clung to the little bundle of her belongings wrapped in Richards' plaid shirt. Old Bishop yanked the rope and waited until the tall slender girl stood next to his horse. When she was close enough, he struck out for her bundle like a cat. He tied it to the other end of the rope. Then he took her wrist rope tightly in his other hand. He drew her hand close to his own and tightened the rope slowly. Mama began forward, jerking at every bite the hemp made in Blueflower's dark skin.

"Never mind," Papa said. "Never mind, Martha."

Blueflower had not even so much as winced or breathed sharply from the pain. The expression on her face remained the same.

"Hah. Mipuwai, Sipapu," Old Bishop said, almost grimacing. He held her hand high as she walked beside his horse. In only one brief moment did she turn back, and it was to see her old friend Hawk Feather stumble beside one of the ponies because it was moving too fast for her awkward stride. Her look back was only for an instant, but it angered Old Bishop. Flattening his hand, he reached toward her and struck his gnarled fingers across her face.

Mama started forward, pulling away from Papa's hand. But she was too late. The crowd was getting in front of her now, turning back toward the wagons. Mama gave a little, painful cry. As Mara's eyes followed the men on horseback moving into the distance with the women prisoners trailing behind them, she saw Old Bishop hit Blueflower again and again. Finally, she turned away and closed her eyes.

"Stirred up, this black soil is so alive, looks like it'll talk," Papa said, leading the oxen by the yoke. He bent down and rubbed a handful of the rich earth now caking his boots. They were approaching the crest of a hill.

"This is the place," Mama said, her voice weary and strained. She rode Sequel, gripping his mane, her feet dangling loosely against his withers.

"So this is the country the Utes kept for themselves," John said, his eyes widening. Over the crest of the hill the legendary Ute valley lay before them like a garden. Mara couldn't believe how beautiful and rich it looked. Below, a river wound out of a steep canyon. Thick groves of trees bright with small leaves and shaggy bushes aflame with yellow bloom followed the river as it wound to the south.

"Beautiful!" Mama said, sounding breathless, no longer so weary. Sophia sighed.

"Incredible," said Papa. Mara was quiet. She hadn't felt like talking much on this trip. There wasn't anything to say.

In the distance, against the steep hills, they saw the smoke of an Indian camp. Down close to the river they saw the last of the Indians disappear into the trees with their new prisoners.

Sipapu turned to look back toward the crest of the hill. She could see the wagon and the people, but she could not see which one was the pale woman who gave food. Squash pulled on her rope, and she walked faster, holding tight to the hand of her daughter Mipuwai. What would become of them now with no man to protect them? If there had never been any white man in the valley, her old Hapu would still be strong. There was not enough space in this valley for both Hapu and the white man. Hapu's spirit returned to her in the night, asking for the healing in her hands.

Hapu. He had been foolish to follow Little Chief. They had never been happy with the Utes, her Hapu and herself, though they had spent long years among this people, from the time when the Utes killed their old Piute fathers and mothers and captured them together. They were strong, she and Hapu, and brave, and the Utes did not kill them. The Utes were not kind to them, but Hapu had not been wise to follow Little Chief and Kickingboot and Dog Foot, the renegades who stole the white man's cattle. Hapu knew. "The white man will find us," he said.

Sipapu felt the fire of the white man's weapons against the edge of her memory. She had seen them kill her Hapu. And the others. She had huddled down behind the bank of the creek, standing with Mipuwai in icy water. Hapu had fallen to the ground, the arrow in his bow breaking under him.

As they walked toward the camp of Arrapene, Sipapu was content that she and her daughter were among the Utes, even though they stumbled at the end of the rope. Mipuwai belonged to the Utes. She was born among them as was her brother Sobeshent, a tall boy, who had died of a white man's disease. Sipapu closed the death of her son, so long ago, from her mind. She closed the white man from her mind. She moved her feet over the rough earth.

Arrapene and Squash were murmuring to the men who met them in camp. Sipapu could not hear what they said. Sipapu did not like the language of the Utes. She did not try to learn it well. "You must speak," Hapu told her. But Sipapu was silent.

Arrapene spoke again, and one man ran back to the large tepee. He brought out a big man wearing a white shirt. It was Walkara. Walkara raised his arms for silence. He looked toward the women, pointed to the southwest somewhere beyond their mountain. Sipapu stood quiet, wondering. Walkara pointed to the women, laughed.

They slept in the tepee of Old Bishop, their ropes tied to the poles. In the cold darkness of the night, Sipapu felt a hand shaking her out of sleep. She could smell strong breath, but she did not know the dark shadow that stood over her. The shadow woke Hawk Feather and Angel Lip and pulled hard at their ropes until Angel

Lip cried out. As the sleep fell from her eyes, Sipapu could see the shadow more clearly. It was fat Squash.

"Har!" Arrapene came into the tepee, then, springing toward Squash in the dim light of the clouded moon. "Not Blueflower!" he shouted. He wanted Blueflower for himself, Sipapu thought. Beautiful Blueflower, daughter of the great Ute medicine man. She did not belong here. If her heart had not followed the young brave with fire in his eyes, she would not have been taken by the white men. The young brave with the fire in his eyes. Sipapu winced and cut off a moan in her throat. Long ago, before the young brave, there had been another youth meant for her. It had been Sobeshent, Sipapu's own son. If Sobeshent had lived, Blueflower would not be a prisoner among her own people now.

But now Arrapene would have her. A bad man. But one of her own. Squash stood over Blueflower. He grunted at Arrapene and bent from his thick waist, reaching down to Blueflower. Arrapene sprang to him and pushed him away. "Go! Take the others. I will follow," said Arrapene. Squash came then and pulled her rope. Sipapu got to her feet as Squash pulled hard on her rope, lifting Mipuwai up beside her. He dragged them out into the night—Angel Lip carrying her baby, then Hawk Feather, Sipapu, and last, Mipuwai, who stumbled, not awake. Blueflower was left behind. Arrapene came out of the tepee and threw down the flap. Squash climbed on his pony, still holding the ropes. He began to ride. The women stumbled behind him in the darkness. Arrapene, Angatewats, and another she did not know rode behind shouting for them to hurry, to run.

As they moved southward along the broken path, the sun began to rise from behind the high cliffs. Sipapu looked down on the valley. Beyond the river was the silver lake and then the far hills. If she were sure of what was to become of them, she could rejoice with the earth that was beginning to awaken to the sun.

While the sun spilled its light on the far hills, Sipapu thought she could see fire in the space between the land and the lake—in the bend of the river. Fires in the far trees. Not Utes. Utes would not have camped so close to the river. That would be the white men. Arrapene and Squash looked from their ponies, pointed toward the lights in the trees.

Slowly the dawn came. The colors of the earth returned. The sky grew blue. Sipapu stumbled over weeds, dry winter grass, her feet stiff with cold. Mipuwai stumbled beside her. Still they traveled the western rim of the valley, high on the hills. Although Sipapu had never seen Walkara's men before, she knew of them. Where were they taking her and Mipuwai, who stumbled to keep up with fat Squash on his horse? Sipapu watched Hawk Father, who, though she was as wrinkled as the dry earth before the rain, still kept pace like a young pony.

The sun rose in the sky. Still they walked. Mipuwai was tired. Angel Lip moaned. Her baby was very big. He grew very heavy. They must stop soon. Sipapu stumbled, and the rope pulled hard on her wrist. The sun was high over her head when Squash and Arrapene ordered them to stop at the edge of a clearing. Sipapu sat on the ground; she would move no more. She twisted her rope around the stump of a bush. The others sat near. Angatewats watched over them from his pony. Squash and Arrapene came down from their ponies and went away. Sipapu closed her eyes and slept.

When she woke, Arrapene and Squash had come again. Other Utes were with them—men who sat arguing with Arrapene and Squash, and women and children who stood in a ring around Sipapu and the others, watching. Sipapu heard hoofbeats in the distance. Arrapene stood quickly and looked toward the south. White men on mules rode into the clearing. Angatewats and Squash, with the other Ute men who had come, began talking with the white men, with loud words, using their hands to make pictures of what they said.

Sipapu looked at the white men. They were not like the ones in the camp, who gave food. Their faces were covered with hair. They spoke in loud voices.

"Five for ten guns," said Arrapene in Ute. Then Sipapu knew that what she feared would be so. They would be sold to these bad white men.

The biggest white man shook his head. "One." He held up his gun. "One." He pointed to Angel Lip.

Arrapene turned his head. "Five, seven guns."

"Seven guns?" said the big white man in Ute. "Five for seven?" he said again, his face scowling at Arrapene. He came down off his mule. The other three white men followed him. They stomped their boots on the ground. The big man had a voice like a bear. He came to the women. Sipapu held her child close to her. The white man shook his head and laughed. He spoke in a rough voice in the white man's tongue and laughed again. "Four!" he said.

Arrapene pointed to the women, named them and counted: Sipapu, one; Mipuwai, two; Hawk Feather, three; Angel Lip, four; baby, five. Five!" He held his hand high, his fingers spread like feathers.

The white man growled, shaking his head. Arrapene counted again, his face angry. "Five!" he shouted.

"Four!" the white man shouted back to him, holding up his fingers.

Arrapene held out his arm to take the guns. His face was dark with anger. The white men took four weapons from their packs and gave one to Arrapene. Arrapene turned it over and over, then pulled it to his body as a mother holds her child.

The white man pointed to Angel Lip. Squash pulled her to her feet. She gave the baby to Hawk Feather. The baby cried, and the old woman sang to it softly, rocking. Sipapu's heart pounded inside her. She would be sold to these big angry white men! She and Hapu's child. Sold!

The white man gave Arrapene another gun and pointed to Mipuwai. "No!" Sipapu spoke then, stumbling to her feet and raising her arms in front of her child. Squash pushed her to the ground and Arrapene carried Mipuwai to the back of the white man's mule. Mipuwai sat, making no sound, her eyes wide with fear as she turned to look at her mother. Sipapu felt Arrapene's hand around her arm. He dragged her to another mule. Forced her to mount. Then Hawk Feather mounted beside her on the last mule, Arrapene grabbing Angel Lip's baby from Hawk Feather's arms.

The white man shook his head. "No more." He put his hand flat up before Arrapene's face. But Arrapene held the child toward him, shouting. "Five! Five!"

The white man shook his head again. Arrapene pounded the earth with his foot. "Five!" he shouted. "Five!"

The big white man went away from Arrapene and climbed behind Angel Lip on his mule. A small man with red hair on his face climbed in front of Sipapu, a tall dark one in front of Mipuwai, a big one with an angry face in front of Hawk Feather. They were riding away. The baby in Arrapene's arms was screaming. Angel Lip leaned from the big man's mule and cried for her child, her arms stretched out.

"Five!" Arrapene ran after them, the child high in the air over his head. The white men did not stop. Angel Lip screamed for her child. Arrapene was running, shrieking into the sky. He held the baby by its feet, high before his face as he ran. The white man did not turn back. Arrapene stopped. Sipapu turned to see him as he stood still, holding the child in the air. Arrapene held it by its feet. For a moment he did not move. But then he swung it up to the sky and down against the rocks. Angel Lip's cry tore the heavens at the child's silence. She closed her eyes and her head fell to her chest. The big man held her and did not stop.

God of our people! cried the soul of Sipapu. Cold filled her heart. Mipuwai had not seen; she had not looked back. The white men kicked their mules, and they rode into the sharp sun.

That first night they had spent in their camp on the river, the settlers had not had time to build much protection. So they kept the fires going continuously and alternated hours of watch for guards with firearms. They had moved south along the flat plains until they came to the river moving swiftly from east to west in its steep banks. They crossed it, the horses and oxen knee-deep. Many people rode wagons or begged a ride with horsemen who made periodic trips. Finally, that afternoon, they were all safely on the other side. Tired and cold and wet, they decided to stay. This spot on the river would be a good place to camp; perhaps for good.

That first afternoon some staked out over two hundred acres and began planting grain. Others cut down young trees and began stripping them. Mara watched the land changing before her eyes, the trees disintegrating into sharp stumps. After a few hours, the meadow looked like a tornado had hit it. Papa called it "destruction before construction." It had to happen, he told them. Something was always destroyed to build something new. They began by marking off the corners of the fort and creating a few feet of a fourteen-foot-high barrier. They worked hard to prepare materials to build the fort the following day. Papa's oxen were put to use dragging the big logs to the site. John borrowed an ax to help with the stripping. While the men worked, Mama rummaged around in the supplies to find some beef jerky and a little flour. She made some thick soup that warmed all of them in the cold evening.

The darkness seemed to descend more quickly than usual that Wednesday evening in late March, their first night in their new home. The black trees along the river looked to Mara like great dark webs. The sound of the rushing water lulled her to an uneasy sleep. No Indians came that night.

Mara slept long past dawn and woke to the sun warming the grass on the riverbank, steam rising from the ground, and trees stirring in the morning breeze as if impatient to break into green leaves. Things would grow here. The land was rich, Papa said. "All around us, Mara," he had said. "Land, rich land. Ours. If the Indians will let us use it."

Mara looked toward the east, watched the sun spread over the crests of the mountains. The mountains looked black in the smoke of morning, then gray, then a mottled brown with bright patches of white as the sun rose higher above them. She thought: even the mountains shift and change. Nothing stays the same. Everyone in camp was busy, but no one noticed her. Standing from her blankets she stretched and looked all around. From where she stood she could barely see the lake, a sliver along the horizon in the west. To the north and east she could see the big mountain, spreading behind the front hills, white with snow. Mara tried to think of Bret, tried to remember how she had felt in his arms. But the mountains and the shadows stood between them now.

That day both men and women spent the morning in the fields planting after they had turned up the dark earth with their plows. They spent the afternoon building a log wall to assure some protection for the night. Bishop Higbee had marked out the fort—to be about seven hundred feet long and half that wide. On both the short ends, east and west, there was room for gates and on the inside of the east gate a corral to protect the cattle inside the walls at night. Each family chose a place inside the fort wall to build their own cabin facing the center of the fort. There were not quite thirty cabins to be erected around inside the rectangle, the back walls of the cabins serving as the outside walls of the fort. Protection would not be complete until all the cabins were built, so everyone helped everyone else.

Papa's oxen were busy all morning drawing the rusted plows. In the afternoon they helped drag trees to the fort. Both John and Ashel helped cut and strip the trees. No one was without work. In the morning Mara worked with the women, carried seed, sowed. Later she helped keep the fires burning, helped boil river water to make soup or flour cakes or dough boys, which the children cooked on green sticks over the coals. The cows grazed. Mara helped milk them, fed the hens, and watched for eggs to gather.

In the late afternoon, Mara brought stones from the river for the mud chimney, and she helped Papa and John settle a few logs around the little space that was to be theirs, on the south side of the west gate. That second day in the valley they managed to build their cabin walls up to about three feet and their stone fireplace up to eight feet. Mama organized some of her things from the wagon in a little space just behind the back wall. "In case the Indians come, we can duck behind our little wall," she said. "And we'll have some food, a few dishes, and blankets."

By nightfall of that second day, one large field had been planted, much of the fort completed. But it would probably be more than a week before everyone would be safely housed. Mara slept with her family that night near the chimney place on the south side of their three-foot-high hollow house. It was like sleeping in a hog pen. But Mara was so exhausted that once she lay on the bedding and covered herself with five inches of thick downy coverlets, she didn't move. The noisy rush of the river rolling only about a hundred feet northwest of their cabin and the crackling of the warm fire in the chimney place crowded out all the sounds of the camp trying to settle down for the night, and she fell into a deep, sound slumber.

It was the crow of a cock that woke her early. She sat up. For a moment she could not remember where she was. There were still hot coals on the new hearth beside her; her eyes grew quickly accustomed to the dark. She could see the three-foot wall to her left and then she suddenly remembered she was inside the fort, such as it was. She rubbed her eyes and was about to lie back down under her warm cover when she saw something moving outside the wall, a dark figure, then another, a smaller one; they were passing stealthily along the river. Indians! Terrified, she dared not move. Again the cock called, long and loud. The sky was gray with dawn. The figures were stealing quietly near the trees. She knew she must do something. So, without making a sound, she slid from her covers to hunt for Papa in the mounds of dew-wet blankets lying side by side on the bare ground. She found him, a large soft lump on the other side of the hearth. She quietly nudged him awake.

"Papa! It's the Indians! I know it's Indians!" she breathed.

Mama turned her head, looked up, her eyes wide with terror. "Get the gun," she whispered, hoarsely.

Papa was quick. John and Sophia woke too. Only Ashel still slept.

"Grab that," Papa whispered to John, pointing at the other gun. The men stole out of their bedding and crept to the wall facing the river. Mara, straining her eyes in the dawn, could see the figures stopped now, humped behind the distant trees. A breathless quiet hung over the noisy voice of the river. In the growing light, the two black heads huddled close together grew more visible.

"My land, it's Spirit of Earth and Rain!" Mama said, standing up.

"Well, I'll be," said Papa.

It was, for sure, Spirit of Earth. And behind her, Rain. Their eyes sharpened in the light of the sun, their gaunt faces intently watching the Eastmans on the other side of their short wall.

"Oh my land, they have got out and run away," Mama said. "We must fetch them and take them in."

"Birds and bee feathers!" Papa pushed his big body up from his crouching position behind the wall. He stayed on his knees. "Land of America! So here they come again out of the dust and the sunshine! Spirit of Earth and Rain." He shook his head. "I doubt you'll ever be without 'em again, Martha."

Mama hardly heard him for bustling about in her bedding, finding her stays and her skirt packed under the quilts to keep them warm. She was up and dressed in two minutes, folding her hair behind her with a few stray pins. When she started out the gate toward them, the Indians backed away in the trees, so she stopped and called.

"Sipapu," she said quietly. "Here. Please come. We won't hurt you. We'll take care of you." Slowly, Spirit of Earth's eyes emerged from the trees, and behind her, the bobbing black head of Rain. "Sipapu, come here. What has happened?" As Spirit of Earth bit by bit revealed her face in the growing light, Mara could see her dark skin was stained with blood!

Mama started forward again, stopped. Spirit of Earth moved haltingly, her limbs jerking under the rough fabric of her torn wrap. Painfully she came toward the gate and toward Mama, Rain moving slowly behind her. Mama met them.

"Sipapu! What has happened to you!" Mama cried. Around the woman's mouth were patches of bloody scabs, and on her wrist raw sores under the ragged remains of a chewed up piece of rope. Rain's wrist bore the same raw sores and the same chewed up rope. "My land!" Mama held both sore hands gently in her own, cradling them, turning them over and over. "You and your poor child. You have come with great difficulty. We will take care of you." Her voice was like music. Spirit of Earth stood patiently while Mama touched her mouth caked with dry scabs.

"Come here," Mama said. "We have some ointment that will help you. And some breakfast. I know you'll like our breakfast. Papa, stir the fire! Mara! Sophia! Warm the pot, and we'll have hot tea and griddle cakes. Stir, Ashel!" As she spoke, she took the two scarred hands firmly in her own and gently led the two brown Indians into the fort through the narrow gate.

After Mama's loving hands had dabbed the blood from the wounds and patched them with an ointment of herbs, the Indians ignored their pain. They tore at the pancakes as thought they had not eaten for a week. As they ate, they gazed at the walls of the house rising.

After breakfast, Mara took Rain and Spirit of Earth on a walk all the way around the new fort. She never dreamed she would be so happy to be with them. She wished she could talk to them to find out what had happened. But seeing their wounds, she did not really want to know. She wanted them to be happy now. She smiled at them. They inspected the fort, touching it on the sides, bobbing up and down to check the way the logs fit.

When they reached the straw and clay pit where the men were mixing the mortar, Spirit of Earth bent down into the straw, smiling and talking rapidly to Rain and Mara. She picked up the straw and deftly, not paying any attention to the bandages on her wrists, wove a tiny basket. She gave it to Mara, who ran with a feeling of joy, holding it up to the sun.

Rain moved out into the fields then, and began gathering yellow wildflowers. With quiet patience, she removed the bugs from the stems and blew them off the palm of her hand into the breeze. She smiled at Mara. "Good-bye," she said awkwardly, one of the first words she had learned from them. "Good-bye," she said to the bugs. Mara laughed.

When Rain ran into the fields from flower to flower, Mara ran to follow her and together they gathered flowers. They brought some of them back to Mama tucked in the little straw basket. The walls of the house were high, now, and the men were pounding on the last supports for the roof. Excited, Mara set the flowers in the empty window.

"It's your house, too," she said to Spirit of Earth and Rain. "It's your house, now, too."

Not understanding a word, both Rain and her mother just clapped their hands and grinned.

Chapter Four

Friday afternoon at four o'clock the Wheeler boys spotted the settler's first visitors from the Great Salt Lake. One of them was a big man on a shaggy horse. The others were younger—two with red hair, and one lean and sandy-haired. Mara recognized Sully from a distance. The others were unmistakably Ivie Richards and his boys. On the last mile into camp, they raced their horses, kicking and shouting.

All four horses were foaming and trembling when the boys and Ivie Richards drew them up sharply outside the east gate.

Mara, Nancy, and Hannah were searching for dry kindling in the huge pile of discarded limbs when the men came.

"Well," Richards said, holding back his horse with some difficulty. He grinned at Mara. "If it isn't a few of the camp's prize beauties!"

Hannah pulled away, jerking a branch from the stack. Nancy blushed. Mara pretended to ignore Richards' remark. Behind them, Brother Allen, Brother Pace, and the Wheelers were coming from their post at the construction of one of the front cabins. Standing tall, Mara looked up at Richards. She was determined to be cool and indifferent.

"Hello, Mr. Richards." She looked at him steadily, hoping

her anger did not come into her eyes, hoping her fear did not reveal itself in her trembling hands. But Richards' stare above his terrible grin penetrated her. She shuddered.

"Well, we come to visit you, girl. I told you, didn't I? It wouldn't be the last." The horse shifted under him.

Mara knew well she wasn't the total reason for his visit. "Can I do something to help you?" she asked as coolly as she could. By this time Brothers Allen and Pace were near.

"Well, Ivie Richards. If it isn't you and your boys. And Sully Tuttle! Hello there. How's things up north? You come down here to stay?"

Richards gave Mara one last glance and turned to the men. She stood without flinching as he turned his big horse so close to her he nearly kicked her with his stirrup.

"I'm thinking of mapping out a farm, building, then bringing down my wife," Richards reported in a matter-of-fact voice.

"Well, there's plenty of land to map. You can count on gettin' some of it."

Richards glanced toward the cabins going up around inside the fort. "You got a space ten by ten me and my boys can set our tent?"

"You're welcome to anything you can find," said Brother Pace. "Help yourself."

Sully must have dismounted from his horse while Richards was talking, for as Mara turned to go back to work pulling the limbs, she found him directly in front of her. His face was red. "Hello, Mara," he said, more deliberately than he needed to. "Indians gotcha yet?" He turned to Hannah and Nancy.

"Not yet," Hannah said, angrily tearing sticks in jerks. Hannah didn't like being at Provost's Hole.

"They got our Indians though," Nancy said quietly, her face as red as Sully's. "But two of them came back this morning to Eastmans."

"That right?" Sully said, interested in the news. "Is that right, Mara?" He turned back to Mara. She stood watching him without hearing what he and Nancy were talking about. She was wondering what he thought about that night at the Hunts'. What had Bret said when he came back? When Sully looked at her, she felt uncomfortable.

"Spirit of Earth and Rain escaped forty-niners who bought them as slaves," Nancy said.

Sully continued to gaze at Mara. "Is that right, Mara?"

It was only last Sunday—not even a week yet since she last saw Bret! But now it seemed he was in another world.

"Mara?" Sully's voice was insistent. It seemed to say, *look* at me. I'm here. Mara looked at him.

"That's one of the reasons we're down here, to find out what happened to the Indians," Sully said.

"What's the other reason?" Hannah said, jerking a limb from the pile.

"Well, me . . . I'm here because I want to stay," Sully said. "Farm. This looks like good country."

"It is good country," Nancy said. She wiped her hands on her apron. She was smiling. "It's a great place. And if the Indians will leave us alone we can do anything here."

"Anything?" Sully asked with a smile.

She blushed again.

"And the others?" Mara spoke at last.

Sully started at the sound of her voice. "What others?"

"Why are the others down here?"

"Like I said, Richards wanted to know what happened to the Indians. And he wants to get farms too. For his boys—his wife's boys."

Mara glanced toward the fort. The two red-headed boys, still mounted on their ponies, were now following Ivie Richards into the gate behind Brother Allen and Brother Pace. Richards wants to know about the Indians. That was it! She knew it. Richards was down here to look for Blueflower. Her heart pounded as her eyes narrowed. "It's not the Indians. He doesn't care at all about the Indians," she said between her teeth, almost so softly that Sully could not hear.

"What's that, Mara?"

"Never mind."

"Is your family's cabin built, Mara?" Sully asked her with that tremor in his voice—as if he worried he would say something she wouldn't like.

"Almost," Mara said absently, irritated by his making up to her. He seemed so thin, so fidgety.

"Which one's yours?"

"Ours is down at the other end, too," Nancy said cheerfully as she began to gather an armful of kindling to carry inside. Hannah gathered hers quickly, a thick, very neat stack which she carefully swept up beneath her chin.

"Here, let me carry that," Sully said quickly to Hannah, but Hannah turned away from him, her head high. "I'll carry it."

"I can manage myself, thanks," Mara said.

Nancy stammered and smiled. "If you want to, you can help me, Sully."

Carrying the rest of Nancy's pile, Sully followed the girls inside the gate and began to cross the length of the fort to the west end. On every side men were hurrying to put up enough logs to give them security for the night. At the west gate, Papa and John were working on the roof.

"Well, bless me if it isn't Sully Tuttle," Papa wheezed.

"Martha," he called to Mama, who was rummaging about inside the four walls. Sully put Nancy's kindling on the ground and followed Papa to the door. "We got a visitor from the City."

"Sully Tuttle! Why, my goodness. Imagine you here." She came to him and took his hands. Why was she so glad to see *him*? Mara wondered to herself. "Well, come in, such as it is. Come in!" Mama said.

Sully bent and walked in through the doorway. He walked over and peered out the one small window at the back of the cabin. "Nice view," he said nervously. He surveyed the hearth where Spirit of Earth and Rain lay sleeping soundly. "Looks good," he said, smiling to Mama.

"Yes, we got our Indians back," Mama said warmly. "Just today." That wasn't what he meant, Mara thought, angry at Mama for welcoming Sully like he was kin or something. "Sit down, boy," she was saying. Sully perched on a crate. They hadn't moved the furniture in from the wagon yet.

"Is Mara back from gathering the wood, Ashel?" asked Mama, unaware that Mara was standing in the doorway.

"She's right here, ma'am," said Sully.

"Bring in some kindling, Mara," Mama said. "Why, imagine a visit from somebody so soon, girl!" That was it. Mama was just glad to have a visitor from the city. Mara carried an armload of kindling inside. Sully jumped to help her as she laid it under the kettle on the hearth. She stood up.

"Mr. Richards came, too."

"Mr. Richards?" Mama's smile faded.

"And his two boys."

"Well, they'll all need someplace to stay, I guess," Mama said almost absentmindedly. Mara could not believe her ears. "Have you a place to stay, Sully?"

Sully looked at Mara, his face red. "Why, uh, no ma'am."

"You're certainly welcome to stay with us until you get yourself settled." From his silly grin Mara could tell that was exactly what he was waiting for.

"Oh, ma'am. How kind of you. I would sure appreciate it. Why, thank you very much. I'm much obliged, ma'am." He looked around him, pleased. Mara looked away from the question in his eyes when his gaze rested on her. He started to chatter again. "Now, if I can help you get the roof on, we can likely do it before dark. Do you have any other tools, Brother Eastman?" He jumped to the doorway and practically tore the latch off. He banged his knee on the door jamb. "I can help you get this roof on before nightfall."

"Why, that I believe you can," Papa boomed. Even Papa seemed glad Sully was there. Couldn't he see what Sully wanted? He had been so angry about Bret. Why was he so happy about Sully?

Sully left to help John, who was pounding at bark shingles.

"Mother!" Mara nearly shouted. Then, between her teeth, "What are you doing asking Sully here?"

Mama looked at Mara. Her eyes were tired. She shrugged her shoulders. "The boy needed a place to stay."

"Yes, but . . ." Mara's voice was a coarse anxious whisper, "we've got Sophia . . . in her condition. And John. And me. *I* count. And we've got them . . . Spirit of Earth and Rain." She pointed to the Indians sewing leather on the hearth. When she acknowledged them, they began to nod and smile. "Where do you think he's going to sleep? There's barely room for all of us already on this tiny floor."

Mama turned away. She was tired, and Mara was suddenly ashamed of herself. From Far West to Nauvoo to Salt Lake, it was simply something you did, and she knew it. You just took anybody in, gave anybody what he needed. You always asked whoever was there, tired or hungry, if they would like to share what you had, no matter how little. But she couldn't stay here with Sully . . . the way he looked at her. And he didn't need to stay here. There were others who could take him in. Others who had more room. More food. Let him stay in the tent with Ivie Richards.

Mama stirred the stew in the pot over the fire. "I'm sorry, Mara. I meant no harm."

"But Mama. He could stay somewhere else." Her mother didn't answer. "Well, *I* can't sleep here while he's here."

Mama sighed. "Do what you think is best. I've invited him."

"Do what I think is best? Sleep in the yard, I suppose. Do what's best? What *is* best? You tell me what it is I should do that's best!"

"Mara, calm down now. It'll only be for a short time. It won't be forever," Mama said, still stirring.

"A short time? I'll just bet. You'll just keep taking people in and giving things out until we've got nothing, not even a place to sleep."

"We have enough."

"We don't have enough space!" Mara cried.

"Mara!" Mama turned toward her now. They stared at each other. Then Mara was suddenly aware that Sully was standing at the door.

"What is it, Sully?" Mama said in her patient voice.

He hesitated and then seemed to stutter. "Ma'am, d-do you h-have a bit of cloth we can use to b-bind up an ax handle?" Perhaps he had not heard. "I-I hope I'm not interrupting anything."

Mara lowered her eyes and picked at the edge of her apron.

"No. No, my boy," Mama said. "It's . . . it's nothing." She went to a crate and drew out a long piece of torn cloth.

"Surely we'll get your roof done tonight," Sully said. "I hope it isn't going to inconvenience you if I share it with you." Mara breathed relief. He hadn't heard.

Mama handed him the cloth. "My boy, as far as I'm concerned, you're more than welcome." Mara shot a glance at her mother. "Someday you'll likely do the same for some of us." Sully took the cloth in his hand and looked at Mara, who looked back down at her apron.

"You know, Sister Eastman," he said, his voice warm, "I really hope so."

When he left, Mama said, "Mara, honey, I think he's a fine boy. Oh, I know you don't fancy him." Mara looked up at her mother, surprised. "He's not pretty like that Hunt boy who's put you right out of your senses." Mara looked at the floor. How could Mama know what Bret was like? He was so good.

"But mark my words, girl. That one has a long way to go before he's ready to settle down. You keep on worrying about him and he'll break your heart." Mama *didn't* understand. Mara would have to keep Bret to herself.

"Now, Sully Tuttle might not turn a pretty girl's head the way Bret Hunt does, but I wouldn't discourage him too much if I was you. You'll be wantin' to start building your own life someday soon. And you'll be needin' to do it with somebody that has something solid to offer you, mark my words. And his feelings for you aren't just passing fancy."

Mara felt Sully's eyes on her all evening. She felt his presence like she felt shadows between her and the sun. Why did he act that way? What did he know of her? She knew all she needed to know of him. He ate too fast. He was clumsy. His days in the streets of London rose to the surface in small fits of violence. When he nodded to the Indians at the hearth and smiled at them, he looked like a red-headed clown.

Mara picked at her food and hurried through the dishes. She stared out the doorway of the cabin as they sat huddled around the fire. Bret. Why hadn't it been Bret who had come instead of Sully? As the family talked in the chimney corner, she would not look at him, though she knew well his wide blue eyes followed her every move. If Bret had come, Mama would see how fine he was. Papa too.

"It's time for bed, now," Papa said, raising his big body that seemed to fill the entire cabin. He was feeling good. The roof had been completed. "Yes, we've done well today, folks. Let it snow, now. Yes sir, let it snow." He looked up at the rough shingles overhead. "There's no doubt some leaks there, but nothing we can't fix." He stretched. "Thank you, Sully Tuttle and John, for your help."

"Oh," Mama moaned, "don't ask it to snow. Please don't ask it to snow. There's still people without a roof!" There were tents up, but it was true many of the cabins were still unfinished. "And the crops! It may freeze the crops! How can you ask for snow when so much plowing still needs to be done?"

Papa shook his head, and he and John and Sully left the cabin to fetch wood while Mama spread out the bedding for the Indians. Then she pinned up a large quilt on the left side of the cabin to serve as a temporary wall for herself and Mara and Sophia. Mara took her shoes off but crawled quickly into her bedding fully clothed. She watched Sophia climbing into a flannel nightgown. Her belly was rounder than it used to be.

"John and I want to get our own place, Mama," she was saying softly. "He says John Mills wants to start a saw mill in the canyon, and we may go with him."

"Sophia! Don't talk yet about your own place," Mama said.

"Mama, I think John wants to go right away . . . maybe even next Monday."

It's too soon to leave the fort," Mama said. "Too many Indians watching us from the hills. Haven't you seen them?"

Mara did not sleep well in the room with a blanket for a wall. Sully was only eight feet away. She was aware of his breathing, a quick hoarse sound, noisy even above the rush of the river, not regular like sleeping breath. She felt his presence long into the night. She was afraid of where he lay in the cabin. She knew he must be awake, too. She lay awake for hours, trying to call up her dreams of Bret to shut out the sound of Sully so close by. At last, in the deep quiet of the early morning, she fell asleep.

"Snow!" Mama's loud whisper from the blankets next to hers woke her abruptly. Mara rubbed her eyes, as tired as if she had not slept at all. It was still dark. Out of the small window at the back of the cabin, Mara could see the big white flakes in the moonlight, as though they fell from a cloudless sky. It was cold. She pulled her cover up over her chin.

In a few moments she heard a shuffling and whispering on the other side of the quilt. "Martha!" It was Papa's whisper. Mama got up, wrapping her cover around her. When she came back around the quilt she brought Nancy Allen and her two little sisters Polly and Elizabeth, who stumbled, half awake, and her two-year-old baby brother Benjamin, who was asleep in Nancy's arms. Nancy's Papa had only begun the roof on their cabin.

"It was cold in the tent," Nancy whispered. They settled down as quietly as they could so they would not wake Sophia and Benjamin. Mama took her bedding away to make room. "I'll sit up with Sister Allen," she said. The little sisters fell asleep as soon as they lay down. Mara could hear Sully whispering to Randall Allen on the other side of the quilt. Mara thought there must be more than twenty people in this little room!

"Is Sully going to stay with you permanent?" whispered Nancy.

Morning came late, its dawn crowded out by the black shadows spilling white flakes over the land. Out of the small west window at the back of the cabin Mara could see the results of the night's silent storm. The trees along the river bent with the weight of the snow. Along the ground, a foot or more of heavy white snow covered the sage, the brush, last summer's trampled flowers.

"It snowed, all right," Mama was saying, looking out the empty window from behind Mara. Some snow had drifted through the opening onto the bedding, into the hearth.

It was still snowing, but lightly now. Sophia, John kneeling beside her, rose and dressed quickly, talking softly. "Do you think John Mills will still be finding a spot for his sawmill?"

"Don't worry about it, Sophia," John whispered.

"But I want to go, too. Can they plant now the snow has fallen?"

"They've planted enough for awhile, they said. They may have to wait to plant more," John said.

Mara knew the greatest concern would be for the crops. She felt the anxiety in Mama, in Sophia and John. The little Allen children woke with excitement and energy, rushing outside to find their parents, who had gone back to their own wet cabin. Nancy followed them sleepily. Mara heard her say hello to Sully on the other side of the quilt. "The snow is beautiful, Sully," she said. Mara did not hear what he said in reply. Maybe if she stayed in her bed long enough, Sully would be gone when she got up, Mara thought.

The whole camp was slow to get moving. The adults were all quiet, their faces stern. Sully had gone with Papa and John to see what needed to be done for those with cabins not finished. As Mara helped Mama with the breakfast she looked out the door. She could see Ivie Richards and his two boys with the Allens around their outdoor cooking fire. At least *they* won't be here for breakfast, Mara thought.

Across the blanket of snow, Mara could hear Richards' loud voice. "What they ought to do is build a platform in the center of the fort and raise the cannon on it."

"What they ought to do is bury the cannon under the ice and raise a little hell on it," Papa said.

"I think they were going to do that today," Allen said. "Although we haven't had many Indians come down."

"Well, you have 'em around," Richards said. "I saw plenty on my way in. They're watching you from a distance. You just got to be smarter than they are."

Mama was quiet this morning, and as Mara moved around the cabin she heard the noises of the camp—and from time to time she could hear Richards. It was as though he were shouting for the whole camp to hear.

"Indians or not," he bellowed. "Me and the boys is going to build outside, mark off some land." He pointed north and east. "Maybe today."

Mara breathed easily. Good. Richards would be leaving the fort.

"Maybe we can get by without killing. I know some is going to try building outside now on a homestead, but they're sure taking a chance going against Brigham Young's counsel." It was Papa's voice. Mara looked out the door.

"You can't live on top of each other in this snow and in a few square feet of fort," Richards growled back.

"It's not going to be easy," Papa grunted as he put Brother Allen's beam in place. "But nothing the Lord asks us to do ever is."

For the next three and a half days it snowed, sometimes thick and wet, sometimes powdery. The sky was always overcast. Daylight came like a gray cloud and left in a black cloud in the darkness of evening.

It was generally quiet except for the occasional laughter of children playing in the snow. Ashel and his friends built a snow fort. On Saturday morning Mara looked outside and noticed Rain tracking along the river with a few small Indian children. They were dressed in ragged skins with huge pieces of fur tied like bundles on their feet. The Indians themselves may not have come down to visit with the settlers, but their children were not afraid. Mara noticed they were dragging dead branches along the snow behind them, erasing the tracks they left.

When Sunday came everyone in the fort attended a very long Sunday School. Bishop Higbee went over long lists of assignments—people were to take different plots of ground to cultivate outside the common fields. "If we do make our own farms, it's wisest not to live on them but to come back to the fort in the evening. I know the Indians don't seem to be bothering us. But God will help us only if we help ourselves."

John had been one of the first anxious ones to begin his own homestead up near the mouth of the canyon where his friend John Mills was planning to build a sawmill. Sully had decided he would go with them.

Richards had left in the same direction on Saturday. The Wilson boys and other scouts who were somewhat acquainted with the area, told of the rich bottom lands northeastward which would make excellent farming.

Over Sunday supper, Mama began to whimper, begging John to leave Sophia with her in the fort. But as feelings of irritation began to crowd the family cabin, John and Sophia had definitely decided to go. "It's not far away," Sophia said. "And I will be riding back and forth to see you often."

"I'll take care of them for you," Sully said, his voice uneven. Mama looked at Sully and said nothing, an amused smile on her face.

"I can take care of Sophia. You don't need to worry, Mother Eastman," John said in his quiet voice.

Sully turned bright red. "Of-of-of course, you can. I mean, I didn't mean. . . ." he stammered. Papa smiled into his soup.

After supper, Mama sent Mara outside for some kindling. Mara was glad of the chance to get out of the crowded cabin gracefully, but she wondered why Mama didn't send Ashel and why Mama wanted more kindling anyway, at this time of day. Before she could close the door behind her Sully was at her heels. Mama *planned* this, she thought to herself angrily.

Closing the door quickly behind him, Sully stood still by the cabin for a moment while Mara lifted the oilcloth back from the woodpile and gathered some sticks into her arms. All of a sudden, Sully leaped into motion.

"Let me do that!" he almost shouted. Startled, Mara dropped the kindling onto the snow. As Sully knelt to retrieve it, an uncomfortable nervousness boiled up in Mara's heart.

"I'll go back in then," she said hurriedly.

"No!" Sully stood up in front of her, the kindling dropping to the ground once more. "I mean, if you would be good enough to hear me out, I got something I would like to say to you," he said woodenly, as though he'd rehearsed it.

Mara winced and began to turn away. He grabbed her arm in a grip—he had no idea how violent—and turned her back. "Please, Mara!" he begged, releasing her arm, embarrassed. As much as his intense face frightened and annoyed her, she felt sorry for him.

"All right," she said. "I'll stay for a moment, but Mama will be wondering. . . ."

"No, it's all right. I've asked her permission to speak to you." It was Mama! Well, he certainly hadn't asked Papa, Mara thought angrily. But Papa wasn't blind. Where was he now, when she needed him?

Mara's anger chased away her fear, and she looked up at Sully. We may as well get this over, once and for all, she thought.

"Mara, I know it's a mite sudden," Sully was going on, "and a mite soon. But I ain't got much time. I-I mean, I'll be leavin' in the morning with John and Sophia and I want to speak before anybody else . . . that is. . . ." He was trembling, whether from the cold or from his emotion, Mara couldn't tell. "Mara!" He grabbed both her arms above the elbows so hard it hurt. "Mara, startin' out in this kind of country a man and woman need each other more than any other time in their life." He looked at her tenderly, his fingers more gentle on her arms now. "I know I was raised in the rough streets of London, but I've learnt to be a good farmer. Ask Mr. Hunt. Ask them all. Hunts'll say so."

Hunts! Why did he mention them? Mara blushed at the memory of Bret that rose in her now. It was a pain, like a knife in her heart. Don't you know how I feel? Mara wanted to shout at Sully. Don't you know it's Bret?

As though he read her thoughts Sully dropped her arms. "Mara, I'd do good for you," he said quietly. "I'm going up north to make a farm with your sister and her husband. I'd be much obliged if you'd take it on yourself to think on coming to live with me." Sully breathed a long sigh, as if he had unloaded himself of a great burden. He stood silent, his eyes on the ground, waiting for her reply.

Mara took a deep breath. "Sully," she began. "I know you're a good farmer, and you're a good, kind. . . ."

"Don't!" Sully was gripping her arms again, his eyes flashing into hers. "Mara, don't you understand? I love you!"

"Oh, Sully, Sully, please," In spite of herself, Mara began to cry. Why wasn't this Bret? Why hadn't they sent *Sully* to England?

"Mara." His voice was quiet now. "I know you don't fancy me much right yet. And I ain't askin' you to marry me right now. I'm just askin' you to *think* on it." He let her arms go. "I won't push you. I won't even touch you. Though I'd like to." He looked at her with such longing that Mara thought for a moment he would leap on her. But he just stood trembling and gazing at her. "I love you enough to wait. I know you're young yet. I know your heart is not ready to settle. But I want you to know I'm waiting." He looked away from her and off into the growing dusk. "I'm going to build me a cabin and map out a farm this spring." He looked at her again. Her fear gone, she began to be fascinated at the intensity of his desire for her. You have to respect him for being willing to be so patient, she thought.

"Mara, I love you. Remember it, will you? And think on me, in the cold spring nights, or in the spring mornings when there's dew on everything and the grass is starting to grow. Just remember there is a lonesome man out there in a warm cabin on the riverbed. Remember he's out there plowin' and plantin' and waitin' for you to come." He stroked her right shoulder with the flat of his hand.

He looked so thin, so young. Mara didn't know whether to laugh at him or cry for him. But he was so earnest. She stood quietly, letting him say all he wanted to say.

"Tell me you'll just think on me, Mara." She looked him in the eyes, feeling a kind of warm pity. Could it be that he had completely forgotten that Sunday night (was it only a week ago?) when she had come to Hunts with leaves in her hair? Could he have forgotten how Bret had ridden after her? Surely he knew Bret had not come directly home when he followed her. Did he know anything of what had happened? Anything of how she felt? Was he doing this to try to bind her to him and make her forget Bret? Well, he wouldn't be able to do that. But he was so earnest. She didn't want to hurt his feelings. It wouldn't hurt just to calm him down a bit. Surely she would think of him once in a while. Perhaps it would make a difference in his life. Help him somehow.

"All right, Sully," she said, looking calmly into his burning eyes. "I'll think of you."

"Oh!" Sully cried, swinging in a circle on his heel, nearly knocking Mara down with his spindly arms. "Glory hallelujah!" He was jumping and clapping like a little child. Then, grabbing her arms again, "Mara! You're wonderful, just wonderful! Hoooweee!"

"Wait a minute, now," Mara laughed nervously, amused by Sully's enthusiasm, but suddenly afraid. "Sully, you're not to think for a moment that I have promised anything more."

Sully stopped his dancing. "No. No, of course not. I know that, Mara. I don't need no promises. I'm not makin' any promises to you, neither. The time for promises will come." He took both her hands now. He seemed so happy, so confident. Surely it wasn't wrong to make him happy. He would see for himself that it would never work, that she could never love him. He would find someone else. Surely someone. . . .

"Oh, Mara, I'll work so hard. You won't believe it when you see what I can do."

She felt a warm feeling for him, almost motherly. It was in her power to make him happy, to help him make something of himself, to help him prepare himself to make some woman a good husband. "You watch out for John and Sophia, now, won't you," she said, feeling almost affectionate. There would be somebody for Sully, someone who could love him, someone perhaps like . . . Nancy. Mara hadn't thought of it before, but Nancy seemed to like him. Nancy would be good for him.

"I will, Mara, oh I will," Sully was saying.

"Will what?"

"Why, watch out for John and Sophia, like you said."

"Good," she smiled. "Good."

Monday the dawn broke though a clear blue sky. Not a cloud marked the horizon. The fresh snow stood in deep drifts along arroyos and washes in the bed of the river. The river was a trickle of ice water draining through the cascades of sculptured ice. Papa packed the wagon behind the oxen as Sophia and John separated their own things from Mama's in the packing crates. Sully stuffed his last piece of bedding into the saddle bag on his pony. Mara was packing a lunch of meat and fried cakes in an old patchwork bag.

On the east side of the fort, John Mills, his young wife Cassie, and their family of small children sat in their wagon, waiting, while Sully, leading, and John and Sophia in the ox cart, trundled across the distance of the fort, waving good-bye to the Allens, the Wilsons, the Wrights, the Wheelers, the Olsens.

Mama and Papa walked with them outside of the fort, Mara and Ashel following behind. Spirit of Earth and Rain came too. The stretches of snow on either side of the river ahead lay like vast lakes alongside a bridge of trees.

"If you're not careful to stick to the river, you might get lost," Papa said. They would be moving along the southeast bank, traveling toward the mountains towering to the east.

Sully, astride his pony, bundled in a brown scarf, looked back at Mara several times as he rode away. Nancy had come to stand with Mara. Every time Sully looked back, Nancy waved cheerfully. It wouldn't do to say anything to her about Sully just yet.

Sully had never felt better in his life. At his side he carried an old Derringer. He rode at the front of both parties, scanning the white distance for any possible movement, feeling like a scout, his mind alert and his body tense. Everything he would do now would be for Mara, for their future, for their children. Their children! Tall sandy-haired boys and beautiful dark-haired girls with delicate skin and deep beautiful eyes. He and Mara would watch their children grow in the wilderness and bring civilization to this wild land. He and Mara! His blood pounded in him and kept him warm on the cold ride. For now that the snow had stopped falling, and the blanket of clouds was gone, the cold was brittle beneath the clear empty sky.

Sully looked at Sophia huddled under several blankets on her wagon seat. She is a nice woman, he said to himself. But quiet and pale. Not like Mara, so bright, so beautiful, so warm. His heart pounded. Mara! This summer Sophia would bear John's child. Next summer, who knows? Next summer—Mara might bear *his*.

ʳ trudged northward along the river bank Sully ˍ ᴊɪɪe Mills children whimpering from the cold. They were moving into a wide trough sheltered by a group of hills to the west as well as the mountains on the east. With low hills rising sharply all around them, they found themselves in a rich area of wooded bottom lands where, amidst the giant trees, there was still enough empty plain spread far and wide to make room for ample farms. It was breathtaking. Sully whistled softly to himself.

Less than a mile from the canyon site where John Mills had decided to build his sawmill, Sully thought he saw movement in the trees by the river. He was certain someone was camped there. As they drew closer, one of the trees in the distance seemed to waver, then fall. As it fell, he saw to his right up on the ledge overlooking the course of the river a small group of Indians on ponies, watching. They were close enough above them that he could clearly see one to be an old wizened gray-haired man. With him on his pony was one of the most beautiful Indian maidens he had ever seen. Her face brought a stab of memory to Sully, but he shook his head. He was not sure he had ever seen her before. The other older Indian was very large, spread over his horse with more flesh than the horse itself carried. Two other younger braves rode with these two. Just as he caught sight of the Indians, they turned on their horses and rode away.

Ahead of the rest of the party, Sully saw smoke, finally a blazing fire, and three men chopping and cutting away limbs from the giant tree that had fallen. They had been setting thick logs on a large new cabin, now almost completed. Sully immediately recognized Richards and his two stepsons. Delighted, he sped his horse toward their camp and toward the fire. The Mills and Smiths followed him. "Look!" he heard Cassie Smith say excitedly to her children. "A fire. We can get you warm!"

"You're almost settled!" Sully said to Richards who came toward him, ax still in one hand, extending his other for a warm handshake.

"Welcome!" Richards exclaimed. "You picked the right place, too!"

"We're moving up to the canyon and setting up a sawmill."

"You found the trees, didn't you. Well, there's enough for everybody here, and the farmland is fine. Welcome."

"Any Indians?" Sully asked, just to be friendly.

Richards' face tightened like a drying lump of adobe clay. "A few," he said without expression.

"They been down here pestering us," the oldest Richards boy offered.

"Or we been up after them," the youngest boy chimed in.

"I've got my Indian wife still here up somewhere on these hills," Richards glared at Sully, at John and Sophia. "I think I found her."

"Well, so you found her!" Sully said good naturedly. Richards' brows were still knit and his voice sullen with a surly darkness. "And it's possible she's carryin' my child."

Sully looked at Sophia. Her face showed clearly her anger and her disgust. John mumbled under his breath, "You dirty. . . ." Sully looked quickly at Richards, but Richards was not paying attention to John and Sophia.

"I'm not sure," Richards said quietly. "But I want to know."

"How can he know!" Sully heard Sophia whispering to John. John was taking her fingers that lay on his arm and warming them in his hand. He did not say a word. Richards and his boys stared at them.

"Well, I wish you luck," Sully said. "If you don't mind, we'll use your fire to cook our midday food. We'll help you raise your roof on your cabin and then if you have a mind to come with us to the site of our camp we could use you to set up."

"Be glad to," Richards said heartily, seeming to break out of his dark thoughts.

The noonday sun was bright on the vast plain of snow. Sully climbed down off his horse, John helped Sophia out of the wagon, and they joined the Mills to warm themselves at Ivie Richards' fire.

John and Sophia had been gone less than a week when they returned to fetch Papa to help build. Mama, who was not feeling well, begged him to stay but Papa felt John needed him more. He left Mara with instructions to get help from the Allens or the Wrights as they needed it. He would return every few days to check on things and to help with the planting and digging for irrigation.

Mara took care of the fires and helped Mama wash the clothing and bedding and prepare the food. With Papa gone much of the time there was little use to cook big meals, and they ate meals based on flour and picked wheat sprouts for greens.

The crops, just barely standing out of the black soil, looked good on the last day of March, but on April tenth and eleventh a cruel frost choked the tiny plants. Shivering and sick, the settlers walked back and forth across the rows, some of them hunting for last stalks of green to gather and cut.

On the morning of April eleventh, Mara was alone outside the fort gathering broken twigs by the river for kindling. She thought she heard horses in the distance. Her heart stopped. It could be Indians, or it might be Papa coming home to check on them because of the freeze. She stood up and peered through the trees. In the distance she could see three men on horses. She could tell from their clothes that they were white men. Breathing a sigh of relief, she stepped out of the trees and shaded her eyes to see who they were, but she couldn't tell.

As she stood in the morning sunshine, two of the riders veered off toward the east gate of the fort, while the other, the largest, rode toward her. He wore rough skins and his beard was thick and bushy. Though it hardly looked like him, Mara could see who it must be. No one else could look so big and shaggy. It was Ivie Richards! Too late, Mara stepped back into the trees, hoping he wouldn't follow her, but at the same time feeling a strange terror that he might.

He was off his horse and into the trees in a moment. "Well, hello, Mara," he said gruffly, coming up behind her. "Isn't this nice of you to be out here to meet me."

"Hello, Mr. Richards," Mara said, not turning around. "How are Papa and John and Sophia?"

"Everybody's just fine. Got froze out. They sent me and my boys back for seed. The rest stayed up to plant what little the Tuttle boy had left. Looks like I'm the lucky one this morning, yes sir."

"We've got some seed in the cabin. Mama's awake. You can go ask her for it," Mara nodded toward the fort.

"Oh, I'll go along in a bit." He came up beside Mara. "It's been a while, Mara. 'Bout a month since we last . . . talked." Mara felt his big hand on her hair. She stiffened, but she didn't run. "I want you to know I still mean what I said, about you marryin' me. Have you thought about it?"

Mara moved from under his hand and went on gathering her kindling. Her face was hot and there was that strange tightness inside of her. She hated Ivie Richards with all her soul. And it was fear that kept her from running. She kicked at a branch with her boot.

"What about it, girl? I asked you a question."

"What makes you think you have a right to ask questions like that of me!" Mara said defiantly, turning to him with her head high. She could feel Blueflower's eyes as though they were her own. "You!" Mara almost hissed. "You would take anyone, like an animal, whether you had the right or not!"

Richards grabbed her by her right arm and her kindling fell at her feet. For a moment the memory of her encounter with Sully by the woodpile came to her. She almost laughed aloud. She would just have to stop going for kindling. "What're you smiling about?" Richards shook her, angry. "I know your type. You women who can't accept the holy practice of plural marriage!"

Mara shook him away. If she would have to handle him without help, she would do the best she knew how. "Holy!" she shouted at him. "What do you know about holy! The way you took Blueflower, was that holy? Did God call you to take Blueflower like she was some slave? Did Brigham Young call you to steal an Indian woman? Is that the holy practice of plural marriage?"

"You watch your tongue, girl!" Richards thundered. Maybe if he shouted loud enough someone would come to her rescue. She was not afraid, so close to the fort. "I married Blueflower!" He was still shouting, coming close to her again. "She had no one to care for her," his voice quieter now. "I married her. Brigham Young didn't say no! And I am still willing to marry you. I can take care of you all."

"Married her! You forced her."

"I married her fairly. A fellow who used to be sheriff in Illinois read it!"

"You call that the holy practice of plural marriage?" Mara taunted.

"She's only an Indian!"

"She's a woman!"

Richards was quiet for a long time. Mara became almost afraid of him again, he was quiet for so long. "She's a woman," he said softly. "And so are you." He moved toward her, his giant frame a silhouette against the sharp sun in her eyes. "You are a woman, too, Mara, and I want you, as my wife."

Mara drew away. She looked through the trees at the fort. Surely someone would hear them. Someone would come soon. Richards reached for her, catching her wrist in his big hand.

"Not thinkin' of leavin' without givin' me an answer, are you?"

"I can't talk about it, Mr. Richards," she said, pulling away. "You'll have to talk to Father about it." Telling Richards "no" would just inflame him, she thought. But if she turned it over to Papa, he could take care of it for her.

"Come here, girl," he reached for her again. "I won't hurt you." He held both her elbows in his thick hands. "Mara, your father and I have been working together for a month. I'm sure he knows I would take care of you." His hands rose up her arms to her shoulders. "You're a beautiful woman, and I only want to take care of you as God meant a woman should be protected."

His voice was so quiet and steady that it unnerved Mara. He was large and shaggy and dirty, but something about him almost attracted her, made her stay. "It's all right, girl. I can love you." His hands moved down her back as he pulled her in against his leather coat. "God wants it for you." His body was large, his breath hot on her head. His hands were on her waist. They moved down.

Mara jumped, pulling away from him, afraid. "Please, Mr. Richards. Please leave me alone." She began to cry.

"You don't have to be afraid, girl. I won't hurt you. I can wait." His voice was still quiet, almost tender now. "Now, come back a minute. Let me show you what it feels like to be a woman." He reached out, one hand sliding across her throat, dropping to her waist, the other hand at the back of her neck, drawing her to him once more. The blood in her whole body beat hard against her veins. Her head spun. She couldn't see clearly through the tears in her eyes. She opened her mouth to protest, but no sound came out. In that moment, Richards leaned down and pressed his mouth on hers, his mouth open, wet. . . .

Mara wrenched herself from his arms with a cry. "No! Let me go! Let me go! I'll tell Mama. Let me go!" She began to run now, out of the trees. In a few moments she saw their Indians at the corner of the fort. When they saw her coming, they stood up and dropped their kindling. With worried looks on their faces, they held out their arms. They cheered when she ran to them. She had never been so glad to see the mother and daughter before. She ran to them and wanted to hold them in her arms.

"I'll see you again, Mara Eastman," Richards shouted after her. "I'll see you again, girl! You've got a lot to learn!"

But his voice was buried in the distance. Mara felt the warmth of her friends. She had never been so close to them. She leaned against their cheeks and smelled the smoke and woodbine in their hair as they safely took her home.

Chapter Five

Sunday when Papa came home to the fort Mara ran out to greet him before he had a chance to come through the gate. When he let himself down, Mara threw her arms around his chest. "Oh, Papa! I'm glad you're home."

"What's this, girl?" Papa said quietly, his voice not really a question.

"I'm so glad you're here is all." They walked to the fort in silence. Mara had told no one about Ivie Richards, except Nancy, who had been horrified. She *had* to tell someone, and she certainly couldn't tell Mama. Or the Indians, although they had put their arms around her and nodded their heads up and down and smiled. She hadn't talked to Richards again since that morning in the trees. He had gone back that same afternoon. Had he talked to Papa? She could not ask.

"Mara," Papa said as they neared the east gate. "Brother Richards has spoken to me. About you." Mara was silent. "Now, I don't know what your feelings are in the matter, but I feel you are much too young to be considering any marriage at all. Much less. . . ." Papa stopped. The subject of plural marriage never came up in the Eastman house. Mama's feelings about it were well known, and no matter how Papa felt—and he had never said in Mara's hearing—he would not be called to live it as long as Mama felt the way she did.

"I mean, it isn't just the Principle. I suppose there are some plural marriages that are for the good of all involved. But Ivie Richards. . . ." Papa was looking off into the distance. He seemed not to be aware that Mara was there. It was as though he were talking to himself.

"Though I guess it really isn't a matter of that any more. I heard the rumor that his wife in Salt Lake City is dead. From grief over Ivie and him taking the two boys down here. And of course that Indian woman. Richards is up there looking for her. Thinks he's got a child coming by her."

Mara gasped. Still, Papa didn't seem to know she was there. They were standing by the east gate now. Everyone was inside the fort, getting ready for the morning meeting.

"And then him taking all that good riverbed land without waiting for Higbee's word on it. Why that's going direct against what Brigham Young has said should be done. And those horses of his. They sure don't look like no wild ponies to me. That's all we need, a white man stealing . . . and then, to think about marrying my daughter Mara!"

Papa looked at her suddenly, his face clouding. "I didn't mean for you to hear all that, girl. It's just that I been thinking all the way here from Sophia's place. No, Mara, I'll not have it. He's a good farmer and a hardworking man, but I'll not have Ivie Richards marrying my daughter. I'll be as good a neighbor to him as any man ever had, but he's not having my daughter!"

Mara clung to her father's arm. "Oh thank you so much, Papa," she exclaimed.

Papa patted her hand. "Let's go see your mama," he said.

After that, whenever Richards came to the fort, Papa came, too. Mara did not know what Papa had said to

Richards, for they still seemed to be friends, or at least polite to one another. But she never found herself with Ivie Richards alone again.

The land blossomed everywhere under the touch of spring. When the spring rains subsided, summer came with fresh color and bloom. Like a crazy patchwork quilt the fields sprang alive with wildflowers. The air grew sweet and warm. Bees began to hum, keeping the air dizzy with sound. Near the fort, the white children ran in the fields with the Indian children. Occasional fights broke out. The Indian children shot arrows at the scarecrows the settlers had put up in their corn, but in general the summer was quiet, the settlers hopeful. Everyone seemed to feel they were going to make it here.

Even Mama consented to leave the fort long enough to visit Sophia and John on their farm, to help Sophia prepare for the birth of her baby in August. Mara and Ashel came, too.

It was easy to see why the families along the river had chosen this spot to cultivate. John and Cassie Mills' garden nearest the mouth of the canyon was lush, springing from the black soil. John and Sophia's farm situated just south of the mill filled the canyon with fields of ripe wheat. Just east and a little north of John and Sophia's farm, Sully had carved out a little space, and then down the canyon nearest to the fort was the huge spread belonging to Ivie Richards. It was all excellent soil, black with rotting leaves, with easy access to all the irrigation it would ever need.

Not only did the farms in the north look beautiful, but Mama said the stone sawmill was one of the sturdiest she had ever seen. Papa had spent a lot of his time with it, staying up with John and Sophia, and his investment was beginning to show. As different families ventured from the fort and began to build homes in outlying farmland, the demand for cut lumber increased and the sawmill people began to prosper. Papa talked about the house he would build for his family someday.

"Anything to keep everybody happy," he would laugh, patting Mama's hand.

One Sunday when Mama wasn't feeling well and Ashel was running with his friends, Papa and Mara walked alone home from Sunday School. "And what about you, Mara girl? What can I do to make you happy?" Mara was silent. Papa went on. "You never have seemed the same since we was called to leave Great Salt Lake City. I'm worried about you, girl. You never laugh the way you used to."

How could she tell him that getting her away from Bret didn't get Bret out of her mind? How could she explain the despair she felt when she thought how long it would be before she saw Bret again, if she ever did? How could she tell Papa about Ivie Richards? Papa would kill him if he knew he had made advances. And Sully. How could she explain how much she disliked the intensity of the silent question always in his eyes?

"I'm growing up," she said at last. Papa accepted her answer with a shrug.

"It's been a hard year. Trouble has sobered us all, I guess," he said.

Mama often questioned her about Sully. "Mara, are you sure you couldn't like him? I see him as a real solid young man. He's made his own farm up to John and Sophia's place. You run from him like he was a leper. And he's just a simple person with a good heart. And that heart has you in it." Mara wondered how much Mama knew, how much Sully had confided in her. "It's time you was looking around and choosing now. You'll soon be the age for marrying."

Mara never answered.

Whenever the fort held a dancing party on the grass in the middle of the clearing, it seemed to Mara that Mama and Papa watched her like two old hawks. She always danced every dance, unless she begged tiredness and sat on a log with Papa or went off alone into some corner of the fort to dream of the farewell party at the bowery. She called up in her mind the dances with Bret. Tried to feel his arms. She dreamed of his body behind hers as they rode Sequel that last night, dreamed of his kiss. But Papa always came after her and brought her back.

One hot August night she watched, annoyed, as Randall Allen and the Wheeler boys fought for places on her dance program. She was only sixteen, but already she was tired of the way every boy over twelve in Fort Utah acted around her. She was just about to tell all the boys she was going home when she felt someone standing behind her.

"Easy, boys." Sully's voice was loud in her ear. "Miss Eastman will dance this one with me." Randall and the others looked up, annoyed. She could tell what they were thinking because she was thinking it, too. Sully was here, and that would mean one thing—he would command every dance with her that he could get. Mara sighed, resigned to her fate for the evening. She turned.

"Hello, Sully," she said in a tired voice.

"Hello, Mara," his eyes burned with that same steady fire of desire that Mara had accustomed herself to by now.

Not until halfway through the evening did Richards and his two boys show up. Like huge bears, they crowded through the east gate. Mara was dancing a round dance with Sully. She stopped dancing and stared. Sully turned to see what she was looking at. Richards was walking directly toward them. He wouldn't dare,

Mara thought, her heart pounding. Not in front of everyone. Not with Papa here. She looked around frantically for Papa. He wasn't there! She looked across the open space toward their cabin. There was a light burning in the window. Papa had taken Mama home! Mama had probably pretended to be sick so that Papa would leave her alone with Sully.

"Don't worry, Mara," Sully was saying, his arm around her waist. "I'll protect you." Sully's protection was not what she had in mind, but it would be better than nothing. "Everyone knows Ivie Richards is sweet on you," Sully said. Mara looked up at him, surprised. How did Sully know? What had Richards been saying?

"Mara, don't let him force you into anything. He can't do anything to you if you don't let him. I'll stay with you. Come on, let's keep dancing."

Richards was making his way through the dancers. As he neared them he reached for Sully's shoulder. "Excuse me, Tuttle. I'll be having this dance with Miss Eastman."

"I'm sorry, Brother Richards," Sully said, turning to Richards and holding onto Mara's elbow. "I'll need to be taking Miss Eastman home just now. Her papa will be expecting her at the cabin. If you'll excuse us." Before she knew what had happened, Mara found herself at the edge of the circle of log benches, heading toward her cabin, Sully nearly dragging her along. "Now wait a minute. . . ." She heard Richards' voice behind them. The music had stopped. Mara turned to see everyone looking at Richards, who still stood in the middle of the dancers. Everyone looked at him, then at her as Sully dragged her away. Richards shoved his way out of the crowd in the other direction.

Sully was mumbling under his breath. "He might steal Indian horses, but he's not stealing my woman! Taking the best farmland. Building the biggest cabin. Well, he ain't getting the best woman. Who does he think he is? His cabin might be bigger, but mine's tighter. His chimney blew off in the wind." Sully gave a laugh that was almost a snort. They were at the Eastman door now.

"Here you are, Mara. Safe."

"Thank you," Mara said, turning to go in. To her annoyance, Sully seemed determined to follow.

"That you, Mara? Sully?" It was Mama's voice inside.

"Yes, Sister Eastman. It's us."

"Well, come on in, the both of you."

Mara was tired; her head was spinning. She wished Sully would go. She didn't want him to say anything about Richards. Papa would get angry, and then there would be trouble. And trouble between Papa and Ivie Richards on her account was the last thing they needed in the settlement right now.

"What's the matter, girl?" Papa asked, looking at her, then at Sully.

"Nothing," Mara said quickly. "I-I'm just tired. Sully was kind enough to see me home."

"Oh, I'm sorry," Mama said, looking more at Sully than at Mara. "Won't you stay for some warm milk and bread, Sully?"

"He was saying how he'd like to be going back to the dance for a while," Mara said, knowing Sully was too gallant to call her a liar.

"Yes," Sully said, his face long. "I'll be going then. Good night, ma'am, sir. Mara." Sully nodded. Nodded again. And at last was gone.

Sully had scarcely left when John and Sophia came bursting through the door. John was waving a white letter in his hand. He led Sophia to a chair by the hearth, and she collapsed into it, heavy with her soon-to-be-born child.

"We were over visiting at Higbees," John was saying, breathless. Good, Mara thought. Then they didn't see what happened with Richards. "And a messenger came from Salt Lake City with some letters. And there's one for you, Mama! It's from Boston!" Mara had never seen John so excited before. She didn't think she had ever heard him say so much all at once.

"Boston!" Mama exclaimed. "Aunt Caroline Astle! Hart, it must be from my Aunt Caroline!" She tore the letter from John's hands and trembled as she opened it. "Get a candle, Mara, quick!" she said.

Mara lit a candle at the fire under the kettle. *"Boston, Mass., November 30, 1848. My dear Martha,"* Mama was reading. *"I know not how to bear such news as I must tell. The judgment of God has passed upon me more than I am able to find words to express. How long it has been since we were together. But I am hopeful that such a space of time will never seem so long again. For I am dying, and as I will return to the heavenly kingdom of God, I shall see my loved ones and anticipate their gentle company in the life to come."*

Mama began crying as she read rapidly ahead. She wiped her eyes with her handkerchief. "Heavenly kingdom." She looked up from the letter. "That doesn't sound like Aunt Caroline." Mama went on.

"It is with mixed feelings that I write this message, as I have some tragic news and some pleasant news. I shall give first the tragic news, hoping to bring you only cheer at the end of my message. I shall explain to you the circumstances under which I am dying, begging for your circumspect aid in a matter of which I must write."

Mama's brow furrowed. "And now it's August!"

"Hurry," Papa said. "Read on, Martha."

"As you know, the foundry passed into my hands when your Grandfather Harding breathed his last and I have

done well with it. Your father had little or no interest, and the entire management and operation of Harding and Astle Foundry Company, Incorporated, of Boston, was to fall into the hands of my son Horace Astle. I know not how to tell you of the heaviness that rests in my heart. I must only blame myself for the lack of character in my son which allowed him so often to misconduct himself. Finally, in an intoxicated condition, he took the lives of both himself and his wife in a foolish carriage accident, leaving their precious three-year-old daughter Caroline an orphan."

Mama's hand trembled visibly now. She asked Papa to stir the fire.

"*As you know, I did not care for your joining the Mormon Church, but, my dear Martha, during these past few months of agony I have received the blessings of heaven. Two young men from the Church came to me and have brought the book which has changed my life. Yes, you will be amazed to know I have accepted joyously the gospel of Jesus Christ as it has been revealed to his prophet Joseph Smith, and I am ready to go into the waters of baptism as I sincerely believe God wills I should. Oh, that I had offered such a course of life to my only son who, spoiled by fortune, dwindled in unrighteousness."*

As he listened, Papa stood with his hand firmly braced on the mantel piece, the sharp tension of his face revealed in the flickering light of the fire. "Your Aunt Caroline!" he said in Mama's silence. Mara could hear a catch in Papa's voice, as though he were trying not to cry. "Sometimes we forget," he said, his voice husky, "until someone like Aunt Caroline reminds us . . . of what we have."

Mama, tears rolling down her cheeks, was going on. "*Now that I know the truth, nothing must stop me from settling everything before I go into the kingdom of my God. There are just a few things left to do. I am going to sell the foundry. Though they may have the advantage of fortune, the future generations of Harding and Astle must find the peace of the gospel and forsake unrighteousness. I trust you alone to raise Caroline, and I must have someone of the family to help me settle the estate before that final day of judgment rests upon me. Please, in all haste, if it is at all possible, and if you find it in your heart and circumstances, will you send Hart to fetch the girl and to help me with the legal settlement of the sale of the foundry. I shall cling to my life until I hear from you. However, if anything should happen that you do not receive the letter until much later, contact my attorney James McQuivey at 9 Seagram Avenue in North Boston. I am your sister in the bosom of Jesus Christ, Your Aunt Caroline Astle.*"

Mama sobbed into her handkerchief. Papa came to her and knelt beside her, patting her back. "There, there, Martha. There."

Papa stood up. "I've got to go see Higbee. That letter was written nine months ago. There's no time to waste." And Papa rushed from the room.

Mama was as silent as stone. No more tears filled her eyes. Seated on the hearth, her back to the fire, she stared at the floor, her hands open on the letter in her lap.

John's quiet voice broke the silence. "So you know what this means, Sophia? Do you have any idea what this means? A foundry! It means a fortune! Sophia, it means a fortune!"

Mama looked up at John sharply, her face dark. Embarrassed, John left Sophia's side and came to Mama. He knelt at her knees and took her hands. "I'm sorry, Mama Eastman," he said. "I'm just thinking of

Sophia, of our child, of all of us. Aunt Caroline has come into the fold. And her fortune will bless the lives of your family. It's a blessing from God, Mama! It's a blessing to you for forsaking family and friends for the truth, for coming west with the Saints of God."

Mama closed her eyes and nodded silently. John went on. "Now, don't you worry. Papa Eastman may be gone for a few months, but I'll look after you. You—all of you—can stay with us. You and Mara and Ashel . . . even the Indians," he said. "I'll protect you all." Mama looked up at John and smiled.

John. Could he protect them all? Aunt Caroline's letter had meant one thing to Mara. Papa would leave. And then who would there be to protect her from Ivie Richards? And who would there be to protect her from Sully? And from Mama's plotting? John was good, though a little quiet. Could she confide in John?

Sophia and Ashel were sound asleep, as were Rain and Spirit of Earth on their blankets in the corner, and Mara was dozing when Papa came back from Higbees. "It's all set, Martha," he said in a low voice to Mama, who sat with John in the flickering light from the fire. "Higbee says he has word that a group of missionaries is leaving day after tomorrow from Salt Lake City. They're going to New York, and he's sure I could go along with them." Then Papa was talking to John. So soon, Mara thought, afraid.

John got up from the fire and went to lie down beside Sophia. Papa and Mama talked long into the night, Mara sleeping fitfully and waking to hear their voices. "It's a blessing from God, Martha," she heard Papa whisper. "And I sense that it's only the beginning of the bounteous blessings he means to send us in this wilderness." Mara heard Mama weeping in the darkness.

The morning was full of preparations. Sully was there

lending a hand. Mara was grateful that this one night he had accepted the hospitality of the Allens. She felt his eyes on her as she helped fold Papa's bedding and pack his clothes into the big cloth bag, but her mind was too full to worry about Sully. It came to her that she might never see Papa again, but she shoved the thought from her mind and tried to keep the tears from her eyes. The preparations were made quickly, and before noon it was time for Papa to go. He would take Sequel and have him sent back with the next messenger from Salt Lake City. Sully and John and Sophia would ride with him as far as their farms. Mama would not leave the fort. She promised John that she and Mara and Ashel would be fine.

The hot summer sun was high. "I-I'll just go in now," Mama said as it was time for Papa to go. He followed her into the cabin. Coming out in a few moments, he said, "Ashel, go in to your Mama." Then he grabbed Ashel's arms and hugged him to his chest. "Be a man, my son. Take good care of your mother and sister for me." Ashel stood stiffly without saying a word, then turned and went into the cabin. Mara knew he was trying not to cry, but he wasn't succeeding any better than she was.

Papa was standing close to her now. "I'm more worried about you, girl, than I am about your Mama," he said. His voice was that same husky voice she had heard the night before. He cleared his throat. "And, it seems to me that whether I like it or not, you're blossoming into someone's lovely young wife," he said gently, putting his big arm around her shoulders. She wanted to turn her head into his chest and let the tears come, but she knew it was hard enough for him to leave as it was. She must not show him how afraid and confused she felt.

"Mara," he said, raising her chin gently with his hand.

"You listen to me. Don't give yourself away to anyone unless you love him with all your heart and unless you know it's the Lord's will. Life is possible without that companionship, but it's a lot easier with it, I can tell you." Mara's eyes filled with tears, and she had to look down again.

"Now, there's still plenty of time, girl. So if you can, wait for me, will you?"

"I'll be all right, Papa," Mara said still looking at the ground. Then, brushing her eyes with her hand and putting on a smile, she looked up at him. "We'll all be all right."

Papa hugged her to him and kissed her forehead. "Walk with us to the gate," he said. He swung up on Sequel and rode up to the ox cart where John and Sophia sat waiting. The Allens and the Wrights and Bishop Higbee were there to see Papa off.

"God bless you, Hart." Brother Higbee shook Papa's hand. "And keep you safe. Don't worry about your family. We'll see to them."

Mara watched them ride out the gate, Papa ahead, John and Sophia next, Sully at the rear. To her surprise, Ashel dashed by her. "Good-bye, Papa, good-bye!" he called. "Watch out for those Indians!"

"Good-bye, my dearest." She heard Mama's voice behind her. "God be with you. Come back soon," she said with a little cry, almost too soft to be heard. Papa stood up in his stirrups and waved to them all. Mama and Mara walked to the east gate and watched them out of sight.

"This is good country, Sully, my boy," Hart Eastman said as they rode together. "It's old country with the lives of our future generations still locked inside of it. All of this earth like a lode holds the precious metals of the life that will come out of our own loins—this earth sired by the sun and nourished by the rain. Someday, whoever rides along the banks of this river will see a vegetable garden or an orchard planted by one of your great-great-grandchildren. Over there will be a factory. Over here, big houses, buildings, stores."

Hart saw that Sully listened dutifully. "Yes, sir, Brother Eastman," he said. But he knew the boy wasn't really listening to what he was saying. He doubted there was anything much in that boy's head at all except Mara, and whatever he thought of his beautiful younger daughter troubled him. What would her life be like in this land?

"If the Indians will let us have this land," he said aloud, "we shall build it into one of the finest cities that ever rose in the wilderness. A city that shall grow in righteousness and glory, to join the vast kingdom of God in motion." And my Mara shall be the fairest jewel in the kingdom. If she will just forget that smooth-talking Bret Hunt. I've spoken my mind to Richards. There will be no more trouble from him. But this Tuttle boy. He's not much. Not enough for Mara! It was difficult for Hart Eastman to imagine the man who would someday claim his dark-eyed Mara. He knew no one worthy.

They were just out of sight of the fort now, nearing the place where he would leave John and Sophia and head for the Great Salt Lake. Sophia. His good, quiet Sophia. Never any trouble—not sharp and fiery like her younger sister. Sophia. About to give him his first grandchild, and he would be away, securing their future back East, where they all came from in the first place. But John would take care of her. During these last few years he had come to trust and respect this John Smith who had won the heart of his firstborn.

"Well, my boy," Brother Eastman was saying. "This is where I must make my good-byes." They had reached the fork where the road to Salt Lake City turned to the left. "Can't tarry if I'm to get to Salt Lake City before the elders leave for the East." He put out his hand. "Good luck, my boy. God bless you!"

"Thank you, sir." Sully wanted to say something. He had to say something now or it would be too late. Brother Eastman would be gone for months, and if he were to speak to him about Mara, he must do it now. But there was something about the way Mara's father watched over her, guarded her, that made Sully afraid to talk to the big man about his daughter. But Sister Eastman. Sully had her ear. Maybe that would be enough. "Good-bye, Brother Eastman," he called as Brother Eastman rode to Sophia and John in the ox cart. John climbed down and Brother Eastman got off his horse. They shook hands and embraced. "Take care of my girl, John," Brother Eastman said, his voice husky.

"I will sir. You know I will."

Then Brother Eastman climbed up next to Sophia. "Oh, Papa!" she cried, burying her head in his shoulder. He patted her hair and her back for a moment, then, releasing her, he climbed off the cart and onto Sequel and was gone without another word.

Sully rode ahead of the ox cart the last half mile to the first clearing along the riverbed where Ivie Richards' cabin stood. Sully was the first to see the Indians at Richards' place. He counted eight ponies.

Sully drew up his horse and John stopped the ox cart just behind him. Richards and his two boys stood outside their front gate holding the ropes on three ponies.

"It's Angatewats!" Sully could hear John's loud whisper behind him. "The young one. The white-haired one was named Old Bishop on a spoof long ago after he visited

Brigham Young. And the fat one is Squash. We met them on the trail our first day out from Salt Lake City. They were with Arrapene. Took the Indian women. The dirty savages! Sold them as slaves!" John's voice was quiet, but very angry. Sophia shushed him. "I don't know the other two," John went on, meaning two young Indians who sat tall on handsome Appaloosa ponies, their brown skin slick with sweat. They held ropes leading two other ponies.

Richards was shouting at the Indians. "They ain't yours! We found 'em wild, fair and square."

Sully swallowed hard. He didn't want to get messed up in Richards' problems, but a man, a good neighbor, just couldn't sit there watching. "You stay here with Sophia," Sully whispered to John. "I'll ride up a bit." Sully nudged his horse forward.

As Sully drew up the road, the two young braves on Appaloosas jerked the ropes they held and kicked their horses. They gave a terrible long, loud cry and galloped away, the extra ponies behind them.

Squash turned angrily to Old Bishop and hurled some words in Ute to him. Old Bishop leaned from his horse and tried to grab the ropes out of Richards' hand. Angrily, Richards jerked them back.

"Leave me and my boys alone," he screamed. "My horses! Bring me back my horses," he called after the two braves who had left. "Tuttle! Well for once I'm glad to see you. Those damned Injuns! Stealing my horses! And what's more, this one's got my shirt!"

Now Richards lunged toward Old Bishop and the Indian slipped from the pony. Frightened, Squash backed away, stood at a short distance, waiting.

"You've got my shirt!" Richards growled, his dark brows pulled together with intensity. "This is my shirt! How did you get my shirt?" Old Bishop was wearing a blue plaid flannel shirt that looked vaguely familiar to Sully, all right. Sully got off his horse near Tony and Clem Richards.

"Take off my shirt, you dirty Injun," Richards seethed.

"Got shirt—woman!" Old Bishop spit back in broken English.

"What woman?" Richards growled, lurching for Old Bishop. The Indian tore out of his grasp, leaped to his horse and grabbed his bow. Not far away, Squash turned his pony and disappeared into the hills. Old Bishop clattered after him, turning back over the rump of his horse as he put an arrow in his bow.

"You won't get away with my shirt, you dirty Injun!" Richards screamed at the top of his voice.

As Old Bishop pulled back on the arrow, Tony Richards raised his gun. Crack! The sound shook the hills. And in the shadow of the green hill, in the near distance, the horse under the old white-haired Indian jerked its front feet upward and swung round. The old Indian's hands flew open; his bow and arrow clattered to the ground. His horse twisted, and Old Bishop, his head flung backward, his mouth gaping open and filled with blood, flew through the air. Free of its burden, the horse whinnied and galloped over the hill as Old Bishop thudded to the grass.

There was a long silence in the hot morning sun. Sully stared, his hands feeling suddenly cold and wet. "God in Heaven!" John said, running from the ox cart.

Sully turned to look at Tony Richards, who stood with his smoking gun, his eyes wide and his mouth pale.

"You've done it now," John said. Sophia sat on the cart, her face covered with her hands.

"None of you touch that Indian," Richards hissed between his teeth. "It's on my property, and I'll dispose of it as I see fit."

"You can't do that," Sully said, worried. "They'll all be here unless you get rid of him right now. We got to get rid of him. Hide him so there's no trace." Sully's throat was dry. A terror rose in his heart. "They'll kill us all!"

John was the first to step forward. He walked slowly toward the body in the grass. "He might still be alive," he said. "Perhaps we could save his life."

Sully followed John. The bullet had split open the Indian's skull. Blood gorged every opening in his head. "No," John said, his voice tight and angry. "No. We cannot save his life, and we'll be fortunate if we can save our own."

"We'll bury him now," Richards said, his voice a strange dark sound.

He won't quit until he's destroyed everything, Sully thought, wishing it had been Richards who had been killed instead of the old Indian, and then shoving the evil thought from his mind.

"You'd better start digging," John said, turning to Richards, his face full of hatred.

Richards stood taller and turned to his boys. His voice sounded far away. "Then run get some shovels, boys," he said between his teeth.

"Merciful God!" It was John Mills. Sully had not even seen him come. He must have run all the way from his cabin up by the sawmill. "We heard the shooting. . . ."

Richards' boys had come back with the shovels. "The Indians don't like it," John Mills said, "you burying their dead." He looked around the group, his eyes full of fear and questions. "They come and get the bodies of their dead. They find the killer and take his life in return." Sully saw the blood drain from Richards' face.

They stared at the corpse of the Indian. The blue flannel shirt was now soaked in blood. "Then what are we going to do?" Richards asked.

"You better hide him, Pa," Tony Richards said, his voice shaking. "Nobody'll know what happened if you hide him; they'll think he just disappeared. Maybe they'll think he ran away to California, with Chief Walker. . . ." Tony babbled in his fear.

Sully knelt down by Old Bishop's body and tore the greasy broken feather from his braid. Long ago he had seen a gang fill a man's body by the Thames and sink it into the water. "Sure. Sure. They'll think he just ran away," he heard John Smith say bitterly.

"Where could we hide him?" Richards asked now.

"You could fill him with stones and he would sink to the bottom of the river," Sully said, looking up from the body. His heart was sinking in his breast. "I saw it when I was a kid in London."

Sully stood up. His legs felt like water beneath him. He thought with every breath he took that he heard footsteps, hooves, Squash returning.

"All right," John Smith said finally. "Let's do it. What other choice have we got?"

Sully's head pounded. He felt sick. How many years he had repented of those nights on the London streets following the gangs into the rat holes. He had wanted to forget all he saw, all he had learned. Still he had remembered.

"You better get back up to Cassie and the children, Mills," he heard John Smith say. "You don't need to get mixed up in this. Go on; they'll need you. You can keep a lookout from up there."

"Maybe you're right, John. Shall I take Sophia?" But Sophia wouldn't go, and Mills went back up to his cabin alone as Ivie Richards and his boys carried the dead Indian to the river out back of their corral.

Sully watched John Mills go past his own place, the place he had built for himself and Mara. What would become of it all now?

"Come on, Tuttle," Ivie Richards growled. "We don't get rid of this Injun and it's your hide, too." Sully ran toward the river where they were stuffing the dead man's shirt pockets with stones.

"No," said Sully. "It don't work that way." Feeling fear that it would never be done fast enough, he drew his knife from the sheath on his belt. He knelt down by the old Indian and silently prayed. "You have to cut him," he said almost inaudibly in his pain.

"Well, this was your idea, Sully. Give us a hand," Richards said.

Sully pulled the flannel shirt up off the Indian's belly and held his breath. He winced and dug the tip of his knife into the dark flesh. Sully felt sick. A pig or a sheep, maybe, but this was a man. He swallowed back the sickness and began stuffing in rocks. "Hurry!" he said, leaning back and choking with the stench and his tears.

The deed done, Sully washed his hands and arms in the cold river. His shirt was bloody. The cold water made his arms numb. He filled his hat and poured the cold water over his head in the barbs of the hot August sun. He was dizzy.

"I don't like it." It was John Smith beside him, washing his hands, too.

"He was going to shoot someone, to shoot Richards," Sully said. And I wish he had, he thought to himself. It would have meant far less trouble.

"We can't be sure about that," John replied, his voice tight. "And now we've killed an Indian. Do you know what that will mean?" He stood up and shook the cold water from his arms, drew his hand across his face, and went to Sophia who sat pale in the ox cart. Sully stood and followed John. The Richards had gone into their cabin.

"It's better he dies than some of us die," Sophia said, staring straight in front of her, her eyes glazed.

"Is it?" John said, staring off across the grassy plain. "Come on, Sophia. We've got to get you out of this wretched sun," he continued in a dazed voice as he climbed up beside her.

Sully stayed with John and Sophia in their cabin the rest of the morning. The men sat tense, not daring to go out into the fields, not wanting to leave Sophia. There was no sign of anybody coming out of Richards' cabin to the south, either, no sign of John and Cassie Mills or their children to the north. Sully stood at the west window and watched. The sharp sun rose high and hot. Sully was restless to be out and doing. He went to the north window and looked up the river toward his place, the place he was making for Mara. Could he bring her there, remembering what had happened today and his part in it?

"They'll be here before long, now," John said, coming up behind Sully. "Would you mind, Sully, joining me in prayer to God for our lives?"

At a little past noon Sully saw ripples in the grass toward the northeast. He saw the bushes on the far side shake, the sparrows fly up. He made out two figures, both on foot, bending, swinging their arms through the grass. Indians looking for Old Bishop!

"They're here," Sully said, his voice hoarse. John came quickly beside him. Sophia gave a soft cry from her cot in the corner.

"They may have hidden their horses in the grove," John said. "Look! The fat one must be Squash. I can't make out the other one behind him. Looks like a young boy, though, not a big brave."

They came nearer, moving fast over the ground with

no noise. Squash carried a bow in his hand, the arrow already in position. "They haven't got guns," Sully said. The Indians neared the clearing inside Richards' field. Suddenly, they both dropped to the ground.

"They found the blood!" Sully breathed. At that moment, Sully heard a shot.

"The fools! The infernal fools!" John shouted. The slender Indian with Squash fell to the ground. "God in Heaven, Sully! They've killed another one!"

Squash was dragging the fallen Indian off. A second shot rang out across the hot field. Squash ducked, let go of the fallen Indian, and ran, his fat body bouncing as he made for the grove.

Richards and his boys burst through their cabin door. John grabbed his gun and Sully followed him out, cursing as he ran. The Indian on the ground was still alive, moving in the tall grass. Tony Richards got there first.

"Pa!" he shrieked. "It's your Indian wife!" Richards ran. Sully ran with John, catching up with Richards.

"Blueflower!" Richards' cry was like a wounded animal. Then, all of them standing in a circle around her as she lay unconscious in the grass, Richards whispered, "I didn't mean to hit no one. I just fired to warn them."

"You warned them all right," John said, kneeling beside Blueflower in the grass.

"What was she doing here?"

"Maybe she kept trying to escape like she always did."

"They're not about to let go of her, are they?"

They heard a rustling in the grove.

"They're coming back!" cried Clem Richards.

"Nah," said Tony. "That's only Squash sneakin' off."

"Move away, Smith," Richards said roughly. "She's my woman. Come on, boys. We got to get her to the house." He knelt beside her and shoved John away. She lay on her side, her belly against the ground, large and round like a melon. Her leg was bleeding. The bullet had gone in just above the knee.

"Come on, boys," Richards barked. "Lift her up."

"You'd better stop that blood first," John said, angry. He pulled out his kerchief and tied it around the wound. Richards didn't stop him.

"Now, get her to the house," Richards growled at his boys again.

"Is it your baby, Pa?" Tony asked as he lifted Blueflower's legs.

"Shut up!" Richards snapped. "How the hell do I know? Come on, hurry up. We got to get her inside."

"Richards." John's voice was even. "Take her to my place. Let her be with Sophia. There's going to be trouble. We can watch out for the two of them better if they're together."

What the devil was John thinking of? Sully wondered, amazed. John Smith was always kind, always good, but this was too much: bringing all Ivie Richards' trouble right into his own house! Sully was sure Richards would never agree to it. He watched the man's face. Surprised, he heard Richards accepting the offer. "Why . . . yes, Smith. Yes, I guess you're right. That's neighborly of you. But your wife. It's about her time."

"It's about *her* time, too, Richards," said John, nodding to the limp body Richards and his boys held slung between them. "We've got two rooms. If you haven't killed all of us with your foolishness, we can at least try to save the lives of the babies."

Like dumb animals, Richards and his boys followed John to his cabin. Sully came behind, still amazed, at John, at Richards, at Blueflower.

"Blueflower!" Sophia cried as they came through the cabin door.

Sully saw her eyes take in Blueflower's swollen belly

and come to rest on Ivie Richards. "You, you. . . ." the sound came from between Sophia's teeth, her face red and angry.

"Sophia," John said gently. "Blueflower is going to stay here with you. We'll dress her wound." They carried Blueflower to the hearth where John and Sophia spread blankets to receive her. Sophia moved awkwardly, her left hand behind her on the small of her back. Richards stood up and then bent back down to Blueflower.

"Get away!" Sophia shouted at him. "Go away all of you! John, help me dress this wound! Sully, bring water from the kettle!" Everyone jumped at Sophia's commands. As she and John worked over the unconscious girl, Sully went to the small window behind Richards. The two Richards boys slumped down in the corner by the door. They waited.

They waited through the hot afternoon. They waited as the treacherous sun went down. A choking darkness followed the dusk. John gave them all dried meat from a barrel and hunks of brown bread. Sophia dipped water from the kitchen bucket and they all drank.

They traded watch all night. Sully's turn came near dawn. He sat silent, watching, his gun trained on the fields, waiting. He felt the hours bringing the Indians closer. He heard Blueflower's soft moans from the bedroom at the back of the cabin. Then, in the dim light, Sully thought he heard rustling along the riverbank behind Richards' corral.

"They're searching the river!" Richards was beside him in a moment, the only one awake. He brought his gun to the window with Sully's. They sat silent as the sky grew lighter, not hearing another sound.

Sophia made them flour cakes and they stuffed them down, swallowing hot milk after them. Still, they waited. Blueflower was only half conscious; she lay in a fever on John and Sophia's bed.

About ten o'clock they saw a swarm of Indians at the crest of the eastern hill. Like an army they advanced in a narrow line, their ponies straining at their bits. Some carried rifles. Arrapene, Angatewats, and Squash led them. There were more than a dozen—fifteen, sixteen. Sully felt the blood leave his head.

"Check your ammunition," Richards hissed. "They'll be on us in two minutes." They all obeyed, then stood in total silence. The line advanced with no sound, no cry. Sully's hands and arms felt heavy as he clung to the rifle. Then he saw Arrapene draw the white shirt from his belt and tie it to his spear. Now the Indians slowed the animals as they rode into Richards' field.

"They want to make peace," John said.

"What are you goin' to do, Pa?" Tony Richards asked.

"Wait." There was a long silence. "But they ain't going to take Blueflower back. That one thing's for sure."

The Indians stopped about two hundred yards away.

"Looks like we're going to have to talk," Richards said.

"Are you going out?" John asked.

"Keep an eye on me," Richards said roughly, and he shoved his gun into Tony's hands. "Now, you go get the horses," he ordered Clem. Clem looked at Richards, his mouth open but not speaking. "Horses. Horses!" Richards shouted at him now. "Sneak around the back of Smith's cabin. Stay low. Get around to our place and take the horses out of the corral!" Clem still stood motionless. "Quick! Do as I say!"

"Pa, they'll see me going all that way!" Clem whined.

"Just keep low. And you all keep an eye on me!" Richards said sharply. John showed Clem out the back door of the cabin as Ivie Richards went out the front.

"Pa! Don't go out there!" Tony shouted behind him.

"It's my mess, boys," Richards said over his shoulder as Sully closed the door behind him.

Sully watched as Richards walked toward the Indians, his right hand to the square. Arrapene climbed down from his horse.

"Agasraki! Blueflower! My woman!" Arrapene's voice rang out across the field as he stood beating his chest. "Agasraki!"

Sully could see Richards shaking his head, but he couldn't hear what he said. Arrapene spoke again. "You kill Old Bishop, take woman." Arrapene's voice was loud on the dry air.

"Not here!" They could hear Richards now, loud, but calm.

"Squash say, man here, in river. . . ." Arrapene swept his hand north and south. Richards shrugged. "Squash say, you shoot woman with big belly."

"My woman!" Richards said in a loud voice.

"What is he doing?" John wondered aloud. But to their surprise it was Arrapene who shrugged now.

"You make big belly?" Arrapene laughed an ugly laugh. "You keep the woman. Nice woman. Not strong. You keep." He laughed again. Sully was amazed. Was this it? Was it going to be so easy then? But suddenly Arrapene's face clouded again. "But give us one who kill Old Bishop!" He shook his fist in Richards' face.

Just then Clem came out into the field, leading a string of ponies. Richards began talking to Arrapene, his hands moving. He pointed to the horses. Sully could hear him say, "No fight. No fight." Then, pounding on his chest, "Peace. We make peace." Richards stretched out his hand to Arrapene. Arrapene did not move. "You take horses for dead man," Richards said. "Take horses." He took the ropes from Clem's hand and held them up.

For what seemed forever, Arrapene sat staring at Richards from his pony. Take the horses, Sully thought. Take the horses and leave us alone. Sully prayed without closing his eyes. God in Heaven, make them leave us alone. Then he saw the ropes tear out of Richards' hands. A whoop split the air, and Arrapene was thundering away, the horses trailing behind him. The other Indians turned their ponies and followed Arrapene.

Richards turned, his face blank, and walked back to the cabin. Only John spoke, "We'll know how it worked in the next few hours," he said.

In the late afternoon, Sully fell asleep. A gunshot startled him, and then the clatter of an ox cart in the road. Outside in the yard he saw John and Cassie Mills and their children hurtling toward the cabin. From the cart, Mills was shooting into the hills. Sully shook himself awake. Herding their children in front of them, Mills and his wife made a dash for the door.

"Open up, John!" Mills screamed. Inside, leaning breathless on the closed door, Mills said, "We decided to try to drive down to the fort, and the Indians fired on us! We saw Richards give them the horses. We thought it would be safe."

"It didn't work, then," John Smith said, his face drawn and worried. "They still want retribution." There was a cry from the bedroom. John rushed in to Sophia. He came back out quickly. "We've got to get to the fort somehow," he said. "It's Sophia. She's getting ready to deliver!"

Sophia's time! Sully felt all the blood leave his head. And the Indians firing on them! Curse Ivie Richards! He had killed them all. The two Johns along with Richards and his boys were running out the cabin door. Sully grabbed his gun and followed them to safe positions behind the Mills' ox cart.

The Indians were not coming closer. John raised his head above the cart, and a bullet whizzed by. The Indians were not firing unless they saw something to shoot at.

"Look, Richards," John Smith was saying. "I've got to get my wife to the fort. I'll take Blueflower, too." Richards opened his mouth to protest, but John was talking fast. "We'll take John and Cassie and their children. We'll need Sully to help. It's you they want. Not women and innocent children. They might come after us if they see we've got Blueflower, but I'll not leave her here with you to die."

"They don't want her. She's mine. They know she's mine. They don't want a woman in her condition with a white man's . . ." Richards stopped.

"That's what they said," John spoke quietly. "Do you believe Arrapene, Richards?"

Richards didn't answer for a moment. Then, "Leave Tuttle. You can hide Blueflower in the wagon. The Indians won't follow you. We'll need Tuttle here. He's got a place to protect, too."

"It's up to him," John said quickly. "Sully, you decide."

Without waiting for Sully's answer, John and Mills rushed back into the cabin. In only a few moments they were back. Staying behind the cart and the animals for protection, the two Johns and Sully slowly brought the cart around behind the cabin. Richards and his boys made for their cabin, crawling though the low grass and then running crouched, breaking a back window to crawl in. Three or four bullets zinged into the clearing, but no one was hurt.

Leaving Sully on guard, John and Mills dashed in the back door of the cabin. Mills returned with his wife and children and hurried them into the cart, telling them to squat down in the back corners. Then Mills went back in and came out carrying Blueflower completely wrapped in a blanket so that no part of her could be seen. Sully helped Mills lay Blueflower on the floor of the cart, near Cassie in the back. Cassie moved the blanket from Blueflower's face. Her eyes were closed, her face twisted in pain.

"Give a hand!" John Smith called, coming out the door with Sophia. Sully and Mills leaped down. As they lifted Sophia into the cart, she cried out, then bit her lip to stop the cry. They laid her on the floor, just behind the driver's seat. John Mills jumped into the wagon in front of his wife, whispered something to her, and then kissed her, kissed the two children. Cassie Mills began to cry.

"What about it, Sully?" John Smith called from the driver's seat. "We can make it if they don't follow. Stay and protect our land, if you feel it right. Or else follow behind on your mare."

His land! His farm for Mara! Sully looked at Sophia, Cassie and her children, Blueflower. What should he do? John snapped the reins on the horses and moved the cart around to the back of the corral and out to the road. Then, looking around quickly, he shouted at the horses and drove into the road in the direction of Fort Utah. As they drove past Richards' place, John Mills suddenly stood up and jumped from the wagon. Cassie cried out.

"As God lives, keep going, John!" Mills yelled, running for the back of Richards' cabin. The Indians were firing on Richards' cabin now. "Get going, Tuttle!" John Mills shouted to Sully who stood by his horse behind Smith's place. "I'm going to stay and protect the mill! If the Indians don't follow them, you can ride back and help us. Now, get!"

Sully climbed onto his mare, dug his heels into her sides, and was off after the cart.

Chapter Six

With the women on the floor of the wagon, his own wife about to give birth to his first child, John Smith raced toward safety. The Indians were still firing on Richards' cabin. Perhaps they would not follow. Perhaps they did not know where Blueflower was. Perhaps they did not really want her, as Richards had said. Why had she come with Squash to find Old Bishop? Was she Arrapene's woman? Was he finished with her now that her condition was so evident? Her condition! Her child coming now, like this!

John Smith was only twelve when old Granny Smith had put his mother to bed for the birth of his youngest sister. They had been living in Herefordshire. His father was at a meeting at William Benbow's, listening to the missionary Wilford Woodruff. He still remembered vividly the darkness of the room, the candle at the head of his mother's bed, and Granny's sour breath as she leaned over him.

"Johnny, get out of here," Granny had said. "If you had any guts about you, you'd fetch your father from Benbow's. Likely meeting it is, till nine o'clock, and his own wife put out by birthin'."

He did not know if Granny had meant he should really fetch his father. A foul February storm raged outside, and he stood at the front door trembling with cold. His mother, between her pains, gasped, "Let Johnny stay. Hatch isn't much good at birth." He saw Granny shake her head. He stood at the door, between staying and going, while his mother cried terrible cries. He had not ever heard her express such pain. The baby died, and, soon after, his mother also. His father joined the Church of Jesus Christ and brought his family to the United States. The memory of the hard painful years that followed rushed through John's mind—the hope and the peace, so quietly followed by fear and running. His father, marrying that woman, staying in Kirtland when the Saints moved on. Meeting the Eastmans in Nauvoo. Sophia. Gentle, quiet Sophia. He had meant to do so much better for her than this! Her first child! And here they were in an ox cart, running from the Indians! And all because of that crazy fool Ivie Richards and his boys!

They had been doing well at the mill. He had met John and Cassie Mills back in Nauvoo and had decided then to learn the trade of a sawyer. Mills had brought his pit saw with him across the plains, and he knew the wood mill business. With the help of Papa Eastman, the mill was doing right well now, and they would have been doing all right with the farming, too, if the Indians would just leave them alone. Now, there was no hope of that again.

The sound of hooves in the distance startled him from his thoughts, and he turned just in time to see an Indian pursuing them, his bow drawn. John ducked as the arrow whizzed past his head. Sophia clutched his feet. Cassie's children were crying. He beat on the horses, but they pulled ahead slowly. He heard Sully at his side. "I can shoot him, John."

"No. Get me something white, Cassie." Cassie stood up in the wagon and tore off her petticoat. "Wave it, Sully!" John shouted. Sully grabbed the white petticoat and waved it wildly above his head. The Indian slowed. Sully waved the petticoat again. "Go on, Sully," John said. "Ride toward him!" Sully kicked his horse, and holding his gun in his hand over his head with the white petticoat, he rode toward the Indian. The Indian turned and rode back toward Richards' place. John turned in the seat.

"Go on, Sully!" John shouted. "Follow him back!" And God go with you, boy, he prayed in his heart.

In the distance, John could just make out the fort. Sophia began to cry out again, the same cries he had heard his mother make so many years ago in childbirth—and both baby and mother had died. It was all John could do to keep from stopping the wagon to hold her in his arms. His own body shook with the sound of her screaming.

"Lift yourself up. Squat," Cassie was telling her.

"There, that's better," Sophia said, her voice weak.

"Hurry, John," Cassie said. "Please hurry. It's coming!"

John beat the animals again. They walked only a little faster. He gritted his teeth in anger. Not here! Not in this dirty ox cart!

Two or three farmers had built cabins outside the fort by now. James Bean was one. John saw him out in his field with his horse and plow. He had built a small wood house on the other side of the river, floating old barrels and a rough mill-hewn raft across the river as a bridge. John waved to Bean in the distance, shouting the warning to him as the cart clattered near.

"No!" the old man shouted back, his face white. "Are they the same Indians that's been trading with us?"

"Yes," John said. "You ought to get to the fort to safety."

"My corn!" James Bean looked over his ripening field as John drove past him. John turned to look back, but

Bean stood still in his field, looking after John as the oxen drove away.

"Some people never do anything you tell them. They have to see it for themselves."

Sophia cried out again.

"It's coming! The baby's coming!" Cassie screamed suddenly. John glanced behind him in terror. Sophia lay on the cart floor, reaching to clutch his feet with a grip like iron. He saw Cassie struggling with the wool blanket, sopping up the blood and water that flowed freely. Blueflower, sitting up against the back of the cart between the children, gazed with wide eyes as the blood flowed. The children cried.

"It's coming!" Cassie shouted again. Sophia spread her legs wide. John turned away. "Push," Cassie said. "Slow down," she called to John. He slowed the oxen to a steadier walk.

He was dizzy. Not here. Not in an ox cart on the run from Ute savages in this hostile land where there was little hope for a child in the first place. His old home in England rose in his mind—Granny Smith's needlework, the needlepoint chairs, the fine old wood clocks, the glass candlesticks. Here there was nothing for his Sophia but dirt and flies. No dignity giving birth in a bloody mess in the back of a wagon with only her grip on his leg to ease her pain.

"Push now, Sophia," Cassie was saying. "Now! That's it . . . the head." Sophia screamed. Then she let go of John's leg, seemed to slump into dull heartbreaking sobs. John slowed.

"Keep driving, John. She's all right!" Cassie called. "It's a little girl!" John turned as Cassie lifted the wet, red, wrinkled creature into the air by its feet. "A fine healthy girl. She'll be a good one for you, John."

His disappointment that the child was not the boy he

had planned for vanished with the baby's first helpless cry. A girl! To be named Martha after Sophia's mother. A child who would be as beautiful as Sophia and as wise as Sophia's mother. He would give her security, a home, and love.

Cassie held the child for John to see. "We won't cut the cord until we get hot water." She placed her hand on Sophia's brow. "It's all right. You did fine. Now just wait a minute for the afterbirth." She wrapped the baby in a blanket she took from one of her children and laid her in Sophia's arms.

John wanted to go to her, to his wife, to their child! But he must get them safely inside the fort first. He was so lightheaded he thought he might fall from his seat. He was a father now! Little Martha Smith lay curled in his wife's arm.

"Perhaps move just a little faster," Cassie said softly. "We've got to get the cord cut, get the baby clean." It was not long until the wagon drew up before the east gate. John hailed some of the men in the corral.

"Can we help you! My word, if it isn't. . . ." Bishop Higbee began. His eyes twinkled as he met John's, then looked at Sophia inside the cart. "If it ain't a newborn. Allen! Come here! Give us a hand."

By the time John was down, three others had come to assist. Cassie held her hands out to stop them. "No lifting until the afterbirth, and I'll cut the cord inside the box."

The women were suddenly there in numbers. One carried a bucket of boiling water. Cassie was not without help now and she pushed hot rags up against Sophia's bleeding body. In a moment two more came to the wagon: Martha Eastman and Mara. As they reached Sophia, they were breathless. John stood at the cart feeling proud and happy as he saw his mother-in-law's excitement.

"It is! It's born! Oh, my darlings!" Martha Eastman looked down. It's her first grandchild, John thought, proud.

Amidst the "ohs" and "ahs" of the others, Martha Eastman cradled the baby in the corner of her arm, watching it with absolute pride and reverence. The pinched features had hardly been smoothed; the brow was still red, the nose small with the wide nostrils that had characterized Sophia. The lips were bowed and sharply defined in the cheeks by deep dimples. The dimples were John's. Martha touched the small hand curled on the blanket. It could not have been more beautiful. As her neighbors smothered her with compliments, she felt crowded by joy. A spreading light reached the roots of her hair and warmed her feet. Perhaps it had been worth it after all, she thought, tears spilling into her eyes. If there had been pain, heartache, anger in the past, the frustration of moving from place to place, the ugly fear, it vanished in this moment. There was fresh peace in the child's sleeping face. "Now there is a chance to begin again, to begin all over again," Martha sighed. "God knows we need that chance. And you shall have it, little darling."

Inside the cabin door she saw John—good John—plumping the bedding on the crates and letting Sophia sink into it. He came to take the baby, and Martha surrendered her namesake reluctantly. But she belonged with Sophia, rightly enough.

"Fresh from heaven," Martha told John softly. She yearned for Hart's presence. How he would love to hold the child, to gaze into the tiny face. "Our very own grandchild, Hart," she whispered.

Mara had turned to follow the others to the cabin. She had touched the child in her mother's arms, the small, fragile hands almost transparent. But before she had gone far, Cassie had called her for help. Not until then had she noticed there was anyone else in the wagon. It was Blueflower!

The same stinging fear she always felt for Richards rose inside her as she saw the beautiful Indian woman's head rolling painfully back and forth in the bloody wagon bed.

"Take these rags, Mara," Cassie was saying.

Reaching for the blood-stained rags, Mara moved woodenly, her eyes fastened on Blueflower, whose beauty had always stunned her. The hair, a sheen of rich black silk, fell like a shawl around her head; her eyes, unlike the usual swollen eyes of some of the natives, were closed shut with large white moons of lids stained by her black lashes that curved along the high cheek bones. Her mouth was a warm copper color, the lips full and trembling with her pain. The soft doeskin shift that fell about her revealed her large belly, stretching the doeskin tight.

"She's wounded," Cassie whispered to Mara. "Richards shot her. By mistake." Other women gathered around now, and Brothers Allen and Higbee came toward them. "Help me lift her," Cassie asked them. "Careful. So careful."

Not a sound came from Blueflower's lips, though her brown face was crossed with an expression of terrible pain. Mara noticed the blood on the blanket she had wrapped around her legs.

Richards shot her! Mara wouldn't have believed that even of Richards. What had happened? And he probably had got her with child in the first place, though she seemed too big for the time she had known Richards. Maybe it was the child of her Indian husband. Did she have an Indian husband? Perhaps one that was killed in the raid?

"We'll take her!" Mara said as they lifted Blueflower from the wagon. "Bring her to our place."

Her head resting on Brother Allen's large arm, Blueflower turned slightly to look at Mara. The moon-shaped lids opened halfway and the large dark eyes seemed to recognize those around her.

"We'll take care of her," Mara said, rushing to her side.

"With your father gone, you have enough with your other two," John Higbee said, carefully tucking the blankets up around Blueflower's body to get them off the ground. Brother Higbee's expression was a puzzled one. Though clean shaven, his face was dark with furrows of worry, concern.

"But our Indians can take care of her," Mara insisted, walking rapidly to keep pace with Brother Allen's great stride.

"It won't be necessary. We can take her," George Allen said. "She'll be due soon." Brother Allen carried her to his own cabin where he gently laid her near the front door. Some of the others gathered around. Mara noticed Spirit of Earth and Rain both watching from a distance with large anxious eyes. She knew they did not dare come too near their friend with so many others present. Nancy went into the house to fetch her mother. Sister Allen, a big woman in a large white apron, took one look at Blueflower and clucked in despair. She hurried to fetch hot water and rags, her little children hanging to her skirts.

"Whatever we do, we should keep her from Ivie Richards," Cassie murmured, kneeling to peel back the blood-stained blanket wrapped around Blueflower's legs. "John and Sophia dressed the wound as best they could. But the ride's been hard on her. It's all bleeding again." As Cassie peeled away the dressing, Blueflower winced with pain.

Mara laid her hand gently on Blueflower's shoulder. "She should never had met Ivie Richards," she murmured darkly. There was a raw hole in Blueflower's thigh. Mara thought she could feel it as if it were in her own thigh. She closed her eyes.

"Richards." John Higbee shook his head. Then he asked the inevitable question, hesitant, as though someone might be able to answer him but would not. "Is that Richards' child?"

For a moment no one answered.

"I guess so," Mara said so softly that only Bishop Higbee heard. His furrowed face fell, the brows met.

"He tries," Higbee said with more charity than Mara thought was necessary. "But since the death of his very own children on the trek west. . . ." The fact that Richards had lost his children tragically hadn't made Mara hate less, but she felt the sorrow in Bishop Higbee's voice for Richards, in spite of his greed and impatience. "Hatred hurts only the one who does the hating," Papa used to say. Yet how could she not hate Richards, watching Blueflower writhe in pain?

In a few moments it would be dark. The heat of the August afternoon lingered like dense smoke in the air. As the others left for their cabins for the night, Mara and Nancy and Hannah stayed outside near Blueflower and talked. Mara fed her beef soup from a large spoon. She could barely turn to eat, but she was hungry, and she sucked the hot soup from the spoon with short breath.

"Were they still fighting?" Nancy wondered.

"John says they left the others to fend off the Indians while they escaped." Mara spoke softly as she struggled to lift Blueflower's head to the spoon.

"Will they come here?" Nancy asked.

"Probably," Mara said.

The moon rose spreading shadows on the clouds. Dusk and the advancing starlight and moonlight lit the roofs of the cabins in the fort with a hazy glow. Hannah was still snapping the tips from the roots she had gathered. There was just enough light. She was breaking them into a basket set between her legs, her full skirts bunched around her knees.

"I hope they're all killed!"

"Hannah!" Mara was amazed.

"The Indians, of course.

"Just the same. Indians or white men. They are all people. And we ought to be kind," Mara said almost automatically. Her heart leapt to her throat as she remembered where she learned to say it. Where was Bret now?

"They're all just dirty savages," Hannah was going on.

Mara nodded in Blueflower's direction. "Hush, or she'll hear."

"She doesn't know English.

"You don't know."

"She never talks."

"But she listens."

Blueflower looked at Hannah, but her eyes remained expressionless.

"She doesn't know anything," Hannah said with more confidence. "Anyway, what could she do? Why does your family put so much effort into saving those old Indians, anyway?"

"Hannah," Nancy reprimanded, "they are Lamanites. If you read your Book of Mormon you'd know they're our brothers and sisters."

Hannah's eyes narrowed above a very thin smile. "I know about the Lamanites," she whispered. "That doesn't make them cleaner or smarter or more pleasant to live with."

"Hannah, you're being impossible."

Now Hannah sighed. "I know. I'm being cruel. I'm just tired of it, that's all."

"Tired of it?"

"Tired of this hole, this place where there is nothing. Even my folks want to go back to Salt Lake City."

For a moment there was silence. Blueflower turned her head from Mara's spoon, and Mara did not feed her again. They had all felt that way so many times. But no one said anything. No one who had been called by Brigham Young dared to complain.

After a heavy moment under the hot dusky sky, under the heavy yellow moonlight that bathed everything in a glow almost like heat, Hannah spoke again. "My father wants to get us out of here. He hates Indians."

Mara and Nancy, with Blueflower lying beside them, were quiet. The voices of people around them getting ready for bed came through the cabin walls. In the house next to the Allens, Mara could hear her own family in their warm cabin. Mara thought she heard Ashel and Mama, then the cry of the new baby.

"I've got to go," Hannah finally said, and she stood from her squatting position around the basket of roots, her large skirts falling to the ground. As Mara said good-bye, she paid particular attention to the thrust of Hannah's white chin, the way she carried herself. Perhaps it was true that Hannah was too good to be here. Hannah was a handsome girl and she knew it. Mara could understand Hannah's feelings about the Indians, but her parents were not like Hannah's parents. "Here we are, living in God's country, and with people of the earth," Papa always said. "These people come out of this land. They are part of this country. The sun stirs up the ground, and they come right out of it. They belong to it; they know it like the backs of their hands and we ought to listen." And then there was Bret, who had said noble words, too. . . .

"Do you think Blueflower will be all right here?" Nancy said almost inaudibly to Mara as soon as Hannah had gone.

"Oh yes," Mara whispered. And she drew the blanket up over Blueflower's shoulder. It was hot, but a dry wind sometimes came up in the evening.

It was just as she came to her own doorway that she heard the horses coming across the river through the water and over the banks to the gate. They would have come at this time of night only in an emergency, and they were coming fast.

Mara opened the gate and saw eight or nine dark horses, some with several riders, streaming through the moonlight. George Allen came outside, then John.

"What is it, Mara?" John asked, seeing her at the gate. Others came running from all over the fort.

John hailed them before anyone else recognized who they were. Then Mara recognized Richards' shaggy mare and John Mills and Sully and Richards' boys. On the other horses were James Bean, his wife and child, and the Purdies, who had also built a house on the outside.

"They are quelled for now," John Mills called from his horse at the front of the group. "But we thought it best to stay in the fort for tonight."

Quietly, so as not to wake everyone, the men dismounted and brought the animals inside the fort. The families began to set up tents in the moonlight. Mara backed up against the cabin as the men led their horses to the corral. Only Sully might have seen her, his darting blue eyes searching the darkness. But he did not stop. She watched Richards' large body move away with his animal, her heart pounding rapidly. She had to protect

Blueflower! She found herself slipping out of the gate and around the back to the willow hovel that Spirit of the Earth had built for herself and Rain against the back of the fort.

"Rain," she whispered as loud as she dared so that her own family would not hear her through the small window. In the darkness of the large lean-to, she caught sight of the two humps of her Indian friends on mats.

"Rain! Hurry!" she whispered. "Hurry!"

By now Rain understood some English. She was sitting up, her eyes blinking away the sleep. Her mother lifted her old head from the other mat in wonder.

"Hurry! It's Blueflower! We must bring her here."

Though Rain understood, she could not speak.

"Mi-oop-joon," Mara breathed some of her own brand of Ute. "Hurry. Help me carry her."

Rain had grown in the six months she had been with the Eastmans. She was as tall as Mara now, and more fully developed. Though she had none of Blueflower's beauty, her head was finely shaped and her broad features were well defined. Her large nose and mouth gave her a look of serenity, a look of earthiness that became her well, Mara thought. She took the hand Mara held out and turned back to say something to her mother.

Looking puzzled, the old woman fingered the thin covering over her body. Along the walls of the lean-to wickiup Mara could see the stacks of Spirit of Earth's remarkable handiwork—baskets and mats and smaller baskets hanging from wires hooked into the willow ceiling. Outside, against the wickiup, hung other weavings of grass, willows, and wool.

Walking so as to avoid drawing attention to themselves, Mara led the Indians inside toward the Allens' cabin. Several people milled about asking questions of John Mills and Sully and Richards, but no one noticed

Mara with Spirit of Earth and Rain. No one was at the Allens' except the sleeping children inside. Mara thrust her hands under Blueflower's armpits. She urged Rain to carry Blueflower's legs with great care. The old mother stood by, her eyes slits in her puzzled face.

"Ka ai wa," Rain said. The old mother took the coverlet dragging on the ground and wound it in her hands.

Blueflower's body was heavy. Awakened, she protested Rain's grasp on her legs and stood on the good foot, slinging her arms around Rain's neck. The two Indians exchanged a few words in Ute. Mara stood on the other side of Blueflower and lifted her along as best she could. Mara turned back to see the men returning from the corral. She could outline Richards' large black shape in the gray dusk. He was the largest man: his snarled black hair rising above all of the other heads including Sully's, whose sandy mop she recognized clearly. They were advancing toward them now. With urgency, she pulled Blueflower forward, felt her breathe sharply in pain.

"Hurry, please," Mara whispered. She passed the Eastman door without stirring anyone and reached the gate just as Richards and the others passed the bastion in the center of the fort that held the cannon ready for any Indian battles that should come.

Quickly, the small group stole outside the gate. "You'll be safer here than in there," Mara breathed knowing she was not understood. The old mother stood by like a helpless child while Mara and Rain ducked inside the wickiup with Blueflower, holding her tightly, letting her down slowly to a mat where she writhed in silence.

"Now, we'll hide her here," Mara instructed Rain. "No one must know. I'll be back in the morning."

Spirit of Earth had not been much good in carrying Blueflower, but suddenly Mara saw that she was perfectly capable of comforting her. Blueflower murmured a few soft words in Ute and old Spirit of Earth knelt to her side. She took Blueflower's hand in her wrinkled fingers and began rubbing vigorously.

"Ka ai wa," she said over and over again. Rain sat down beside Blueflower's legs and settled them on a soft blanket.

Mara studied the Indians on the dirt floor of the willow lean-to outside the fort. The bright moon lay shining needles of light on the women in the darkness. They huddled together speaking low comforting words. Mara let down the deerskin door to cover them. Then she looked up toward the trees, watching the moon behind the black fingers of leaves. Perhaps the Indian women would be in danger outside the fort. But for now, this was best, Mara thought as she neared the fort gate. Just as she reached the gate and pushed it slightly to enter the fort, several men's voices cut through the night air.

"We'd better lock it. No telling what they might do."

"They want blood," another voice said. It sounded like John Mills.

As Mara touched the door, someone leaned up against it and slid the inside bolt into place. Her heart beat rapidly. How was she going to get in? Her fingers touching the door felt cold. For a moment she stood frozen, fear flowing into her like a river.

"They might be after us from now on."

"I can't stay locked up here!"

"Think about it next time your boy's about to kill an Indian."

They were all voices Mara knew she had heard a hundred times but in the flight of her senses she could not place any of them. Should she knock? Even if she were to rouse her family, there would be all the questions, then the arguments, and probably Blueflower would have to go with Richards—her husband. But if Mara hid her, Richards might go back to his place without her. Her heart beat wildly now. Unable to think clearly, she turned her back to the door and stood against it waiting for silence, for the right moment, for time to think of a good reason she might have been outside the fort gate at this time of night. Reasons crossed her mind. But all of them would have led her mother to question her. And she knew she would finally tell her, and although Mama would hate to see Blueflower returned to Ivie Richards, she would be scrupulous and open, and she would do what she thought was right. "Why he's her husband," she would say. "No, he's not a very admirable man, but he'll probably take better care of her than she's had from her own people. And she is probably bearing his child." She could just hear her mother's voice. Mama had been hinting that she knew something of what Richards felt for Mara. She had said more than once that Richards needed to find Blueflower to cool him off. No. Mara could hope for no help from Mama in hiding Blueflower.

Mara felt desperate to save Blueflower. In every way she could feel her pain. Perhaps Mara would never be able to pay her debt to the woman who carried the child that might have been hers.

When her heart slowed, Mara studied the night. It was close and hot, but a slight breeze cooled her cheek. The trees seemed to close down on her, their branches profuse with moving leaves. The moon carved shadows into the ground with a vague light.

She could hear more voices inside the gate. Only one person seemed to be moving there in the stillness. If only it were John or Mills, she might get by with an excuse. Oh, let it be one of them, she prayed silently. Her blood leaped inside of her as she decided to knock. She gave a soft rap, as though its softness would protect her.

"Someone?" she whispered. "I was locked out."

No one answered. But the movement behind the gate stopped. Mara knew someone was there. She rapped again, softly.

"Who is it?" someone said.

"Mara Eastman."

The person on the other side of the gate did not answer, but the breathing seemed almost audible. Mara's heart beat hard. Then she heard the bolt slipping smoothly through its hasp.

The man opened the gate slowly, peering into the moonlit darkness.

"Mara," the man said softly. She could see only his dark hair until he lifted his face. Her body flooded with fear. For a moment she felt Richards' large hand like an imagined shadow. But it was only John. Sophia's John.

"John! John!" she whispered, about to cry. She stopped the tears in her eyes. John reached out to her. Nervously, gratefully, she took his hand.

"What are you doing?" he asked her, startled. She felt she could tell him, though she wondered if he would understand her. He listened patiently, his long face turned to the moonlight, his brows deepened in thought.

"Mara, you're right, of course. I took Blueflower away from Richards once today myself." He patted her hand, held it between both of his, looking at her with a smile. "You're a regular angel of mercy, you know," he laughed quietly. "Now let's get you home without Mama asking you a lot of questions."

In a flood of relief, Mara pressed John's hand in return. "Oh, John," she began to cry. "It's so good to have someone to trust, a man who isn't . . . who is . . . oh, John, thank you." And she buried her head in his shoulder. She felt him release her hands and bring his arms around her. Her heart beat against his chest as he held her safe.

"Mara. Mara. I *will* take care of you. Don't you worry. I'll take care of you all. As long as you need me."

"Well, I suppose you marrying in the patriarchal covenant to Mara Eastman is a remote possibility." Bishop John Higbee turned a sober face to John Smith; his eyes narrowed above his weather-roughened cheeks. "You're aware, of course, that Martha and Hart Eastman were always against participating in plural marriage. Of course, it's an ordinance by choice for those who are called, for those who feel . . . worthy." He spoke the last word with hesitation, turning away from John's gaze.

"Will you support me in my request to the Eastmans?" was all John could ask. The silence seemed formidable to him as he waited for Bishop Higbee to rise from his large desk and walk to the front window.

"Yes," Higbee said thoughtfully. "Although I should caution you that I will only support what all parties feel is desirable. There are the feelings of many to consider. Sophia first of all."

"But perhaps if she felt it was a calling. If she felt you as our bishop thought it best, that might give her strength."

"Perhaps." The bishop turned and placed his hands on John's arms. "John, my boy. It is not myself who calls to the ordinance of plural marriage. It is the Lord. And it is your communication with him which seals the feeling you may or may not have that it is right for you. It is a frightening and awesome responsibility, and one I am sure you do not take lightly."

John remained silent, peering intently into the gray eyes of his leader. Bishop Higbee had been an example to them all, a hard worker, a good provider, a loving husband and father to his families. He himself showed to all what sobriety, what effort, what unselfish love was necessary to keep several families fed and happy. He did not preach; he never forced his ideas on anyone. He merely went about doing what everyone knew he felt was pleasing in the eyes of the Lord.

And now, he made it clear that even if he were to feel inspired to call John Smith to live the Principle, the responsibility of deciding to enter into plural marriage would be John's and Sophia's. And then there may be others whom John would feel it appropriate to bring into his family.

"It's the women who decide after all, John. The women have a very great burden of heart in this matter. And that isn't all. It is very difficult to be peaceable with another woman when you know you must share the affections of your husband with her. Each woman has her own way of doing things as well. Even such simple things as cooking and washing. . . ."

"But that's why it would be so perfect!" John broke in. "Sophia and Mara are sisters, with so much in common, yet a difference in temperament that lets each have her own place. They have grown up knowing how to share affection; they know how to work together."

"Yes, John. Being sisters in blood helps women to understand what it means to be sisters in the covenant. But, John, sharing parents' love is not sharing a husband. Would you like to share Sophia with another man? Would you let her go to another man's bed with a light heart? How would you feel if she were to bear another man's child? We must try to understand how the sisters feel in these matters. Plural marriage is a great strain on a man's strength and his . . . tact. But it is a greater strain on a woman's heart. Do you think Sophia is ready, John? She has just given birth to her first child, not twenty-four hours ago. Should you not give her some time of joy to share with you alone?

"Bishop, I don't understand. You sound as if you would discourage me from the new and everlasting covenant, the blessings of which you yourself enjoy."

"Covenants are better not made than broken, John. I'm just trying to help you understand what it is you are seeking."

John left Bishop Higbee troubled. He had only wanted to do the right thing. Holding the frightened and beautiful sister of his wife in his arms the previous night, it seemed so obvious to him what must be done. Mara, the beautiful, spirited child. How had he missed what a lovely, generous creature she had become? If she had never fallen into his arms that way. . . . But she had. And what was the honorable thing to do now that his heart pounded when he saw her? Perhaps it was wrong of him to feel this way. Perhaps he must simply pray for God to purge his feelings and return them to their former state. But no. Mara needed to be protected. And the bishop had said he thought the Lord would approve if John's heart was right.

John had heard Sully Tuttle curse about Ivie Richards' lust for Mara. Mara, pursued by that devil. "I will save her from him, from all that could harm her," he said half aloud. Now that he had gone so far as to suggest to the bishop that he be called to live the Principle, a course he knew was frowned upon by the Eastman family, he would not turn back.

But there were three women to convince that what he wanted to do was right, was the will of God. And he was not sure of his power to win them. Perhaps, if it were truly the Lord's will, he would turn their hearts, if they would listen. He felt more sure of Sophia than of Mara. And more sure of her than of Mother Eastman. He would wait for the right moment.

For a while the Indians did not leave them alone in the fort and Mara was afraid. Soon, Mara's fear passed into restlessness. The settlers never shot, and the Indians didn't attack the fort outright, but they seemed to be growing restless, too, annoying the settlers continually—throwing rocks through windows, killing cattle, chasing harvesters from the fields. Everything and everyone seemed to Mara to be waiting, waiting for something to break, to change—waiting and sweltering in the August heat under the ruthless and necessary sun that, striking the earth, continued to wrest their lives out of the soil.

There was the new baby. At least tiny Martha brought something new, something exciting, but even she slept too much to be very interesting. Sophia, worn out from the birth in the ox cart, slept too. Mama busied herself with her two sleeping charges. Ashel played. So there was only John. Good, kind John who had not betrayed her, who had helped her convince Mama that Blueflower was best where she was and had told the other inquiring neighbors that Blueflower's own people had taken her, which was true. Surprisingly, nobody, not even Richards, asked further. Maybe Richards was so guilt-stricken that he was glad to be rid of the evidence.

Mara hadn't had much trouble from Ivie Richards since the business with the Indians, either. Not that he hadn't tried, but whenever Ivie Richards came around, John appeared as if by magic. He couldn't have shown more care and concern than if he had been Papa himself. John wasn't big like Papa and Scott Hunt . . . and Ivie Richards. He wasn't tall and handsome like Bret. Bret, so far away. So long ago. But John was good and strong. And she had felt that night when he let her in the gate, felt for the first time since Sophia married him, that her sister was a lucky girl to have such a man as

John Smith. At least she was safe from the likes of Ivie Richards and Sully Tuttle. Sully, every-present Sully, buzzing around like a bothersome fly. Oh how she wished the Indians would go away so Sully could go back to his marvelous farm and leave her in peace.

Because of the Indians, not much harvesting could be done. August wore on under the unyielding heat. And then, late in the month, the ruthless sun brought the familiar curse—crickets. They came without warning on a hot, dry afternoon. Swarms of them crossed the wheat fields like a cloud of dust, darkening the sky. They blazed like a fire across the new grain, the ripe corn-fields, stripping, cutting, and chewing their way into the heart of everything the settlers had grown.

John was one of the first to see the crickets coming out of the south, crossing the fields like smoke. "We can stop them with ditches," he shouted. "Or fire!"

Mara worked with every other able-bodied soul from the fort all afternoon and far into the night. She beat the insects with her shovel, beat them as they crawled into the ditches the men dug. They dug the ditches deeper and deeper, but the ugly black creatures filled them rapidly, building bridges of legs and wings. Thousands of insects died, but thousands of others stripped the land. And no seagulls came as they had come the year before to the valley of the Great Salt Lake. Mara kept searching the sky, but she saw only clouds.

Clouds! Mara stopped. Rested on her shovel. It was almost morning. She heard the low buzzing sound of the crickets across the dawn. Clouds like the wings of angels! At last there were clouds in the unrelieved clearness of the August sky. Perhaps the rain would be the answer to their prayers.

But before it became an answer, it first wreaked its destruction. The clouds burst, and within a few moments

Mara was drenched and standing in mud. John came to her. "You've worked so hard, Mara," he said in such a kind voice through the rain. "I'm very proud of you." He put his arm around her shoulders. She wanted to sink against his chest. He would not notice her tears in the rain if she cried now. She was so weary. First the crickets and now the rain.

The gutted and charred land now crumbled into swelling, spongy mud. Mixed with the bodies of dead insects, it clung like tar to shoes, rakes, wheels, and hooves. Bishop Higbee ordered the men to dig a ditch close to the fort to allow the river to drain, as the water was rushing over the banks and collecting in huge puddles of murky, black, tarry clay.

Not until after the flood came into the wickiups did they find Blueflower. Seeing the water rise toward them, Mara had rushed to the willow lean-to as soon as John left her to dig the big ditch. The Indians were wet and muddy. Water was collecting on the floor. She had to find John. Turning to go back out into the rain Mara came face to face with Ivie Richards. He stared at Mara above his soggy beard, his dirty hat dripping rain onto his shoulders.

"Water is collecting on their floor," Mara said as matter-of-factly as she could. She took a shovel and began digging, the mud clinging to the hem of her skirt. In a moment, John was at her side, digging with her.

"Here," Richards growled. "You ought to let a man do that. Your feet will get wet." He put his hands on Mara's.

Mara clung to the shovel. "They're already wet."

But he did not take his hands from hers on the shovel. "Not as wet as behind your ears."

John stayed close. "It's all right. The Indians are her special friends. Let her do it."

Richards reluctantly let go, drawing his hands slowly over hers, his rough skin scraping her knuckles. "When you grow up, someday, Miss Eastman. . . ." Richards was saying. John struck his shovel into the ground. He stood glaring at Richards with a threat in his eyes that Mara had never seen before.

"If you had eyes in your head, Smith, you'd see what a beauty you had here in a sister. Yes sir, just on the edge of ripeness, too," Richards said, his grin visible through his dripping whiskers.

"If you had eyes in your head, Richards, you'd see she wasn't interested in the likes of you!" John was shaking, his fists clenched. Mara trembled, afraid of Richards, but almost as afraid of John's intense anger. Mara wanted to stop it all, before something happened.

"Hush, John," she said quietly, reaching out to touch his sleeve. "It's all right. Brother Richards doesn't mean any harm, I'm sure."

"The lady knows her own mind," Richards smirked. "In her own mind she don't want to see a pretty boy like you sprawled in this black mess."

If Richards hadn't chucked John under the chin like he was a baby, maybe John wouldn't have hit him. As John caught Richards with a blow to the chin and another one to the belly, Mara cried out, "Oh! John, please! He'll hurt you!"

"Here, here!" Bishop Higbee must have seen it from a distance. He was running toward them, followed by Sully. But they didn't get there soon enough to keep Richards from smashing John's head. John swung again, but Richards ducked and John fell headlong into the mud, Richards hitting him on the back of the skull as he fell. Seeing John fall, Mara's hatred for Richards overcame her, and she swung her shovel into Richards' side. Richards groaned and his legs buckled under him.

Unconscious of her skirts and the gummy black mud beneath her feet, Mara knelt in the rain and lifted John's heavy head into her lap."Are you all right? Are you all right?" She shuddered as he shook his head to open his eyes.

"Mara." Her name was like a moan on his lips. She wanted to touch his wet cheeks and smooth away the pain with her fingers. But she thought it wouldn't be right.

Bishop Higbee and Sully were holding Richards by the arms. "We'll have none of that with you brethren," the bishop was saying in a patient, tired voice. Mara looked up. Richards' eyes were full of fire. "We need another hand over at this ditch," the bishop said as they pulled Richards away.

John raised his head from Mara's skirt, leaning on his elbow in the muck. "Are you all right, Mara?" he asked.

"I'm fine," Mara said, wincing at the sight of John's bruised and muddy head. "But you look awful!"

"Almost lost my head." John laughed at his joke. "But nothing's missing," he said, feeling his jaw.

"I hope not." Mara smiled with him. She found she had to fight herself to keep from touching his jaw, too. As he raised to his knees, she knew she wished he had stayed for another moment, knew that she had enjoyed holding his head in her lap more than she had enjoyed anything in a long time. She was afraid.

"Anyway," John said rising to his feet and holding out his hand to help her up, "now that I have made a complete fool of myself, I think it's time to get something to eat."

"Oh, John, you didn't make a fool of yourself!" Mara protested. "Taking on Ivie Richards like that . . . in my . . . my behalf. . . ."

"But he beat me, Mara," John said quietly. "He won the scrap."

"Oh, no he didn't, John," Mara said, and immediately felt too much warmth in her words, too much for the husband of her sister. What was she doing? What was she feeling? Her face felt hot through the rain. She stammered, "I mean, I . . . I'm not hungry . . . I. . . ." Then, as if she had just waked from a dream, she remembered the Indians. "Blueflower!" she cried. "They'll be drowned! And Richards! He'll find her!"

"No, we'll finish our dam. It will hold the water for a while. Richards won't be back." Then, rubbing his head, John looked at Mara and said her name. "I'm not as worried about Blueflower as I am about you." He stopped rubbing his head and put his hand very gently on the side of her neck.

Mara returned his gaze with fear and a question in her eyes, and in his eyes, she thought she could see a stab of pain.

The opportunity for John to disclose what was on his mind came when he and Mara entered the house at noon. He went to Sophia, sitting by the fire nursing the baby. She kissed him warmly, and then looked at his clothes.

"How could you get so black? You're filthy," she cried. "Mama, put some water on!"

"And I'm not the only one," John said, glancing back at Mara. Sophia's eyes widened at the sight of Mara's skirts. "We dug to keep the river out of the Indians' wickiup."

Mama Eastman, mixing the biscuits, shook her head. "No way to keep clean in this mudstorm."

"That's from more than digging," Sophia said. "What is that bruise on your cheek, John?"

"Oh, Richards gave me a fast right, but you should have seen Mara hit him with a shovel." John laughed. The others joined him. Ashel started to laugh and clapped his hands together. John grinned at Mara. She returned his glance with brightened eyes.

"Richards! Might have known," said Mama Eastman. "But what business had you fighting him?"

"Just keeping him out of our hair," John said, looking at his wife's mother.

Martha Eastman's eyes narrowed. "Or out of Mara's hair." Her voice was level, but John sensed in it a dim anger. What had she guessed?

"Look, Mama, you ought to get this little daughter of yours married off, and you won't have any more wolves howling around." John tried to toss the words flippantly, lightly. But his heart began to beat loudly. It would have to be now. He would have to speak now. If Mama Eastman guessed on her own, she would set herself against it, and that would be the end. But if he could suggest it in the right way. . . .

"Mara! I'm ashamed of you!" It was Sophia. "In the first place, you ought not to be digging, cutting wood, hauling like a man. But fighting like a man!" Sophia's voice hung on the warm smoke in the room. She took the baby from her breast and laid it gently in its crate. As she covered it, she lingered over the tiny body. "Mara ought not to be conducting herself like a man. John's right. She ought to be married. She ought to be having a baby! Mama, can't you convince her? Mara, Sully's been wanting to bring you to his place for so long! If you'd marry him you could come and live close to us in the canyon." Sophia raised up from the baby's crate to look at her muddy sister. "And besides, I need you now."

"I've already tried telling her," Mama Eastman said. "And that man Richards after her all the time with his black heart."

Mara had turned her back to the others and stood stirring the soup over the fire. John's heart beat rapidly now;

he glanced around at the three women in the room. Ashel stood by the hearth feeding the small flames. He must say something now. But what? He hadn't spoken to Sophia alone yet. He should do that. But here they were, urging Sully on Mara. Not Sully. Not for Mara. "Perhaps . . ." John began. "Perhaps Mara would come to live with us anyway," he tried. "She would not need to marry Sully. I don't believe she loves Sully. Do you, Mara?"

Mara didn't answer. She looked back toward the door. John knew that Sully would probably be wanting lunch, but he had not come yet.

"There's a possibility. . . ." Suddenly John was afraid. All of them at once—Mama Eastman, her gray head bobbing over the large table of crates as she set out tableware, Sophia as she came to the table to help Mama, and Mara, her back turned, her head toward the door, waiting for Sully? He had to speak now. He took a deep breath.

"There's a possibility," he heard himself say. "That is, I've been thinking about this for some time." All three women looked at him now.

John's heart thudded in his chest as Mara gazed toward him. He had promised himself not to encourage her until he had talked to Sophia and Mama. But her eyes melted him. She was so much in need of him, and of Sophia. And they needed her. Mama Eastman could surely do all right with her neighbors, with everyone else from the fort around her, and with Ashel. "There's just a chance," he stammered, trying again, "that it would be wise for us. Well, I've been thinking about this for some time, and I know, Mama Eastman, you're not really in favor of it—at least you haven't been in favor of it for yourself. . . ."

Mama Eastman drew herself up from setting the table, a fork poised in the air, and stared steadily at John's eyes.

"I mean . . . I know you are dedicated to the Church,

Mama Eastman, and the authority of the prophets. And it's not that everyone can't make their own choices. You've made your choice. But perhaps for wisdom's sake, in the present circumstances, and for Mara's sake . . . and even for Sophia's sake if she could find it in her heart to . . . I think God would help me. . . ."

"My stars, John," Mama Eastman interrupted. "A lot of words and I don't have a notion of what it is you're trying to tell us." Something in the bland way she said it made him believe she knew very well and was just trying to make it harder on him.

"I mean to say that if I got everyone's permission I would ask to court Mara with the intention of honorable marriage in the new and everlasting covenant." John stopped to catch his breath. "And of course wait until Papa Eastman is home, and be assured of the permission of the Church." He paused again. No one spoke. They all looked at him with amazement. He went on. "There are blessings promised to those who enter the ordinance of plural marriage." He caught a sudden shadow in Mama Eastman's face, and she stood silent as the noon sun began to peel back the shadows and the clouds. "I feel it would be a good answer to certain . . . ah . . . er . . . problems Mara has at the present time, and that Mara would be the perfect answer to Sophia's need for help with the baby, and that I could keep the family together and protect Mara. . . ." And love her, he continued, but to himself. Oh yes, he could love Mara. Would Sophia accept that? "I haven't talked to anybody yet but the bishop, and I believe I have his blessing."

He looked at Sophia now. She sat down on the edge of the bed and stared, but the softness had not left her face. Dear Sophia! Mara clung to the soup spoon and slowly turned back toward the soup, but she did not stir it, or even move. Mama's eyes narrowed.

"Well, John," Sophia spoke first, a softness, a lightness in her voice. "I'm sure that you are just trying to make us all happy, but. . . ."

"But it isn't something the Eastmans have ever done." John said hurriedly. "I know that. It's new. It's an idea. Just something to think about."

There was a long silence now. At last, Mama Eastman spoke. "You're quite a young man, John," Mama said quietly. "I can only feel you are suggesting this out of the generosity of your heart. You, of course, know how genuinely interested Sully has been in Mara, and you have been aware that she has not returned his favor." Mama looked at Mara now. "And so I commend you for a kindness unselfishly offered out of the beauty of your soul, even though you are aware that the Eastmans have never participated in plural marriage."

"Though it is one of the Lord's commandments," Sophia said, surprising everyone. Mama Eastman gazed at her, speechless as she continued: "If I were called by the Lord to enter it, there is no one I would rather be with than Mara." Sophia! His gentle Sophia! Even knowing her goodness as he did, John had not expected her to be such an angel, so full of understanding, so willing. He took courage now.

"It would be up to Mara, too, of course. If anyone at all objected to it, it could never be." John waited. Through the hesitating sunshine, the rain still fell on the roof, dripped in pans on the cabin floor. He gazed toward Mara, who still had not turned around. "I have loved Sophia so much," he paused, his voice closing up again. "We have so much love for one another, so much love to give. I felt we had enough to share. . . ."

Mara turned now. Her face was pale with no expression, unless it might be fear. She did not look at John. She looked at Sophia. Her eyes filled with tears. Gentle

Mara, John thought. Perhaps this is not what you had waited for. Second wife to your sister's husband. But you don't love Ivie Richards, or Sully Tuttle, or any of the young men in the fort who pursue you. I know you don't. And you are weary of their pursuit. You need rest and protection . . . and my love. Oh how I would love you, Mara. John tried by the power of his thoughts to win Mara to him now. She stood so beautiful, so alone, looking at Sophia with tears in her eyes.

And then she was running to Sophia, kneeling, clasping her sister's knees in her arms. "Sophia! Oh Sophia! I would not mind. I love you both. And to share little Martha. If you would not care?"

Sophia put her hand in Mara's hair. Mama Eastman stared at her daughters. John felt such gladness, his blood seemed on fire. The room seemed bright, full of sun, though the rain beat down outside.

Mama Eastman dried tears from her eyes with the corner of her apron. John went to her and put his arm around her shoulders.

"Well, John," she said. "I suppose, if it's what everyone wants, we can work it out somehow."

In the afternoon, Mara heard a commotion from the wickiup. The lean-to roof was attached to the back of the Eastmans' cabin about seven feet high, and it gently sloped down to about three feet in front.

"We've forgotten Blueflower!" Mara cried, grabbing Papa's slicker and running out into the rain. John was close behind. Moving as fast as they could, their feet sticking in the wet clay of the fort clearing, they were out the gate and around to the wickiup. Bishop Higbee and George Allen were already there.

"Our dam has broken!" Mara cried. "They're flooded!" Brother Allen was carrying Blueflower out. She was covered in mud to her waist. Peering into the darkness of the wickiup, Mara could see Spirit of Earth and Rain stacking mats high in one corner over some pieces of muddy pottery. The fire pit was a murky puddle. John led the old woman and her daughter out into the rain as the mud oozed into their wickiup, thick and heavy, burying the mats, tearing at the willow stakes that held the tightly woven walls of the hut upright.

"This won't hold much longer," said Bishop Higbee, tugging gently at one of the stakes. The stake, as useless as a piece of wet straw, came out of the mud in his hand, and the willow ceiling slumped to the ground. Spirit of Earth gave a cry at the collapse of her home. John tried to comfort her as she sank onto a clump of sodden grass at his feet.

"Let's get them inside," John said. Mara held Papa's slicker over Spirit of Earth's head as John led her and Rain into the fort. Ahead, George Allen carried Blueflower.

"So that's where this Indian disappeared to," Brother Allen said over his shoulder. "We can take her or one of the others if it's too much for you at your place."

"They don't like to be separated," Mara called back in the rain. "Thank you, but we're used to them. We'll take care of them."

Mara hadn't seen Ivie Richards since they had come out, and as she walked patiently along trying to keep the rain from Spirit of Earth, she hurried inside, hoping Richards would not appear and make trouble. He must be inside the Anderson's place, Mara thought.

Mama was at the cabin door with her arms out. "Bring them in, oh, bring them all in, the poor souls. We should have had them in hours ago, with this rain." Mama shook her head and clucked, taking Spirit of Earth into one arm and Rain into the other and leading them to the hearth. John helped Brother Allen settle Blueflower on a blanket near the corner of the chimney. Sophia came to her with some swaddling cloths and began to clean and wrap Blueflower's wounded leg. Blueflower turned her face away toward the fire, biting her lip in pain, making no sound. The smell of wet deerskin filled the room.

"It's all right," Mama was saying soothingly, as she patted Spirit of Earth's hair with a dry cloth.

"We'd be glad to help, now, Sister Eastman," George Allen was saying. "You just say the word. We'd be more than pleased to take one."

"Thank you, thank you, Brother Allen, but we can manage. We've plenty to handle all of them," she said. And before Brother Allen was out the door, Mama was bringing dry flour biscuits and cups of leftover venison soup to her Indians.

It was only after the Indians had been settled that Mara noticed Sully, who had come in, she guessed, as Brother Allen left. With a nervous glance at Mara, Sully rushed to Mama's side. "Let me take them biscuits for you, Ma'am," he said. Mara didn't look away from Sully when he searched for her eyes. She felt a peaceful feeling of confidence in her new role as the prospective second wife to her sister's husband. She had no need to fear Sully now. And in that moment, watching him help Mama so dutifully, she felt a new compassion for the lanky red-haired boy. He had always seemed so young. She could never have married him. But he had tried so hard!

Then, kneeling near Rain with the plate of biscuits in his hand, Sully let out a shout. "John! It's coming in the cabin walls!" Mara rushed with the others to the spot. Sure enough, behind the crates near the back wall where Sophia usually lay with the baby, a thin, black muck oozed along the cabin's edge. Water began to trickle into the center of the floor, and where Mama had stashed old rags to keep moisture from crossing the floor, there were now little piles of mud. Mara stood, her mouth open, amazed, feeling helpless. For a moment, no one moved. Silt began to push the drip pans from their places on the floor.

"It's coming!" It was Mama's old whine. "Oh, dear God!" She clasped her hands together. "The flood's coming into the house!"

Sully and Ashel moved away the bed, and Mama and Mara mopped up the water seeping into the room with old wet rags. "I'll dig a deeper ditch around the cabin!" John called, rushing out into the rain. Mara followed him and Sully followed them both. The lean-to had slid into the mud. John was digging furiously. Mara grabbed her shovel, still lying in the mud by the lean-to.

"It's all right, Mara," John looked up. "Let Sully help me. Sophia's right. It isn't becoming of a lady."

"There's another shovel," Mara said, pointing to three shovels left by others who had been digging earlier. "I'm able."

"John's right," Sully said, coming to her. "Mara, let me take your shovel."

"There's another shovel," said Mara, annoyed.

"Yes, but you ought to let me . . ." Sully stood, his arms out to her.

John watched Sully for a moment and then said quietly, "Sully, it's all right. Let her do it if she's got a mind to."

But Sully didn't give up. He turned to John. "She don't know what is her own mind," he says. "I'd just like to help." He turned back to Mara now, his eyes those same pleading eyes. "I just want to help you, Mara. You know I just want to help you." His red hair ran onto his forehead in little wet strips. John was behind him now, his hand on Sully's arm. John's voice was husky, full of compassion.

"Sully, she is going to marry me."

Sully blinked, his eyes still fastened on Mara. His hands fell to his sides; his shoulders sagged. He was quiet for an unbearably long time, his eyes softening, like those of a disappointed child. "Marry . . . ?"

"Yes. Mara and I are going to be married."

Because this afternoon had been so filled and she had not yet spoken a single word about it alone to John, Mara had in the last few hours felt dizzy, not fully comprehending that her future had been made today. But now she felt with a jolt what had really taken place. She and all of her family—with the exception of Papa—had agreed to her betrothal to the man standing beside Sully: this strong man with his thick back and muscular arms. His blue shirt sleeves were rolled tightly above his elbows, where his brown arms glistened in the rain. His hands were large and strong, and his fingers tapered to flat ragged nails and calloused fingertips. The cords of his neck were thick, and his shirt, open on his chest, revealed a mass of thick, wiry brown hair. She noticed the square cut of his jaw as he spoke to Sully. He had large soft lips, now curved and tense. His nose was straight, with very little curve and such a high bridge that his brown eyes seemed hidden under his thick brows. His thick brown hair, wet from the rain, lay in smooth waves down his neck and on his forehead.

Mara stared at John feeling a wild leap in her blood and a fantasy of yearning for his strength. It was true, then! He had asked for her; she would be his. Now he was making the announcement! The frustration of the crickets and the rain, the destruction of the Indian wickiup, the worry she had felt for Blueflower, the intensity of the last few hours made her feel weak now.

"It's all right, John," she said, watching the light fade from Sully's eyes. "He can use my shovel. I guess I am tired."

"Mara," was all Sully could say.

"I never promised you," she stammered.

"You promised me," Sully nodded slowly.

"Not really. I said I would try. Well, it doesn't work, Sully. I don't love you." She winced inwardly, feeling his pain.

"And for a . . ." Sully stared at John now, his eyes narrowing. ". . . For a marriage to a man who can never really be your own." His voice began to crack, now. "What do you think you are doing? Have you really thought about what it is you are giving up . . . sharing your husband with another woman? Have you even thought about it? I don't believe it, Mara. I don't believe it and I won't believe it until it's done!"

"She knows her own mind better than you're willing to admit, Sully," John said, in that wonderful smooth authoritative voice of his. "She wants to join her sister and me for eternity."

Mara's heart thudded. John released his hand from Sully, who took the shovel. He placed his arm around Mara's shoulders. "I love her. I just haven't told her yet." He smiled at her, his brown eyes liquid with light. Trembling, she stood in his arms. It was all true. Her life with John had begun.

"I won't believe it till it's done," Sully said.

Chapter Seven

On September 14 Brigham Young, having come down out of the stormy north hauling wagonloads of life-saving supplies, stood in a Sunday conference session and announced that the fort would have to be moved. If dismantling it was more practical than milling and hauling new lumber, that was fine, but no city could be built on a mud flat. To make city-building a possible activity near a fort, the fort would have to be moved and rebuilt and located about two miles east of where it now stood if it were going to be safe from flooding. The move must begin tomorrow if not yesterday—the good Lord wasn't going to keep a toad dry who didn't have more sense than not to sit on a lily pad.

Monday the sky dawned as fresh as spring. The storm sailed over the mountains to the east as though it had been ordered to find its victims elsewhere. With it, the crickets left, too. Taking the situation in hand, Brother Brigham ordered a few to follow him east toward the plain.

"Well, if the Indians are still angry, that's all the more reason to build sound walls," his voice boomed over the questions, the fears. "Keep your guns loaded and by your sides. Build hearty, with speed."

Eighteen men rode on Monday with Brother Brigham to map out the site for the new fort two miles east of the old. Mama bid Sully and John a strained good-bye as she wrestled with the news of another move. Mara thought she heard Mama breathe in with little gasps, like crying.

"Are you all right, Mama?" Mara asked, knowing Mama's thoughts. "It's just something that must be done."

Mama choked back any angry tears. She rocked fast and picked the threads out of an old coat of Papa's she was making over for Ashel. "Yes, I suppose so." Her voice seemed broken. "If it's the last, even then. Hart wanted to build outside the fort. Why couldn't they wait for that? Wait until we were sure enough of the Indians to move outside the fort and build homes?"

Mara didn't know what to say. She placed her hand lightly on Mama's shoulder. Mama wadded a handkerchief and dabbed at her nose.

"It's just something that must be done," Mara said, more quietly now, feeling the ineffectiveness of her repetition. But she hadn't known what else to say. Mama sighed and returned to picking out the seams of the coat piled in her lap.

In Papa's absence, it would be up to John to dismantle, move, and build the Eastman portion of the fort. Sully, a changed person since John had told him of Mara's intentions, seemed closed and guarded now, his eyes as furtive as a weasel's, his mouth drawn and tight. But he did not leave the Eastmans. He would often say to Mara when no one else could hear: "You're not married yet." Bullheadedness seemed to drive him to a desperate hope. Mara felt compassion for him, and she tried to be kind while showing him consistent firmness in her decision.

John and Sully destroyed the old cabin to build the new. They took the cabin walls apart to save as much lumber as possible, although some of it was ruined by too much rain or broken by the misplaced stroke of a hatchet or an ax. Ashel helped the men load the lumber into the ox cart, carry it to the site of the new fort, and pile it in a position at the new site similar to their place in the old fort.

Mama and Mara supervised the packing while Sophia nursed the baby and prepared the meals. Spirit of Earth and Rain helped, better at managing the supplies than Mara would have expected. They were excellent help in grinding the corn. They slapped the corn cakes, laughing and jumping up and down in rhythm over the stone. Spirit of Earth, in the process of teaching things to Rain, shared her knowledge with the others.

Blueflower hobbled about now, still with a great deal of pain. Sometimes, while dressing the wound, Mama would touch the red inflamed tissue on the Indian girl's slender thigh.

"Is that healing proper, Sophia, do you think?" Or she would ask Sister Allen about it, who knew something of nursing. But Sister Allen was so overwhelmed with the task of moving her large family that she was little help.

Many hours of the day, Blueflower just sat, holding a large blanket around her shoulders, a tent which hid her large belly, growing larger every day. There were times when no one saw her for several hours because she had gone somewhere close by to build a twig hut in which she would give birth to her baby. It was the custom, Rain managed to tell them all. Blueflower was very conscious that her baby was coming, but it did not stop her from joining with the others in meals and in preparing food. She ground the corn and fried flat corn cakes over the fire. When the others laughed, she smiled; when they sang, she sang with them. When John brought venison he had killed, she was better than anyone else at skinning it and cutting it into chunks for cooking. She could also prepare rabbits, her quick hands more agile than Spirit of Earth's gnarled ones and more experienced than Rain's.

When almost half the lumber had been transported to the new site and John and Sully had managed, with the help of Brother Allen and others, to raise the portion of the fort wall that served as the back of their cabin, John brought the women to the new site in the ox cart with most of the furniture, cooking utensils, and bedding. After the rains, the weather began to grow hot again. Now the main function of the fort wall was to provide a spot of shade until the cabin was finished. As though the heavens heard their collective prayers, the rain did not fall again for a long time.

The Eastmans had taken the spot just inside the south edge of the west gate again. Because the gates were needed for markers, they came up first, distinguishable in the spare skeleton of the fort rising slowly on the wide plain. As well as planning the large-scale markings for the width and breadth of their new city, the settlers also planned more room for the new fort; even the Eastman cabin was to be a few feet larger. For a second time, placing the stones in the fireplace and on the chimney became Mara's tedious task. Without Papa, everything took longer, but not really as long as she might have expected without him. For John was filling his role as man of the family with admirable strength of purpose and will. He was dependable, fast, and thorough. Perhaps little Martha motivates him, Mara thought. Or maybe, she hoped, he wants to impress me. He seemed a powerhouse, capable of doing everything.

As he worked mostly with the men, Mara did not see much of him. He was gone for long periods in both locations either dismantling or building until almost everything was moved. Finally more and more people were ready to stay at the new fort.

During that first week after their decision, John's announcements to friends, Sophia's kind anticipation, and Mama's vague smiles seemed to assure her that her marriage was truly going to be, but as time passed it was more and more difficult for her to believe that she had promised herself as John Smith's second wife. Mama had agreed with John—in fact, she had set it as a stern requirement—that the marriage should not take place until Papa and Caroline had returned from Boston. And no one knew when that would be.

So, for Mara, although there was talk of marriage plans and talk of what the responsibilities would be between her and Sophia for the baby and the household, nothing seemed very much changed. John still worked with her, smiled at her, greeted her with the same kindness he had always shown. As the darkness grew earlier each evening, he sat as he had always done with the women and with Sully and Ashel, and now the Indians, around the warm hearth, feeding the flames, talking, often holding the tiny baby in his hands and cooing to her, his eyes bright with pride. And each night, as the time came to retire, as he had always done, he rose with Sophia to the section of the cabin behind the blankets where they settled in their large bed in the corner, its springs creaking with their weight. Sully looked after them, sitting glumly by the fire. Then he would often watch Mara with a piercing glare, his eyes small slits beneath his brows, his long hands that had always been so nervous now clasped loosely between his knees, his whole body motionless.

As each evening passed in this manner, Mara grew more and more puzzled. At first things had often seemed strained, but now they seemed forgotten, as if no more were to be said about it until Papa's arrival; and that was more difficult for her to bear. John hardly ever spoke of the marriage to her anymore. His smile was always sincere; he sometimes took her hand and held it warmly for a few seconds, hardly different from the Sunday handshakes she often received from the brethren. But he did not really treat her differently from the way he had when she was just young Mara, Sophia's sister, and Mara grew more and more concerned about the promises she had made. She wished Mama had not insisted on putting it off so long. A questioning, growing unrest began to rankle in her heart.

Sully watched as though he knew exactly what was happening, and he seemed to gloat over Mara's impatience, crouching like a hungry panther waiting for the right moment to pounce. Sometimes when Mara caught him staring at her with the old intensity, he turned away with what seemed to be a sly grin.

Comparing Sully to John always strengthened her commitment to John. She often watched John's efficient strength and power with admiring eyes, and she drew closer to Sophia as they sometimes talked about his habits, his favorite foods, his plans for the mill next spring as soon as the good weather should arrive. But once in Mara's dreams the face of John Smith changed into the face of Bret Hunt. Bret. On his mission in England. Far away.

October saw the new fort completed and a new and larger outdoor shelter built for the Indians. Instead of hanging the wickiup on the exterior wall, John and Sully decided to help Blueflower with the twig hovel she had been building to give birth to her baby. They helped her to make it larger than she had planned, and they furnished it with willows and a rain-tight roof. The mother-to-be did not seem to mind when John and Sully invited Spirit of Earth and Rain in to live with her. Having saved what mats and pots they could rescue from the muddy debris of their lean-to, the Indians furnished their little wooden house with warmth and care.

While they were moving to the new place, Mara saw Ivie Richards riding up and, her heart beating loudly, waited for his temper to flare, but he sat still on his horse and did not so much as flick away the flies. His eyes narrowed as he watched the Indians in the ox cart, but though he saw Blueflower, he also saw the breadth of her belly, and he must have thought she would be better off with her Indian friends than with him and his two boys. So he never said a word. Mara was somewhat startled at his behavior. She wondered if he had known where Blueflower had been all this time. She felt a little foolish, but she never mentioned anything to anyone, and took it as a matter of course that Blueflower was theirs to take care of in the new location.

Mama smiled much of the time, now, saying she felt deeply in her bones that the next time they moved it would be to the new home Hart promised he would build for them. She walked out with Bishop Higbee and several other brethren and neighbors on a crisp autumn day in late October to pick the spot she wanted for the Eastman homestead. Mara went, too.

The city fathers had mapped a wide road just to the west of the new fort, moving from north to south, just a little way outside the Eastmans' west gate. Many of the lots along the new road were already spoken for. As Mama walked southward, she gazed with interest on the spot where John Higbee indicated they would build a church, a school, and other buildings. Five blocks west of where the tabernacle was to be built, Mama chose the spot for her house. It was across the street from the city park, on the corner lot still facing Main Street. From that day on she was hardly able to contain her excitement for the time when Papa would return and they could begin building. She spent hours outlining every detail of the home, and when John thought no one was listening, he reminded her that she might as well plan for a mansion. "The sale of a foundry is bound to bring in plenty," he said quietly. He and Sophia chose a lot just south of Mama's, and they seemed just as excited as she was. They didn't talk about the sawmill anymore.

No one asked Mara if she liked the lots they chose. No one seemed to care how Mara was feeling. She began to hurt inside, not really understanding why, except that when she gazed cautiously toward John, hoping he might see the longing in her eyes, he would only smile at her briefly and then quickly look away.

She spent time with Nancy and Hannah raking dead autumn leaves over their lots outside the fort to fertilize their future gardens. Sometimes they husked the late harvest of corn. She found herself unable to confide in either girl anymore. Neither one was very happy about Mara's promise to enter plural marriage. Nancy's older sister was a third wife in Salt Lake City, and so Nancy, although she had a romantic idea of her own about a girl's first love, said it would be all right for Mara if that's what she really wanted. But Hannah, even though her own sister Kate had married Scott Hunt only a year ago, seemed withdrawn and scornful.

"I'll never enter into plural marriage," Hannah exclaimed, turning her fine white chin upward and tossing the black curls against her neck. "My sister Kate was a fool. Even if she has money and position, it's not worth sharing any man."

"Do you think he really loves you?" Nancy asked with kindness, watching John from a distance working in the fields.

"Oh, I'm sure he does," Mara said trying to sound sure, but noticing with pain that the words came out weak, without conviction. She dropped the subject with her friends and tore the husks from the corn with fury.

On a cold day in late October, the Indians became very ill.

One morning as Mara went to take the Indians some flour for their breakfasts, she found Rain sprawled outside on the cold, dead grass in a pool of vomit. Spirit of Earth peered from behind the deerskin door fastened to the willow hut and with sharp dark questioning eyes beckoned Mara forward.

"Ka ai wa," Spirit of Earth managed in her gruff, ragged voice.

"Oh, Rain," Mara ran to her. "What is wrong?"

Rain raised her square face from the ground and Mara felt her forehead. It was burning. Mara tugged at Rain, half lifting her back into the hut. Rain dragged herself forward reluctantly, but when she reached the doorway of the wickiup, Spirit of Earth cackled, "No, no, no Mipuwai," shooing Rain away. At first she was puzzled, but Mara soon realized that Spirit of Earth was trying to protect Blueflower from the sickness. The same feverish intensity that appeared in Rain's eyes burned in the old wizened gaze of her mother. Concerned about Blueflower, Mara left Rain outside and ventured through the deerskin doorway. In a corner on a pallet Blueflower lay, also burning with fever. She rolled over toward Mara and pointed to the blood-soaked, stained rags on her leg. Mara picked at them, but knew immediately she must fetch sister Allen or someone who knew more. The wound, puffed and red, looked as if it had been reinfected if it had ever healed at all.

Whatever sickness the Indians had manifested itself in the settlers in the form of dysentery. Though it was a short-lived variety, it seemed that almost every man, woman, and child caught it and had to suffer with it for two or three feverish days. So far the settlers had been fortunate to have had no serious epidemics, and they felt grateful that this one was not more dangerous than it was.

Mara was first in the Eastman place, and then Mama. From Mama, the illness spread to Sophia. Sophia tried hard to protect her little Martha, but was unsuccessful. The men seemed not so severely affected, although they too vomited and lay inert and unproductive for a time. Once she felt better, Mara began helping Sister Allen to care for the many others who were sick. Because the dysentery had come in the fall, the cold weather soon curbed its rampage, and almost everyone got to feeling better with the exception of Mama Eastman and her little namesake, the baby Martha.

Mara had never before worried about her mother's health. But for many days, she fought to control her fears as her mother developed a frightening hacking cough and a pale whiteness around her eyes. Day after day she lay inert on the bed, her arms moving limply from side to side as she turned.

The baby was not much better. Sophia, ill herself for a time, clung to the child in a half-hearted manner, in too much pain to nurse and afraid that by nursing she would infect the baby. Finally, when she did feel better and nursed the baby, Martha vomited and would not eat. Everything Sophia put into little Martha's mouth came up again quickly, a sickly green consistency. John called Sister Allen in, and the brisk woman, taking one look at the tiny child, sighed.

"She's got it bad. Little ones can't take such a high fever. Give her soda."

The soda didn't seem to do a thing. Mara helped Sophia warm and cool the little child by changing cloths for her. Blue with cold, the baby shivered, her little limbs rattling. In the next few moments her body would grow as hot as a flame. Frantic, Sophia finally asked for the herbs Spirit of Earth had gathered, but the herbs would not stay down, either, and during the next week, little Martha, only two months old, wasted to a sickly pale color, blue with veins.

John became fiercely panic-stricken. Every day for seven days he brought Bishop Higbee or various other leaders into the cabin to administer to Martha and to Mama Eastman, but they remained the same.

On Sunday he left the cabin early in the morning. Mara slipped out to follow him while the others slept. She kept him in sight until she saw him drop to his knees in a clump of trees, his hands clasped, his head first bowed and then lifted to heaven.

At the close of the Sunday evening meeting, Mara and John hurried back to the cabin where they found Sophia sitting on the side of the bed humped over as though unconscious, her hands dangling on either side of her legs, her face hanging in her lap against the tiny motionless body of baby Martha.

"Sophia! Martha, what has happened?" John screamed. From her own bed, Mama groaned. "I couldn't lift her up. She was too heavy. The baby's dead."

"Oh, dear God." John grew pale; his eyes, washed out, looked gray. He gently laid Sophia back against the pillows and bedding and took the tiny body from her lap. "Oh, dear God."

Mara stood trembling with grief. It couldn't be! God wouldn't have let it happen!

"The baby's dead," John said softly over and over again. "The baby's gone." He touched its body, rubbing it, rocking back and forth on the edge of the bed, patting it over his shoulder, but the tiny lump of cold flesh did not respond. Mara might have tried to comfort him, but his eyes grew vacant and cold. He instructed her to dress the child while he saw the bishop. Later that evening he returned and hammered a wooden crate into a tight box.

While Sophia and Mama slept, Mara dressed the tiny body in its beautiful new white clothes. There was a little dress that Sophia had made for her from an old crocheted doily once used to decorate a chiffonnier. Mara winced as she drew the pale and tiny hands through the open sleeves. Once or twice Mama raised up out of her own bed and cried, begged Mara to bring the baby to her. She held it and then fell back against the pillow, still weak with fever.

"Oh, my baby, my baby," she cried.

Sophia didn't wake until dawn.

On Monday morning Bishop John Higbee pronounced a solemn burial sermon over little Martha, another little child, and an old woman; all had died from the dysentery. They buried them a few hundred yards from camp in a little grove the bishop felt could make an adequate cemetery for a time.

"They are all now with our Father," he said quietly. "Their journey is done."

Shaking her head from side to side, Sophia began to flow with tears. John took her away while Brother Allen dedicated the graves.

Feeling weak with shock, Mara slumped against the hearth for a few moments before beginning to prepare the midday meal. Ashel fed the fire. Mama had not gone to the ceremony. She lay listlessly on her pallet, her thin white wrist raised and flattened against her hot brow.

"Was it beautiful?" she murmured. "Was it befitting my little namesake?" Mara felt too heavy to respond.

"Was she beautiful when they closed her away? Did she seem too tiny for the box? Was she still rosy in her cheeks?"

Martha had been blue even before her death. Mara could not answer. Ashel was there and he came to Mama's bed. He placed his hand on Mama's head, and she took it in her palms and chafed it nervously.

"It's all right, Mama," Ashel said, sounding afraid.

"Was she still rosy?" Mama turned to him, barely opening her eyes.

"She was a pretty baby," Ashel said.

"She was. She was a pretty baby," Mama said. "She was a beautiful baby. She was named Martha after me. My first grandchild."

Her mother's incoherence frightened Mara. Mama had never been like this before. She wished Papa would come. John could do nothing but spend his time consoling Sophia. So, alone for two days, Mara nursed Mama until her fever finally broke. That was on Thursday and, amidst prayers and anxious wishes for good health from the sisters of the camp who came in and out, at last Mama sat up one day. Sister Allen showed her a pair of hair cutting scissors she had sent for from New Jersey. They had come in a brown paper bag tied with string. She also showed Mama a looking glass with an ivory handle.

"Birds and bee feathers," Mama said looking at herself in the glass. "Cut it quick before it eats me alive." After that, she began to sit up in the rocker and take an interest in the world again.

And then on Thursday morning Blueflower's baby was born.

Chapter Eight

Thursday, November 4, 1849 was not a cold day. There was enough yellow sunshine in the hills to make the valley as bright as a bowl of flowers. Mara did not connect the sounds of crying she had heard in her early dawn dreams with Blueflower until later. It was at about eight o'clock in the morning while she was hanging some clean clothes out on the wire clothesline on the west side of the fort when she saw Rain bolt toward her with fear on her face.

"Kah de iu!" Rain stammered in Ute.

"What?" Mara gasped, unable to get meaning from the few broken words she ordinarily would have been able to understand.

"Agasraki!"

She knew Blueflower's Ute name. Picking up her skirts she ran toward the wickiup where Spirit of Earth stood outside waving her hands madly in the air.

"Agasraki!" Spirit of Earth cried. "Kah vah. No where. No where."

Mara ducked and peered into the dark hut. Spirit of Earth had been telling her Blueflower was nowhere to be found.

"Agasraki iu kah ai wah," Rain translated. "Lig bah."

"Leg bad," Mara understood. She did not have to be told how badly infected Blueflower's wound still was.

Rain and her mother were telling her that Blueflower had tried to build another small hut not far away where she would not be heard when she screamed in her pain, but they did not know if she had been able to finish building it because her leg had been so bad.

Mara, lifting her skirts, pounded toward the clump of willows to the southeast where the city fathers had promised to build a tabernacle someday. Her bones felt heavy in her flesh as though at any moment they would jar themselves loose and puncture the soles of her feet. Rain followed her and Spirit of Earth hobbled far behind.

Ahead of them in a small clearing of bushes stood an interconnected circle of twigs—the beginning of Blueflower's hut. Inside of the circle, lying flat on the ground with her face against the earth, her hands clutching the cold autumn soil, Blueflower writhed in pain, and beside her in the hollow of her arm lay a tiny black-haired boy.

"Get blankets, Rain," Mara said, looking upward. The sun hit her eyes with its fire. She could barely see the Indian girl. "Quick! Blankets! Fetch John, Sophia!"

"John. Sophia," Rain repeated and ran toward the fort. Mara touched Blueflower's head. The girl groaned. Seeing Mara, she tried to roll over, but her body would not respond. Mara pulled away some old rags and dried herbs from her legs. Under her body flowed unstaunched rivers of bright red.

"Blueflower!" Mara said. She tore at Blueflower's legs and the girl gasped in terrible short gulps. The half-healed wound on the leg had broken open again and pus oozed out alongside a sluggish stream of blood.

"You're losing too much blood! Hold this between your legs!" She pushed the cloth in place and Blueflower's hands after it, but the whitened hand fell loosely against the dusty ground. Feeling her own head beat with pain,

Mara tried to hold the cloth with her elbow as she tore a few loose pieces of fringe from Blueflower's deerskin tunic. She pushed the cloth against Blueflower's open wound and, lashing the fringe together, wound it tightly around her thigh.

"You're losing blood. Please, Blueflower, try to help."

Her pleas were in vain, for the young Indian girl had turned over and, pushing the child away, clenched her fists in angry pain. She breathed rapidly in deep gasps, and then held her breath until her face was blue.

"Please, Blueflower, help me."

"Hah nah." The Indian girl opened her large eyes now and lay her head back against the ground. Her dark rich hair fell in a ripple about her shoulders. The veins in her neck pulsed under her skin.

She lay quietly now, as though waiting, and her hands, once tightened, relaxed. Mara's eyes began to sting and she too hurt all over. It seemed she hurt in the same places that Blueflower hurt. The baby began to stir. Mara reached for the tiny naked body lying in the folds of Blueflower's tunic.

"Hah nah. You, you." Blueflower spoke the only word of English Mara had ever heard her use. Her voice, not familiar to anyone, was liquid with a silver sound. "Sobeshent," she indicated the baby with her feverish eyes. "Sobeshent."

"Hush, they'll be here soon."

For the first time in her life Mara held a tiny Indian baby. Its small head, about the size of her Papa's fist, was round and still wet, capped with slick black hair. The baby was breathing softly like a tiny animal in her arms. The joy of the feel of it was crowded out only by her concern for Blueflower and that no one—John, or Sully, or anyone—was coming.

"Sobeshent," Blueflower said once again, this time

more softly, her voice hanging in the air, sounding far away. She looked once more at Mara, into Mara's eyes. This time she said nothing, but Mara saw a light pass through the dark glass of her gaze. And then she saw the light go out as though someone had blown out a candle.

"Blueflower!" Mara called, clutching the child in her left arm and pressing the slender olive-skinned hands with her right hand. "Blueflower!"

But as though slipping away on silent moccasined feet, Blueflower was gone. Stunned with grief, Mara held the child in her arms without moving. Then she let the tears fall when she heard Rain and John and Sully and the others as they came.

Blueflower's burial was quiet. John and Sully dug the grave only a few feet from the place she died. Spirit of Earth and Rain came to dress her and, breaking Blueflower's personal possessions to "release" their spirit to go with her, they placed scraps of clothing, pottery, weaving, and jewelry around a small willow stand they fashioned in the shade of the bushes. Spirit of Earth fell on the ground near Blueflower's head and chanted longingly. She stroked her cheeks and neck with an herb she had pounded into an oily paste.

"Ha nah. Don dai. Oh Hah nah," she wailed softly. She stood only when she heard Mara whispering the baby's name as she held him in her arms. "Sobeshent." Spirit of Earth rose then to look at the child, and tears streamed down her face. Mara glanced at Rain's eyes as she sat daubing the blood beneath Blueflower's legs with a bloody rag.

"Name of my dead brother—son Sipapu, friend Blueflower. Die a tall boy," Rain said.

Brother Allen came later, and Nancy. When the grave was dug, Brother Allen and John lifted the body into it, and Brother Allen said a brief prayer.

The sun rose over the warm autumn hills. By noon it was known all over camp that Blueflower had died and had left her child with the Eastmans. Mara could not take her eyes off the tiny child who slept and slept as though it would never awaken. "Sobeshent. Sobeshent," she said softly. "Sobeshent." Blueflower had pointed toward Mara as though she had wanted Mara to take the child. And she named it "Sobeshent," the name of Rain's brother who had died as a boy. Mara had never heard Rain mention her brother before. She whispered the name to the child over and over again, and stroked his smooth and fragile hands, his shiny thick black hair.

Back in the Eastman cabin, Mara showed the baby to her mother with whispers so as not to wake Sophia who was still in a stupor from the loss of her child. Lately she had withdrawn for long periods into her bed behind the hanging blanket. When Mara brought the baby in, Mama lifted her head from the bed of crates where she lay just recuperating from her illness.

"The baby!" she exclaimed. "Blueflower's tiny baby! Is it all right?" She pushed aside the tip of the blanket that covered its face.

"A little boy," Mara whispered. "Sobeshent. He's just fine."

Mama, unable to keep her head above the pillow for long, lay back down and shut her eyes. "I wonder . . ." she said softly so that Sophia wouldn't hear her. "I wonder . . . a baby whose mother has died. And we have a mother whose baby has died." She glanced upward, her eyes meeting Mara's. Her eyes, for the first time since she had been ill, for the first time since little Martha had died, brightened with light. "Sophia. But don't wake her." Mama said. "And don't push her. She is distraught with grief."

As Mara prepared the food for the family, Sophia still slept. She had slept all morning while they were at the burial, and she had stayed asleep while John had gone to the corral to stack some of the summer's hay they had gathered for the animals to eat should there be much winter snow. She continued to sleep until after noon.

Not until about one o'clock did she emerge from her small hiding place, her dark eyes sunken above her sagging cheeks. She appeared lifeless, as though the blood had been drained from her body. Her smooth white forehead was platted with wet hair, her brows drawn together. She did not see the Indian baby now lying near Mama in her bed, but she stumbled to the table where Mara was placing large hunks of unleavened bread and pouring a little milk from a tankard John had milked that morning from a neighbor's cow.

When she saw Sophia, Mara's heartbeat quickened, for she was hoping to surprise her sister. Still unsure how Sophia would react, she had decided with Mama that she would let it happen naturally, slowly, without too much excitement or urgency. But her heart would not be still.

"How late is it?" Sophia said. "How long have I slept?"

"Past the highest noon, anyway, isn't it, Mama?" Mara answered.

"That long. Oh, my!" Sophia moaned, pushing her hair back from her face.

"Sophia, did you see the little Indian child?" Mara said quietly. Sophia sat at the table without moving, her back to Mama. She looked at Mara.

"Blueflower's baby," Mara said.

"I know," Sophia said without color to her voice.

"It was born this morning."

"I know," Sophia said again without looking around. "A boy." She choked on the last words.

Mara was taken by surprise. "You know? How did you know? Did John tell you?"

"Yes," Sophia answered. The quality of her voice commanded silence. When no one said anything, she added, "But he didn't need to tell me. I heard Blueflower cry out in the night. It woke me."

For awhile Mara stirred the hot soup in its tankard on the table. Sophia did not turn around. Her dark eyes drooped to Mara's hands.

"Don't you want to see the baby?" Mama said weakly from the cot. Still Sophia did not move. She sat on the edge of the crate, her head in her hands. The quiet seemed ominous until Ashel and Sully came in from the field.

"We got enough corn for a little while," Sully was saying. "Ashel here knifes some of them kernels from the cob like he's shavin' bark off a whistle. It smells good, Mara."

During supper no one said very much about Blueflower or her baby. Not until evening did Sobeshent begin whimpering. It was a tiny cry, a faraway cry, as though the delicate body, only one day old, were from a different world or a faraway star and had not quite caught up with where he was supposed to be on November 4, 1849.

Mama, sitting on the bed now with her soup dish and cornbread in one hand, reached toward him with the other. "Maybe water, Mara," she said. "Do you have a bit of sponge?"

Mara rummaged around the kitchen items in the cupboard crate. She found the sponge and dipped a corner of it into the hot water over the fire.

"Let it cool," Mama said.

Mara waved it about, blew on it.

"Just see if the little dear won't suck on it," Mama said, tucking the infant into the corner of her arm.

"Sweet little tiny one," she whispered. "Only I think he'll be tall. Tall and thin. Look how thin he is." She lifted his little hand and unwound a long slender arm. The baby's cry became more than a whimper now as he pulled his arm back into the coverlet. When the sponge had cooled, Mara put the corner of it into Sobeshent's open mouth. He grasped it quickly and sucked at the warm liquid. It satisfied him for a few moments. When he was quiet again, Sophia left the cabin to hunt for John. Mara felt a coldness from her, like an icy wind.

The baby slept again until almost eight o'clock, sucking occasionally at the little sponge. But at a quarter past eight, he began crying in earnest. The water no longer satisfied him, and he turned away from it, his wide mouth open with an angry, hurting cry.

While Mama lay weakly on the bed, Mara held the baby close and rocked him. Sully and Ashel and John came into the house. John's eyes were sober and glassy. He did not come to the baby, either.

Sophia, with her back to the others in the room, stared out the window.

"Sophia, please," Mama finally said. No answer. "Sophia, you must be in pain; the child could at least relieve your discomfort." Still Sophia did not speak. "Well," Mama sighed, "we could try cow's milk and the sponge, but oh, Sophia, my darling, the Lord giveth and the Lord taketh away. And the Lord giveth. . . ."

John's eyes were dark with sleepiness, care, and mourning. Mara watched him. He seemed about to speak. He turned to Sophia and said something so soft Mara could not hear. Sophia stood, her curved back seeming to tighten. "Sophia, please." John's words were even softer than Mama's.

The room seemed so still, so full of sadness and despair, that Mara felt as if she were drowning in it, felt she must run outside to get some air. She held the baby close and rocked him, his screams a soft whimper now. And then Sophia turned toward her, her body trembling. Slowly, she walked to Mara, her eyes dark. She leaned over in the firelight and reached for the baby. Mara held him out to her, and his mouth searched the air.

Sophia took him in her hands. The blanket fell from him, revealing long spindly legs, no bigger round than willows. His tiny toes stretched and waved in the faded light.

"He's no bigger than a prairie rat," John breathed.

Sophia placed her hand under his toes and drew his legs up close, holding them in her fist. Then she turned and covered him with her arms, and drawing him in a little bundle close to her breast, she moved behind the blanket to her bed.

Mara heard the baby breathing fast, heard little soft rooting noises, and then gulping and spattering as he drank in his first meal. And then she heard Sophia's stifled sobs, and her heart broke for her sister.

Sophia and the baby were asleep behind the blanket. John sat without moving beside the fire, staring into its hollow coals, into the shadow and light, the blue and dancing flames. When he rose he tossed his willow into the fire, and, staring at Mara, turned toward the door. "I'm going for a walk, Mama," he called back. As he tugged to shut the wooden plank he turned once more into the room, his face pale. "Why don't you come too, Mara?"

Mara stood wiping the soup pot with a dry towel. Her heart began to beat hard. Her head was light; her ears buzzed. As he left, she stood not breathing. Then she glanced toward Mama. Mama nodded, slightly. "Go on, Mara. Ashel can finish the cooking pots."

Mara flung down the towel, whipped her shawl from

the hook by the door, and, passing a stern-faced Sully, hurried into the cool November evening. John was ahead of her, ambling toward the west gate.

"It's not very cold for November."

Mara was still not quite by his side. He walked with a lunging stride, his hands deep in the pockets of his jacket. "But I suppose it will be cold soon."

Mara didn't know what to say so she said nothing. Ahead of them in the west long jagged clouds half hid the moon. Against the far hills, the mist had settled like soup, its streaming froth lit with a smoky light. The November evening was a sea of air and land on an undefinable horizon. They passed through the gate and into the open fields.

Matching her stride with John's, Mara hung quietly behind him, her arms folded under the shawl. With her heart still pounding she took all she could from this moment alone with John. She saw him as she often did in her dreams on lonely nights. She outlined his silhouette under the motion of his stride, his body, powerful and light. What would he say to her? His voice seemed to be far away, and his thoughts even farther.

"Perhaps we can take Blueflower's baby for our own, and for a time it will appease Sophia." His voice was thin, and he did not look back at Mara.

When she finally reached his side and strode close beside him, he slowed. Out in the fields he stopped and turned toward her. His white face was bleached by moonlight, his dark eyes tired and sad.

"Mara," he said, taking her elbows in his hands. "I haven't said anything to you lately . . . about . . . about our marriage. I've been so . . . troubled. Sophia has needed. . . ." Mara's heart stopped. "I've wanted to wait until Papa came." His voice trembled on the edge of a deep sob. "But I need you now."

Mara didn't breathe. She had dreamed of being alone with John like this ever since that first night out by the gate. She had wondered why he had never approached her and if he ever would.

"We've only begun our lives together," he said softly now, his hands trembling on her arms. "And we must wait to be married." He paused. "But Mara, I know you. . . ."

She felt a surge of compassion, as though in only a few moments she had grown from a child into a woman who could comfort this man who stood beside her, his breath warm on her face, his rough-shaven face only a hand's breadth away.

"I love you, Mara," he said, and she felt his body tremble. "I've never told you that alone. Once said like this, it's hard to hold, and I've wanted to wait. But I can't wait any longer. I love you."

Mara's bones melted as he drew her into his embrace. He pulled her by the small of her back, close into his body, and the warmth of his thighs, his arms, enclosed her fully.

"Mara, I love you. And Sophia . . . and I need you so desperately." He was almost sobbing now, his mouth searching her neck, her shoulder, his lips opening and closing against her. The fire raced along her spine. He held her in his arms, and she responded, breathless, tears welling into her eyes, the feeling almost painful.

"And you have been waiting so patiently," John continued. "Mara. My Mara."

Without words she clung to him, softly breathing, holding his head in her hands, raking her fingers through his hair, covering his ears, his neck, with her own wordless mouth.

"John. Good John," she finally breathed.

Then he took her face in his hands and leaned slightly

away from her. They looked at one another. There seemed no time, no place, just the two of them. "We'll do everything for each other," he said softly. "All of us working together can do it. We will conquer this wild place and all its sadness." He looked strong and stately, his body taut as though prepared for a life of protecting. After a moment of stroking her hair, he said warmly, cocking his head to the side and smiling a gentle smile, "This kind of thing will be hard to stop now. Mara, you are so beautiful," he whispered.

For several moments they clung to each other in the yellow mist stirring under the moon. The clouds sank to the earth around them like shadows, surrounded them like smoke. Though it seemed that only a few moments had passed, they spent almost two hours together walking down the rows in the fields, talking together, stopping to embrace. John took her head in his hands and smothered her with kisses.

"You are so lovely, my angel. And it won't be long until we're together forever, for eternity."

With their arms linked around each other, they passed across the space in the park marked off for the church. Then they walked south toward the lots they had chosen for Mama's and Papa's home site, and then John's own.

"I thought of you when Sophia and I chose the site, Mara." He turned to her. "Mara, forgive us. You are a part of us and we should have had your say, but," and he whispered now, a warmth in his eyes, "I wanted to wait. And I want to build you a house of your own." Mara threw her head back and laughed with joy; her hair fell back from her face and she felt the moonlight in her eyes. She took John's hand and they raced with one another like children across the rough ground.

"I've never been so happy," she said.

"Never?"

"Never."

"Don't tell a soul, or it might go away." John teased her. He took her into his arms once again. "Oh Mara, keep laughing and smiling like this. Promise me you will. Life is never easy. But your smile feeds my soul!"

"Oh, I will," she promised. "And this must last forever!" She laughed again, feeling a happiness deep inside, a joy she had not felt before. For one brief moment the image of Bret Hunt passed in her mind, then vanished quickly. She was holding something precious in her grasp, and she must not spoil it now.

"Forever. Forever. Forever." Each time John repeated the word, he kissed her face. And he held her as though he wanted never to let her go.

As soon as the harvest came in, the settlers began counting out stores of supplies for themselves. With the arrival of new families almost every week, the numbers in the fort had expanded almost beyond the reasonable amount of grain they had grown. But it was too late to grow more. Now, as though it were seeping upward from the pores in the earth, the cold of December like an icy smoke surrounded them. The frozen grass shattered with footfall.

Representing Brigham Young, Parley Pratt came down from Great Salt Lake City to visit just before the winter set in. Pleased with the number of buildings, the new fort, the city streets plotted and planned, he smiled and told everyone in a Sunday evening church meeting, "I can report to Brigham Young these very sturdy cabins, almost sixty of them, all behind good walls; and adequate harvest in spite of the floods, the crickets, the late freeze." People smiled. People cut and pinned with pine pegs new shelves against their log walls, stacked them with little clutches of sage and herb teas, dried currants, roots, alum and rosemary, chloe, and mint—mint and watercress had grown along the river in profusion—lily roots dried and stored in bags, boxes, and barrels.

"The Indians bothering you much?" Brother Pratt asked Bishop Higbee after the meeting. Mara and John, who were close by, heard his question.

"Once in awhile they come down and kill our cattle, or ride their ponies across our fields, or yell at us inside the walls."

"But surely, if you never fight back, they won't stay angry with you for long."

"Surely," John Higbee said, and he and John exchanged grim smiles Brother Pratt did not see.

"Keep to yourselves," Brother Pratt smiled. And he nodded and blessed the sick and the children and then went his way.

On a quiet day not even a week later, the settlers saw the Indians come down from the hills again, this time carrying a white shirt flying from a wooden spear, a flag of peace. Ope-carry and Big Elk, two local chiefs, rode little Appaloosas. Several others followed them: Squash first, his soft flesh rolling under his tight deerskin pantaloons, his jowls fat as a chipmunk's cheeks; Arrapene next, solid as a rock atop his large mare, his gray face drawn. Behind Arrapene two Indian women rode a pony, and following them two other young braves with Angatewats.

As he had done consistently for the past two months, Bishop Higbee closed the gates when the Indians came down. But this time when he bravely stepped outside the fort to talk, Dimick Huntington and several others joined him. John pressed his ear against the gate and reported the conversation to those gathered inside the fort. Richards and his boys stayed behind the others.

"They say we still owe them the life of the man who

killed Old Bishop," John said. "But this time they'll take ten cows and twice that many bags of corn." He paused. The people muttered. They barely had ten cows in the whole settlement! John went on. "The bishop is telling Huntington to say no, all we can give them is a few bags of corn." John paused again. "Dimick is talking to the Indians." Mara, standing with Ashel and the Allens, hardly breathed. "They say no deal. Ten cows, twenty bags of corn, or they take the cows and corn without permission," John reported. His eyes briefly glared at the hidden Richards.

"We do not wish to fight." The settlers inside the fort could hear the bishop's voice without John's report now. They could hear Dimick's clipped and firm words as he spoke with the Utes.

"Then they'll take seven bags of corn," Huntington said.

"It's more than we can afford," Bishop Higbee said with a broken voice. But the settlers went to their cabins, silently, and brought out the corn. When Bishop Higbee opened the gate, the seven bags of corn were ready. Bishop Higbee, Brother Allen, Brother Conover, Brother Weaver, Dimick Huntington, Sully, and John carried the corn out and offered it to the Indians, who took it without smiles, one bag on each pony. Then the Indians turned, hit the flanks with their bare heels, and rode back into the eastern hills.

The gift of corn solved nothing. As the colder weather in the hills brought them down into the camps, still the Indians came to the fort to throw stones, threaten, and call names. The settlers were forced into their cabins behind locked fort gates for days at a time. Often some young braves rode in noisy clatter around the fort walls, screaming. Sometimes they came to the windows. Peering in with angry faces, they hissed, "Pale face old women no fight. Bloody old women."

Mama, still lying weak on her cot inside the cabin, turned from the window just above her head and covered herself with her blanket if she heard Indians coming. She would ask Ashel or Mara or Sully or John to cover the window.

One evening as Mara was preparing supper while her mother lay silent with fever and her sister nursed Blueflower's baby, she thought she heard the thunder of Indian horses not far away. A few moments later, she heard shouting just outside the fort, but not Indian voices. Still, frightened of seeing a brown face peer in at her, she did not look out the window. She stood to the side of it and let its deerskin cover fall. As it fell, she thought it unrolled into an orange light. A pale glow filtered into the window, unusual for sunset, or the light of a December moon.

She bravely lifted the skin and, peering into the dusk outside, she saw a fire. The Indians must have set fire to Blueflower's hut that John and Sully had helped to build where Earth and Rain lived. Afraid, she climbed into Papa's sheepskin coat and rushed out into the fort to find John or Sully. But the men had already seen the blaze and had fetched rakes, tarps, and buckets to put it out. On the way to the fire, she met John returning, his arms holding a wet quilt over two stooping figures.

"Sipapu!" Mara cried out, running to them. "Rain. I'll take them," she told John.

John gave the blanket to her and turned back toward the fire with the other men. Mara could see the flames rising above the fort wall. It would be too late. Their hut, their mats and pots—all would be gone.

Mara, still holding the blanket around Spirit of Earth's shoulders, led her and Rain toward the cabin. Huddling together, the Indians crooned mournfully.

"Ah nah. Ah nah," Spirit of Earth grieved. Rain breathed in and out noisily as she pushed the wet hair back from her face. Though unharmed, both of them chattered with cold under the wet blanket that had doused their singed clothing.

From her cot under the window, Mama sat up as they came in the door, and holding her head in her hands, she began to cry. Mara stopped just inside the door wondering if Mama was well enough or if she should take them somewhere else this time.

"No, it's all right," Mama said as though reading her thoughts. "I'll be well soon. Bring them in. Yes, it's bound to be crowded. But I wouldn't have them go anywhere else."

"I can take them . . . to the Allens, maybe," Mara started.

"No, no. I can't think of it. Welcome, friends," she said weakly rising to meet them.

"Don't get up, Mama. I can take care of it. I'll take care of them." Mara led the two Indians into the room. They smiled and nodded, bobbing up and down and clapping their hands. "Thankee, thankee," Spirit of Earth said. Wearily, Mama smiled and tightened her fingers on their hands. Then she lay back on the cot against some pillows she had propped up under the window. To Mama's right, the foot of Sophia and John's bed lay behind the blanket curtain that separated their corner from the room. Sophia stirred now, just finished with nursing the baby. She opened the blanket and stared at the Indians, her face bleak and dull. Then she looked at Mara, questions in her eyes.

"It's all right. It's all right," Mama was saying, crying softly.

First Mara removed the wet blanket from the Indians' shoulders. They stood shaking near the fire.

"Ashel, get the fire going better," Mama said weakly. Ashel began stoking it, staying out of the way of the Indians, their damp clothing reeking with the wet odor of burned deerskin. The heat of the flames fanning upward began to dry the wet burned fringes of Spirit of Earth's long cloak. As a powerful stench began filling the cabin, Sophia coughed from her corner and Mama turned and began to get out of bed, wrinkling her nose.

"It will have to come off," she said to Mara, to Ashel, to Spirit of Earth and Rain. "For their own sakes. It's time," she said to assure herself, and she tottered uneasily toward them.

At that moment John and Sully entered the tiny room, their faces dark with soot. Mama caught herself near the bed, getting her balance again. As though counting everyone, she gazed around the circle. Then she came to Spirit of Earth and touched her wet singed garments gently. "We'll need to take them off, Sipapu. Off. Off." Mama made herself understood by tugging on them slightly. John and Sully looked at one another, then at Mama. Her eyes rose to John's and she indicated with a motion of her head that the men should leave. John and Sully backed toward the door without a word, then turned and were gone. Ashel followed them. Mara stood, her arms dangling helplessly beside her. Mama was not agile on her feet, but she had strong nimble hands, and she worked quickly releasing the wet skins from Sipapu's arms and legs.

How long had it been since they had first cared for Sipapu and Rain? For nine long months Mara had never seen other clothing on them, nor had she seen them remove these crusty old skins dried and dark in places from sweat. She had seen them bathe in the river on hot days in the summer, washing their garments along with themselves. But if they had ever removed their clothing, it had been in the privacy of the lean-to at the other fort, or in Blueflower's hut that John had fixed up for them, now burned to the ground. Perhaps they had never removed it. They were like animal babies shedding their skin.

The light in Sipapu's eyes grew keen when Mama made herself understood and had placed her hands on her garments. Sipapu was still the quiet withdrawn Indian woman they had tried to feed so long ago, the wizened snappish face darkly furrowed and lean with old memories.

"Uh," Sipapu grunted softly, smiling and placing her thin gnarled hand over Mama's quick warm one. Mama stopped and glanced upward.

"This is something we need to do now you are staying in our house with us for the winter," Mama said without hesitation. "Help me lift this, Mara," she called to her daughter.

"Uh. Nah," Sipapu said, placing her hands more firmly on Mama's. Her knuckles whitened with tension. She no longer smiled.

"No. No," Mama said again, insistent. But it was no use. She could not lift the long tunic unless Sipapu would raise her arms. Still weak from fever and nauseated with the odor of the singed animal skin, Mama sat back on her heels a moment and brought a weary hand to her brow. Then she stood slowly. From the bed, with the tiny baby in her lap, Sophia was shaking her head. Mama motioned for Sophia to lay down the baby and come.

"Sipapu, we can't take your clothes unless you let us," Mama said wearily, standing beside the hunched old woman now. She wrinkled her nose. "They smell bad." Then she held her nose with her finger and thumb. "Bad. Bad. Please let us put you in something else."

Sophia was rummaging through some of their old clothing now. Mara stood hesitantly beside Rain.

"Remember, we wanted to give them a bath the first time they ever came home with us and they wouldn't let us near them at all." Mama talked softly as she knelt again to lift the tunic from Spirit of Earth's old bowed legs. "I've stood this old smell long enough; we've been having them in our house off and on now for about a year—one of the reasons I had Papa and John build the lean-to and fix up the hut. But I want to love these dear creatures. I won't let them go."

But Spirit of Earth would not move her tough old hands. She locked them against her thighs and without saying a word stared daggers at Mama.

"It isn't going to work, Mama," Sophia ventured hesitantly. She held an old pair of Papa's dungarees and a shirt loosely in her hands.

Mara felt uncomfortable standing by. And yet with Mama ill, needing help, she felt she ought not to leave. She touched Rain. The girl turned her large dark eyes toward her, filled with concern, pain. "I know, Mama," Mara offered. "Sophia, get my . . . no, never mind." Mara, deciding to fetch it herself, dashed to her trunk under Sophia's bed, sorted through it quickly and brought up the white lawn dress her mother had given her, the one she had worn at the farewell party at the bowery the night before they left Great Salt Lake City. "Here, Mama. Here, Rain." Mara went to Rain and turned around, showing Rain her own skirts. They fluttered about her ankles as she twisted, almost danced with her feet. Rain stared and her dark eyes began to light.

"Put on the kettle," Mama whispered now to Sophia, her own eyes brighter. "We'll give them a wash."

"Isn't it pretty, Rain?"

"Bitty," Rain understood, nodding. She smiled.

"For you," Mara pointed to the dress, then to Rain. "Dress for you. Clean. Get clean. Then we are clean for Christmas!"

Mara knew Rain understood nothing about Christmas, but she understood what Mara was going to do with the dress. Rain was growing up. She was almost as tall as Mara, and her body looked more like a woman's now than a child's. The Indian girl looked at the dress, at her old mother, at Mara, and at the dress again.

"We'll take your old burned clothes," Mara said softly as though Rain would cooperate. The girl, with her eyes fastened on the soft drapery of the dress, smiled faintly and did not resist as Mara lifted her limp hand. The singed and wet tunic came off with difficulty. It caught and jerked and stuck on its way up. But Mara helped Rain to remove it over her wet head. Under it hung a few rags tied to Rain's waist. Mara removed them with her deft hands. Spirit of Earth stood by, her mouth closed, her eyes staring in narrow slits of suspicion. Mama stood by her and began to try again, a soft question in her eyes as she gazed at the old mother. This time Spirit of Earth's gnarled old hands relaxed and Mama took them in her own.

"We won't hurt you, Sipapu. We've known you for a long time. We won't hurt you." Silently, Mama lifted the old deerskin tunic up along the earth mother's thighs. Beneath her ragged dress were the tops of old knitted stockings on the calves of her legs. No doubt retrieved from some forty-niner, Mara thought. Her wizened tawny legs were almost a foot apart at the knees where they bowed out and rose into thin sagging flesh.

Controlling her displeasure at the odors, Mama continued to lift the tunic over Spirit of Earth's gray body. She was thin and sagging, except for a protruding belly which looked misproportioned for the rest of her frame. Against her ribs the gray flesh draped like paper, her small breasts sagged.

"We love you," Mama said, patiently, pulling Sipapu's tunic over her head. "We love you." She drew her hands over Sipapu's wiry dark hair, and tossed the old burned garment to the floor. "You don't understand any of this, but you are the daughter of the Book of Mormon people. You are like our own. We love you." Mama's voice was soft in the still room. Rain also stood before the fire now, her large bones finely shaped under smooth nut colored skin, the soft roundness of her body visible on every limb. Sophia brought the warm water. Mama and Mara dipped towels into it and began to wash.

"Hart would say you are a part of this earth itself, stirred up by the sun. Where you come from, the Great Spirit you worship is our same God. He came to visit your people. Your many times great-grandparents may have seen our Jesus." Mama talked without stopping, her hands quick and sure over the bodies standing before the fire. First she washed Sipapu's hair with water and soap and had her lean over the tub to rinse. She washed behind her ears and around her dark neck, along her shoulders and arms, her trunk, along her thin legs and old flattened feet. Then she wrapped Spirit of Earth in a clean towel. When she came to help Mara finish with Rain, she touched the girl gently, almost reverently.

"You are a strong one, Rain, and old enough to bring children. You must teach your children who they are."

Without pausing, Mama handed Mara a clean towel and then brought out two pairs of soft white full-length warm underwear, new ones she had been saving. "You are God's children, and we are called to take care of you for a while. Just a while." Working patiently, without stopping, she lifted Spirit of Earth's dark gray foot from the rag rug on the floor, now wet with suds. "You are truly the Spirit of this earth we are standing on, for you were born here, and we will remember that, Sipapu," she said, now buttoning the buttons. "But you don't need to carry so much of the earth around with you."

Sipapu's eyes were softer now, her gaze changed. With everything clean, her hair slicked against her head, she looked like a newborn baby or a small otter just coming out of the water for breath. "And nobody will hurt you or take you away and sell you into bondage. We'll take care of you until Rain, here, can find herself a young buck who wants to take you both and give you a home."

At Mama's words Mara remembered Papa telling them that without an Indian man in the family, widows and their children were often left to starve. "Out of practicality," Papa had said. "They don't have the resources. They don't know the gospel like we do, either."

Once in the soft white garments, the faces of both Sipapu and Rain relaxed, almost smiled.

"Bitty," Rain said again when Mara held the dress to her. She climbed into it almost shaking with delight. Her wide face came through with a broad grin; her eyes beneath their puffed lids sparked with fire.

"Beautiful, Rain," Mara said with genuine delight. "Happy Christmas from me."

"Oh, it is almost Christmas, isn't it?" Mama said remembering and looking about the tiny cabin with a sigh. "And without Papa home. We'll have the two of you for our gifts at Christmas time." She spread Rain's skirt. Mara buttoned the dress along Rain's back. Rain stood stunned in the middle of the cabin floor, unbelieving, unable to move. She grinned. Her hands touched the dress over and over again.

"Happy Christmas from me," Mara said again.

When they were completely dressed, Mama wanted to add some old slippers of hers and Papa's for shoes. It was at that moment that Sipapu suddenly knelt on the floor and began searching for her old moccasins. Mama had taken the shredded moccasins and wrapped them in the bundle.

Sipapu searched under the table. She scraped around on the floor for a long time before Mama pulled the threads of the old moccasins out of the pack. Sipapu grabbed them quickly. She tore at one of the old laces and pushed her fingers deep inside a seam pocket close to it. She pulled out the bear's tooth she had taken from Blueflower's necklace nine months ago. Then she pulled out the bead—a lacquered thorn. She crooned over it and rubbed it in her hand. She put it in the pocket of the dress and put her hand over the pocket. Then she smiled.

Chapter Nine

Without much sugar or many candles there was no way Mama could have duplicated past Christmases, even if she had been feeling well. This year because of her persistent fever, the energy she had given to her Indian friends, the sleep she had lost at the wakeful cries of Blueflower's baby during the night, and on top of all of this, Papa's absence, she was more lifeless than Mara could ever remember her. Weak, Mama lay on her cot under the window, her back propped up on pillows. Often, she broke into small sobs, her shoulders shaking.

Mara, Sophia, and Ashel took upon themselves all of the burdens of the housekeeping. John and Sully brought the wood, milked the neighbor's cow, cared for the oxen, prepared and cured the dried meat, and cut new lumber for next spring's building. The Indians ground corn, cooked many of their own native corn and dried pemmican dishes with Mara and Sophia and spent many hours at sewing projects, working on pieces of deerskin, animal hide, or what they called "maru," even re-using some of the better pieces from their old clothes. Sipapu made a necklace of the bear's tooth for Rain and sewed the thorn on the front of her new tunic over her heart.

On Christmas Eve, John burst into the small cabin carrying a snow-covered pine bush. It filled the room with a fresh sweet odor. He shook its icy boughs. The cold air and the moistness filled Mara's lungs and she breathed deeply, remembering last year's Christmas in the valley of the Great Salt Lake.

"Can we have popcorn? Can we?" Ashel cried out, fairly dancing in the small space in the center of the room.

"Oh, I guess we've got a few kernels left of popcorn," Mama said, sitting up on the bed, smiling one of her rare smiles. She had been calling for Papa lately in her feverish sleep, still hoping he would come home for Christmas. Mara, remembering that Papa had told her to wait for him for at least five months, wasn't sure whether to worry about him or not. Sophia said he wouldn't come back in time, and they ought to have Christmas and enjoy it as much as they could. So Mama never talked about Papa if she was fully awake.

"We'll have popcorn, and then I'll tie my old ribbons in with it to make a Christmas garland!" Sophia offered gleefully. There had been a change in her countenance since she had begun to nurse the tiny orphan baby.

Mara and Ashel gathered little red berries off the bushes in the hillsides and strung them on long threads with homemade thorn needles. "I have only two needles of my own," Mama said, "until the next supply comes from Great Salt Lake. I'll let Spirit of Earth and Rain learn with them until they know how to sew themselves some new clothes."

The cold weather had brought them together for long evenings by the crackling fire when John or Sully would tell stories about Haun's Mill or Liberty Jail, or Mama would read the Book of Mormon if she had enough breath in her lungs. On this special evening before Christmas, Mara and Sophia put little cinnamon bags in all the stockings. In the morning Sipapu and Spirit of Earth held the cinnamon to their faces, breathed deeply, and would not let go. Mama had written each person a small letter on paper she had kept from Nauvoo, telling them about their ancestors, her own good father from Boston, her Grandfather Arrington, and the great-grandfather her own Papa had told her was one of the men roused up by Paul Revere to fight at the battle of Concord and Lexington.

"Now keep what I give you and show it to your own children," she told them. To Spirit of Earth and Rain, Mama gave bars of the homemade soap she had made last summer, and to John and Sully new cravats for church, sewed from an old suit.

Bishop Higbee had seen that the church room had a popcorn-decorated Christmas tree with one or two candles. The Saints held a supper on Christmas day with as much food as they could fix from the rations they allowed for themselves: dried beef and pork, jerky, puddings made of potato and honey, slabs of bacon, bits of corn cake, and finally a few plum puddings from the dried prunes they had guarded jealously from their trek across the plains.

John took Sophia on one arm and Mara on the other on his way to church. Sully and Ashel flanked Mama. Even Rain came with them, smiling shyly at people who made a fuss over her beautiful dress.

"We are blessed," Bishop Higbee said from the pulpit, his voice catching. "Our Father knows we can make a place out of this land to be an ensign to the world of nations. We will raise our children in righteousness and there is nothing we can't accomplish. Let the Indians come. They are our friends. We accept them. We want to live in peace with them. We will bear all pain but the pain of being driven again."

"Amen." The hushed agreement fell on the lips of those who heard with all the might and strength of their weariness.

"We will not be driven again," Bishop Higbee emphasized, closing his eyes in prayer. "Now we will build our cities, and our Father knows it is for the last time."

With the other young people, Mara and Ashel and Sully began caroling. They went from cabin to cabin wrapped warmly in scarves and coats, and in the snowless December cold they sang of the Savior's birth. Garth Williams accompanied them with his fiddle, the music ringing on the air. Mama said she swore she could hear the Indians come down out of the hills and stand around listening outside of the fort while the young people made their Christmas music.

"It's time to tell everyone about the Savior," she smiled wanly from her bed. "They don't know it, but they had ancestors who saw the Lord himself." Ashel wanted Mama to tell about it. Too weak, she asked John to read. In a tight circle around the hearth, John read in his rich full voice from Third Nephi.

And it came to pass, as they understood they cast their eyes up again towards heaven; and behold, they saw a Man descending out of heaven; and he was clothed in a white robe; and he came down and stood in the midst of them; and the eyes of the whole multitude were turned upon him, and they durst not open their mouths, even one to another, and wist not what it meant, for they thought it was an angel that had appeared unto them.

"He came here?" Ashel asked in wonder.

"Oh yes," Mama said, closing her eyes, propped against the big chair. "He has sheep in many folds and we are only some of them."

"The missionaries told us that!" Sophia said as she contentedly rocked back and forth with the tiny Indian baby. "You heard about that!"

"But I don't remember it," Ashel said.

"Well, you remember it now," Mama said. "Jesus came

down, maybe here on this very spot. And you take a look at Spirit of Earth and Rain, and imagine those people then were their great-great-great, many times great-grandparents. Imagine how it might have been when their ancestors sat around just like this and out of the clear sky Jesus came down, and they could feel the thorn prints on his brow and the nail prints in his hands and feet, and they could thrust their hands in his side."

"When Jesus was born, Spirit of Earth's many times great-grandmama stayed awake a whole night when there was no darkness," Sully said.

"And you look at that tiny baby boy of Blueflower's lying in Sophia's arms. Someday, to his great many times great-grandchild, and to yours standing alongside him, Jesus will come again." Mama closed her eyes and leaned back against the chair. "He will come and take us all home."

"Are you all right, Mama?" John said, rising.

"Maybe I need to lie down now," Mama said a little breathlessly. "If I could ever shake this fever I would be fine." John stood by her chair, "First I want to kneel," Mama said, "while you pray. And pray for Papa to come home soon." Slowly, using John's strong arm for support, Mama let herself fall to her knees. "And please pray that Blueflower will gather together the angels of heaven to guard her baby and that Spirit of Earth and Rain will come to love us as much as we love them. And pray for all the Indians that someday their children's children will know who they are."

John did.

In the weeks following Christmas, more Indians came into the vicinity of the fort, forced down by cold and hunger to forage for food. Knowing the settlers still had grain, they pounded on the fort gate. If the settlers refused them entry, they shouted, beat incessantly, and often shot their guns into the fort. Twice in the week after Christmas, two of the white men's cows were grazed by bullets from Indians shooting through the fort wall. Frightened, the leaders gave them two more bags of grain, but Bishop Higbee said that was absolutely all they could spare.

Spirit of Earth and Rain stayed close to the Eastman hearth and showed no signs of casting their lot with their own people on the outside. Inside the cabin, Spirit of Earth taught Rain, with Mara and Ashel looking on, how to weave a small drinking bottle out of skinned willow sticks which she called an "oush." She carefully tested each layer of twigs that moved in and out of the slender upright twigs fastened to the base. Spirit of Earth tested it by looking at it through firelight to see if there were any holes. If she found any, she pried the opening apart with a chip of bone, and placed a bit of cedar bark into it to stop it up. When the bottle was completed, she filled it with some pine pitch from the firewood, followed by hot stones which she rattled around in the bottle. The stones melted the pitch, spreading it evenly on the inside of the bottle, waterproofing it. When the pitch dried, it was shiny like glass. Everyone from the family took a drink from the bottle. The water tasted cool and fresh with a hint of pine flavoring. Spirit of Earth presented the vessel to Mama, who beamed with pleasure from her cot.

"Your Christmas," Rain told Mama when Sipapu grinned.

"Oh, you didn't need to do it," Mama said.

"Your Christmas," Rain repeated.

Often in the evenings, Rain and Mara and Ashel played the "stone in hand" game Rain had taught them. Passing a little stone from one of them to the other, someone would finally hide it in his fist. All would hold out either right or left fists and make a "one-bet" on who had the stone. A "two-bet" would mean they were guessing also on the person's other hand. Even John and Sully liked to play occasionally, or they would arm wrestle with Ashel, and with each other, making bets who would win.

For Mama, who was still ill, and for Sophia, who soon after Christmas showed signs of having caught Mama's fever, the favorite evening was filled with quiet talk in front of the fire. Mama relished sitting and closing her eyes, listening to John read the scriptures or to Spirit of Earth's soft murmuring while Rain did her best to translate into English. Sophia listened too while she nursed Blueflower's baby Sobeshent, and Mara thought of his bloodlines. Was Ivie Richards his father? Or was he the child of a dark-skinned handsome Indian brave?

"Sobeshent," Rain said. "Name of my dead brother—friend Blueflower. Brother die many moons past—tall boy. Sobeshent. Name growing green, like spring."

"Sunshine in spring," Sophia said softly to the child. He was growing plump and round on Sophia's milk which was rich despite her own illness; his little legs and arms filled out with soft nut brown flesh. "Spring. He grows in the sunshine. That's a good name for Blueflower's baby."

"Ute wrap baby tight to keep still, put dried birth cord on head." Rain translated for her mother, making a circle around her head, meaning headband. "When spring come, we made him Kan, put him outside, to breathe good air." Rain explained that "kan" was the old Piute name for the baby case, the cradle. It was made of willows and the baby stayed laced in it tightly for a long time. "Weenoonse a pope," Rain said. "The Piute fathers did this, way back to Mokis."

Rain listened as her mother spoke in her strange melodic tongue. "Sobeshent know Ute," she translated. "Like Rain brother Sobeshent born in Utes. Sipapu Piute. Hapu, Rain father, Piute. Hapu sit—friend—friend Blueflower father. We teach Sobeshent his people. Blueflower father great Ute medicine man. Sit, hear Spirit." Rain looked up for a moment and closed her eyes. Then she began telling Spirit of Earth's story again. "Sobeshent grandfather die in white man camp. Winter kill great mother. We eat mouse, snake, seeds. No more food. Winter kill. We eat white man cattle. White man kill Hinte, man of Blueflower. Kill all man."

Mara strained to understand everything Rain said. Hinte, Blueflower's man! Maybe Sobe wasn't Ivie Richards' child, then! And what did Rain mean about the great mother? And who was the great medicine man who was Sobe's grandfather? And why were Sipapu and Hapu, Piutes, living with the Utes? Mara had so many questions to ask. But she kept them to herself, waiting for a time when Rain could speak better. For now, Rain had done so well, had tried so hard to tell them what Sipapu was saying. Mara did not want the girl to think she had not done well.

Mara looked at Sophia. She was gazing at the tiny brown boy she rocked in her arms. John had told her that Sophia had begun to love the little creature in spite of herself, though there was never the same light in her eyes that there had been when she had held their own little Martha.

Only two weeks after Christmas, the Indians slaughtered two of Zeb Anderson's oxen. Ivie Richards, who had stayed with Anderson, had borrowed them to haul wood.

"They might have been our oxen," Mama Eastman gasped when she heard the news.

"No," said John, his hatred of Ivie Richards rising in him once more. "We would never have left ours in the care of Ivie Richards." He had been grateful all winter that Richards had left them alone. Since the birth of Blueflower's baby, they had hardly seen him except once or twice at church. He was probably afraid we would think he had some obligation to the child, John thought bitterly, the way he had always insisted that Blueflower had been his legal wife.

But no matter if Richards did think he was the baby's father, the baby was theirs now. His and Sophia's and Mara's. It might be the only way of saving Sophia's life. Richards and his boys had no way of nursing it, or caring for it, anyway.

"We can't deal with the Indians no more," Richards said angrily in a church meeting one Sunday late in January.

"There is no doubt they have become troublesome almost beyond endurance," Bishop Higbee said softly, taking his position at the pulpit. John knew how hard it was for Higbee, standing continually between the anger of the settlers and the ideal position of kindness and patience—and martyrdom some called it—insisted upon by Brigham Young.

"I believe we need to talk once more to Brigham Young," Miles Weaver suggested. "Getting his permission for even one small disciplinary action would likely secure our peace."

"Well spoken!" seconded Zeb Anderson, angry because of his loss.

Bishop Higbee searched the group. His eyes were quick, but in them John saw hesitation. Could he ask this group who had endured so much to endure more?

"May I say something, Brother Higbee?" It was the quiet controlled voice of Peter Conover. "We was promised that we never would have to be driven again." A murmur of agreement rippled through the crowd. Conover continued. "The Indians are spitting into our windows, shooting at us if we leave the fort but for a moment. They call us cowards and old women because we are not willing to fight. There is a point at which our women and children and ourselves can no longer bear it. Yet if we move again is there a place we can go?"

"Hear, hear. Yes." The agreement passed through the congregation. John was glad Mama Eastman had not come today, for any talk of moving caused her great discomfort.

"No, we should not be driven again, as we are promised," Bishop Higbee said quietly. "Perhaps it would be wise to get permission from Brigham Young to give the Indians the fighting they seem to want." A hush fell over the crowd; there was not a breath as the bishop spoke unevenly. "Although we may have no blessing from the Lord to guarantee that none of us shall lose our own lives. . . ."

Early on the following morning, January 31, 1850, Peter Conover and Miles Weaver left on a mission of request to the main body of Saints in the valley of the Great Salt Lake.

For days, without news of any kind, John grew morose with anxiety. There was a choking feeling among the people of the fort, a restlessness that was no longer quiet. Once they had permission to fight, they would be ready. Even Ashel felt it, and he begged John to let him practice shooting with the other young men inside the fort corral, although Mama forbade it. John had mixed feelings. In his evenings in front of the fire as he listened to Spirit of Earth and Rain, he understood the gaunt Ute people fighting their own unsuccessful bout with the winter, with vanishing game, with encroaching white settlements. He thought then that he understood Brigham Young's point of view, and he was willing to accept it, until some taunting old Indian man would creep outside past their window and throw a handful of stones against the glass, or shout his terrible sounds, or take a pot shot as John and Sully left to cut wood in the groves. And then, too, when he let himself, he would think of how it was that the Indians—their Indians—brought the dysentery into the camp that took his little Martha. But John could not allow himself to think on that. He must believe it was God's will that the little girl should be taken from this life of woe. Perhaps she was too pure for this world. And then, he knew well that white men's diseases had been killing Indian children for three hundred years.

"It isn't going to be easy," Mama said from her cot, staring vacantly into the fire. "We knew it wasn't going to be easy. As long as they bring plenty of men from the Salt Lake settlement. As long as they fight away from the fort. John and Sully, promise me. . . ."

But there was nothing anyone could promise Mama. For more than four weeks now most of the men had abandoned fields and outside activities to stay close inside the fort. Only a few of them left to gather news. Weaver and Conover were the only two who had braved a trip to the Salt Lake Valley since before Christmas. No one knew what might happen or even where the Indians were located, except that they were somehow closer now that winter had set in. And so they waited for word from Brigham Young.

They did not have to wait long. On the icy cold evening of February 8, Weaver and Conover rode into camp with George Grant from Great Salt Lake City, their big horses sweating and cloudy with steam.

"We got more'n thirty volunteers," Conover announced

to the men gathered inside the fort. "They'll be here tonight, marching around from the west side over by the river."

In not more than an hour, the settlers, straining to see past one another in the dark from the west gate, caught sight of the militia moving like shadows against the silver distance of the lake, two ox teams drawing huge Conestoga wagons, men marching, some riding ponies. By seven o'clock, they had arrived, steaming and wet from a cold rain. The women heated kettles of hot broth and fried biscuits and johnnycakes. Men rode or walked out to meet the volunteers and empty the wagons of ammunition, tools, clothing, food supplies.

John led Sophia, holding the baby tightly under a cloth, to the gate. Mara, Ashel, and Sully followed them. George Grant barked instructions while the men entered the fort or alighted from their animals whose shaggy fur was gray with ice.

"No, we didn't see none of your Indians on the way in," George Grant shouted to someone. "For us being here you can thank Cap'n Stansbury from the United States Army who needs to make a few surveys. He convinced our peace loving prophet we ought to put a stop to it all."

Amidst the snorting of weary animals, the stamping of heavy boots, the movement of the crowd to empty supplies into the dry cabins, Mara surveyed the militia and found her heart pounding rapidly. Her guess had been right. Coming toward John was Bret's father Scott Hunt, with Caleb, the son who was her own age. Caleb had grown. He was tall and slender like Bret, not massive like their father. Excitement crowded into her throat. She had thought all memories of Bret were gone, but the sight of his father and brother stirred her more than she believed possible.

"Well, Scott Hunt!" John greeted him warmly.

Hunt drew his thick shaggy gloves and took John's hand. "We meet again," he said simply, a warm smile crossing his frostbitten cheeks. Then he took Sully in his arms. "Sully, my boy. How have you been?" He released Sully and stood back from him to get a good look. His light shaggy hair crowded into his eyes from beneath the large white-winged felt hat on his head. His blue eyes scanned Sully, a long, fond look. Then he saw Mara, Sophia, and Ashel. He smiled and nodded to them.

"It's good to see you all well. Your mother?"

"Mother's ill," John said. "She's in the cabin."

A look of concern crossed his face. "I'm so sorry," he said. "Have you heard from Hart?"

"No, no word yet."

"Well, it's slow getting news from the East, you know," Scott Hunt's eyes narrowed and he smiled into John's face, without conviction Mara thought. "Well, John," he said turning to Sophia. "Congratulations! Let's see your child! He took hold of a corner of the baby's blanket and peered into it. Sophia held the baby slightly away from her body.

"Our . . . our baby Martha became ill," John said hesitantly, "and passed away."

Scott Hunt's smile faded. He drew his hand away from the shock of Sobe's black hair. "No! I'm so sorry." He raised his bright blue eyes. "Oh, I'm so sorry."

"This is the Indian maiden's child . . . Blueflower. She died."

Not a muscle in Hunt's face moved. But in his eyes there was something. . . . He stared at the child, at John. "Yes," he said slowly. "I remember Blueflower." Mara felt a sudden pain. Scott Hunt's eyes glazed over. She felt that a moment from the past was repeating itself: her first sight of Blueflower, the argument of Scott

Hunt and Ivie Richards, and finally Blueflower's bleeding face.

As well as Caleb, another man seemed to be with Brother Hunt, a tall thin spectacled man in a charcoal gray walking coat and shiny leather gloves. On his head was a stately dark hat, finely made, now soggy with rain.

"Meet Dr. Blake," Brother Hunt indicated with a nod of his head. "One of Captain Stansbury's men who'll do medical service with the militia."

Dr. Blake drew one of his gloves and held out his hand. "Glad to meet you, Mr. Smith."

"A medical man from Washington," John said hospitably.

"Sully, our good friend who lived with us for several years," Scott Hunt said turning to Sully, "now wants to settle on his own here at Provost's Hole."

"Glad to meet you, Sully."

"Sophia, John's wife. Mara, her sister. Her brother, Ashel."

"Of course you'll stay with us," John said.

Mara caught her breath. Where on earth would they put him? John was as bad as Mama.

"We'll be glad to," Scott Hunt said. All of them? Mara thought she wouldn't mind sharing their cabin with Bret's father and brother, but. . . .

"I think there would be room" John hesitated. Sophia glared at him.

"Well, we just need space enough to stretch out on the floor," Brother Hunt smiled, "and we thank you for your hospitality."

Just as the men entered the cabin, Mama rose from the bed, clutching her heavy robe tightly about her shoulders. Seeing her guests, her face lit up.

"Captain Hunt," she shook his big hand warmly, her eyes brighter than Mara had seen them since Papa left.

"Martha," Brother Hunt smiled and came to her, took her hands in his.

Mara watched him, remembering how much her family had admired Scott Hunt and his family in the Salt Lake Valley. She looked at Caleb, standing with Sully by the door. He was taller, not the gawky fifteen-year-old she remembered. He looked so much like Bret it took her breath. Everything was settled, happy. Why was she so excited to see the Hunts?

"If we had only come for a pleasant visit, instead of an uprising," Hunt was saying. At that instant he saw Spirit of Earth and Rain huddled in the corner.

"Our Indians," Mama began.

"Still with you," Hunt stared first at them, then at Mama. "You're charitable people," he said.

"Blueflower is no longer with us."

"I explained," John nodded.

"The Indians took the old grandmother and the young woman and her baby. . . ." Mama said. "And Rain tells us . . . Angel Lip's baby was killed. . . ."

"Mama, please," begged Sophia. Mara knew how much it hurt Sophia that the Indian baby had been killed. She had cried out that nothing must happen to her baby.

The next two hours were filled with catching up on news as they ate hot biscuits and broth. Dr. Blake sat quietly listening, and Mama put on her best grammar for the eastern visitor. That night on the cot Ashel slept with John, Sophia and Sobe (Sobe was their short name for Sobeshent), and Mara with Mama in the big bed. Scott Hunt and Caleb, Dr. Blake, and Sully stretched out on bedding on the floor. Not an inch of floor space was unoccupied.

Tingling with excitement in the full room, Mara could not close her eyes. She lay awake for a long time listening to the silent sleet against the roof, feeling the breath and the heat of bodies in the crowded space. "And tomorrow we'll stop them," Scott Hunt had said calmly about the Indians. Mara remembered being fascinated with the size of his hands, which he folded and unfolded in front of him as he leaned into the fire, his elbows resting on the tight deerskin breeches stretched over his large knees. She found her memories of Bret rising in her more clearly than they had for months. The excitement of that one foolish night thrilled her once again. She loved John. She was sure of that. He filled her with a confidence and joy she had not felt with Bret. Yet, it was with John something like she had imagined it would have been with Bret.

Sully teased her unmercifully, and more and more bitterly as time passed. "A strange woman who'll take half a man when she could have a whole." And she had to admit that often, when she watched John and Sophia together, her heart would sink with a deep longing and need. But the alternative had always been Sully.

Now she thought about Bret. He had been gone almost a year on his mission. He would be returning . . . someday. But she had never heard from him. "Bret is doing well with Uncle Jeb," Scott Hunt said at Mama's questions. "Bret is doing very well." Mara had looked from John to Scott Hunt and back again. And Mama looked at her. As much as Mama had warned her to keep from thinking about Bret, she wondered if Mama really did want her to marry John. Marrying John would cut her off from Bret forever. And someday Bret would be like his father.

She admired the man Scott Hunt, whose presence filled the room, even in sleep. He was large. Larger even than her father, larger than Ivie Richards. But solid and clean. Now Mara lay trying to distinguish his breathing in the dark. She could make out the sounds of her family, of John, of Sully, sounds she had heard every night for so long. She listened carefully to everyone in the room. It was Dr. Blake who snored, but with a light wheezing sound. He had been strangely curious about Mormons, and about Indians. Mara felt like some sort of specimen under his questions. Especially his questions about "polygamy."

Scott Hunt's visit brought Mara not only painful memories of Bret that clouded the view of her marriage with John, but also memories of her home in Great Salt Lake City, a home she had in less than two years come to love. She suddenly felt trapped here as though she had lived and breathed Fort Utah so long that she could no longer remember the city, the people she had known, the large houses built with glass and with stairwells, or the beginning of Brigham Young's beautiful houses and Scott Hunt's two-story farmhouse on the southeast Main Street. She remembered Nauvoo, the city streets, the imposing homes and stores, the temple lot. She remembered what it had been like to have curtains at the windows, plush furniture, carpet. It would be like that soon in Great Salt Lake City. But here, in the barren wasteland of this Indian country, would anything ever be beautiful, civilized? Was she grasping at John for some way out, for some joy in the bleakness? Was she falling into his life to escape her fear of Ivie Richards, her annoyance at Sully Tuttle? John was good, kind. And she knew she loved him. But was life in the covenant what she really wanted?

All this she wondered in her crowded heart in the darkness of the cabin. What should she do? Turning uncomfortably in the bed beside Mama, she listened to the faraway crow of a cock and felt the mute sun begin its climb over the hills. For a while she drifted into a restless sleep.

The day began with the unexpected blat of an old tin bugle, a bawling noise that woke everybody.

"You're not going, Ashel," Mama said out loud, as soon as the horn sounded. "You're staying right here."

Ashel was creeping about the cabin with his shoes in his hands. "Caleb's going."

"You're not going."

The morning buzzed with excitement as the militia prepared to move. After a short breakfast of bacon and bread, they mounted quickly, thirty-one militia, fifteen men from the fort, all armed with muskets, rifles, and ammunition.

John took time to tell the women good-bye. "Take care, Sophia," he instructed as he kissed her. He kissed Mama, too. As he led Sequel away from the cabin toward the east gate, Mara and Ashel followed him. Before he mounted he turned to Mara. She was looking at him, and he must have seen the confusion in her eyes, left over from her sleepless night.

"I'll kiss you too, Mara," he smiled warmly, as though joking with her. "After all, we're betrothed, and the whole fort knows it." He paused. As he leaned toward her to take her face in his hand, she caught herself drawing away slightly. "Aren't we?" He looked deeply into her eyes now. There was no time for questions. Mara did not say anything. Her heart turned over. She tried to smile. His lips neared hers in a warm sweeping motion. Then he caught her mouth and steadied her face with his hand. "I love you, Mara," he said so quietly no one but Mara could hear. "When the Indians are no longer a problem I'll take you and Sophia to our place." Mara shook her head slightly. "No, John, please don't worry about me."

As he mounted Sequel, John gazed down at her. "Good-bye," John told Mara and Ashel and turned away.

Mara watched him as he urged Sequel to move. The men gathering in the group outside the east gates calmed their animals which were stamping and snorting in clouds of steam. Though there was no rain, billowing white clouds settled along the tops of the mountains, forming a shadow that hung over the valley for miles.

Mara, Nancy, and Hannah, along with Ashel and most of the other young people, stood outside the east gate until the men left for the hills.

John turned on his horse, staring at Mara until she was almost out of sight. He had been puzzled by the look in her eyes. He turned forward in the saddle and breathed the morning air deeply. There would be time for Mara when Papa returned and they could marry. Someday he would build a house for her. He turned his eyes upward toward the grassy meadows. Eight months here and he loved this valley with its formidable mountains, its laughing rivers. He would have many happy children here in these hills.

At the bend of the frozen river, as it turned north to wind its way into the canyon, a smoky thread twisted and curved through the gray trees.

"I believe it's Indians," Conover said. "They was here when we went up."

On the opposite side of the ice-clogged river, James Bean's abandoned cabin hid in the winter woods, smoke rising from the chimney.

"First we talk," George Grant gave command. They raised a white shirt on a rifle and moved steadily toward the riverbank.

"Halloo!" Peter Conover shouted.

Not a sound was returned. But John could see the outline of a dark face in the front window. Then several dark faces.

"I knew there was a lot here camping at one time." James Bean's voice was soleful, resigned. He stared at the home he had been so proud of.

Except for the sound of a few horses stamping and snorting, the militia was quiet, their eyes steady on the small house.

"Halloo!" George Grant shouted a second time. Now John could see heads bobbing in the windows. The door of the cabin opened slightly. The old chief Ope Carry appeared, his eyes dark with suspicion. He turned back into the room and with a gesture of his head beckoned the men behind him to follow. Dressed in warm skins and with leatherbound feet, two or three men emerged slowly, bows and arrows in their hands.

"Tell them we want to talk," John Higbee said to Dimick Huntington. Huntington spoke to Ope Carry, who returned his short answers, difficult to hear, the expression on his face unchanging.

Huntington turned to Higbee. "He says they've talked enough. They want the man who killed Old Bishop. I told him that would be no good, two men dead instead of one. He said then there will be more who die."

"Tell them we want peace, Dimick, we must have peace," Higbee was pleading now.

"No justice, no peace," Ope Carry said in English.

For a moment the morning was dead quiet, then John heard a sudden zing as an arrow shot across the river. Ope Carry turned on his horse and shouted a string of what must have been Ute curses. A horse in the militia reared. A rifle was fired. John turned. Behind him several men raised their guns. He turned back. The Indians scrambled into James Bean's cabin. Negotiations over, Huntington drew back his horse. The animal nearly stumbled with the quick movement of the tight reins. Huntington's face blanched as he swore.

"No choice," George Grant shouted. "Then fire!" The militia let go. A volley of shots left smoking rifles as a rain of ammunition fell in James Bean's windows, on his walls.

The men, feeling the pent-up anger of their persecutions, fell into the smoke with fury. Full of despair, John gazed about him, confused. Indian arrows rang from inside the cabin walls, crossed the river with deadly speed. Then rifles sounded. Around him, John saw men spring from their horses. One or two fell. One of the Wheeler boys was shot in the belly. He doubled over in pain.

George Grant began to scream. The Indians inside the house had too much advantage. "Back. Back!" His words were muffled in the painful sounds of wounded and outraged men.

John leapt from Sequel to kneel beside the Wheeler boy. "You hurt awful bad? We can take you back with us." John lifted the limp body into his arms. Then he was aware of noise—a singing noise that took him by surprise, and a terrible thud against his back. It threw him off balance. And then he felt the pain below his left shoulder blade. A strange sudden nausea swam upward and blurred his eyes. "Oh dear God," he said aloud. He was aware of shouting and rough hands, the movement of an animal beneath him. And then nothing. Blackness.

Voices, sobbing, shouting, warmth, a fire, the unbearable pain. When John awoke he saw Sophia bending over him, the tears choking her voice. "Oh, he's awake!" He's coming out of it. Mother!" she almost screamed.

"John, oh my darling." He felt Sophia's fingers on his face.

"Sophia?" He could see her clearly now. And someone else.

"We're going to get them, John. We're going to get

them tomorrow." It was Sully, his voice sounding far away. Someone else was wringing rags stanched with blood. His blood? Mara. The pain surrounded him, and he closed his eyes again.

All that afternoon and into the night Sully helped build the movable fortress. They cut and scraped heavy logs and tied them into a buttressed V-shaped wedge. They tacked blankets to the inside surface to protect them from shots that might penetrate the wood.

In the night, Sully sat with the Eastmans as they watched over John. Captain Hunt and Dr. Blake came to eat, and then later, in the middle of the night, to get some sleep. All night long there were groups gathered in the center of the fort, talking, planning. The Wheeler boy was dead. As the sky grew gray from the early light of dawn, Sully dozed.

The soft moan of pain from John's lips woke him. Sophia and Sister Eastman stood over him. Mara looked on from her seat by the hearth. She had not gone to him when they brought him in. He had barely recognized Sophia.

Sully had nothing against John Smith. He was a good and fair man—except perhaps in this one matter of thinking himself a fit husband for Mara when he already had one perfectly good wife. But Mara's intentions to become a plural wife were failing, Sully could see that. He would wait as he had for so long. He would be patient. Mara needed to be loved by a man who could love her with all his soul, with no holding back and no place else to give himself. Only he, Sully Tuttle, loved her like that. Not John, not Ivie Richards, not even Bret Hunt. He would wait. She would come around.

"It doesn't look good." It was Dr. Blake talking as he saw to John's wound. Sophia covered her face with her hands. Mara turned to the fire. Sully could not see her face.

"They ought to be killed," Captain Hunt said.

"Exterminated is the word," Dr. Blake agreed.

"It's what they seem to want." Captain Hunt turned and walked out of the cabin, Dr. Blake on his heels. Sully followed them.

The February cold hung over the valley in loose foggy clouds. At eight o'clock the militia could barely see the Indians in Bean's abandoned home. Slowly the sun warmed the fog away.

At about nine o'clock George Grant ordered the Indians to come out peacefully or be killed. Only a few moments after that the first arrows zinged overhead. Grant ordered "Charge!" They charged this time and came down on the house with fury, shooting and shouting. Sully, Scott Hunt, Dr. Blake, Caleb, Brother Anderson, and some of the others lifted the wooden fortress in front of them and moved toward the house steadily, unharmed. Rifle shots flared all around them, penetrating the wood, sometimes hitting through to the wool blankets inside the wood shield, then dropping to the ground.

Sully dared not look from his position behind the moving shield. His heart beat wildly in his chest.

"Take them!" Scott Hunt said, cocking his rifle. "Forward!"

Sully helped carry the wedge forward. Then they crouched behind it, ducked, shot over it, and ducked again. One of the horses had rolled into the cabin, blood spilling from its throat. They shot into the windows of the cabin. Several Indians were hit. Some of the other settlers had neared the house and were shooting inside the door.

"Ahh-hh-hh." Sully heard bloodcurdling screams. They came from the direction of the Indian Big Elk. He was crying like a child, waving his arms madly, trying to get the notice of the other Indians. The Indians were running. Sully stopped firing. He watched amazed as the Indians scrambled outside the house waving their arms furiously as though they would protect themselves with their hands. There had been more than twenty-five of them in the small house, not counting those who had been killed.

"After them!" George Grant screamed. Arrows still flew wildly through the air. Before they retreated, the Indians kept shooting while one or two of them knelt to the dead horses sprawled out on the ice or in front of the cabin and quickly carved large chunks of meat from the flanks and thighs. "Take them all," George Grant shouted from behind the fortress. He ducked just as an arrow grazed his cheek. Another Indian fell. Then another.

"They're trying to ambush us from behind!" Scott Hunt shouted. One group of Indians ran toward the lake, another group separated from them and headed for the canyon to the east.

"Divide the militia!" Grant shouted. "Abandon the fortress! Follow them."

Sully came from behind the wedge now, cautiously. Hunt sprang ahead of him, Caleb following. They sprinted across the frozen ground behind the Indians, who escaped with amazing speed.

"If we don't get them, they'll never leave us alone!" Grant shouted, following Sully, Hunt, and Blake. About fifteen others with them tore down into the gray fields. The rest followed the group into the hills.

Sully caught sight of Ivie Richards and his boys pounding down behind him. "Hiyee!" Richards shouted noisily. He was enjoying the chase.

From bushes or clumps of trees Sully often heard the sounds of hiding Indians. He stayed close to other trees, or he crawled on the ground.

After about an hour they reached the trees standing by the lake, and through the trees they could see the vast open ice that lay for miles like a silver sheet.

"We'll get 'em at the lake," George Grant said softly from behind Sully in the bushes. The sun glowed faintly.

"Don't go out there very far, just shoot from shore," George Grant cried out to Tony Richards, who lumbered toward the Indian who had fallen as though dead on the cold ice. But it was too late. Reaching the Indian humped over on the ice who lay on his belly as though in great pain, Tony stood over him. Very much alive, the Indian raised his body on his elbow, drew his bow, and shot Tony Richards in the bowels. The boy lowered his rifle and shot the Indian in the neck. The Indian dropped his bow. His hands loosened suddenly like limp claws, and he fell back against the ice, blood spurting from his mouth.

Then Tony Richards wavered. His body leaned unsteadily on wooden legs. Blood began to soak his clothes. Ivie Richards screamed and tore to him. Tony rocked forward; then he doubled over, and fell. He was dead. The Indians have the man they wanted now, Sully thought, stunned. It should be all over now.

With a terrible fury Richards and Clem sped across the gray ice chasing other Indians who slipped away. Sully, Blake, Hunt, the others, followed them. The shots rang out against the bleak gray hills on the other side of the lake like the clattering of pebbles thrown into a deep well.

"We're getting them all!" Grant shouted, his raised rifle cutting them down one after another as the brown figures slipped and scurried on the ice. One after another, like decoys in the distance, they fell. Sully raised his gun, shot. Loaded. Shot again. Every time he aimed, a brown figure fell. He thought of John Smith, of his farm, of Mara. He shot again. He would make this place safe for her.

Sully stayed close to the lakeside, his gun smoking, his ammunition spent. He watched Hunt and Grant and some of the others move toward him now across the frozen water. Sully began to breathe evenly. A wave, almost a shudder passed through his body. For the first time since they left the fort this morning, he realized it was cold. He drew his collar around his neck. The afternoon light reflecting from the lake flashed in his eyes, blinding him. A heavy blackbird or duck swooped into a clump of trees. The men continued walking toward him, their faces shadowy beneath the setting sun. Richards carried Tony in his arms, lurching, stumbling forward. As they neared, Sully heard the murmur in their voices. He felt strangely apart from them, apart from the lake, the trees, apart from everything that had happened in the past two days. The bodies of the Indians scattered across the lake seemed so silent, so finally silent. Sully followed Hunt and Blake back to the fort just as the sun slipped into the yawning darkness of the western mountains. They had killed them all. Every single one of the Indians was dead.

The Wheeler boy and Tony Richards were the only ones killed among the settlers. No one was killed at the canyon where the others had chased the group of Indians into the hills. That was not many killed, they said, considering the circumstances. Of course there were the six wounded—including John Smith.

Sully heard the crying before the men came to the door and Sister Eastman let them in. John lay on the cot under the window, Sophia kneeling beside him, her head on his chest, her arms around him. She was sobbing. Sister Eastman stared at the men and choked the words. "He's dead."

A lump rose to stop the air in Sully's throat. He looked at Mara, who stood at the hearth with Spirit of Earth and Rain. Her hands were clutched in front of her, the knuckles white, her face white, too. There were tears in her eyes. She didn't see Sully. She looked like she saw nothing. Had she loved him? Sully wondered.

No one said a word. Captain Hunt came to John, took his hand. Dr. Blake followed, checking the pulse, feeling the brow. John's body lay silent.

"No," Hunt murmured, shaking his head. "Oh, no."

Sophia's sobbing was the only sound in the room.

Then Captain Hunt spoke again. "Do you have his clothing?" Sister Eastman nodded, her eyes wide with anguish and pain. "Dress him now, set him outside. It won't be good in the morning."

But Sister Eastman gestured toward Spirit of Earth and Rain. "They rubbed him with herbs." She sounded hesitant, questioning. Sophia clung to John's hand.

For a moment Hunt was quiet. "But that can't last long." He paused. "Outside is best. They're planning to bury the others in the morning." Sister Eastman's face was a question. "The Wheeler boy and Tony Richards. He was killed at the lake."

Sophia lay shaking over John. "Don't take him away. Don't take him away."

Sully, still watching Mara, saw her turn away, her head down. Her hands went to her face. Her shoulders shook. He wanted to go to her, to comfort her, but he was afraid. No one paid any attention to her. Sister Eastman held Sophia while Hunt and Dr. Blake dressed John.

"We won't leave you until it's taken care of," Captain Hunt was saying to Sister Eastman, who looked at him with eyes full of grief.

As they finished their task of preparing the body, Sophia again threw herself over her dead husband.

"He's not there, my darling. He's gone with Martha," Sister Eastman said, trying to hold Sophia back. "Let us take him outside."

"But I need him," Sophia said, her voice weak in her throat. "I won't leave him!"

"He'll be loved and needed in heaven. . . ." But Sister Eastman choked on the words.

Chapter Ten

"I'll be going with Stansbury for a couple of weeks . . . to finish out the survey," Dr. Blake was saying. "If I had help . . . I could probably finish up before Stansbury's party gets here tomorrow."

"We'll be leaving tomorrow ourselves," Captain Hunt said. "I've got to get things ready here, but Caleb . . . and maybe Sully. . . ."

The voices of the men in the room rose and fell. Sully heard them as though they were far away. He watched Mara, who was sitting by the fire, her eyes staring, her face white. He longed to take her in his arms, to comfort her, to touch her cheek. . . . But she sat so still. He could only send his heart out to her, love her with his eyes. He thought, once in a while when she looked at him, that she was grateful. He knew she could see the love in his eyes.

The sound of his name on Sister Eastman's lips startled him. "Not Sully! You wouldn't take Sully away? Not now! He's all we've got now."

"Me, Mama," Ashel said, standing at his mother's side.

"And Ashel, oh, my darling," she said, drawing the boy to her. "Yes, you."

"What about it, Tuttle? Want to go with me and take some of them Indian specimens back to the Institute?" Sully became aware that Dr. Blake was speaking to him.

"You wouldn't be gone long. Not long." Blake looked at Sister Eastman.

Sully stared for a moment at Dr. Blake. He looked like a big rat, a wiry gray moustache on his lip. "What?" Sully asked, not sure what he had heard.

"The Institute, in Washington, D.C. They want a scientific study done, and they will pay handsome for the skulls of Indians from this part of the country." Dr. Blake's moustache twitched when he talked.

"A study?" Sully did not understand.

Captain Hunt spoke then. "On these Ute Indians, son. You and Caleb can help Dr. Blake with his specimens. We can jimmy a sledge out of the shot-up wedge. . . . I'll get these ready here. We can leave when you get back. You can decide whether you want to go with Dr. Blake to Washington or not." He turned to Sister Eastman. "Martha, won't you try to think of coming with us? It's not safe here, for you, and the girls and Ashel and the baby. I know it's hard for you to think of going, but we'd be pleased to have you. Come, just until Hart comes home. With John gone, and if Sully goes with. . . ."

Captain Hunt stopped at the sound of Sophia's sobs which broke out again from behind the curtain in the corner. She had been quiet since they had carried her away from John's body and brought her into the house. His body and those of the Wheeler boy and Tony Richards were laid in the center of the fort beneath the awful cannon. Thinking of John made Sully's head throb. A good man, a good friend. Mara would never have married him.

Sully could hear Sophia fighting her sobs. He looked at Sister Eastman, her eyes wide and dry. "I don't know," she said, shaking her head. "I don't know. Perhaps we *should* go, but. . . ." She stared past Captain Hunt, looking at nothing, her face gray, tired. "I'm tired of going. . . ." she

"Hart's letters will come here," she said from what seemed far away. Captain Hunt rubbed his hand across his face. "Think about it," he said. He walked to the door of the cabin and went out.

Sully's head felt thick. I won't leave you, Sister Eastman. You can count on me, he wanted to say. But he couldn't make his voice work. It seemed to belong to someone else. And he hadn't been listening well. What was he supposed to do? Help Dr. Blake? Go to Washington, D.C.? What was it? Would Captain Hunt take the Eastmans to Salt Lake City? Take Mara? He looked at Mara once more. She was looking at him, but she turned quickly away. She *had* been looking at him! A slow excitement pounded deep inside him again. If only Mara would come after him. He would get up, walk out the door, and she would come after him. He would hold her, stroke her hair, love her. She stood looking into the fire, her back to him. Sophia's sobbing broke into moans now, long painful cries that tore Sully's heart. He felt crowded, helpless, confused. He wanted to get out of the small cabin, full of the sounds of Sophia's cries. Why didn't Mara look at him? Why did she turn from him when he had so much to give? What stood in the way now? Not her grief for John. She hadn't loved John like Sophia had. It would be proper for her to come to him now. It would be all right. But Mara did not turn to look at him again. Please, please, Mara. Come to me. Sully stood, went to the door. Still Mara did not look at him, did not come to him. He opened the door and went out into the cold night alone.

Sully walked a long time in the dark. When he came back to the cabin they were all asleep: Captain Hunt, Caleb, Dr. Blake, Sister Eastman, and Sobe. Mara was behind the curtain with Sophia. Sully lay down on his mat by the door and closed his eyes.

He woke to the sound of hammering. Everyone else still slept. Sully rubbed his eyes and got up. He was tired. His short, restless sleep had been filled with bad dreams. He went outside. In the cold gray light from the moon, Dr. Blake was just finishing with the sledge. "Give a hand here, boy!" Blake called to Sully in a loud whisper as Sully closed the cabin door behind him. He was trying to tie the makeshift sledge to his shaggy horse. Sully helped.

"Now," said Dr. Blake, "let's see if this thing goes." And he urged the animal forward. "Yes, that should slide along the ice all right."

Caleb came up behind Sully and handed him a hunk of dry bread. His voice was sleepy. "Pa says you better eat this, Sully."

"You ready to go, boys?" Dr. Blake had mounted his horse. Sully followed Caleb to their ponies. He was so tired. It was hard to climb into the saddle. Riding behind Dr. Blake in the darkness, Sully chewed on the bread. "Stansbury ought to be here by midmorning. I got to be ready by then," Dr. Blake said. Dr. Blake talked, but Sully didn't listen to what he said. His head ached. Caleb rode in silence beside him.

Dr. Blake talked and Sully thought of Mara. He had listened for her from his mat. He thought he could hear Sophia crying. He heard no sound from Mara but her quiet breathing and, once, a deep sigh. He dreamt of John, smiling, strong, standing with Mara by his side. He dreamt of John's cold dead body, Sophia sobbing on its chest. Sully shook his head, but the memories of his night's dreams would not go away. They swam in his head in the cold moonlight.

The dark shadow of Dr. Blake with the sledge moved out onto the slick ice. The lake glowed and faded in the moonlight as clouds moved across the sky. Sully thought about being on the earth in the shadow of the sun. It reminded him of the only conversation with his mother he could ever remember: he had asked her which was more important, the sun or the moon, and where did the earth come in? And she said "Can you say who is more important, day or night, Mother or Father?" The lights were equally important, one for night and one for day. As for the earth: she said the sun could do no virtue to itself. If the rays of sun never stirred the ground in the earth, nothing would happen. One was not greater than the other. There must be a connection. . . .

Sully felt his horse's hoof strike the ice. Connections. "Mara," he said softly to himself. He pulled on the reins and the hoof slipped back onto the rocky shore. Dr. Blake dismounted and led his horse along until the sledge was beside a dark heap on the ice. Sully could just make out the Indian. From where it lay, it could be the one that killed Tony Richards. Sully dismounted, Caleb beside him. Dr. Blake was stepping carefully towards the dead man.

"Come along, boys!" Dr. Blake called as he drew a long knife from his belt and knelt on the ice. Caleb stepped out onto the lake. Sully followed. Dr. Blake raised his knife over the head. The Indian lay in his frozen blood on the ice. As Sully drew even with the sledge, Dr. Blake plunged the knife into the Indian's neck. Sully saw it, but it seemed far away, like part of his dreams. He shook his head. There were dark stains on Dr. Blake's knife and hands. Sully heard Caleb speaking beside him in a tight, sick voice. "It's all right, Sully. Pa says . . . it's . . . for a . . . study." Sully stared at Dr. Blake's bloody hands.

"Get me the file!" Blake shouted at them. "We'll need it on the bone. Come on, give a hand!"

Caleb didn't move. Sully heard himself speaking. "You can't do it like that. I'll do it." He moved forward, swallowing the nausea that suddenly filled his throat, made his eyes swim. Sully reached into the sledge and grabbed the ax. His head was clearer now. He told Blake to move.

"It will take all day that way," Sully said. "Let's get this done." He swung the ax down, the bone cracked, and the head fell off. The head rolled onto its side, the open eyes staring across the shadowy ice. Caleb ran, retching, slipping on the ice, to the shore.

They worked until dawn. As dawn broke, Sully still swung the ax, thinking of nothing, his head clear, feeling empty, his body not tired anymore. Caleb helped now, holding the dark heads with his knee, or under his boot while Sully swung the ax through the air and down with perfect aim. Twenty-eight, twenty-nine, thirty. Dr. Blake counted them. They collected more than thirty heads. Sully felt the energy in his blood. He did not know how long they had been there. There was no time. He felt powerful, almost elated, his frustration and confusion gone, his bad dreams floating out of him into the cold morning.

Dr. Blake picked up each head, looked at it, turned it over in his hands. He tossed them into the big canvas sacks like cabbages. The sun rose. The ducks and gulls swarmed upon the blood as it thawed in the sun. Like vultures they swarmed, cawing, screaming, beating their wings.

"You know, I could hit good in my time," Dr. Blake shouted to the boys. He grabbed his shotgun, raised it, and dropped a black mallard with one clean crack. With a cry the duck folded its wings, doubled, fell in a heap of feathers on the ice.

"Fine old bird," Blake said, his wire whiskers twitching. "Fine old duck," and he lifted the body high enough to inspect it. "Once I could break its neck," he said, and shot again. This time the spot against the sky hurtled to the ice, its neck split.

"Now looky that! You can't beat that, boys!" he smiled.

Caleb raised his gun this time. Once. Twice. On the third shot a heap of brown and blue feathers turned and rolled crashing to the surface of the lake. Another one. Four, five, six. Ten.

"Wonderful!" Blake shouted, hauling the ducks one at a time to the sledge and tossing them in on top of the heads. Blake's shaggy horse stamped, pawed the ice, and strained to tug the load on the sledge. It stuck, slipped, then struck an uneven break in the ice, lurched forward. At the shore, Blake led the horse slowly up off the ice. The sledge strained, moving hard along the rocky slope. As they reached higher ground the wood pulled apart where the nails had split it. One of the sacks of heads at the edge slid, the top opening.

"Get me the ax again," Blake ordered. He pounded at the nails with the heel of the ax, but they split the wood apart; the weight of the load pulled the sledge apart. The sacks of heads and ducks rolled to the ground. Blake stood up, his eyebrows knit above his black eyes. His fingers rubbed the gray stubbled chin. "I can't waste time here," he said. "Stansbury'll be in camp today. I need to go with the survey. Can you get them in crates and bring them to me? When I get back to Salt Lake City? In a week or so?" Sully's head was heavy again, as though the weight of all this death pressed down on his brain. Dr. Blake's voice sounded strange to him; it seemed to come from half a mile away. "You know the place. The big hotel."

"I'll . . . I'll already be there. We're going back today." Caleb sounded uneasy. "But Sully . . . what about you, Sully?"

Sully nodded his head, his heavy tired head, saying nothing. "Let's leave 'em, then. Pick 'em up at your convenience," Dr. Blake said, and with the ax he chopped the rope cleanly, mounted his horse, and began to ride away. "You can decide about coming with me to Washington, Tuttle," he called back over his shoulder. "I could use you."

Caleb followed Dr. Blake. Sully, dizzy, mounted and gazed at the sledge full of bags of heads, dead ducks, blood. He stared, not thinking. Then he turned his horse around and rode toward the fort.

When they reached camp, Stansbury and the survey party were already there. There was a commotion of loaded wagons. Several of the fort families were leaving. The Wrights—Hannah with her mother, father, younger brothers and sisters. The Andersons, the Carmans. They had given it up here. Sully was not surprised at the families who were leaving. He knew Hannah for one who thought she was too good to be here. Not like Mara. Not brave. Not strong like Mara. Mara wouldn't go. Even if Captain Hunt *could* persuade Sister Eastman. . . .

Sully's whole body ached. He wanted to lie down, to lay his head in Mara's lap. He wanted to feel her hand on his forehead. He rode with Caleb past loaded wagons to find Captain Hunt. Mara might be here somewhere, waiting to say good-bye to Hannah. . . .

Mara! Sully saw her, sitting on the front board of Captain Hunt's big wagon, a blue bundle in her arms. She did not look at him. Ashel stood beside the wagon. Captain Hunt rode up on his big mare. "You got back just in time, boys," he said. "We're about ready to roll out. Caleb, ride over to Bishop Higbee and get the letters he wanted me to take, will you?"

Sully stared at Mara. She turned at the sound of Scott Hunt's voice, saw Sully, looked at him with blank red eyes, not smiling, and turned away again. "I'm taking her and the baby home with me, son." Captain Hunt was speaking to him, his voice low. "I wasn't able to persuade

Sister Eastman to go. . . ." Sully stared at Mara. "As heaven is my witness I tried my best, but I guess Sophia's going like that. . . ." Sully turned his heavy head to Captain Hunt, opened his mouth to speak. Sophia?

"I'm sorry, son. I'd forgotten you didn't know. We found her this morning . . . she had frozen . . . no one heard her . . . she went outside the cabin to John in the night. . . ." Captain Hunt took off his big hat and ran his hand through his hair.

Sophia dead! Sophia, too! Sully looked up at Mara, sitting so still, hunched over the baby, her eyes half closed.

"Sully." As he heard his name, Sully looked into Captain Hunt's eyes. "Sister Eastman is beside herself. She won't leave. This is the way she wants it, and there's nothing else I can do. Ashel will stay with her, and the Allens will be next door. But she'll need you, Sully. She'll need a man in case of . . . these Indians are not finished yet, my boy. You know that. Will you look out for Sister Eastman, my boy?" Sully looked at Captain Hunt, but he could not make a sound come from his throat.

"She likely won't notice you much for a while. Won't talk. Won't move." Captain Hunt shook his head. "She's fond of you, son. If she could count on you . . . if you would look after her. . . . When she is ready to be among folks again, the Allens will bring her to Salt Lake City." Captain Hunt looked across the fort enclosure toward the Eastman cabin. "She's in a bad way, Sully. I wouldn't take Mara away from her like this, but with Sophia gone, there is no one to nurse the baby. My youngest wife Kate. . . ."

Sully's heart fell into a dark emptiness. He looked at Mara on the wagon seat. But I can take care of her. I can keep her safe, he said, but only to himself.

"Don't say anything to Mara just now, son." Captain Hunt reached out and put his hand on Sully's shoulder. "She's. . . . I'm taking her with me for a while."

Sully stared into the cold morning. Captain Hunt rode to the rear of the wagon where Caleb was tying his horse. He took the letters Caleb had brought from Bishop Higbee and put them into his coat. Caleb climbed to the driver's seat next to Mara.

"Caleb tells me you'll be coming up for Dr. Blake soon." Scott Hunt reached out and took Sully's hand between his big leather gloves. "We'll be looking for you. It's always good to have you home, son." He clapped Sully on the back. "Good-bye, my boy," he said. Still Sully could not speak. "Martha will be all right. Just stay with her for a while. Help Ashel keep the fire going. The Allens will bring in food. When she's ready, they'll bring her up. We'll all be together up home before long."

Captain Hunt waved his hand and rode away. "Move 'em out, Caleb!" he called over his shoulder. Caleb slapped the reins and the wagon began to roll.

Sully stared after them: Scott Hunt in his big fur coat, the wagon as Caleb drove it north, away from the east gate. Caleb turned to wave to Sully. Mara did not look back.

"See you before long with the spoils, eh boy?" It was Dr. Blake, shouting to him as he rode to join Stansbury's survey party, headed southward.

All around, people were still saying good-bye, stomping snow from their boots, shouting good wishes to one another.

"Oh, how I'll miss them!" Nancy Allen stood beside Sully, holding to the bridle of his horse. She waved to Hannah as the Wrights' wagon rolled by. Hannah sat huddled in the wagon, her face like a pinched cherry under her bonnet. "I'll be so lonesome for them," Nancy said. "Both going! Hannah and Mara, too!"

Sully blinked his eyes in the cold as he watched Scott Hunt's wagon drive out of sight.

All morning Mara watched the tiny sleeping face in her arms. She watched, thinking of nothing, as Sobe slept, warm in his blanket. Caleb said he was sorry about Sophia and John. Mara nodded, not looking up from Sobe's face. Caleb was silent then, and Mara was grateful. She didn't want anyone to speak to her about it. If no one spoke of it, and if she did not think about it, if she could get away from it, perhaps it had not happened.

The sharp hot sun was high overhead when Sobe woke and blinked up at Mara with his black eyes. No, Sobe. Go back to sleep. But he looked up at her now, his eyes wide. The great pain rose in Mara's heart. No, Sobe. Go back to sleep. If he looked at her, or smiled, she would feel the pain. She would cry. Go crazy like Mama who would not come with them. Like Sophia, who slept on John's coffin. Sobe knew her face. He smiled now, the dimple coming in his left cheek. Mara held him to her so she could not see his face. It was hard to keep the pain there where she had pushed it down deep inside so she couldn't feel it anymore. It was hard when Sobe smiled at her. She held him to her and rocked him. She looked out, for the first time since they had left the fort, up and out across the flat land to the pass in the mountains to the north. It had been almost a year since they had come through the pass—all of them. Papa and Mama and Sophia and John and Ashel. All of them together. If she did not think of today, of yesterday, it would not have happened, and they would be all together still. If Papa would only come home.

Sobe stirred against her. She rocked him faster, holding him tight. Perhaps he would go to sleep again, not look at her, nor smile. She looked up ahead toward the pass.

She had not wanted to come to Provost's Hole. Fort Utah. Provo, they thought they would call it, as if a new name would make it better. She had been afraid. But she had not been afraid enough. Sophia had been afraid. She had not wanted to bring her unborn baby and her new life with John out into a land of wild savages. But John. John was good and faithful. They came. And they died for it. Now they were all dead. Baby Martha, Sophia, John. Could she remember that John Smith had taken her in his arms and kissed her? How had it been that she had loved him, had wanted to be his wife? Now she could not remember. How had it been for Sophia? How did Sophia love John? Mara had not been able to look at Sophia's frozen body. Sophia had not stopped crying for him until she had gone to be with him. Now they were together. Side by side in wooden boxes in the ground.

Bishop Higbee had said, "Brother John and Sister Sophia and their beloved little one . . . a family in eternity. A family in the great family of our God." Mara had stood holding Sobe in the cold, watching Mama. Mama stood between Brother and Sister Allen, staring at the wooden boxes. Scott Hunt spoke to dedicate the graves. ". . . this plot of earth to be a resting place until the morning of the first resurrection. . . ." The Allens held Mama. Mara was afraid Mama would fall down, would tear herself away and fall across the grave.

"Amen."

They held Mama back from the graves. "Oh, dear God in Heaven!" she had cried. "Why have you taken them?" They carried Mama away then—as they had carried Sophia away from John the day before. Mara stood alone in the cold, holding Sobe, then, as now.

Suddenly Sobe cried, pushed against her breast. Poor

little one. She lifted him to her shoulder, patted his back. She could not look into his face. She must be strong. Not foolish and weak like Mama. Mara shut her eyes. Sobe struggled to pull his hands from the blanket. She brought him from her shoulder and loosened the blanket, freed his fist from his shirt for him. He brought it to his mouth and sucked it, turning it in his mouth. Sobe. She looked at his brown face. He closed his eyes, sucking hard on his fist. "Already you know you must wait for what you need," she thought. She tucked the blanket tight around him and rocked again. "What will become of you? Now that the white man has killed your first mother and the red man has killed your second mother, what will become of you, son of Blueflower?"

Mara gazed into the bright winter sky to the north. She remembered the first time she had seen Blueflower. Another cold morning. She had come running from her Papa's cabin where Ivie Richards. . . .

Mara held Sobe away from her and looked into his face. No. She would believe Sobe's father was the Hinte of whom Rain had spoken. Blueflower's Indian husband. Not . . . Richards. Mara fastened her eyes on the road ahead. She looked up at Scott Hunt's broad back where he rode with the others in the front of the company. He too had hated Richards. Scott Hunt was taking them away. Away from Mama and the grief that made her insane.

They had tried to bring Mama. Brother Hunt had come to Mara as she walked with Nancy back to the cabin after the service. "Gather some things together, Mara. I'll take your family with me."

They had brought Mama into the cabin, and Bishop Higbee and Scott Hunt had laid their hands on her head while the Allens held her arms. "Our most gracious Father in Heaven," Bishop Higbee had prayed. "Bless this our dear sister in the hour of her great grief . . . give her strength. . . ." She had stopped screaming and crying at last. She fell into her chair by the fire. "Go away, all of you," she had said. Her voice was hard, low. It frightened Mara. Everyone had gone except Sister Allen and Brother Hunt. Sister Higbee took Sobe and Ashel. She would feed them and prepare them for the journey.

Mara had packed quietly in the small cabin as Mama stared into the fire: her best dress, her underclothes, nightshirts for Sobe. She put them into her big valise. She moved slowly to the crate that held Ashel's things. She was afraid Mama would see what she was doing, make her stop. Brother Hunt went to Mama, knelt by her chair and took her hands. She did not push him away. He spoke softly. "Martha, this is no place for you now. Hart would want. . . . You and Mara and Ashel and the baby safe. At least until this Indian trouble is over. Until Hart comes home."

He held Mama's hands for a long time, waiting while she stared into the fire, saying nothing. Please, Mama. Please say yes. Scott Hunt's invitation was for Mara like an offer of life when she felt she had already died. But Mama just stared into the fire, her eyes wide like a madwoman's. "Mara, go so Kate can nurse the baby." Scott Hunt rose, motioned to Mara to continue with her packing.

Bustling inside the door, Sister Allen brought some scraps of cloth to her. Anxious, she sat her in the chair by the window and began cutting them into pieces. She gave Mama a needle and thread. She sat with her for a while and sewed while Mama stared out into the bleak sky.

Mara felt angry. She couldn't leave her mother like this. Forcing herself to move her feet toward her mother's side, Mara reached down for her mother's hand, but Mama waved her away.

Mama's voice trembled now. Mara was afraid she

would cry. She held her breath and prayed she would not. "Please, Mara. You want to go, don't you?" The pause frightened Mara. "You want the baby to be nursed, don't you? And safe? If the Indians find out he is one of them. . . ." Her words choked off.

Mara heard her own voice as though it were far away. "Yes," she had said. She tried to push down the pain. She was free, going north, in the protection of Scott Hunt. Away from Mama's crushing grief. Mama would be all right. As soon as she had commanded Mara to leave, she had begun sewing pieces into the quilt. Sister Allen cut up the scraps and spread them out. She got along so well with Sister Allen—and Sully. Sully would make her smile. He always did—skipping around, making up to Mama the way he always did. No wonder Mama nagged her to marry Sully. As if Sully with his longing, hungry gaze did not needle her enough. He made her feel she owed him something. She hated him for making her feel that way. All she felt was that she wanted to be far away from him.

Sobe fussed, turning his fist around and around in his mouth. Mara held him and rocked him harder. But at last he flung his fist from his mouth and cried. She found the sponge in her satchel and poured water on it from Caleb's water jar. Sobe sucked it hard for a few seconds and then pushed it away with his tongue, crying again. Mara bounced him and crooned to him, but by the time the company made its midday stop, Sobe was crying loudly, and Mara could not quiet him. He turned his head toward her, opened his mouth for food that did not come.

Almost as soon as they stopped, Brother Hunt came to them with Hannah Wright and her mother. "Let Afton help you with the baby, Mara," he said, smiling at Hannah's mother. Mara was grateful for his thoughtfulness.

Afton Wright was not tall and beautiful like her daughter, but she carried herself with the same cool deliberation, that same haughty air of superiority Mara knew so well in Hannah.

"All you have to give him is a sponge?" Mrs. Wright asked briskly. "You haven't even tried spooning him flour and water? He ought to be old enough by now. Four months? He's old enough." She was thin and dark, her movements quick, almost military. Hannah stood silent, obeying her mother's orders as quickly as they were given.

"Give me the flour, Hannah, and a spoon." They mixed the flour and water into paste, and Mr. Wright tried to spoon it into the baby's mouth. Sobe spit and sputtered, but Mrs. Wright kept spooning it off his face and into his mouth. Mara watched, feeling grateful, but impatient.

"I guess he'll be all right now," she said. "Thank you." She reached for the spoon, but Mrs. Wright pulled it away from her.

"I'll finish," she said abruptly, sounding almost angry. "It's hard to judge when a child's had enough if you don't know what you're doing," Mrs. Wright said, finishing up with short quick scrapes of the spoon over the baby's chin. "You should be able to handle it yourself now, though." She stood, wiping the spoon clean with much more vigor than it needed. "Of course, if you're staying at Hunts' you'll have more than enough help."

Mara had never had much to do with Hannah's mother before. Mrs. Wright kept herself aloof from the others in the settlement. She did not even like to be called "sister." She was "Mrs. Wright" to everyone Mara knew. Now Mara began to understand why. Hannah might be snobbish and spoiled, but her mother was downright cold and hard. Maybe it was because she knew it would be her daughter Kate, Scott's youngest wife, who would take on the additional burden of nursing this baby when they reached the city. But she never mentioned it. "Yes," she said as she climbed down from the wagon box. "If there's anything at Scott Hunt's, there's more than enough people. Come along, Hannah."

Mara watched them go, wondering why Hannah and her mother treated her this way. Hannah was supposed to be her friend, yet she had hardly said a word to her, standing there with her chin high, her nose in the air, balancing her black bun on the top of her head like a china teacup. And why had Mrs. Wright spoken in such a tone about the Hunts? Kate had been adamant about wanting to marry this Scott Hunt.

Mara remembered Kate Wright's marriage. It was about a year and a half ago. It was an elegant occasion, the candles burning in the vestibule of the Hunts' new house. She remembered how she had felt watching Kate, no cold dark beauty like Hannah, but pretty enough, and blonde. She remembered that she had watched Bret that night. It was one of the first times she could remember noticing Bret in particular among all the other boys. Why would she be marrying the father, she remembered thinking. She's just the age of the most handsome son!

Bret! It had been a long time since she had thought about Bret. And now she was going home, to his home, to be a part of his family. Mara felt a hidden excitement inside. She tried to push it away. It was wrong that she could be thinking about Bret this way when John and Sophia. . . . But Fort Utah, the pain, seemed so far away already. Sobe closed his eyes. He must be tired from battling the harsh woman with the strange food, Mara thought. As she rocked Sobe she let her thoughts go to Bret. There was only Sobe to remind her of all that had happened since Bret had kissed her good-bye, almost a year ago.

Mara watched Hannah and her mother climb into their wagon. They needn't have been so harsh, Mara thought. It's not as though I could do anything to hurt them. Hannah has never been so cold and mean before. I could see it, from such people, if I had done something to them. Are they angry because I am leaving Mama? Not likely. They're running away, too. Is it because Kate won't want to nurse Sobe? Surely she won't be forced to. Is it because I'm going with Scott Hunt? It's not as though I'm going to take Kate's place or anything. . . . Could that be it? Do they think I'm going to Salt Lake City to marry Scott Hunt myself! For a moment Mara wanted to laugh. And then her heart nearly stopped inside of her. Marry Scott Hunt! "I'll take you, then, Mara," he had said, in such a kind voice. "To be part of my family." Mara had thought only of his comfortable house, his large happy family, his tall handsome eldest son.

But if she thought about it, Bret would not be home for a long time yet. It could be years. Caleb and Joshua were both older than she, though Caleb by just a few months. Perhaps it would not be seemly for a girl of her age—a woman with a child to care for—to remain long in a household of so many men unattached. She was not at all interested in marrying either of Bret's next two brothers, but his father? Marry Scott Hunt? He had four wives already. Still, he was good, handsome, one of the richest and most prominent men in the valley. *Did* Scott Hunt have some idea of marrying her when he felt her mourning for John was over? She thought to herself suddenly that it would be a great honor.

"Is everything all right, Mara?" Mara nearly jumped from her seat at the sound of Scott Hunt's voice. He had ridden up beside the wagon seat. "Did the baby take something?"

"Yes. Yes, thank you, Captain Hunt. He's fine." Mara felt almost breathless.

"But what about you? You haven't even come down from the wagon. Wouldn't you like something to eat? It has been a long, hard morning for you. Could I bring you something?"

Mara felt surprised, almost foolish at her feelings. She could hardly speak. She was afraid she might blush. "Thank you, Brother Hunt. I'm all right."

"Well, I'll tell Caleb to bring some of that bread and cheese he's eating over there with the Andersons. You should eat something." He turned his horse and rode away. Mara gazed after him, at his broad back and the blonde hair that curled down his neck under the white hat. She looked away, her heart pounding.

Caleb climbed up beside her. "Pa says he thinks you might be hungry. Here." Caleb seemed almost shy. Mara held Sobe in one arm and took the cheese from Caleb. She took a bite. It was good.

As the wagon began to roll, she looked over her shoulder at Hannah and her mother sitting stiffly, waiting for Brother Wright to come and get them underway. They did not look at Mara, though Mara had a definite feeling they had just turned away. Marry Scott Hunt? Mara thought to herself. I could. I just might do it.

Not since their wagon train had first entered the valley of the Great Salt Lake had any spot looked so good to her as did the great city that next day in late February of 1850. Her grief for Sophia and John was partially replaced by a gnawing excitement. She could not believe how many new homes had been built in just a year.

As the wagon rolled down into the valley, Mara could make out the tall white Hunt mansion far ahead. She could not see her family's old place. Scott Hunt dropped back to ride beside her for a few moments. "We've done quite a bit in a few years' time, haven't we, Mara?" His voice was quiet, full of satisfaction. "We've been building fast this winter, before the spring planting takes us away from it."

It seemed to Mara that the valley was full of neat houses. And Scott Hunt's stood taller and more beautiful than all the rest. She saw the shiny weather vane on the roof, and behind it, the blue hills frosted with sparkling snow.

Mara had not seen the Wrights leave the train, but they were already gone when Scott Hunt and Caleb left the ammunition wagons at the central place and said good-bye to the rest of the militia. When they turned the wagon down their street, Mara's heart beat hard. What would they all say, seeing her here alone with a baby in her arms? Would *they* think she had come as Scott Hunt's future bride? She thought of more than just Kate Wright, now. There was Sister Hunt, Ella—the mother of Bret and the other tall sons. She thought of Chloe and Polly. How would they all receive her? What would they say?

"We're home, Mara." It was Scott Hunt, reaching up to take the baby. He held Sobe in one arm and reached out with the other to help her down from the wagon. There it was: the gate with the big drive to the stable, the white three-story house on the knoll. She gasped in spite of herself, surprised at how clearly her last visit here came back to her now. The warm night. Sully finding her. Her wild ride with Bret! Home? Suddenly she wanted desperately to go down the street and around the corner to her own home. Perhaps someone would take her to see it later—the place she had lived. The place where Bret had kissed her good-bye.

"I hope you'll be happy here, Mara. I believe you will love it as we all do." Scott Hunt's big hand was on her arm. He gave Sobe back to her, helped her forward toward the gate.

"Why, Mara Eastman! What's this we have here, Scott?" It was Ella Hunt, wiping her hands on her apron and embracing her husband. Scott Hunt took her in his arms and kissed her. He stood with his arms across her shoulders as she turned to Mara and peered into the tiny bundle. "Blueflower? Of course I remember Blueflower! Beautiful girl. Oh, bless his little heart. What a sad time of it he's had. Sophia! And John, too! Their own little baby! Oh, my child." Now Ella Hunt moved from her husband and put her arms around Mara and Sobe. "Poor little one. Two, three mothers. Barely four months old."

As Mara listened to Scott Hunt explain and Sister Hunt respond, her heart broke inside her. Now, as Sister Hunt held her, she was afraid she would burst into tears. Sister Hunt looked into her eyes. "Oh, my dear child. I had not heard you were promised to John. My dear little one." And she held Mara and Sobe to her. Mara wanted to lean into her broad shoulder and cry.

But now the children came. And Chloe and Polly, both with child, came from the big garden behind the house, wiping their hands on their skirts. Scott Hunt drew Chloe into his arms and kissed her. Polly came next. The children came from every side, and he seemed to take them into his arms all at once. He laughed, kissing each one.

"The boys are over at Johnson's helping with the barn, dear." Ella Hunt still stood with Mara, her arm around her waist.

"Mara Eastman is to be part of the family," Scott Hunt announced to them all.

"Oh, dear, I wish you could have persuaded Martha to come!" Ella said.

"Goodness, yes," said Chloe. "But we're so glad you're here!"

Scott Hunt was looking up at the windows of the carriage house. "Kate's not there, Scott," Polly said softly.

"She asked . . ." Ella began, her voice sad. "I . . . I told her she could go to her old place to greet her folks. She took one of the horses not ten minutes ago."

"The children?" Scott Hunt asked.

"With her."

Scott Hunt shook his head, and taking Polly's elbow began to walk to the house. Ella and Chloe came behind with Mara. "If that's what she wanted," he said.

"Come, Mara," Ella said. "Let's get you settled and see to this little one here." And Mara walked between two of Scott Hunt's wives up the stairs.

The warmth of Scott Hunt's big family surrounded Mara. Chloe and Polly and their little children filled her with an excitement she had not expected to feel. She felt secure, happy. This felt like home. She would love it here.

Polly mixed broth for Sobe while Ella and Chloe finished preparing a magnificent meal of beef pie, creamed potatoes, hot bread, pickles, smoked bacon, and carrot pudding. They wouldn't let her do a thing but sit and hold Sobe. Children surrounded her, asked her questions, peeked at the tiny baby in her arms, laughed and giggled until Chloe told them to be quiet, there was too much noise, and then Ella announced it was time to get washed up for dinner.

Mara fed Sobe his broth and rocked him to sleep in the kitchen rocker. Now he lay sleeping in a cradle in the corner of the dining room, and she joined the family standing behind their chairs at the large dining table just as Scott Hunt took his place at the head. She saw him look around the table—at the delicious, plentiful food on the sparkling china, at the scrubbed faces of his family. He looked proud, and Mara knew he had a right to be. Tall, handsome Ella, her big boys with their sandy-colored hair, only Bret missing. Chloe's four daughters and her two boys, all small and dark like their mother except for Chloris who looked like Scott Hunt with her cascade of blond curls. Polly and her five little towheads, round and pink like her. There were three empty places at the table. Ella motioned to Mara to take the one across from her, at Scott Hunts' left, next to Joshua. Bret's place? she wondered, her heart skipping a beat. Or perhaps Kate Wright's?

"Caleb," Scott Hunt spoke once they were all present. "Would you please thank God for our safe return and for this food."

Caleb prayed slowly, with a sincerity that touched Mara. She had not thought young men knew how to pray like that. ". . . and thank thee, Father, for bringing us safe out of the battle . . . and for Mara and the baby. In the name of thy Son, Jesus Christ, Amen."

After supper there was some discussion about it, and it was decided that Mara should stay in the carriage house with Kate. "It will be quieter for the baby," Ella said. For the first time since her arrival, Mara felt afraid. She did not think she would be welcome company for Kate Wright.

Not until late that evening did Kate come to the room over the carriage house with her two small children, one toddling up the stairs behind her, the other in her arms. Mara had lit a candle and was writing a message to her mother at the desk under the window at the far end of the bedroom. She heard Kate, and rose just as she opened the door.

"Hello," Mara spoke hesitantly. "Brother and Sister Hunt, I mean . . . Sister Ella . . . and . . . they said it would be best here. I'm sorry. I hope I didn't surprise you."

"I saw the light," Kate said simply, turning to close the door and catch the lock. There was a long moment of silence.

"I-I just came from Fort Utah today . . . with your family . . . in the same party, I mean, with your mother and. . . ."

"I saw them." Kate was not as tall as Hannah, and she was rounder, fair like their father. But her bearing and temperament were much the same as her mother's and Hannah's. Mara had hoped that in spite of the fact that Kate had chosen to greet her parents without first seeing her husband there would be some of the Hunt family's warmth in her. But now Mara was overcome with disappointment. All the pleasure of living with the Hunts might be overshadowed if she had to spend her time here, with Kate.

Kate gave Mara no word of welcome. She fussed over the tiny baby who lay asleep in her arms and set him on the large bed.

"I knew that was your bed," Mara said softly. "I took the cot for myself and Sobe. I hope that's all right." Kate did not answer. Mara tried again. "Your children are beautiful." The little girl at Kate's heels ducked behind her mother's legs when Mara looked toward her. Mara searched her mind for something to say to fill up the awful silence. She would never breathe anything to suggest that Sobe was the hated Ivie Richards' child. It crossed her mind that Kate might already know of that possibility. But she would never mention it. Now she was afraid to mention Sobe again at all. She had a sinking feeling that Kate would never yield. Still, he was a tiny helpless child like Kate's own baby. It might give her a chance to be generous; it might give them something to be friends about. She took a deep breath.

"I-I suppose it would be too much to ask, but Sobe . . . he was nursing with my sister until . . . it was just yesterday . . . and I know you are nursing your own. . . ."

"Mr. Hunt has mentioned it to me," Kate said and she raised her green eyes now to Mara. "I can nurse the baby as he asked me until you can wean him." She looked away again. "Of course, it would be much better if you just wean him very soon. Ella can show you."

Mara was stunned with the cold quiet of Kate's voice. Even Afton Wright had not given her such a chill inside. How had Scott Hunt come to marry such a woman?

"My own baby is just two months old, you understand," Kate said, arranging the covers around him. "Of course, his needs would come first. But I am willing to try to accommodate yours, if that is what Mr. Hunt desires."

The toddler that clung to Kate's skirts began to whimper. Unsmiling, Kate bent down to pick her up.

"I don't want to be a burden," Mara said. "But we have . . . the baby has been through so much, and Brother Hunt offered to. . . ." She stopped then, for Kate's eyes narrowed, and she took deep breaths, as though she were controlling herself with great difficulty. For a long while she did not say a word. Then she stood and faced Mara.

"Mr. Hunt is a very generous man," she said. She took another deep breath. "He is building me a house. It will be ready in a few months. I believe we can get along until then."

The coldness washed over Mara's heart like a shower of ice.

"Do you have enough bedding?" With the same quick motion of her long slender fingers that Mara had seen in Mrs. Wright, Kate pulled a blanket from a drawer. "It's warm for February, but don't expect the good weather to last."

Mara accepted the blanket as graciously as she could

and turned toward her cot. Sobe was sleeping. With her back turned, she draped the blanket around her shoulders, moved the extra bedding Ella had given her, and climbed into bed. She curved herself around Sobe. She touched his smooth warm head over and over again. She prayed he would not wake hungry in the night. Kate had not even smiled.

Mara's retreat to Salt Lake City with Scott Hunt hurt Sully. He could only comfort himself with the thought that he would see her again soon, when he took the specimens up to Dr. Blake. He doubted he could bring her back then, but he could see her. Dr. Blake wouldn't be back in Salt Lake City for a week or so. Until then, Sully would take care of Sister Eastman. She would be all right with the Allens after that. Captain Hunt had said that the Allens would bring her to Salt Lake City when she felt better, but Sully knew that Sister Eastman would never leave Fort Utah. Whenever Sister Allen mentioned it to her, her answer was always the same: "I will not go." And it sounded to Sully like she meant it for sure. When Captain Hunt could believe this, he would send Mara back to be with her mother, when the baby was a little older. There was no sign of more trouble with Indians, either. In the meantime, Sully would see Mara at Hunts'.

The very afternoon Mara left, Sully had found four old crates and set about fixing them up. The next morning he yoked the Eastman oxen to the cart. Ashel wanted to go with him, and finally Sister Eastman said he could go. "Go on, get out of here, both of you," she said. She was always on edge, most of the time not speaking at all, then suddenly sad and tearful, or at other times hard, angry, pushing people away. "Yes, go on about your savage business. Go, Ashel," she said as Ashel ran to follow Sully out the door. Ashel stopped at the sound of his mother's sob. "I don't understand. . . ." Her voice was full of tears now. "Even savages who slaughter innocent sons and daughters are children of God." And she buried her face in her hands, her shoulders shaking. Ashel ran to her, but she lifted her hand and waved him away. "Go on, son. Go on with Sully if you must, and leave me be." After a few moments she picked up her needle and threaded it, squinting in the light from the window. She bent over the pieces in the quilt. She gave a threaded needle to Spirit of Earth and scissors to Rain. Awkwardly, holding the paper pattern, Rain cut the tiny pieces. Spirit of Earth stitched them together. When Mama waved him away, Spirit of Earth waved her bony hand, too.

Ashel was quiet during the ride to the lake. Sully knew that losing Sophia and John had been hard on him, too, though no one had paid him much attention. He had been close to John. John had been a good brother. It would have been easier for Sully if John had not been such a good man. Sully promised himself that he would try to take John's place. He would be a good brother to Ashel, too.

They got to the lake in good time. It looked to Sully like some small animals had dragged off a few ducks, but everything else was just as they had left it. None of it seemed to bother Ashel. Not the headless Indians on the ice, not the bulging sacks of heads and the ducks on the shore. It took them only a few minutes to load the sacks from the sledge to the crates in the ox cart.

On the way back to the fort, Ashel talked a little more. "Can I go with you to take them to Salt Lake?" he wanted to know.

"I don't know," Sully said. It pleased him that Ashel wanted to be with him. Mara would take notice that her little brother liked Sully. But he was afraid Sister Eastman wouldn't let him go. "We'll see," he said. "Your mother won't have nobody else down here but you when I go. She wouldn't take it kindly if you left her."

"It won't be for a while yet. She'll be better," Ashel said. And then, in a voice that sounded too old to Sully to be coming from a ten-year-old boy, "Besides, she don't really need nobody right now. She wants to be alone with it."

Likely you're right, Sully thought. Captain Hunt had told him to look after Sister Eastman. He would do it. For a week or so anyway. Maybe he *could* get her to come with him when he went up, though he didn't figure she'd be pleased about riding with a load of dead ducks and bloody Indian heads.

Ashel was pulling on Sully's sleeve. "Come on, Sully. It'll only be for a little while, wouldn't it? I could stay with Mara."

Sully's heart pounded. Mara. . . . He would see her again soon. He did not promise Ashel anything. He drove back to the fort thinking about Mara.

As they came up to the west gate, the snow began to fall. Not small dry flakes, but big wet splatters. It came slowly at first, and then the sky opened up and let go. Sully and Ashel hurried to the corral, stretched the canvas over the cart, and got the animals inside. They rushed back to the cabin. The white had settled on their shoulders.

"About the biggest flakes I ever saw," Sully said as he hurried Ashel into the cabin.

"Does it mean we can't go to Salt Lake City?"

"Hush, Ashel," Sully said with a quick look at Sister Eastman, who sat by the fire squinting into her quilt pieces. "It takes a lot to stop me."

It snowed. For days. The sky was gray with foggy

clouds, and the snow fell heavily, blew into great wet drifts. Finally, when the sky cleared, it stretched clean and blue for as far as a person could see. But the damage to the roads had been done. Heavy, wet snow stood two feet, three feet, sometimes four feet in the dells. Sully could not go anywhere. He stayed in the Eastman cabin and stripped the bark off the lumber that he cut to make crates. He made a little pine bench so that Sister Eastman could stand to reach the high cupboards.

During the next ten or twelve days, as the snow melted, Ashel often said it was time to try to make it to Salt Lake, but Sully knew he would have to wait. Wait and look after Sister Eastman, who did nothing but work at the quilt in front of the fire and sometimes sip a little broth if Sister Allen made her do it. Sister Allen came often, and brought soup enough for Spirit of Earth and Rain, who wove baskets in their place by the hearth while Sister Eastman spread the quilt pieces on the table.

Ashel pestered him about going to the City with him like a baby after candy. "Stop that talk about going to Salt Lake City, child," Sister Eastman said one Wednesday afternoon, suddenly turning from the fire. "We're not going anywhere."

"I'd be pleased to take you with me, Sister Eastman, when I go up with the . . . specimens. Dr. Blake will be expecting me as soon as I can get there. I'm overdue now. I . . . I've got to go as soon as I can. I'd be happy to take you if. . . ." But Sister Eastman had turned back to her quilt in silence.

The days wore on. Sully thought he might go crazy if he couldn't get out of there. He had to see Mara. What was happening with Mara?

"Why did Mara go with Brother Hunt, Mama?" Ashel asked one day when Sister Eastman seemed a little better, seemed to feel like talking some. "Why did he want to take her so bad? Is he going to marry her, Mama? Is Mara going to marry Brother Hunt?"

Mara? Marry Captain Hunt! Sully felt the room begin to turn. A strange fear seemed to sweep around him. He gripped the edge of the table where he sat eating supper with Ashel. He looked at Sister Eastman. She stayed bent over the quilt. She did not seem surprised.

"He wanted us all to come, Ashel. He's a good man. Important man. Wealthy. He takes good care of his family. Mara could do worse."

"That would be something!" Ashel said, sounding excited. "To have Mara living in that big house! Do you know that William Hunt has his very own horse and he's only just the same age as me? And him and Joseph have their very own room with a real bed with a straw tick on it? And they have. . . ."

Sully's head spun as Ashel talked on with excitement. At last Sister Eastman stopped him. "Enough, Ashel. Captain Hunt has made no offer yet." She sighed. Her voice was tired, but it didn't suggest tears as it usually did. "Still, unless I miss my guess, he'll be making an offer before she's been there long." There was a long pause. Sully could hear Ashel slurping his soup, Sister Eastman sighing over the quilt by the cracking fire, and the pounding in his own head. "She could do worse," Sister Eastman said again, not looking at Sully. *Me, me!* He wanted to shout. *Sister Eastman! Have you forgotten about me?* How could she be sitting there talking about Mara marrying Captain Hunt when all the time she had been favoring me? Maybe she *had* gone crazy like they said.

Through the long evening Sully tossed it in his mind. The more he thought on it, the more sure he became that Mara would never marry Scott Hunt, no matter what Sister Eastman thought. The Hunt family was happy, and it was true, Scott Hunt did know how to keep a woman happy, if any man could keep more than one woman really happy. No. Mara would never play last fiddle to four other women, especially when one of them was that iceberg Kate Wright. Mara might, for a short while, have thought about sharing a man with her sister. But that was a lot different. No, she wouldn't marry Scott Hunt. Besides, Sully was sure that Captain Hunt was just showing kindness in taking Mara and the baby. He was like that. He was too kind for his own good sometimes. His kindness had brought him no happiness when he married Kate Wright, that was for sure. Everybody saw it was his name and his money she was after. Captain Hunt *was* an important man. Next to Brigham Young, his wives had about the finest things in the valley. But Aunt Ella, Aunt Chloe, Aunt Polly, they were good women. They worked hard. They didn't put on airs. They loved the Captain. They loved each other and each other's children. Kate Wright was different. Scott Hunt had not come after her. Sick of Ivie Richards, she had come after him. And he was too kind. He wouldn't really want such a young girl. He was not that kind of man.

It was true that Mara was better, finer, more beautiful than Kate Wright. Oh, yes, much more beautiful. Sully's blood began to pound just thinking of Mara's beauty. But Scott Hunt had his fill of young wives. He would not marry her. Especially if Sully told him that he loved her. Nobody on God's earth could love her as much as Sully Tuttle. Not John Smith, not Scott Hunt. Not even Bret. Sully thought briefly about Bret. But he knew Bret very well. He didn't worry about Bret.

Sully would win her once and for all, long before Bret came home. He would plant his piece this spring. There would be a rich harvest. Enough to sell. He would have riches no woman could resist. All for her, her alone. She would see how much better it would be to belong to him. He would go to see her, and he would win her heart.

In the night, Sully woke suddenly from a bad dream. He had seen himself with an ax, chopping heads that rolled in blood. He had risen from the bloody lake, flying, reaching out to Mara, who slipped away as he touched her with his bloody hands. He flew higher, so high that it was as though he had merged with the sun. He could see the valley stretched out below him for miles. He could see Utah Lake, a frozen dot far below. He flew through the pass into the valley of the Great Salt Lake. He felt the cool breezes blowing into his face. He looked down, saw Hunts' big white house as he had left it a year ago, the weather vane turning in the wind. He thought he saw Mara in Scott Hunt's bedroom taking hold of the cloth, ready to pull it down. He saw her look up, wave to him as he hovered in the air. Then she pulled the shade to the sill and closed him out.

Sully woke in a sweat. The weather had been warmer. He would leave today. It was Thursday, a sunny March day, clear and drying, but the ground still wet with melting snow. He would take Ashel with him and leave Sister Eastman in the care of Sister Allen and Sister Higbee. Spirit of Earth and Rain could help, too. She would be all right.

"I can't see you leaving just yet, Sully. I can't see Ashel leaving and you both going through that Indian country. I can't see it."

"We must go now, Sister Eastman," Sully said in his kindest voice. "We got to get back in time for planting. And those specimens. I promised I'd get them up there. They're going to be. . . ."

"Oh, not yet, Sully. Just a little further into spring."

"But I have to go now, Sister Eastman." Sully knew

Sister Eastman trusted him, liked him because he worked so hard, even if she did think now that Mara might marry Captain Hunt. "The earlier we go, the sooner we'll get back for planting," he said.

"Oh, I'm sure you know best. But oh, do take care." Her voice was high and thin on the air and she wrung her hands. "Ashel, you take care."

With those words, Ashel drank his gruel like milk, ran and threw his arms around his mother's neck, and bolted for the door. "Come on, Sully!" he shouted.

"And bring me news of Mara," his mother called after him.

It was still early when Sully hooked the oxen to the cart. He picked up a corner of the canvas back over the load. The weather had been cold enough most of the time to preserve the specimens and the ducks, but with the heat from the warming sun, an awful stench had begun to rise from the boxes. Sully turned away and swallowed hard. He turned his head when he tied the canvas down.

"It smells bad," Ashel said.

"Never mind it," Sully said. "We'll be getting rid of the meat in good time. Just get the oxen moving."

It was a long day. The mud sometimes rose as high as the axles, and Sully and Ashel both had to tug at the oxen to pull free. Not until they passed the point of the mountain did they see Indians—a few on ponies just off the crest of the western hill.

"Slow billy," Sully chanted. "Ashel, take the gun out of the wagon box and hold it just below the board. Don't let 'em see the gun."

Ashel sat stiff with the gun in his hands. "I thought we got 'em all," he said.

"Those are Snake Indians—a different breed," Sully breathed hard. "They hate the Utes."

"What will they do to us?"

Sully didn't answer for a moment. "Anyway, we didn't get near all of them. They are all over these hills, and the war ain't over." At that moment Sully ducked as an arrow whizzed by the cart. "Looky there!" he exclaimed. On the ridge above them stood five or six Indians on ponies looking across the valley at the Snakes. As soon as Sully saw them, they turned their horses back toward a trail close to the edge and began shouting into the echoing hills. The Snakes came rushing from the low ridge like dry leaves, northward, screaming war whoops.

"Well, glory be," Sully said in almost a whisper. "It wasn't us they was after." Ashel caught his breath. "They was after each other."

Ashel still carried the gun. He clutched it against his knee, his knuckles white. Sully moved the oxen forward cautiously under the hill. When they reached the last curve of road under the mountain point they looked over a quiet valley. Too quiet, Sully thought, and the hair of his neck stiffened.

Suddenly Ashel cried out, and four big Indians on ponies rode down on them in the bright slant of the sun.

Sully ducked, but no arrow sped over them. The Indians slowed and rode silently to the wagon. Sully stopped the oxen and stared. He had never seen Chief Walkara, but as sure as he could have picked Brigham Young from a crowd of white men, he was sure that the man on the giant horse was him. He was large and handsome, with turquoise rings and white plaiting in his thick braids.

"Take me to Salt Lake Cit-ee," the chief said in stiff level English.

Sully's mouth would not close from fright. His hands were shaking. "Yes, sir," he said. "Yes, sir."

"I talk to Mormon chief."

Sully, still shaking, gave a whack with the reins. "Har! Go on!" he shouted to the oxen.

Ashel, unable to hide the gun sufficiently, stared with wide eyes. His face was as white as paste. Walkara rode alongside the wagon and leaned over toward him, reaching for the gun.

"We take gun," he grunted. He pulled it from Ashel's grip and hefted it up to his saddle. Then he turned with a grimace. "What you got in wagon?"

Sully's heart came to his throat. "Meat," he said as carelessly as he could.

Walkara wrinkled his nose and steadied his horse back away from the load. "Bad meat," he said, and rode at a distance.

Sully whistled silently through his teeth. "That was close," he whispered.

"Take me to Brigham Young."

The hair on Sully's head prickled. Beside him, Ashel sat as stiff as a bugle all the way into the city.

They passed south Main Street like a hearse on the way to the graveyard, Walkara and his men close behind them. The people stared, and Sully thought he saw one of the Hunt boys in the distance turn quickly away on his pony. Perhaps he would notify Captain Hunt of their arrival.

The March sun beat down on their uncovered heads at the hitching post in front of Brigham Young's stables. Ashel stared at the prophet's house, his mouth open. "It's so big!" he said. Only a few children were playing in the yard.

"Far enough," Walkara grunted, and dismounted his horse. "Stay!" he ordered the other Indians, who stopped, their ponies snorting and pawing at the ground. "Wait!" he said to Sully.

Sully looked from Walkara to the four Indians behind him and wouldn't dare to do anything else. A moment later Walkara disappeared into the entryway to the office of Brigham Young.

Sully and Ashel waited in the wagon. People on the street stared at the Indians, and no one stopped anywhere near Sully's wagon. The afternoon was silent; Sully and Ashel were still too frightened to speak. Finally the doorway to Brigham Young's office opened, and Sully's heart pounded.

"I'm sorry, but we can't take up your battles with you!" a booming voice crossed over the yard. "I've told you that before, Walkara. You want me to fight your fights for you against the Snakes."

"I don't give up, Brigham Young," Walkara said gruffly, not moving from his position on the stairs. It was obvious Brigham Young was trying to get rid of him graciously, but the stubborn chief had planted his feet firmly on the stoop.

"You say you came with this man and his wagon," Young nodded toward Sully. "But I'll send Rockwell home with you." Brigham Young turned and snapped his fingers. A child came to him out of the yard. He spoke to the boy a minute, and the young fellow ran like a wild rabbit toward the east.

"Thank you, boys," Brigham Young nodded to Sully again. Sully snapped to attention.

"Boy," Sully turned to Ashel quietly. "You probably been spoke to the only time in your life by a prophet of the Lord."

Sully didn't wait to see what was going to happen to Walkara when Rockwell came. At Brigham's nod, Sully whipped the oxen round and drove toward the Utah Hotel. He drove around the corner and parked on the west side.

The hotel was squat and square with big shuttered

windows on the first floor and a porch turning the corner from the Main Street side to Brigham Street. Sully bounded out of the cart and untied the canvas. Holding his breath, he pulled out one of the crates. Ashel hefted the other side, and they stumbled up the stairs.

Government men were having coffee in the large room inside, most of them in smart blue uniforms with once-starched shirts looking gray from so much western sun. Sully, still holding his breath, looked around, nervous. Eyes turned his way, but it looked like no one had yet caught a whiff of his load. If he hurried, maybe no one would.

"Dr. Artemus Blake," he stammered at the desk.

A tired desk man peering out from beneath spectacles and visor nodded his head toward the stairs. "Second floor to the top of the stairs, two doors to the right."

Sully watched the man's eyes. Sure enough, on his last breath they began to water, and his nose puckered up. When Sully and Ashel lifted the crate the man peered over the edge of his bin. "You need some help?" he asked slowly.

"Uh, no. We'll be fine," Sully said, and they stumbled up the stairs.

Dr. Blake answered the door. "Welcome, my lads. I've been waiting for you. Of course we had this confounded snow." He turned then, and pointed to the table. "Set them on the table. Weren't there more?"

"They're out in the wagon, sir."

"Fine! Fine! My, they did ripen," he said as they set down the crate. Sully thought he saw his eyes begin to water, too. "A fine crate you built, my boy." He talked as he pulled at the top slats to open the box. Sully and Ashel stood staring, unable to say a word. He was opening it up!

"Well, they certainly come in one piece, all right. And well aged." He rummaged around in the box and drew out a loose duck's wing. He pulled it to his nose. "Hmmmm. Just right," he said, his eyes welling up with tears. "Say, would you like to stay for dinner?"

Sully's stomach turned somersaults under his ribs. "No! Thanks. Not hungry, sir. No, but thanks very much." Even if he was as empty as a desert rain barrel he couldn't have eaten a crumb now. It made him sick that Doctor Artemus Blake had even mentioned dinner.

With military heads turning in their direction, Sully and Ashel brought up the other three crates, set them just inside Dr. Blake's door, took Dr. Blake's shiny silver dollar with thanks, and bolted for the ox cart as if it were the last train out and leaving on time. They turned the cart around and headed for the south of the City as fast as the lumbering old critters could take them, Sully feeling like he was going to vomit all the way. Ashel was green. He kept his hand on his mouth.

It did Sully's stomach no good to see Mara. When he drove into the yard he caught sight of her at the clothesline behind the carriage house, pinning white sheets out in the afternoon sun. He drove the cart into the gate and stayed in the yard to wait for her. The children ran to him screaming. They hung on his arms and legs, and shouted "Sully! Sully!" They loved him. He almost cried, it made him so happy. At last, from behind the carriage house to see what the ruckus was, came Mara.

"Mara!" he almost gasped walking toward her. He wanted then and there to take her in his arms, to live out all those thousands of his dreams.

"Sully! Oh, it's so good to see you! And Ashel!" Sully's head spun. It's good to see you, she had said! And her eyes were bright with happy surprise. Sully felt he could leap with one step from the earth into heaven.

"Mara!" Ashel was running toward her with an excited shout. He stopped in front of her, awkward, his hands in his pockets. She put both arms around him and hugged him tight. Sully could have died for envying Ashel at that moment. Then the whole Hunt family was out the door, the boys, Aunt Ella, Aunt Chloe, Aunt Polly. They were all around him and all over him, and Sully could do no more than watch Mara lead Ashel to the back stoop and set him down for a talk.

The Hunts loved Sully Tuttle, Mara could see that. They always had. She remembered it from before, how the children—and Ella too—doted on this tall awkward boy who almost looked like a man now. They fixed his favorite meal of rabbit pie that night, and everybody listened to his every word as he told of their encounter with Chief Walkara. The big boys pounded on the table, and Scott Hunt roared with delight to hear of Dr. Artemus Blake's iron stomach. Ella clapped her hands together at the story of the boys being spoken to by President Young. "You'll remember that all of your life, Ashel," she said. "You'll remember all your life you've been spoken to by a prophet of the Lord. There aren't many people on this earth that have been."

Sully watched Mara all through the meal. But she found herself enjoying his gaze for the first time. He seemed so relaxed here with the Hunts. Not awkward or foolish. She saw him with a new respect, here where he was respected and loved so. And he reminded her of home.

"And so you'll be plowing now soon, you think?" Scott Hunt was saying to Sully. "And if the Indians leave you alone I suppose you think you'll have the finest farm on the river?" Brother Hunt laughed.

"Oh, they'll leave us alone for awhile, now," Sully said, his voice sounding confident, but not boastful. Mara watched him out of the corner of her eye. He sounded happy. "And yes, sir, I believe I'll have the finest farm on the Provo River." The big boys cheered Sully.

"And if you want to drive them back with you, take a pair of Herefords. We have a new breed of cattle now."

Sully looked at Scott Hunt, who narrowed his eyes.

"Sure, Sully." Then he winked strangely. "Go check them out. They're behind the east fence."

Sully turned to Mara. "Would you go with me, Mara?"

She looked at Scott Hunt.

"Walk with him a few rods, Mara. Talk over old times," Scott Hunt said. The big boys cheered.

Mara sat stunned. The women were smiling at her. Polly took the baby out of her arms.

"It will take half an hour or so."

Her hands felt clammy. Kate was staring at her.

When they reached the porch, Sully said "Your mother misses you. She has finished the quilt. She stays in the house and is putting up another quilt with Spirit of Earth and Rain." When he put his hand on the door, the knob slipped out of his fingers. He reached back to grab the doorknob and slammed the door. It shook in the frame. When he let go, he stumbled forward and tripped on his own foot, and just barely caught himself on the rail. Mara looked out at the yard. She looked up at the moon. Something had changed. She looked back at Sully's eyes. She couldn't believe how she was feeling. She was not going to laugh at him at all.

"You sure you don't want to come back with us?" Sully asked her.

She was missing Fort Utah. She was missing her mother and she thought about Spirit of Earth and Rain. She clung to the railing on the porch and walked slowly into the yard down to the corral. She smiled at Sully. "Not now, but maybe soon," she said. She could see that his eyes were twinkling in the light.

"Oh don't get me wrong. You don't have to come now. The invitation is open any time."

She remembered how the little Hunt children had gathered around him and tugged on his sleeves.

"I hear Scott Hunt is thinking of building new houses for all the wives, including Kate," Sully said, looking at her from the side.

Mara watched a calf drinking from its mother. Another calf stood by the fence and moaned. For a moment she was thinking about Sobe being weaned by Kate.

"It will be better when Kate has her own place," he said.

Mara watched him carefully. How had he known she was thinking about Kate? She smiled. "I know," Mara said. She had never forgotten what Ella had told her: "We would rather be together like this than apart, Chloe and Polly and I. It's a great comfort to have sisters who love you to share in your trials and your happiness. But Kate. She was just infatuated with a handsome older man. She doesn't understand the Principle."

"Do you understand the Principle?" Sully said softly.

Mara thought her heart was pounding and she didn't know why. Sully didn't touch her. And for the first time in her life she thought it would have been just fine if he did. On the way back into the house, she hurried ahead of him. Sometimes feeling him too close to her, she ran several steps at a time.

At first they were just little things. Before Sully left, Mara found the umbrella tucked under the shoe rack in the closet. She might have believed Kate that it was her Aunt Mabel's old umbrella, except that it was marked with a price in melted wax on the brass handle.

A week after Sully and Ashel had left, Kate put a stack of very nice towels on the foot of Mara's bed and a picture frame with the words printed on paper inside of the glass: "Grundy's frames forever."

The next day when Kate was at her parents' house again, Mara heard Ella say "Be fair, girls."

Polly and Chloe and Ella sewed their clothes in the front room together while the children gathered around them. Two little girls were poring over a book. Another little girl was practicing the violin.

"Did you see the towels?" Polly asked Mara.

"Yes. Weren't they hers?"

"She's been buying things for her new home. And Scott wanted us to wait until all of us could do it together."

Mara saw Ella's eyes. She was busy with her needle. "It will be better when Kate has a home of her own. You'll see."

"There are no walls, not a set of towels I would want more than to feel like a sister," Chloe said. She said it softly over her thimble. She bit her thread. Polly smiled and touched Chloe's hand. Mara wondered about it. She saw love she never believed could happen. When she was in the room with Scott Hunt's family she felt like she belonged there and she would have married him in a moment—if he would have asked her.

But nothing happened. Sully visited again. The boys flirted with her at the table. She was neither a woman nor a child, a wife nor a sister. At two o'clock in the middle of a dark May night, Kate herded her crying children in and left them for a moment while she went outside to a paid coach and with the coachman hauled up a marble-topped table. Mara woke and turned over, drawing more covers over the little weaned Sobe, weaned by necessity because Kate was seldom there. When he didn't wake, Mara breathed a sigh of relief and buried herself in the cot under the covers. She opened her eyes when she felt the bed shake. Kate was pushing the table between the cot and the window. Now Mara would not be able to go around but would have to crawl over.

The following week, Kate brought a dutch oven and put it on the table. There were bags of pumpkin and sunflower seeds sitting in it on a stack of furniture ads clipped from the newspaper. She had marked one of the ads with a piece of tapestry and a note that said "Here."

Almost every evening for the next three weeks Kate spent the nights at her parents' home. Sully visited again. He talked about home, but he didn't ask Mara to come with him. When he left this time, she decided she would make a decision.

At midnight in June Kate went in and out of the room nine times hauling the shell of a dresser and its eight drawers. She put the shell beside Mara's cot and piled up the drawers on top of it. In the morning Mara could not pull her covers to the top of the bed. She stepped over a little stool with a piece of unfinished needlepoint still hanging tacked to the edges and under the stool were three rungs rolled up like sausages and tied with string.

At breakfast Mara climbed out of the cot and took Sobe down to the kitchen. Scott Hunt was just leaving. He looked at her eyes and must have seen something there. "I need to talk to you tonight, Mara."

After supper he walked with her as she carried Sobe to the carriage house. Sobe was growing into a very charming child, constantly grinning, flashing his three white teeth. Mara delighted in him and spent hours playing with him. He loved the prickly grass on his hands as he sat on the ground and bounced and patted the earth.

"Is it going all right with you, Mara?" Scott Hunt asked in his kind, strong voice. "We haven't talked much about you, about your future, have we?"

Mara turned to him. He looked down on her with eyes full of such kindness that Mara wanted to cry.

"Mara," he said, lifting Sobe from her arms, "I don't know what you understand about the Principle, since you have not lived in a family accustomed to it." He paused. Mara was silent, the blood beating in her head. "It's a very difficult thing for me to speak to you about it," he went on. "But you must be aware that you are a woman now, Mara. With a child to care for." He paused again, turning away from her. He seemed almost embarrassed. "If I am to keep you here, you and Sobe, I should in all seemliness take you as my wife." He waited for her to speak, but she didn't know what to say. She could barely stand, her heart pounded so. He lifted Sobe to sit on his shoulder. At last he went on.

"I know you have considered plural marriage, because you were willing to enter into the covenant with John Smith." He paused again. "But I am thinking that marrying your sister's husband and marrying into a family such as mine are two very different matters."

"Yes," Mara said. Scott Hunt, looking down at her, waited for her to say more. But still she did not know what to say. Marry Scott Hunt. It was what she had thought about for several months. He was as much like a great prophet from the Bible or the book of Mormon as she could imagine—a man such as she imagined Nephi or Alma or Moses must have been. A man much like Brigham Young himself.

"You see, Mara," he was going on, "properly, plural marriage is not just a matter of a man and a woman coming to love and respect each other and promising to be faithful for all time and eternity. It is matter of the wives agreeing to love and respect and accept one another as well." He sighed deeply. "And that is a very difficult thing."

He paused again for a long time, as though he needed her to say she understood what he was saying—or at least as though he were trying to say just the right words.

"Yes, I think I understand," she said.

He stopped at the stairs to the room over the carriage house, put his foot on the first step, and held Sobe on his knee. Kate was not there tonight.

"Mara, you are growing into a very beautiful and good young woman. I would be proud to have such a woman as my wife." Mara gasped in spite of herself, whether from pride that he would consider her worthy or fear that she would have to say no, she could not tell. For she knew that no matter how many separate houses there were, she could never share a husband with Kate Wright.

"But," he went on, and a wave of relief swept over Mara and made her so weak she had to sit on the steps. He stretched his free hand to her and helped her to the third step. Sobe turned and reached for her, nestled his head into her shoulder. Scott Hunt smiled. "He loves you, Mara," he said. "And so do I." Then the tears came, and Mara could barely blink them back. She desired this strong, good man. She wanted him to take her in his arms and hold her, make her forget there was a Kate Wright Hunt. Make her believe it was possible for her to be his wife. But Scott Hunt looked away from her and out into the brilliant sun setting over the lake.

"Yes, Mara, I love you. But I must love you as a father and a brother. I must not let Kate break her covenants. Or her heart," he said quietly. He narrowed his eyes in the sinking sun. "I believe I shall never take another wife, Mara." He looked at her now. "I must help Kate to live the Principle." He looked long into her eyes. "Though she will consent if I ask, in her heart she cannot accept another wife."

Mara blinked away her tears and cleared her throat. "I know," she said. And the disappointment in her voice surprised her.

"Yes," he sighed again now. "Yes, I'm sure you do. And it

has not been good of me to keep you here without speaking properly about this, letting you wait and wonder what should become of you here. But there was Polly's new baby, and the new houses." Scott Hunt shook his head. He looked into her eyes and smiled. "In truth, Mara, it was foolish of me to be thinking I am the only man in the world who could take care of you and the child." There was almost a twinkle in his eye now. "From what I see, there is more than one young man of my personal acquaintance who has more than a passing fancy for this young beauty."

Mara blushed. What did he know? Bret? Joshua? Caleb? Sully? Surely anybody could see how Sully felt about her. And Joshua and Caleb were becoming almost annoying as they stole glances at her when they thought she wasn't looking. But did he know about Bret? Had he wondered about Bret's running off into the night—so long ago? She had almost forgotten that this man was Bret Hunt's father, that the Bret they talked of every night at dinner, whose letters were passed around the family until they were almost worn out, was the same tall young man who had kissed her good-bye at her gate fourteen months ago. Only fourteen months! It wasn't possible. More like fourteen years. It was hard to remember such a person as Bret even existed.

"I mustn't be selfish, Mara." Scott Hunt's voice sounded relieved, light again. "I can't have *all* the good women in the world." He laughed his wonderful laugh.

"Now," he said, looking into her eyes, his voice solemn again. "You must tell me what you want to do."

"I think I should like to go home, to Fort Utah," Mara said with an honest feeling she was glad to be able to express, hoping she did not sound ungrateful.

"This is your home, here, for as long as you want," he replied. "You know that."

"Yes, but I think it best for me to go back with my

mother," she said. "You cannot know how grateful I am to you. . . ."

"We shall miss you, Mara," he said, putting his strong hand to her hair, then taking it away again. "You have been an angel here, a breath of air for us. And this happy brown baby! You do well with him, Mara. You can be proud."

Mara stood up, as happy as she could remember being. Scott Hunt's goodness was like a tonic to her. "How can I ever thank you for all you have done for us, Brother Hunt?" she said.

He was quiet for a moment, his face drawn, his eyes absent, as though he were far away in his thoughts. "You *can* help me, Mara. You can help me try to save my wife, my poor Kate."

And as she mounted the stairs to Kate's room, Mara knew that her leaving would be the help he needed for now.

Chapter Eleven

Mara prepared to leave with Sully in the middle of July. During the four months she had stayed with Scott Hunt's family, Sully had made three visits, always brief, always exciting, always filled with talk of home, of Mama and Ashel, of Spirit of Earth, and of Rain, who was growing more beautiful every day, could now speak English well, and was going to school to learn how to read. He told the boys about his adventures, about the Indians he saw, about his arguments with Ivie Richards. He talked to Mara about Nancy and how she had made scarecrows for his fields that looked like the warmed over corpse of Artemus Blake.

Mara knew how much Nancy liked Sully. Mara had always tried to encourage Sully in Nancy's direction. Now she found herself slightly jealous as Sully laughed over the good times he and Nancy had together. Nancy would have enjoyed Sully's talk, his busy, descriptive hands. Mara found herself enjoying him now. He was the flavor of home. And after her final decision to return to Provo, she became excited at the thought of seeing Sully again.

She knew she would miss the Hunts. She loved each child, and Sobe delighted in all his playmates. Ella and Polly and Chloe were so good to her, taught her so much. And when her plans to return were made clear, things even improved with Kate. Much to her amazement, even Hannah came to see her one day, for the first time since she had been at the Hunts!

Still, when Sully came the third week in July, Mara knew it was time to go home. Sully stayed for two days while he prepared everything and she said good-bye to the good neighbors and close friends.

From the wagon board, Mara looked back and saw Scott Hunt's eyes. If they had been the eyes of the prophet himself, they could not have been brighter. As she looked at him, she understood that perhaps more than anyone else in her world, Scott Hunt was capable of pure caring—about her, about her happiness. As Mara waved good-bye to all, Kate Hunt appeared with her two children. She came to the side of her husband, her baby in her arms. Smiling, Scott Hunt took the baby from her and put his arm around her shoulders. Little Alice clung to his leg. And then, not quite smiling herself, standing a little stiff, Kate waved good-bye to Mara, too.

On the long ride home, Sully talked. He seemed full of confidence. His spirits were high. Mara was excited to hear that Mama had received a letter from Papa. He was doing well in Boston. Aunt Caroline had not yet passed away, and Papa was having some difficulty resolving the legal ends of the estate, but things looked good. It might take another few months to finish up, he had said. Since the letter had been sent three months ago, Sully said Papa was probably on his way home by now. Sully thought it would be good for Papa to pump some of his fortune into Provo. Goodness knows the area could use a little prosperity.

Sully began talking about himself. It was the first time Mara had every really heard Sully tell the details of his early life before, and it was interesting to her.

He'd never had any rich relations himself, he said. His mother was a poor devout Irish Catholic who died on a ship out of Donegal. He could never remember her talking about his father. All he knew was that his father's name had been O'Hara. He found himself at age seven taken in by a brawling family called Tuttle who brought him to New York City and put him to work and fed him until he ran away. Still only ten, he found himself in a factory where he tagged onto an old man named Heber Wilson who took a liking to him and smuggled him into his wife's kitchen. He took up with a rough group of boys until the New York Police came armed with a warrant and a summons looking for a "scrawny kid with red hair." The Wilsons hid him, and he stayed out of courts and foster homes. He was only thirteen when he heard the Mormon missionaries at a street meeting on Long Island. He left soon afterward for Missouri where the Hunts took him in.

Mara knew Sully had been an orphan on the streets of New York. But she hadn't known the details. She felt a new sympathy. She herself had suffered hard and frightening times in her childhood, but she had always had her family. Sully went on. He told about good times with the Hunts in Nauvoo and in the Great Salt Lake Valley. He began to talk of his farm in Provo. He talked of Ivie Richards' sprawling place and how much better his own was. He talked of his hard work and his plans for the future. Mara's head began to ache from Sully's incessant talking, and she grew weary. He hadn't stopped for hours. Sobe was cross. She bounced him and sang to him, but he would not settle down. Still Sully talked, as though one minute's silence between them would be fatal.

As though he sensed her impatience, Sully changed the subject to something more exciting. He began to talk of his encounters with Indians and of the violence he had seen. Then he got on the subject of Ivie Richards and his stepson Clem who, after Tony Richards' death, kept hoping to return to Salt Lake City. Sully told how the Richards family might let him farm their land. I'd be glad to, he had answered, for he planned on marrying soon and raising a big family. He stared at Mara. She turned from him. He must know she would guess his thoughts. When she was silent, he continued with something else. Mara wondered at herself for the feelings she had nourished for him these last few months. She had even let it pass through her mind that it might be possible after all to make her life with him. Now it all died inside her as his talk first bored and then disgusted her.

As though he sensed he was losing what he had gained, Sully began to talk faster, of nothing. He chattered his nonsense as though he were a runner near the finish who could not let up for fear of losing face. How foolish he is! Mara thought. He doesn't know the first thing about winning a woman's heart. If he would just be quiet! And the cool confidence he had shown at Hunts' was gone. Couldn't he tell when he was no longer interesting?

Sobe's fussing finally got to be more than Mara could stand. Without waiting for Sully to pause for breath, Mara finally said, "Sully, please. The baby wants to go to sleep. If we could be quiet for maybe an hour. . . ." She was sorry for the exasperation in her voice, but she couldn't help it. It was the first relaxing moment she would have on the trip.

Sobe finally went to sleep on her shoulder. Mara didn't put him down in the wagon for fear Sully would take that as a sign to start talking again. She knew Sully was sulking beside her, but she didn't care. He deserved it for being so inconsiderate. Mara listened to Sobe's quiet breathing and to the gulls overhead. Sully began to whisper. Mara shushed him. It was a long quiet afternoon.

Even when the baby woke toward evening and Sully began to talk again, Mara told him she was tired and had a headache and she would be grateful for quiet. When they stopped to make camp for the night, Sully sat silent by the fire, staring into the flames. He didn't look at her as she fed Sobe his cereal. He mumbled thanks and blushed as Mara handed him a plate of the stew Ella had sent with them. Mara was sorry then that she had hurt him, but she didn't know what else to do. She realized how much she must have encouraged him by her smiles and her attentiveness on his visits at the Hunts'. And she really had enjoyed him. But now it was all as before.

"I should never have told you so much about the kind of life I lived as a child," Sully said into the fire as they ate their stew.

"No, Sully, that was interesting," Mara said. He had it entirely wrong. He did not understand. He could never understand. Mara felt sorry for him. But she knew she could never love him. She could never endure life with Sully Tuttle.

They made good time into the valley the next morning. They would be home a little after noon. They had reached a point where they could get a good view of the fort. Mara was feeding Sobe as Sully stood in the cart to look ahead. Suddenly he sat down. "Mara!" he said, his voice low and tense. "Indians. Bands I've never seen before. They've set up camp across the road!"

Mara started, her heart pounding. She looked ahead. She could see smoke from cooking fires. "Mara!" Sully was standing up again. "Horses!"

Mara put Sobe down in the back of the wagon and

stood to look. She could not believe what she saw. Far away, the ground was moving in dark waves. It looked to Mara like the roiling herd of buffalo they had seen on their trek across the plains. "Wild horses!" Sully breathed. "I've never seen anything like 'em!" They watched, amazed, in silence, as the wild herd rolled across the valley. And then Sully spoke again, shouted, "The crops! They'll kill the crops!"

He snapped the reins across the horse's back and Mara fell to her seat as the cart jerked forward. "Sully! What do you think you can do about it?"

"Mine is up . . . up . . . further. . . . Maybe they haven't. . . ." He spoke to the air, not to Mara, and said no more. The cart rambled down from the crest of the hill. In about five minutes the Indians had seen them, and now four large Indians rode toward them. Sully whispered for Mara to climb into the wagon bed with Sobe and then hand him up something white. He grabbed the diaper she handed him and waved it wildly above his head. Mara did not recognize any of the Indians who drew up in front of the wagon. An old one in front spoke. "Mor-mon?" His thin voice came from deep in his wrinkled throat. He was the most wrinkled Indian Mara had ever seen, older even than Old Bishop. His tiny eyes hid deep above his protruding cheek bones.

"Mor-mon?" the old Indian repeated.

Still Sully said nothing, but he nodded his head.

"Walkara fight." First he pointed to the horses, then to a camp to his right which spread down into the valley of Sully's place (of John and Sophia's, too, Mara thought with a pang) and then up into the hills. "Walkara fight Mor-mon. Brigham Young no fight Snakes."

Mara held Sobe tight to her breast, his black head covered with a blanket. "Walkara fight Mor-mon," the old man repeated. Then he pointed to Sully. "You tell Brigham fight Snake. Walkara mad. Brigham no want fight Snake." Mara understood at last. Sully had told them at Hunts' of Walkara's demand that Brigham fight the Snakes, but Brigham Young was determined to remain at peace with the Indians. Now Walkara must think he could strike here, away from the militia, and force Brother Brigham to do his bidding in order to protect his own settlers. But where did all these beautiful horses come from?

"Walkara chief. Big chief." The old Indian pounded his chest. "Bring back horses from sea. Fight white man." The Indian's arms stretched wide, then he pounded his fists together.

Mara felt cold fear. She could see the reins shaking in Sully's trembling hands. He turned to look at her, his face white with terror. He turned back. There was not a white man in sight. Indians surrounded the fort in the distance. How would they draw the cart through an ocean of wild horses before the eyes of Walkara and his bloodthirsty band? *Oh Father in Heaven, save us!* Mara prayed silently. There was no other help.

"Who is your chief?" Sully was speaking to the old Indian.

"Sowiette." The old Indian pointed to the camp, to the largest tepee set in a ring of colorful skin tents. "Sowiette fight Snakes. Mor-mon no fight Snakes."

So Sowiette's Indians were here as Walkara's allies! "You come," the old Indian said, and he turned toward the camp. With an Indian on every side, the cart rolled across the dry summer ground into the camp. Mara's heart bumped against her ribs, against Sobe, who mercifully slept soundly. What would Sully say to Sowiette?

He told her to stay in the wagon with the baby. Immediately a group of women surrounded her, poking and staring and chattering. They came so close she could smell their strong breath. She prayed Sobe would not awaken. What would they do if they saw she held an Indian child! She saw the men lead Sully into the chief's tepee. He looked back at her with a bleak look of fear in his eyes and then disappeared.

It seemed to Mara an eternity before Sully appeared again. With him was a handsome Indian with a very dark brown complexion. That would be Sowiette. Sully turned to him as they emerged from the tepee. "Brother," Sully said, extending his hand. A slow smile spread across Sowiette's face. Mara thought he looked amused, as though he were about to burst into laughter at this skinny nineteen-year-old red-headed white boy with his hand out. "Brother," Sully said again. Slowly, Sowiette raised his hand and gripped Sully's. Mara nearly burst into tears with relief. How had he done it? For a moment she was overcome with amazed admiration for Sully Tuttle.

Sully scrambled onto the driver's seat. "What. . . ?" Mara began.

"Sh-h-h!" Sully whispered to her. "Sowiette doesn't really want to fight us. He wants to fight the Snakes. I'll tell you later." And he sat shifting in his seat as about twenty young braves with shiny new rifles gathered around them. Mara climbed up next to Sully, holding sleeping Sobe tight. Sowiette disappeared into his tepee again. The summer sun beat down on them. Sobe began to cry. Mara pulled a biscuit from her apron and gave it to him inside the blanket. She dared not uncover him in the Indian camp. Sobe gnawed on the biscuit, content. Mara's own stomach growled from hunger. "I'm starved," Sully whispered. But they dared not move to eat.

They waited an hour, more. "He's taking his own sweet time," Sully said almost inaudibly between his teeth. But at last Sowiette appeared from his rites in his tent, leaped onto a handsome Appaloosa, and rode to the edge of the camp to look over the valley. Then he beckoned the others to follow.

Down inside the valley, Walkara was camped overlooking the fort as though ready to pounce upon the settlers at the least provocation. Sowiette, a handsome figure on his tall horse, led the party directly into the center of the waves of horses, which parted like Moses' sea. Mara held her breath painfully as the cart rocked toward the fort. She breathed easily only as the Indians left them to move toward Walkara's camp. Sowiette nodded to Sully, indicating that if he were going to get into the fort, he should go now . . . to the south. Sully turned Sequel away from Sowiette's warriors and made his way through the wild horses toward the fort gate.

"It's me, Sully Tuttle," he yelled. A voice behind the heavy wooden fence hooted with excitement and slowly the gate squeaked open.

"Heaven's name! How did you get through?"

"Sowiette is only interested in war with the Snakes. He's pleading for us now, but don't count on his luck for a few hours!"

Just as Sully leaped from the horse and drew the cart away from the Indians and into the fort, one of Walkara's burning arrows zinged into the wagon bed.

Startled, Mara jumped back. The arrow was smoking in the straw. She clutched Sobe to her breast and tried to back away as the straw flared. And then she tore the blanket from Sobe's body, set him back on the wagon seat, and flew with the blanket over the flames. She stamped and staggered and knelt on her smoking skirt to smother the fire.

By now Sully was with her, his large hands beating about. The men inside the fort pulled the cart quickly in and leaned against the gate to close it. Several of the wild horses had nosed into the gate and were shut in. Brother Allen slipped the large lock into its grip. Another burning arrow flew into the fort yard. Another hit the stand where the cannon stood. Each time an arrow entered the fort the men beat out the fire with canvas, with brooms, and with rakes wrapped in rags soaked with water from the rain barrels.

Someone shouted from a window, "They're coming with fire to the walls!" A shot rang out and the pattering of feet faded into the hot afternoon. Another shot, more running, the sounds of the horses. Then it grew still. The settlers stood like a forest of immovable trees, waiting to breathe. After a moment Mara snatched Sobe away from the cart and turned toward the cabin. Ashel ran toward her. Following him was Mama, her arms outstretched, and behind Mama, Spirit of Earth and Rain.

With morning, its cool blue sky and the slow sun over the eastern hills, the Indians had gone—all of them, Walkara and his horses, and the champion Sowiette. Even the rows of tepees on both the northern and eastern hills were nowhere to be seen.

Mara woke early to care for Sobe as usual, but Mama was much better, and she was so delighted to see Sobe that she sent Mara back to bed. Mara slept while Mama fed Sobe. She half woke to hear Ashel, Sully, and Spirit of Earth and Rain working silently around her, hushing household sounds with deliberation and care.

The return to Provo was like a silent falling into darkness and peace. Without dreaming, Mara slept. She slept off and on for almost three days. She did not understand how she had come to such weariness, but she enfolded herself into its warmth with acceptance and even joy. It was as though she now returned to her childhood. As much as she loved Sobe, loved caring for him, she now gave up all responsibility with total gratitude and peace. Her mother's renewed health comforted her, and she relished lying still on the cot as though she were asleep, watching from narrowly opened eyelids the movements of her mother in the tiny cabin, preparing food, polishing silver, and playing with the baby Sobe who seemed to think that having many mothers was glorious business. Even Spirit of Earth and Rain occupied Sobe as they wove or peeled bark from willows in symmetrical strips for their clever work. They were completely patient with his heartless attacks on their corner, and they held him and dawdled him until he no longer believed he could sit and play for a few moments by himself but must have a constant companion and constant entertainment. Ashel loved him—playing with him, poking his ribs to hear his giggle, dancing, and pulling faces and crossing his eyes at him, which Mama put a stop to at once.

After the days of sleep came the dreams. Now Mara, feeling rested, feeling free from the tension she had suffered in living so closely with Kate, began to find herself dreaming freely of places she had never been, of beautiful flights in the air, walks in far away gardens. She found herself dreaming of Papa, dreaming of the house they would build, dreaming of Georgian pillars, green shutters, hedges trimmed with a king's shears.

And as her dreaming brought Mara peace, so did peace come to the Utah Valley settlement. As a dead quiet settles over the forest after a fire, the people were left alone after all their troubles.

Sully said he thought Walkara's band was not far away and still camping in a south canyon near Hobble Creek or near the new Fort Payson, but at least no one in Provost's Hole saw many of them, and when they did come in, they very often appeared in small groups and merely begged for food.

For the first time since they had come into the valley a year and a half ago, the settlers of Provo felt able to breathe. "They know we mean business," Sully said often. He was proud of his success with Sowiette. He was regarded as somewhat of a hero in camp, though Mara knew it was a mystery even to Sully what had really happened in Sowiette's tepee that day. "I told him we wanted peace," Sully told her. "He said, 'Walkara fight too many.' And then we came out." Mara was pleased that Sully didn't try to make more of it than there had been.

On the day of Walkara's raid, Sully had without hesitation claimed the four wild horses that nosed through the gate as his own. A few others raised half-hearted objections that they were Walkara's horses and wild at that and that such booty was open to public bid. But after arguing awhile with Sully, who claimed firmly that since he had brought them inside the fort, they were his, most objectors backed down. Hadn't Tuttle saved them all by talking to Sowiette? He deserved the horses. The horses were ferociously wild, anyway, and if Sully Tuttle was willing to break his back to tame them, it seemed only fair they should be his.

They were his pride and joy. For a week he had worked with them unceasingly at the fort, Ashel and a few of his friends tagging behind him. First Sully broke the large black mare; her mouth bled on the hack.

"She's beautiful," Mara said, the first day she came out of the cabin, staring, half afraid.

Sully led the mare he called Tar round the fort corral several times in between each attempt to climb onto her broad back and ride. Sully was not bad with animals, and when Mara was able, she brought Sobe with her and stood to watch him calm his wild prizes. Rain and

Nancy often followed them, too—Nancy always effusive with praise for Sully's skill.

Mara's favorite was an Appaloosa with five spots on her face. It looked as though a big grizzly, after dipping his paw in ink, had tried to grab her nose. "Pawface" tamed in no time at all, and Sully let Mara ride her outside the fort after the first week. Pawface didn't like a saddle. But bareback, Mara could take her through any pace without coaxing.

Ashel liked the brown stallion they dubbed George Washington, and Sully let Nancy or Rain ride the old runt he called "Mrs. Artemus Blake."

Rain proved herself to be skillful with horses, and she helped Sully train all of them. On hot August afternoons, Rain, Nancy, and Mara rode the mares, while Sully rode the stallion George Washington. Ashel often followed on Sequel. They delighted in discovering deer and Indian trails in and out of small canyons, through rivers, creeks, alongside the lake. Rain remembered some of the country from her childhood, although she had spent most of it north of Provo a few miles.

Alone, in the early mornings while Sobe still slept, Mara began to take Pawface to the east to ride the crescent of the hills, tasting the sweet air, shaking loose with long miles of a pure wild gallop until her breath stung in her ribs and the flanks of the horse foamed with sweat.

Pawface was bright and well tempered. Mara loved her and begged Sully to let her stay when he went up to harvest his crops. He was reluctant, but Mara knew he could not say no to her, and he left Pawface in the corral whenever he was gone. He also left instructions that only Mara was to ride her, unless there was an emergency, in which case it might be all right for Nancy or Rain to ride her. He took his other horses with him to his canyon farm and trained them for pulling loads, for plowing, for drawing carts.

Although much of the settlement crops had been damaged by the herd of wild horses, the canyon farms had been unharmed and yielded a bountiful harvest. Sully was pleased at the amounts of wheat and corn he continued to gather for storage.

Toward the end of August, Sister Eastman received another letter from Brother Eastman dated June 10, 1850. Sully was at the gate when the messenger from Salt Lake brought it, and he delivered it without delay:

My Dear Martha:

This is to inform you that your Aunt Caroline Astle has passed the way of all flesh on June 8, 1850.

Although I have addressed several epistles to my family I have remained insecure of their destination, receiving only two of the eight letters you told me you wrote here. I was pleased to make note of the possibility of Mara's marriage to Captain Scott Hunt. If she is set on a plural arrangement, he will without a doubt make her a good man. However, if I am not mistaken, he has four or five grown sons. Would there be any possibility of her settlement on any one of them?

I am still overcome by my sorrows for our beloved Sophia and her dear child whom I never did see and for good John Smith. But as I have filled my last two letters with my grief, I should come now to the matter of my return to Provo with the four-year-old Caroline, who is a handful if I might be allowed to express such a sentiment.

The estate was barely settled to the satisfaction of your Aunt Caroline Astle when she called missionary Heber Williams and myself to bless her at her bedside after which, looking peaceful as an angel, she left this earth as though she chose the time of day herself, which might possibly be the case, as she chose everything else in her life, except the death of her son.

Little Caroline and I will return with Heber Williams and three other missionaries on their way back from Boston to reach Salt Lake City on or near September 1. If it is at all possible I would beg of you to make some arrangements with Sully Tuttle, Hunts, Allens, or some other parties to bring our oxen and cart and if possible, one or two others to help transport some furnishings and items of construction—windows, sashes, doors, which I will be both bringing from Boston or purchasing in Salt Lake City for the construction of our home.

It is impossible to believe I shall soon be home. And if all providence smiles, we shall be together again my beloved Martha. Yours truly in our Savior Jesus Christ.

Hart Eastman

September 1 was now less than a week away. Excitement was high at the Eastmans'. Martha often clapped her hands with happiness and pure pleasure, and she tried to work things out with Sully down to the last detail. In hearty response to Brother Eastman's letter, both Sully and the Allens offered to drive their teams and empty wagons to Salt Lake City, and Stephen Allen, Nancy's brother, offered to drive the Eastman team.

Sister Eastman worried that if they made it to Salt Lake City by the first of September, Brother Eastman might not be there and they would have to wait. Sully did not mind waiting at Hunts', but Brother Allen was very busy with harvesting, so he and his son preferred to stay in Provo until they received news that Brother Eastman had surely arrived. Then they would drive their own wagon and the Eastman wagon to pick up Brother Eastman's things.

The men were so busy with harvesting that Sully wondered if Mara and Ashel couldn't both go with him to Salt Lake City to wait at the Hunts. Ashel jumped with excitement at the prospect, begging Sully to let him ride George Washington.

"Well, George Washington and Tar will prob'ly be drawing the cart," Sully said, almost absently, waiting for Mara to say she would also go. Mara stood outside the cabin with the baby in her arms. "And you and Ashel could see your Papa and come back on the horses to fetch Allens," Sully offered.

Sully's hope for Mara's love had never died, but the last few weeks had been hard for him. He had been so hopeful when he saw her at the Hunts'. Her face had lighted when she saw him; he was sure of that. But something had happened on that trip home, something he said. He was not sure what. Since then, Mara seemed detached, distant. Sully had rejoiced at the chance to lend Pawface to her. His heart pounding for love, he had watched her handle the high-spirited animal with reverence and awe. He envied every motion of the horse under her slender body as she touched the withers, stroked the neck, patted the sleek dark mane.

But Mara's attention to the horse still looked like attention to the horse. He had to admit none of it seemed to be misplaced need for Sully, the master. Sully brooded, and he hoped for Mara to come with him to Salt Lake City. Sister Eastman could care for the baby. Mara could ride Pawface.

But Mara said no.

"It would be too dangerous for them to come all the way back here alone, anyway," Sister Eastman said to fill the awkward silence as Sully stared at Mara, his disappointment turning at last to anger. "Just go on, Sully. If somebody isn't coming back to bring the news about that time, bring Papa all the way home. Allens can go up any time, or Papa could go back himself."

Sully's eyes darkened, and he stared at Mara for a long moment. Lately she had not even looked at him. Sometimes he hated her. She had caused him untold pain. She would never know how much. He hated her now. But under his hatred was the deepest grief his heart had ever known. For after his hopes had been so high, only to be dashed again, a strange and terrible awareness began to grow in him—an awareness that Mara might in very fact never be his.

"Perhaps Nancy or Rain or both would go with you," Mara suggested in a mild voice. "I have the baby, and Mama needs help to get ready."

Sully stared without speaking. In his confusion he couldn't be certain his heart felt hatred or riveting love. But he felt certain of the pain. Nancy or Rain. He had always known that Nancy was fond of him, although he always ignored it. Surely Mara knew of Nancy's feelings too. She was her best friend, after all. For the first time he admitted to himself that Mara had always tried to urge him to care for Nancy. A strange hot anger twisted in him as he looked into Mara's steady eyes. No light reflected there for him now, that was certain. Nancy. Well, then, he would teach his heart to accept things the way they seemed to be. Perhaps he could *love*—if not *love*, at least *accept*—Nancy.

He was aware then that he and Mara were alone. Everyone had gone and left them there standing alone in front of the Eastman cabin.

"You don't really care about me. You never did, did you Mara?"

Looking older somehow than she had ever seemed before, Mara said in a voice that was to Sully maddeningly patient, "Sully, I care about you but not in the way you hoped I would. Sully, I have always known I would never be able to marry you. Please believe me. Someone who loves you will bring you so much greater happiness." She paused. "And I know someone who does." She paused again, and Sully thought she looked afraid. Yes! After having me to fall back on all this time, she is afraid to lose me once and for all! But she went on. "Nancy does."

Sully swallowed hard and stared. It was done. In this grinding instant he found in his heart a jolting shift, as though a great door were closing.

"Then you are saying no. For sure no."

"For sure no, Sully."

"Always?"

"Always." And she turned and went into the cabin, closing the door behind her.

After Papa had been in the fort for a few days Mara realized how much she had missed him. Papa was home. It gave her comfort—she was no longer alone. His big rough presence filled up the empty spaces, even the emptiness in her heart for a time.

"Mara girl," Papa had said, when she came to greet her. "My little dove who's had such a hard time of it being shuttled from heart to heart."

Mara let him hold her in his big arms for a long time. "Papa," she said over and over again. She felt as though a long hard journey had come to an end for all of them. Now they would have a big new house. Papa could begin any business he chose to begin in the valley.

"Now you won't be needin' to get yourself married, my little angel. Stay home with us a while. Someday there'll be somebody."

When Papa talked like that, Mara thought about Bret, about his strength, his courage, about the man he would be, and in a strange reverie that took her away while she fed or rocked Sobe, she began to feel she had always been in love with Bret, that Bret was the man she would eventually marry. She began to realize that all of the other affairs of her heart had been the result of her needs, her own romantic notions, the power of others over her. Now that she was growing into a woman who knew her own mind, she began to know that in her own mind, body, and soul, she wanted Bret, and she would wait for him, no matter how long it took. Bret, who would be all that was good in Scott Hunt, but would be hers alone.

She would not need to tell anyone. She would wait. Other men might come into her life, but they would not be important, just brief flirtations to pass the time. She clung to a dream she manufactured out of nothing but memory. She clung to it with stern hope, knowing that someday, if she prayed for it, hoped for it, and worked for it, she would see Bret again, and they would be together forever.

So, conscientiously, she forced herself to do other things with her life, to share Nancy's courtship and eventual engagement to Sully, to think of the new house, the children—Ashel, Caroline, and Sobe.

Nancy was ecstatic with happiness. At first she was careful as she talked to Mara.

"Mara, are sure you don't mind if I talk about Sully? I am so happy."

"Nancy, I'm glad for you and Sully," Mara assured her. "Nancy, I couldn't be happier. I really could not have married Sully. You know that. We are not for each other."

Once she understood Mara's feelings to be genuine, Nancy beamed with joy. "Oh, Mara. I love him so much. He is a hard worker, and his farm is so beautiful. And he tells such interesting stories. Did I tell you that after the harvest he will give me Pawface?" Mara looked quickly at her feet to hide her shock at the sudden realization that Pawface was not actually hers. "But he also told me he would let you ride," Nancy said kindly, putting her hand on Mara's arm.

Pawface. Sometimes Nancy's excitement cut into Mara's heart, and she wondered to herself if she had not made a mistake. At these times, she brooded and rocked Sobe for as long as he would sit still. And she deliberately thought about her feelings for Bret. She bent her thoughts with her will to remember that dark night a year and a half ago when she had told Bret good-bye. Then for a few days, she would be all right going about her work, listening to Nancy's happy talk, knowing deeply in her soul that Bret would return someday and it would be a glorious day, and that she would never be sorry she had not married Sully.

The new house occupied all of them. With some of the clean, newly-cut lumber Papa had brought down on one of the wagons, he and the neighbors at once put up a very large square shed on the Eastman lot that was to serve as the "carriage house." The goods from all of the other wagons were emptied into it, and Mara, with Nancy and Mama, thoroughly examined with wonder and delight all that Papa had bought with the first of their fortune from Aunt Caroline.

Mara had never seen such lovely things. Papa not only brought lumber, but wagons full of windows, doors, doorknobs, cement, and pounds of nails. He also brought all of their old furniture that they had been storing in Salt Lake City. And best of all, more than a dozen lovely pieces from Boston: a mahogany sideboard, a secretary, a Chippendale table, and a set of dining room chairs, two or three bedroom sets complete with chesterfields, dressing tables, featherbeds, mattresses, and bedsteads delicately scrolled with masterful work, handcrafted, stained and polished until they shone like mirrors. He brought two settees as well as mirrors, clocks, dishes, buckets, pots and pans, knives, silverware and soup ladles, candlesticks, a cruet stand, wedgewood tureens, baskets, and trunks full of linens, draperies, unused materials and old dresses and hats, though slightly dated, richly and expensively designed and cut.

Of course, along with the goods came the little four-year-old Caroline, a tiny flaxen-haired, pearly-toothed china doll who was "as spoiled as a bad egg in an abandoned hen house," said Papa. It was all Mama could do to keep from spanking her the first few days.

"I don't want to!" she said constantly when asked to do any simple thing—eat, dress for bed, pick up her clothes.

"Well, you might just have to lay the rod on her, Martha," Papa said. "Lay the rod on her. Goodness knows I've lost patience with her a hundred times."

Although he had spanked her plenty, she seemed to like Papa, and would mind him occasionally. But as for the rest, she looked at them with disdain, holding her head in the air and pouting, refusing to be civil. Sometimes when Papa came in the door, she ran to him and hugged his legs furiously, glaring at the rest of them.

Mama said she felt like spanking never worked very well but sitting in the corner might help. When little Caroline cried and said "I don't want to" in a nasty pouting way, Mama took her by the hand, led her to the corner, and said, "Now you sit there until you can behave yourself."

Sometimes Caroline cried so loudly for so long that Mama took her sewing or their whole supper out into the fort yard on a warm autumn night and ate or sewed or played games while the spoiled four-year-old screamed her head off in the cabin for thirty or forty minutes.

"You sure you know what you're doin', Martha?" Hart Eastman would glare at his wife beneath his gray whiskery eyebrows. "I would lay into her with a hearty rod until she promised to quit it."

"I don't want her to hate her new home," Mama said with patience. "She'll finally catch on she has to learn to control her own self."

For a while Mara stayed away from Caroline. She let Mama take charge. But after a time, when Caroline wanted to hold the baby, she began to try to pay some attention to her, and a surprisingly soft little girl began to emerge. As Mara grew to love the soft child hidden deep in little Caroline, she disliked more and more the ugly tantrums, the balking. Sometimes, no matter how much they tried, Caroline would not behave, but there were more and more good times, and it seemed possible that Caroline might be pleasant to have around . . . someday.

It soon became obvious that Caroline's favorite friend was Ashel. Since Papa was her other favorite and he spent so much time away from the fort, she soon learned to tag onto "Asho."

"Asho, take me for a walk," she insisted every day. With the patience of Job, Ashel tucked her small hand into his and walked with her across the fields to the river to watch the pigs or throw stones into still ponds. He often took her to the site of the Eastman lot where the new home was going up rapidly, adobe brick after adobe brick.

"Keep her out of the way," Papa would call to Ashel, and the boy would dart to pull Caroline out of the way.

She never seemed to be angry with him but delighted at his rough handling, throwing her curly light blond head back and gurgling with laughter. "Asho. Stop it, Asho. Don't tickle me," she would howl.

There was a time just before Christmas that Ashel begged to join the men in finishing the floors and painting the walls.

"Well, I don't know," Papa said. "You've been a bigger help keeping Caroline out of the way."

"Let him work," Mama said. "He'll feel more like the house is partly his."

So Papa furnished Ashel and Mara and even Nancy and Sully, who said they would help, with paint brushes, and they white-washed the large lumber shed and the trim on the windows and doors.

Completed just before the cold weather set in, the house was one of about seventeen new homes scattered in various locations across the site of the new city of Provo.

At town meetings, Ellis Eames, the first elected mayor, praised the citizens for their good work and assigned them conscripted time for roads and public improvements. Even Papa took one day out of every week for a while to build city roads, clear timber, fence, and begin work on a new home the settlers were preparing for George Albert Smith, whom Brigham Young promised he would send. They set the imposing new home on the northwest corner of First North and Main. Papa's lot was south of the park on the northeast corner of the block. Two big windows downstairs and the main bedroom window upstairs looked down on the site of the new park.

The men diverted a stream of water from the river and brought it down alongside the east edge of the park, and also along the east of the Eastman lot. When the ditch was completed and the autumn river coursed into it, they held a banquet on the park side, roasting a large piece of meat and sharing biscuits, homemade butter, and tanks of milk.

"We been working hard and reaping some of the benefits of our hard work," Ellis Eames announced to everybody at the picnic. "Now we all still owe the city at least one day a week, and we'll be ready with more roads by the time George Albert Smith arrives." Brigham Young's promise to send a general authority into the area meant the city of Provo was truly settled.

Smith's home was completed the following spring. He was scheduled to conduct the ceremony for Nancy and Sully's wedding then, but problems in Salt Lake City were to keep him there until August. His absence did not hold back the glorious plans for the local ceremony, however, to be followed by a sealing on Ensign Peak in the Salt Lake Valley.

It was a balmy, beautiful spring, ripe with fruit blossoms, and the Allens created a community affair on the greening lawn of their new home in the block south of the Eastmans, an imposing salt box similar to the Eastmans' house, with the addition of a fancy stone wall. The Allens hired the Gibson brothers to provide fiddle music, and from three o'clock in the afternoon until after midnight they served a buffet spread out on linen tablecloths draped over four tables in their large yard. It was an unending stream of delicious beef, ham, chicken, deviled eggs, and loaf after loaf of sweet breads, cheese breads, cakes, berries, raisins, and custard pies.

Mara watched Sully marry Nancy with mixed feelings of longing, pain, and loneliness. The few bits of news she had heard of Bret came only accidentally from travelers from Salt Lake City. Occasionally her father, who came back with another load of goods or lumber, had heard something from Scott Hunt which he passed on, that

Bret and his uncle were doing well in the mission field, that they wrote seldom, but were planning to return in the spring of 1853, still two years from now.

Only once Mara had made the mistake of mentioning her feelings for Bret to her mother. It was after a night of dancing and Mara had refused to walk home with Rob Wheeler.

"He's eligible, Mara, and he likes you. Can't you accept ordinary nice boys?" her mother asked, a tone of impatience in her voice. She had never forgiven Mara for letting Sully go.

"I really think I'm in love with someone else."

"Who?" Mama said immediately.

"Oh. . . ."

"Anyone around here?"

"No, not really."

"Mara, you're not . . . not mooning over Brother Hunt or any of his boys now, are you?" Mama waited, but Mara didn't answer. "I know you had eyes once on that oldest Hunt boy, Bret, the one that's on the mission. Mara, you ought to forget about him. It was a passing fancy. He won't be back for two more years. You ought to think of practical things, think about someone close by, someone you can see, talk to, get to know. You dream too much, girl. Real life will pass you by while you dream."

Mama's words cut to Mara's heart with a dull edge of pain. She did not say anymore, because she blamed herself for betraying her own secret.

"If you keep hanging onto dreams, you'll be disappointed, mark my word, girl."

But even though Mama's sharp words cut Mara's heart, she clung to the pieces of her knowledge of Bret. He would remember. True, it did not seem right to expect a letter from him or some indication now that he would see her when he returned, but Mara knew in her heart that she loved him and that it would work out when he came back.

That summer of 1851, Papa entered into the Deseret Manufacturing Company with George Allen and three others who formed the corporation for business purposes and decided their first enterprise would be a hefty crop of sugar beets. When they had fantastic financial success that first season, they made plans for other agricultural pursuits. In the spring of 1852, they opened up the Western Commerce Bank and built a small hotel. Papa was prosperous at last, just as he had always promised. Mama was as happy as Mara had ever seen her. And Mara bided her time.

Chapter Twelve

Sipapu saw the bones of the house rising in the flat wilderness. She saw stones one by one in neat rows in the chimney, the large clay blocks baking in the July heat and fitting carefully into wet mortar. She did not help with the building, but she and Mipuwai watched it cautiously from a distance as they dug for roots, peeled bark, or gathered a few wild berries in the low hills.

Soon the walls climbed into the sky. Other houses around the city rose. The men worked both day and night making brick, cutting timber, fencing. They cut the desert into places for houses, sheared the ground of growth, until no animals lived under or over the ground. The earth was changing before Sipapu's old eyes.

Sometimes, watching it, Sipapu remembered Hapu and felt his old spirit breathing with her breath. Hapu would have squinted with his cat eyes at the land shaved and raw and squared and marked. He would have stared at the houses. He would have sat for many hours at the fire thinking it over. Hapu could no longer speak to his woman, but he would have said, "White man busy without listening."

He would not have thought it good for the white man to move in with his way of building, his way of living, while the dark man stood by in the hills and watched the town from a distance, afraid to go near it, not understanding it, knowing it was here that some of his brothers had been killed.

"Hapu," Sipapu thought to herself, calling on the spirit of Mipuwai's father. He was sometimes very close, so close she could have reached out and touched his wrinkled cheeks. In the day as she skirted the town with Mipuwai, gathering berries and watching, she felt that his eyes were close. Like a butterfly his presence darted around them, staring at Mipuwai.

Mipuwai. Sipapu also watched Mipuwai. Like a strong, young cow, she was ready for children. With Mipuwai she could touch the earth so many years from now through the whisper of herself that was growing in her daughter. But something else was happening to Mipuwai, and Sipapu watched it carefully, talking in her deep heart as though talking with Hapu who stayed close. It was what was happening when Mipuwai sat with the white girl on the grass in the fort and watched her draw words on the slate. Sobeshent played beside them, laughing, chasing the dogs or chickens. Sobeshent. Son of Agasraki, Blueflower. Would he grow tall and strong as her own son, Hapu's son, their Sobeshent? Sipapu let her mind rest on the memory of her son. Promised by Hapu to the Medicine Man as husband for his daughter, for Agasraki. Her tall son, raised among the Utes, but filled by her and by Hapu with the Piute ways. Her son, dead in the thirteenth summer of his life of the white man's fever. Sipapu's pain closed out the memory of her son.

Sipapu watched Mipuwai practice drawing the white girl's letters. They were not the old Piute figures Hapu had etched on stone, nor the spiraling scrolls of the Pahvant Utes, the rainbow, the deer dancing. They were strange shapes for the strange words of the white man.

Sipapu watched Mipuwai follow the white girl on the horses, her black hair flying like the wind. Where are you going, Mipuwai? Sipapu asked in her heart. Sometimes she asked the girl, and there were stiff words under the breath that tightened her heart and caused her old limbs to hurt.

"You are Piute. You are not white man."

"I go with them," Mipuwai said, her bottom lip trembling, "with Sobe." Mipuwai carried Sobeshent on her back while she rode the flying horses in the fields. "I will teach him to hunt," she said crossly.

"You teach him to hunt? You know nothing of hunting. He should learn hunting from his fathers. The People."

The words Sipapu spoke echoed in her mind. Sobeshent belonged to the earth, to the People. Her fears of being again sold into slavery by her own people diminished under the greater fear of being lost from her own life forever. She could always escape again from slavery. But if she should die with no one around her who knew how to bury her properly, she would never see her own people again.

She would like to have taken the baby Sobeshent back to his own fathers, to teach him their ways, to see he could understand. But the white girl and the good woman kept Sobeshent as though he were their own. All that belonged to Sipapu was in Mipuwai.

For these many moons Sipapu had accepted this life as breath, food, and the small pleasure of watching Mipuwai grow. But now Mipuwai's growth troubled her, and into her heart came small angers: Mipuwai did not like the ways of the People, she liked white man's writing, the clothes the white girl gave to her to wear. She laughed, like the white girl. If Sipapu could not take Sobeshent, she could at least keep Mipuwai.

For Rain, there was not a thought of turning back. For Rain, the rising house was like a new tree in the empty field, a new place to hide in the storms, a place to go with people who never came with hands empty of food. She did not think of Hapu, but she thought of Mara, of Sully and Nancy, and Sobe and the flying dark horses in the wind. On long mornings waking on the cot outside the fort in the heat of the summer, Rain waited, and believing her mother to be asleep, rose out of the bed, seeking the rich fields and the water and the space. The days were filled with gathering harvests, creating with her hands, working and playing with her friends. And the letters, the writing, the stories she learned to read in the school.

Rain was sad when Spirit of Earth would not move into the Eastmans' new house. "Take the cabin then, please, for yourselves," the white Mama had said. Sipapu did not answer. But they stayed. In the big fort. Rain knew it was better. The ground corn would spoil Mama's fine carpets. Rain knew the Eastmans would always take care of them. It was better to stay in the cabin. The big house was not far away.

On most days, Rain wore her favorite dress—her Christmas from Mara so long ago. (Mara gave only a few more clothes to Rain because Sipapu did not approve.) She took the leather thongs from her hair and braided it fresh. Then she ran to fetch Mara for school. She stood outside Mara's high north window, and she waited until Mara came. She was taller than Mara now. She carried her books with pride, and her slate, covered with words made from sounds Sipapu would never understand.

For many months Sipapu woke to watch Mipuwai leave, watched from the cabin window while her daughter walked to the log school with the dark-haired white girl who had fed her when Hapu had been killed. For many months she waited and watched her daughter grow, until finally Mipuwai was a woman. One day she could wait no more in her old heart, and she spoke.

"I will take you back to the Pahvant. We will find a man of the People for you."

"I will stay here," Mipuwai said, her face frowning like the white faces frowned.

"We must go. Someday soon we will go."

Sipapu watched the hills. Some day she would have to go back into the hills. She was afraid. But she must go. Her time with the white man would soon be over. She must find a man for Mipuwai. If they did not sell her and Mipuwai as slaves, she could offer her daughter as a woman for one of Arrapene's men. There would be a happy old age for Sipapu then, with a man to care for her among her own people until she went to join Hapu.

Sipapu grew angry at her need of the white man's food. She ate little. The white girl led Mipuwai into the fields to work, taught her to make clothes clean in the way of the white man, taught her to make food in the heat from the big black stove. Sipapu must go back—must take Mipuwai back to the People.

She spoke her desires to the Great Spirit that covered them all in the vast land. She called to the spirits of her Piute mother and father, to Shenobe, the great mediator, who would speak for her to Tovats, the world father. She called to Hapu. And finally, she spoke again to Mipuwai.

"It is time. You will never have a white man. You must go back to your people."

Mipuwai's eyes shone fire. "I will. I will live with the white people. Maybe there will be a man. . . ."

"A white man for you?" Sipapu laughed. "A white man will not want you!" Mipuwai looked at the ground. Sipapu's heart ached inside her for the pain in her child's eyes.

It was May. "May." Rain spoke the word Mara had told her. She liked this time of spring and beauty in the valley.

She woke to smell a morning washed with the night's rain. "Rain." It was her name. She was glad. Rain made the earth clean and new and brought life. She sat on the cot and looked to her mother's mat on the floor. But Sipapu was not there!

Sipapu was gone, like a falling star that dropped out of sight and left no sign. She had taken everything; not a piece of her life was left behind in the bare house. How could she carry it all? She was gone.

Startled, Rain listened. She listened to the sounds of morning around her, the sounds of tiny insects in the sun. She heard the white men in the fort stirring, their whips cracking, their hands moving pots and pans in their cupboards, stirring their coals, beginning their morning lives. She heard all of these sounds. And she heard the faraway voice of Sipapu in her heart.

Sipapu waited for Mipuwai in the shadows by the deep, swift river. She prepared herself to wait hours, days. The water in the river, the yellow flowers in the new grass—she saw them. She felt a new spirit enter her old body and cleanse her. She could feel the hills calling her now, and the blood and the dust of her own people calling her. She belonged to this land. It was hers. It was in her. She would no longer live in a dark house of wood and cold stone.

By the time summer was gone she and Mipuwai would be with a man who would hunt for them, feed them as her people would do. And Mipuwai now was old enough to bear a child.

As the sun came through the new leaves, Sipapu saw Mipuwai, small in the distance. She came, as Sipapu knew she would. But slowly. She had been four summers with the white man. It was hard for Mipuwai to come to her now, this she knew. But she came.

Sipapu waited, watching, until the girl came close. Then she rose from the thicket and turned toward the place of the graves of her Hapu and her Sobeshent. She knew Mipuwai saw her, knew she followed behind as Sipapu led the way back to the People.

Sipapu knew that after the massacre, many of the old Battle Creek People had gone. Only the families of Dog Foot and Squash still camped in the ravine, their few women weak from winter, their dogs ravenous, Arrapene and Squash and his brother Kickingboot overseeing the hunting and the harvest. They were greedy and selfish; they were Utes; but they were People.

Sipapu saw Squash and Kickingboot on their gray ponies. They hid in the brush, but Sipapu knew they were there. They waited until the two women drew close and then they appeared. Sipapu's heart beat hard in her breast. She knew her safety would depend on the desire one of the men would have for her own child.

She saw that Squash knew them at once. He leaned his fat body down from his pony to stare into Sipapu's face. Then he dismounted. "It is as I thought. It is the old mother and young daughter that we sold as slaves."

Sipapu's fear locked her mouth. Her body trembled. Then the eyes of Squash looked into the eyes of Mipuwai. He looked at her tall body. "Uh-h-h." He made a long sound of pleasure in his throat.

Then Sipapu saw Kickingboot's eyes resting on Mipuwai as well. Kickingboot, the youngest brother of Squash, had lived with Arrapene and Walkara until two years ago. He was still a young brave.

"You escaped from the whites." It was no loss for Squash, for he and Arrapene had received the white man's weapons, Sipapu knew that. The mouth of Squash trembled as he smiled. "Good. We can sell you again."

Sipapu's heart filled with fear once more. "No," she

said, standing in the shade of Mipuwai, knowing within herself she could bargain for their lives. Her old hand shook as she took the elbow of Mipuwai. "My daughter would made a good wife," she said in her best Ute.

Squash grinned. "We got women." But he looked at Mipuwai. His eyes filled with a gray darkness, as in a dream. Sipapu's heart beat fast.

Kickingboot dug his heels into his pony and rode in a circle around them. Then he dismounted and came to stand beside his old brother. He was much younger than Squash. Sipapu saw his brown skin stretched tight like leather over strong muscles. His eyes looked at Mipuwai. Sipapu knew Mipuwai was not like the starved women in the camps. Sipapu had seen them prowling by the river. They were like death. Mipuwai was tall, round, strong.

Squash spoke to Kickingboot, his eyes narrow. "Winn-iwah's sister will not like it, my brother."

Kickingboot answered, his eyes pleased with the beauty of Mipuwai. "Atsiback is two years now without child. This one would make fine strong sons. She pleases me very much."

Sipapu's heart was glad. Squash spoke again, his voice strange. "Take her, then, Kickingboot, my brother."

Mipuwai trembled. She would be shamed, Sipapu knew it. She was like the white man. She would not like this now. But she would see that it was right.

"Yes. I will have this woman," Kickingboot said at last.

Sipapu nodded. "With mother," she said.

"Mother will come, too!" Squash laughed. "After two years with the old father of Atsiback, and now you are to have the mother as well!" Squash was not a good man, Sipapu thought. He enjoyed the troubles of others.

Kickingboot did not speak for a moment. At last he nodded. "The mother will come, too." And now Sipapu breathed a great sigh of relief. Her old days would be safe now.

Rain walked into the camp with Sipapu, by the side of the man Kickingboot. She cowered in humiliation. Her mother had bought their lives with Rain's body. She knew it was necessary, but she was ashamed. Kickingboot brought them to Atsiback, who was small with large eyes too big for her face. She stood outside a gray, leaning wickiup. Thin women and starved children stared at Sipapu and Rain in wonder. Arrapene came then, just as Kickingboot greeted Atsiback, who did not open her mouth.

"Rain," he said to her.

"And her mother," said Squash. "Women from the field."

"Women who lived with the white man," Arrapene said quietly as he walked toward them.

"Kickingboot will take the daughter," Squash laughed. "And the mother."

The hut was dry, dusty, too warm. The hot air choked Rain. They passed the pipe, the men in a circle. "We must make the gift to Kickingboot," Arrapene said. Rain did not move. She sat, aching, her body feeling broken, watching the bright eyes of Sipapu, watching the young brave Kickingboot who was to be her husband. He looked like tough leather. When the men left the hut, Rain and Sipapu sat on the ground facing Kickingboot. In the background Atsiback squatted silent as stone.

They ate dried beef over a low sputtering fire. It took a long time. Atsiback ate slowly. It lasted long after dark. Finally Kickingboot waved Atsiback and Sipapu away with his hand. Atsiback's large eyes grew larger. "Go!" Kickingboot said, waving his hand once more. He stared at Rain. Rain's heart beat hard against her ribs.

Atsiback's eyes glowed in the firelight. She looked hard at Kickingboot. Her breath came in long slow sighs. Rain watched her. Like a lean wolf Atsiback rose on her legs and slipped away. Then Sipapu, her eyes bright, stood too, and was gone.

Rain sat with Kickingboot for a long time, staring. He reached for her at last, touched her face, lifted her chin. His eyes told her she was pleasing to him. He wanted her. Then he turned to his pipe, and the smoke wavered and rose in the light above the fire. He nodded toward the low mound of bedding on the far side of the old lean-to. It was dusty, ragged, black with soot. Rain first removed the leather from her thick braids, strips from the hides of Sully's old cow, Jane. She had a sudden thought of Sully, of Mara, Nancy, Sobe. Her heart folded like a broken straw. The man smelled of heavy grease. Like horse grease, like butter. His skin was very slick, almost shining. He sat smoking for a long time, and watching.

Finally she removed the old ragged dress Mara had given her so long ago. The man Kickingboot was watching. She felt his eye on her as her clothing fell away. Then his hands came. Her heart froze again. The fingers seemed gentle, but as rough as gravel. Then Kickingboot pulled her toward him with strength, holding her body against his thighs as he knelt. He took her arms in his strong hands and he pulled her into the bedding. Rain felt a falling away, a pain, and a fear, but pleasant feelings she had never known before.

Morning came like a loud light that would scar all of the senses. Rain woke hurting but stunned in a new sense of feeling, her body alive with sensations. And she woke calling in her dreams for Sipapu. Although Atsiback had gone to the lean-to of her old father, Sipapu lay on a mat on the ground outside the wickiup. Now Rain rose as the large man slept, his knees drawn toward his chest. She felt the whisper of Sipapu's breath drawing her to her mother, to the circle of life she knew that still surrounded her. Wrapping herself in a blanket, she slipped toward Sipapu's bedding on the cool new grass close against the back of the wickiup.

Sipapu lay silent but unsleeping.

"Old mother," Rain whispered. Sipapu's hand clutching an old blanket up around her neck began to loosen; the gray fingers reached out. "Old mother," Rain whispered again. She took Sipapu's fingers and pressed them. "It is done."

Sipapu was silent for a few moments. She held Rain's hand. "It is good," she said at last. "He will give us children." That was all she said. But it seemed to Rain that for Sipapu this was all the meaning of life. Children of her own kind. Rain looked at her mother. In her face was a spirit of rest Rain had not seen since Hapu went from them. It was right that they had come.

They lay like two children on the mat together waiting for the sun to rise over the great eastern hills. The others in camp did not rise early.

"Sobeshent," Sipapu finally said quietly. Rain had been thinking of Sobe, too. She missed him. But they could not take him from Mara. She loved him as her own. "Now that we are safe, even with such as Squash and Kickingboot, we must bring him to his own people."

Safe? In her mind Rain called up the picture of Atsiback. But she knew that for Sipapu, safe meant away from the white man with a man to care for her in her old age. Still, they could not take Sobe away from Mara! But Sipapu insisted. "Tell Kickingboot about Sobeshent. Now."

Obedient, Rain returned to Kickingboot's bed with fear. But remembering the gentleness of his hands, she crept into the blankets beside him. He did not awaken. He had not been loathsome to her. She had suffered pain, but he had been strong, and sometimes pleasant.

Now he was her husband. Carefully, she lay against his warmth and listened to his breathing. He turned toward her. She placed her hand on his hip. He turned and drew her body into his arms.

She whispered quietly to him. The sun rose, light filtering through the willow walls.

"I remember Blueflower," Kickingboot mumbled, waking. "Hinte's woman. Maybe it's Hinte's baby." Rain nodded. "We'll go, then." Rain's heart flooded with gratefulness. Kickingboot drew her body close to his again. His large gentle hands fondled her, touched her, and drew her to him until she touched him along his body from head to toe. "A good woman," Kickingboot said. "You stay with me. We'll keep the Ute camp strong with babies." And in the morning he brought her to his body again.

For two weeks Rain saw childless Atsiback watch her from her old father's hut. Rain had the sickness of conception. The camp felt the anger and jealousy as families chose between Kickingboot and Atsiback. The old Indians, and Arrapene, and Squash and Kickingboot tried to appease Atsiback with gifts. But the anger grew in her face. One day she came to the hut to grind corn on her stone. Rain was there at grinding before her. Atsiback pushed Rain and Rain fell over the stone, hitting her hip and her belly hard as she fell. Two days later, the life in her body made great pain, and was rejected while Sipapu, in gray silent tears, looked on.

When he heard, Kickingboot looked from eyes burning with black fires. The only child he had ever made had been destroyed by a jealous woman. He stood tall, his feet spread apart.

"Atsiback must go," he said in thin stiff words, his lips tight against his teeth. Atsiback, her large eyes wide with fear, stepped back from him and clutched the wall of the wickiup with her small hands. Kickingboot moved forward angrily.

"Dog! Atsiback, get out! You will make the mountain walk to die!" The anger in his voice shook his whole body. He began kicking her. His large foot pounded against her.

Rain rushed to him. "No," she cried. "Please no. Don't hurt her." But Kickingboot threw Rain back roughly. Atsiback slumped frightened against the hut, limp as leaves.

"Atsiback will go to die in the mountain."

Not the death walk. Though she had herself been full of anger at Atsiback only a few moments ago, Rain felt a shudder in her body. Arrapene nodded. Atsiback trembled as Squash and Kickingboot took her between them and led her away. They gave her some food, but took her by horse so far back into the mountains that she would not find her way by foot for many days, and perhaps never. Even the old father had no power to stop them, though he beat his breast and cried aloud. His daughter no longer belonged to him.

Rain felt panic and fear. But she did not say anything. She watched, wondering, not wanting to make more trouble, and still suffering from a terrible sadness and pain in her own body. Atsiback's treatment was not strange for the People, but Rain had lived long enough with the white man to be startled by its pain.

After a few days, Kickingboot asked if Rain still wanted to fetch the child Sobeshent from the white man. Kickingboot had often stolen children from other tribes of the People. It was his occupation in the trade of slaves. But he had never stolen a child of the People from the white man. He thought carefully. He considered making a raid on the Snakes to find a child for trade.

Careful not to offend his pride, Rain tried to make Kickingboot forget about stealing a child for trade. "Perhaps if we ask the family they will see the boy should be with his own people. We can take him peacefully." She spoke more from Sipapu's confidence than her own. In her heart she feared Mara would never give up Sobe. But she must try. Sipapu would not rest until Blueflower's child was with his own people.

Kickingboot's eyebrows came together. Dark shadows hung in his eyes. For a moment Rain was afraid he would make the raid—she feared his interest in slaving was greater than his interest in getting Sobe from the white man. He sat in silence, questioning her with a dark stare. "The white man does not give away children," he told her. He looked hard for a long time. Rain waited almost without breathing. But a child of the People. Perhaps they would return a human being to his own.

"We will take guns and many men," Kickingboot said at last.

Rain feared she had already stripped her husband of some pride, so she said nothing. If there were no guns with the People, there would be no guns with the white man, and no death. But in Kickingboot's eyes she saw fear, fear of the white man, though he hid it well. He would do it his way if he did it at all. And Sipapu would not rest until they tried. Not even Rain knew how much Kickingboot could trust her hope that they could take Sobe back to his own people. She waited in silence by the fire. Kickingboot must do it his way.

They took five of the best rifles. Rain knew the white men always wondered at the new rifles the People carried, and at their never-ending supply of ammunition. They took the rifles and eight men into the white man's town. Kickingboot, Squash, Dog Foot, Arrapene, Atsiback's old father, and three young braves. Sipapu and Rain rode in front, the men behind.

It was a hot day. It was the middle of summer. Lizards crawled in the corn. Rain knew it would not seem strange to the white man to see People coming into their town. For several months Arrapene and Kickingboot had been going into the white man's town to ask for bread and flour. The white man had been generous with his food. It had been a good year for the white man. But Rain knew the settlers would be surprised at so many People coming together, and she knew they would be surprised to see her, and Sipapu.

Her heart beat hard inside her. She would see her friends: Mara and Ashel, the white Mama. Maybe Sully and Nancy would be there. Rain was afraid of her happiness at the thought of seeing her friends. What would they think of her, gone from them to be with her own people? They passed the fort, the cabin where she had known so much happiness. She saw the Eastmans' big white house, so much bigger than she had remembered. She could see Mara's window, where she had waited every day. It was only three months that she had been gone, and yet she felt like a stranger. They left their horses in the street near the big park.

A fearful longing came into Rain's heart as they walked toward the big house. She knew that she wanted to go back to this house as a friend, to stay. And she knew that what she was doing now would make that impossible. The door was opening. Ashel stood with dark wondering eyes. "Ashel!" she cried out with joy, in spite of herself. Behind him in the room she saw Mara's face, brightening as she saw who had come. "Rain! You've come home!" And through the tears that filled her eyes, Rain saw Sobe run toward her, his arms high in the air.

Mara's joy at seeing Rain quickly turned to fear as she

saw the tall dark Indian at Rain's side and the men with guns behind them.

"Food!" the dark Indian demanded. "And the Pahvant boy." The Indian shoved past Rain and Spirit of Earth through the door. Too late Mara saw Sobe on his little fat legs running toward Rain. She saw the Indian reach for Sobe and lift him up into his large dark arms. "Food!" the Indian shouted again. "We take Papoose." And he was out the door and back down the stoop behind Spirit of Earth and Rain.

They had come to take Sobe! Rain! For a brief moment Mara searched Rain's eyes for an answer. Her friend. Rain's eyes were full of tears, but they looked past Mara into the air. Rain! Spirit of Earth! No! They would not take Sobe! He was hers if ever a child was. He was in her blood; his blood and Blueflower's was still on her hands, and when she remembered her debt to Blueflower, it was in her heart. Mara screamed. She shoved past Rain and out the door. Sobe began to kick and cry. The Indian who had been standing close to Rain held him in one arm and grabbed Mara's wrists in the other hand as she reached up to him.

"Give us the child." It was Mama's voice behind her. Mara turned. Mama stood in the doorway, Papa's gun in her hands. A crack tore the air. The gun in the hands of a thin old Indian smoked. It was a misfire. The big Indian Kickingboot, who had been holding Sobe, fell to the earth with a horrible scream. Sobe dropped to the ground, crying with terror, and Mara grabbed him up, held him tight to her. There were more shots from the Indians. Then Mama screamed. In her panic, a shot from her own gun ripped across the yard. The fat Indian Squash turned, ran toward the horses in the street like a fat duck. Arrapene backed away, shooting into the smoky air. All the Indians were shooting and running now.

Mara held Sobe tight, afraid to run, not sure which way to go. The big Indian twisted in his blood at her feet, his hands twitching open. His throat rattled, and he was still. Then through the smoke Mara saw that Spirit of Earth had fallen forward on her face in the long grass. Rain screamed as though her heart had been torn from her body. She did not run with Squash and Arrapene and the others, who had reached their horses now and were riding away. Mara ran through the smoke to the house, carrying Sobe crying in her arms. Mama stood on the stoop, staring with horror at the heap of rags lying still in the tall grass. "Was that. . . . Have I . . . ?" She leaned forward and from her throat there came a strange, choked sob. The gun fell from her hand and clattered down the steps. "I didn't mean to. I was afraid. The gun went off. I didn't mean to." Mara was afraid of the sound of her mother's voice. It seemed to come from another world. Mara looked from her mother to the body of Spirit of Earth where Rain lay screaming and touching her torn breast where the thorn sewn to her dress lay in the blood of the wound.

You will remember how it was in the first years, Father. We were not fat in the stone hills. The rainbow never came in the summer. There was too much snow in the winter. You told me yourself with your hands "This land is not rich. But we live here." I was born here. The sun strikes the ground and we grow a little corn, a little squash working with the family of Little Chief and Arrapene, Walkara's brother, chief of us all, and Shenobe, chief of Walkara, and Tovats, father of Shenobe, ruler of heaven.

The sun tills the land like a table, stirring the life in it, beating it with sharp points of light, then covering it with ice, scraping it raw with wind, war, ravaging tribes, the white man. No pleading to heaven stops the sun. No tears stop the drought, fill the womb with men. The sun never planted a child for me. The land, the heaven whispers us across the dry earth like ground weeds in the fall. Until we whisper death and die.

Lost in these thoughts, Atsiback followed Tabby Yaquay, the sun, as it set on the other side of the hills. She followed the river, still full in the midst of summer. She fished to eat, squatting in the dirt, her eyes on the movement below the clear water. At night the hills closed around her; she thought she knew the way to the Dog Foot camp. She would have known it with her eyes covered. But she came almost an hour's walk too far south, through the big canyon to the north of the white man's village. And she came upon farms like woven mats in the little valley. Unsure of her direction, she slowed, listening to the summer sounds. There were hens, the cackling, rushing flutter of hens pecking, eating. There were dogs barking, the whine of a pony, men talking.

She carried the fish with her on a woven willow rope across her back, moved toward the largest cabin in the valley where the two white men, the older and the younger, saddled and mounted their large Appaloosa ponies. It was morning, as clear as a hot summer at noon, the blue sky deeper than starshine, the air heavy with bees.

The white man saw her through the trees. He pulled sharply to stop on his horse and stared into the bushes. He dismounted and moved toward the brush.

"Where you goin', Pa?" the young one shouted.

"Thought I saw an injun. A little injun lady. . . ."

Her heart beating senselessly, Atsiback withdrew from the trees. Frightened, she held out her fish and muttered one of the only words in English Kickingboot had taught her to use. "Trade. Trade."

For a moment the white man stared. Atsiback was

tired, battered by thorny hills, nights of wandering, days without much food.

"Trade?" the white man grinned. "Fetch some flour, Clem," he called to the young one. "Fetch this old lady some flour and we'll trade for her fish."

The boy brought him a limp white sack. "Give her the flour, boy. And we'll have fried fish for supper."

Atsiback dared to reach for the flour, her eyes staring with appetite that knows no fear.

"We'll take 'em all," the man said, his voice rough and hard to Atsiback's ears. He reached for the string of fish. Then Atsiback heard the hooves coming from the south. She heard the shout, saw Squash, Dog Foot, and Arrapene, behind them her old father, and then warriors running, as from a scene of death. Kickingboot was not with them.

Squash stared at Atsiback with eyes of defiance. "Atsiback!" His voice shook her bones. She stepped back, the fish still in her hand. Her old father's eyes shone at the sight of her, but he did not move to her.

Squash leaned his heaviness from his horse, dismounted and strode to her. In a moment he saw the flour in her hands and knew of her trade. He stared in anger at the white man. He turned, raised his hand, struck Atsiback's face. The pain pushed her to the ground. "Woman of Squash," Squash growled. Then she knew Kickingboot was dead.

"Aw . . . she's making a trade," the white man said. Atsiback knew the word "trade."

Squash, silent, angry, came toward Atsiback again. He reached out to hit her once more. The white man, reaching quickly, held his arm.

Atsiback rose, raised the string of fish high above her head, swung down on the neck of the white man, beating him once, twice, three times. Then she kicked his legs. He pulled back, stunned at her fury against him when he had tried to save her. He would not understand, Atsiback knew. But she must defend the brother of her dead husband. She belonged to him now. Squash hit the white man again.

The white man called for the young one, who came fast, bringing guns. Arrapene, Dog Foot came to take the guns away. They fought. The white man took a gun from the young white and beat the head of Dog Foot. Dog Foot fell; there was quiet. The white man and Squash stood staring at one another.

Finally Atsiback moved. Squash grabbed her arm, wrenching her away, but all the time keeping his eyes on the white man's cold face. He pushed Atsiback onto his pony and stood for a moment in front of Dog Foot's bleeding head.

No one spoke. Arrapene and two of the others lifted Dog Foot to his horse, leaving a trail of blood. Still staring at the white man, Squash moved toward his horse. He mounted, pushing Atsiback out of the way. Still, she was condemned by the People, so they left her, riding quickly away.

Holding Sobe, Mara watched her mother make a knot in the center of the rope and pin it to the corner of the quilt. She pinned a piece of rope in each corner, slipped the quilt over the mahogany sideboard and tied each corner tightly to a leg.

"Give me the other quilt."

Mara gave it to her. Since Mama believed she had been the one to shoot Spirit of Earth, she never spoke except to command. She tied the other quilt over the secretary. Father and Sully walked each piece of furniture down the stairs into the cellar under the new house. Holding a lantern as high as he could, Ashel followed them, and waved the light into the dark corners. It flickered against the cold earth walls shining like a candle in an eerie cave. Mara lay Sobe on the floor and followed them carrying the linens and the towels they would not need when they returned to the fort to live for a while.

"This will be the end of the Indians if they start war over such incidents," Papa said.

"The victim of Richards' temper died in camp," Sully explained.

"Well, we sure enough buried one here alongside Spirit of Earth," Papa said quietly. "We buried both of them. There's been some wrongs. . . ."

In her tears Mama had explained over and over again that one of the Indians in the group had accidentally shot one of his own braves. Hearing the shot, she had panicked and pulled the trigger without clear direction. Without knowing where it was going, the fire had pierced Spirit of Earth. In tears, in quiet, Mama explained how she had accidentally killed Spirit of Earth. It had been unintentional, in a moment of fear and pain.

"There were other Indians shooting," Papa had said. "There were more than two or three guns out there. You don't know."

Shaking, Mama had leaned over and buried her face in her hands. Finally, she had had to pull Rain away from the body of her mother when they dug the grave. Finally, in the darkness, in stunned silence, they had had to draw the grief-maddened daughter into the house away from the terribly clear moon. The bishop sent the Allen boy as a messenger to instruct everyone on the street to move to the fort as soon as possible. All of them would have to move, now. There was no telling for how long.

With her arm around Sobe, helping him to untie his shoes, Mara tried to sit with Rain at her place beside the quiet hearth. She touched Rain, but the girl threw her hand off with a sharp shrug of her shoulder. She kept her face turned toward the stone wall. "Rain," Mara said.

But with any words she spoke, the girl began a deep sharp moan in her throat. Heavy with grief, Mara spoke to herself in her mind. Rain. There have been wrongs, terrible wrongs. We had no intentions of destroying your people. We were also driven. All we wanted was to live and we thought—we were wrong, but we thought it all the same—that we could live beside you, using the land beside you. We thought we could share your land in peace, if we were kind, and left you what you needed. We thought we could make it better for you. But life stirs strange phantoms out of the earth. And while we find life on your land, we bring you death. It is not what we wanted, not what we planned. Yes, it's true we were not always wise, always good. We knew you needed space to live the way you live. But we thought that we could teach you to live our way and that you would find the same happiness we find in order and cleanliness. Our order and cleanliness. We didn't stop, dear Rain, to see you had an order of your own, a harmony with the land. We didn't listen to you very well. Rain, oh Rain.

These were some of the sentiments Bishop Higbee spoke at Spirit of Earth's burial service. They buried her on the hillside with the others early in the morning. Even Sully came down from his farm with his new bride, Nancy. She stood close to him, and he held her hand. Carefully aware of any movement in the hills, Bishop Higbee held his hat against the sun to shade the Bible in his hands. He wasn't reading the exact words. The people in the town who came to risk being with them shifted and stared at the graveyard, brown with winter grass. "From dust thou art, to dust thou shalt return," Bishop Higbee murmured. "We must never forget that Spirit of Earth, like the earth itself, gave all she could give to us."

Rain had not come. She had sat as though frozen in

her place by the fire. Mara did not speak out loud to Rain, because the girl would begin a terrible gurgle of pain in her throat and tear at her hair, "Gah nah, nah nah." As long as Mara sat silent, the girl sat with her face against the wall.

While they placed their most valuable things in the cellar and locked them up behind the thick doors, Papa carried the Book of Mormon in his hand. In the evenings at the fort, they sat around the main room together. Mother worked with her needle while Papa thumbed through the pages of the book. "Nephi told it to all of us," Papa said. "You see, it's all very much according to prophecy. It's all there." He read thunderously from the Book of Mormon: ". . . *they shall be scattered among all nations and shall be hated of all men. Nevertheless, after they shall be nursed by the Gentiles, and the Lord has lifted up his hand upon the Gentiles and set them up for a standard, and their children have been carried in their arms, and their daughters have been carried upon their shoulders*. . . . Maybe there is nothing we can do to stop the way God sees how things are going to be. If the Indians start war over those incidents, it will be the end of the Indians," Papa repeated. He carried the Book of Mormon to the window and lay it open on the sill.

Mama pressed the linens in the trunk and pushed the lid over them. Her face was red from so many tears. "It's no excuse. It's no excuse. Prophecy is no excuse. We could have created something different for them. Oh, dear Lord in Heaven!"

For several days while the militia from Salt Lake City was gathering at the fort, and Walkara's warriors raided the hills, the families in the area spent most of their nights moving cautiously in and out of the fort as they felt they must. Mama wept over her beautiful things as they locked the house each afternoon. Finally Papa grew angry with her and reminded her they were only things. As many of these "things" as they could move, Mama moved to the small house at the fort. She worked tirelessly. In the fort at night she closed herself off with her needlework, hanging in the shadows of her pain. She turned one way. Rain turned the other against the hearth.

Mara grew tired of it. So did Papa. Finally, one sunny morning as they breakfasted in their old room at the fort, Papa stood up and threw the newspaper high into the air. "Do you want to ruin your own life over it? And ours? What do you want to do now? Things can't be changed. Can't be stopped." He waved the newspaper in the air. "Even Brigham Young's letter to Walkara is doing nothing to stop the impending war." It was true. News had reached them that a man was killed at Fort Payson. Cattle disappeared, died. The Indians were gathered in the hills. The sound of vengeance echoed in the hills. "You want to let the Indians kill you? They would. It's done, Martha. We have to live. We have to pick up from here and live. The best we can."

"We could have created something different for them. Look at our darling Rain. She has done nothing but cry since she has returned."

From her corner by the fire, Rain looked up. Her eyes were as blank as they had been these last few days. She began the same slow painful croak deep in her throat. When Mara had come to her with food, she had turned her back and curled toward the wall. The first day Mara had left it, Rain had not touched it. But for the last few times, when Mara had returned, she noticed that the food was gone.

"Could have. Could have." Papa got up and walked the floor. He flourished his handkerchief and pushed his nose up into his face. "Pickled hog feathers! It's done!

Look ahead. There are too many people living to ignore them for the past. Look, the sun rose today!"

Afraid Mama and Papa were going to prolong their argument, Mara turned her head away and picked up Sobe in her arms. She wanted to get away from this talk of war, from the devastating heaviness of all that had occurred. Away from the constant low sob in Rain's throat. She wanted to take Sobe with her.

"Where are you going?" Mama asked.

"I'm taking Sobe for a walk in the sunshine," Mara said. "We won't be gone very long."

"Don't you dare go out of the fort without someone," Papa said. "You know that, don't you? You wouldn't. . . ." He was batting the newspaper against his legs now.

Mara assured him. "Of course I won't. I promise," she called back as she slipped outside the door. The sun was hovering over the eastern mountain. The large square central yard of the fort was empty. No one else had come out yet this morning. That was how she wanted it. She had come out here before to think about Bret and imagine him here, walking in the empty sun. She would wait for Bret. Someday he would come. In the meantime, she was everything to Sobe. Everything. Mara held the tiny toddler close to her cheek. She kissed him. She loved the salty taste of his arms, his tiny nose. How she loved him! And now she had found out how much she loved him. For they had almost lost him, and she had clung to him morning and night.

"Sobe. Little green growing," she laughed and held him up to the sun. He laughed and giggled with her. She walked with him still in her arms over to the cannon in the middle of the fort. It stood black and imposing on its high platform, like an idol, a monument to something Mara did not want to think about. She looked up, instead, at the flag on the pole above, slapping in the breeze. Because the cannon was about as high as her head, she could stand Sobe's feet on the cannon, let go quickly and let him fall into her arms. He loved it. She repeated this trick several times—thinking to herself that this was the way everyone in the settlement should somehow deal with a weapon of war on a platform in a fort. He cooed and laughed, having great fun.

"Sobe Sobe Sobe, my Sobe," Mara talked to him and bounced him and kissed him. She did not see Rain coming up behind them.

"Mara?"

Mara turned swiftly around. It was Rain, squinting into the sun. Mara caught her breath and said a silent prayer.

"Come and stand in my shadow, Rain," Mara said. "We're playing a game."

Rain moved closer to them. When she stood by them, she touched the side of the cannon, and then Sobe's foot. "I'm going to stay with you," she said in simple words.

Mara let go of her breath. Slowly, she reached out to hold Rain's hand while it touched Sobe's foot. Rain did not move her hand.

"See how he laughs," Mara said to her. "He doesn't know anything has gone wrong. Or that anything will go wrong. Life has just barely begun."

Rain began to smile. As the smile began, Sobe reached out and touched her cheek.

"He remembers me," Rain said.

"He loves you," Mara said. "Will you help me love him?"

There were still tears on Rain's cheeks, but she wiped them away with her hand. "I love him, too," she said. "He's ours."

"He belongs to everyone! Don't you, Sobe?" Mara lifted

him high again and he fell into both pairs of arms. "Sunshine in spring." Tangled up with each other, Mara and Rain began to laugh. They stood in Sobe's shadow, shielded from the sun.

This is the end of Thorns of the Sun. *Mara's story will conclude in the next volume,* Shadows of Angels.